THE Guardian

BOOK THREE OF THE GIVEN TRILOGY

MICKEY MARTIN

Right from its opening chapter, The Given Trilogy never sugar-coats the brutality of its world. Instead, the series shows us the strength and determination of the characters within it. These books shines a light of hope in the deepest darkness, and prove that love, compassion and the tight bonds of friendship can heal any wound, and overcome any obstacle. Be prepared to clear your reading calendar, because once The Given Trilogy has you in its grip, it won't let you go.

Multi-Award Winning Author, Carolyn Wren

A pulsating dark romance that is gripping and addictive right from the start. Damon Night, OMG. I'm in Love! The Guardian flowed smoothly from The Given to Dark Angel, and my only disappointment was that it was the last book of the series. No doubt, one of the best trilogies I have ever read.

Louise Manna

We all wish we had friends like Lilliana and Damon. We all wish we had a love like Lilliana's and Damon's love, too. But never in our wildest imaginations could we foresee what horrors lay in store for Lilliana and Damon as they set about trying to rid the world of its most dangerous criminals. The wheels have been set in motion in this, the shocking third and final conclusion to Mickey Martin's trilogy, The Guardian. Martin weaves an unforgettable plot of romance, horror and suspense, never straying far from the greater message she wishes to leave us with; that is, how we can all contribute towards making the world a better place through love, healing and forgiveness, despite all the darkness that exists in the world. A well-crafted, heart-stopping philosophical and psychological thriller engineered with Martin's lofty writing style, fertile imagination, and higher purpose in mind.

Susan Wakefield, Editor

From the first page to the last The Guardian enthrals and captivates the reader. Diving head-first into the dark and sinister Underworld that has become Lilliana Night's reality, The Guardian has it all - love, lust, depravity and that good old-fashioned fight between good and evil.

Just when you think Lilliana has experienced the best and the worst the world has to offer, she is thrown into the depths of a world unimagined. Separated from the man she loves and surrounded by The Given's most skilled and prestigious undercover security team Lilliana sacrifices everything she holds dear for that one chance to bring down the syndicate that ruined the lives of so many for so long.

Through every chapter of The Guardian the reader is immersed in Lilliana's world; willing her to conquer these demons she must face to protect her home and family. Friendships are strengthened, family grows and the unpredictable world of The Given sees evil rear its head again and again.

Without question The Guardian, the much anticipated third and final instalment in The Given Trilogy delivers. I was spellbound, so wrapped up in the world of Lilliana and her family at The Given there were times I was on the edge of my seat, others I was reading through my fingers. At every twist and turn I was there as if I were part of that world.

Mickey Martin's writing is as engaging as her characters. In each book of the Given Trilogy the reader grows with Lilliana and the friends who become her family. As an avid reader I have read many trilogies and often thought the author should have stopped at Book One. The Given Trilogy, hands down, is one of the best trilogies I have ever read and will re-read at every opportunity!

Sally Taylor

First published in Australia in 2020
by Making Magic Happen Academy

www.makingmagichappenacademy.com
www.karenmcdermott.com.au

Cover design by Ida Jansson

National Library of Australia Cataloguing-in-Publication data:
The Guardian/Making Magic Happen Academy

978-0-6489847-8-8 (sc)
978-0-6489733-4-8 (e)

Other titles by Mickey Martin

THE GIVEN TRILOGY:

Book 1: The Given
Book 2: Dark Angel
Book 3: The Guardian

Writing as Michelle Weitering
Thirteen and Underwater

Acknowledgements

Where to start. This is a big one. Of course, I'd like to thank my Mum for having me… I have to start there, right. And what a woman you were Mum. Much love and thanks sent to you, in Heaven, My Angel.

Releasing this trilogy into the world, has been an epic journey in itself and I could not have done without the support of so many individuals that have had my back all the way, and celebrated the birth of this trilogy with me.

To all my amazing, wonderful readers: All I ever want to do, is create an amazing, uplifting world for you to escape into, for an hour or two. Whenever I create a character or a plot, it is with your enjoyment in mind, always. Thank you for reading my books and all your support! Must mention a special thanks to Chris Heithersay, Leanne Rowan, Rebecca Lou, and Kaylene Bradshaw. xx

A massive thanks has to be sent to a lady, who graciously agreed to read the first handful of chapters when the idea of The Given first emerged. Sally Taylor, it was your excitement, honest feedback and requests of, 'I want more! Give me more!'… that spurred me on to write this trilogy. I know I'm not the only one who will want to say thank you, to you, for that! Your friendship is gold, and your unwavering support, encouragement, along with copious pots of tea and colourful conversations these past 17 years, has been like celebrating Christmas every day! Thank you my friend, I love you. xx

Jade Weitering, I have had so many women tell me that Damon Night, is there No. 1 Book Boyfriend. But I could not have written such a beautiful Hero into the world, if you weren't mine. The word, Love, isn't enough. You are my everything. xx

To our gorgeous boys. Jesse and Zane, we are so proud of you. You aren't just our world… you are our entire universe. My sweet Zane, thank you for making me laugh like a lunatic, every single day. You effortlessly lift my soul with your kind, decent heart. xx My darling Jesse, your strength to face your fears and worries in this world of ours, makes you my Hero. Keep writing your Rap, you've got so much to say that could help someone else heal one day. xx

Thomas and Ireland, your Aunty Mickey adores you both, and treasures the relationship we share. Thank you for always believing in me. I love you as if you were my own. xx

To the almighty Dream Giver; Karen Mc Dermott. Where do I start? Connecting with you has been one of my life's most gloriously, serendipitous occurrences. From Frankston to Perth, travelling to Ireland and back, your generous heart, and powerful knowing, is a gift from the heavens to be sure. I can't thank you enough for knowing I can do this, and so much more. Your endless support along with your glowing smile and kindred-spirited heart - makes mine glow constantly. Thank you sweetheart. I love you. xx

To the entire, glorious team at MMH PRESS, I send love and thanks to you, for all your efforts behind the scenes. xx And a massive thank you to Ida at AMYGDALA DESIGN, for making The Given Trilogy's covers so stunning. xx

To my Editor Susan Wakefield. Thank you so very much for all your hard work, in helping me make this book shine. Your talent in what you do astounds me, as you know and I truly thank you for your patience in gifting me with your knowledge regarding the editing world. I'm so excited about our future projects together! xx

To my friend, Susan Wakefield. Although it's been a difficult year, with social distancing, I thank you, for every phone call and voice message filled with laughter and tears as we've shared our incredible lives together. So blessed the day we met as we attended the PWC photo shoot two years ago. Who would have known an instant connection would have been made, by two nervous, grieving women, as they sat together on a book shops steps; as they stepped out of their comfort zone, all for the greater good. Chills right there. I love you darling. Thank you for your unconditional support. xx

Carolyn De Ridder, thank you for loving Damon as much as I do, and celebrating this trilogy with me. Even with your every day, full-to-the-brim, overflowing schedule, you still found the time to support me whenever I needed advice or direction. Your generosity making the most fabulous book trailers, for this trilogy, and sharing images of our beloved cast, has added to the celebration along the way. Cannot wait to connect again in person. Thank you beautiful Lady! xx

To my two sisters; Leah and Louise. Your strength and resilience to overcome what you both endured throughout your entire lives, makes me feel so honoured to know you both.

Leah, boy, what a ride we have had since we shared the womb. I am so thankful that we have arrived at a place in our lives that is filled with nothing but peace and love. I am so excited about our path ahead together, and I hope you are as ready for it, as I am. It means more than the absolute world to me, that we are embarking on our new project together. I love you. Cheers to our next visit to Cavan. xx

Louise Josephine Mana. My Bella! Over the past 27 years, our friendship has been one of my greatest treasure's. The laughter we have shared, as we've travelled through life's arena together, has been beyond therapeutic. You are my rock, and more. Thank you for always, always being there for me, no matter the time or your schedule. Keep the dream alive baby… we are going to Italy! So much love and respect! xx

Maraika Mason. It was essentially your loving guidance, patience, and support, that gifted such beautiful, strong, caring, and sensitive men into the world. Thank you for being such a gorgeous

Grandmother to our boys, and also for being the best Mum in law a girl could ask for. I love you dearly. Your support, not just to me, but to all those amazing writers on F.B means the world. Thank you. xx

Kez Wickham St George. You gorgeous lady! You lighten my heart and make me laugh woman! We connected at Crom, and our friendship has blossomed since. Thank you for being such an enigmatic soul. I so look forward to our writing adventures ahead in the future and connecting face to face. Love you. xx

To my MMH PRESS Author-Shareholder comrades: I love that we are on this journey, of celebrating books and sharing stories together with the world. I couldn't imagine anyone else making this journey as much fun.

Adrea Peters, your light, love, and beautiful heart shines on others in such a comforting way. You are right….Everyone needs Everyone! I thank you for being you and gifting the world with Truitt Skye and your vibrant Quantum Thinking. You are supreme!

Jennifer Sharp, your kindness radiates and your generous heart shines as you help so many publish their beautiful books into the world. Your Guide to successful Authorship is a gem! Thank you for your gorgeous energy and support on the F.B. Cannot wait to meet in person one day. xx

Tanya Southey, your talent floored me the day I received your poetry book, StreetWise-52 Word 52 Weeks. These poems especially touched me, The Week of Change, The week of Music, The Week of Judgement. I could go on… thank you for your gift. Poetry can heal the world. xx

Kelly Van Nelson. It was you who first pushed me out of my comfort zone, inviting me to speak with you at the Docklands Library in Melbourne, 2019, when we first met. Speaking about resilience, whilst trying not to cry my eyes out or throw my guts up, due to my fear of public speaking… was resilience in itself. Spending time with you at the AusMumpreneur awards was such a joy as we connected over laughter and sharing stories. Watching you smash the world with your phenomenal poetry, delights me no end. Thank you for being another amazingly brave advocate for important issues in our world.

Punch and Judy will change lives. xx

And for all the loves in my life, who quietly offer me their support with their kindness and love, I thank you from the bottom of my heart, for you each play a role in lifting my life and adding to any celebration.

Nadine Mendoza, Rachael Hecker, Paul Mason, Taylor Clan, Nicole Sirianni, Grant Weitering, Dean Turner, Coreena La Gallienne, Liz Hicklin, Lindsay Coker, Karen Kildey, Kelly Clark, Adam Wallace, The Fletchers, Ashley Quick, Kylee Robertson, Kim Krajewski, Brendon Clark, Michelle Hales, Kylie Slane, Astrid McCallum, Helen Parker, Sonia Bellhouse, Danielle Line, Kylie Sass, Patricia Lovell, Julia Kaylock- and so many others. Please forgive me if your name is not above…but know, you are in my incredibly grateful heart. xx

A special thanks to one of my mother's dearest friends, who has gushed over everything I've ever written, Edna Royal -Thank you for making me feel like your favourite - Danielle Steele! Xx

Much Love to You all. Xoxo

The road we walk is a gift, no matter the terrain
The journey is our reward – It will shape us all
How hard or soft we tread, is up to us all as individuals
Kindness, love, and Healing will be the footprints I choose to leave
behind as I walk towards
My final destination,
Until my next journey…
begins…

MICKEY MARTIN

CHAPTER 1

Lilliana Night stood surrounded by beloved faces bidding her farewell, her heart heavy at the thought of parting from any of them.

She turned, heart fluttering as Damon Night stepped through the crowd that parted for him.

Reaching for her, his intense blue eyes hungrily swept her up in love and lust. He ran his strong fingers gently along her arm, making her shiver, then stepped against her, bending his dark head towards hers, whispering. "It's time to wake up, darling, we're almost there."

Lilliana moaned softly as she tilted her head, anticipating his kiss as his fingers tightened around her arm, squeezing. He was hurting her, but she didn't care, she just wanted his kiss. She stood on tiptoe to reach him, their lips almost touching as he shook her arm.

"Damon?" she whispered.

"Lilliana, wake up."

The dream disappeared as he squeezed her arm again. She sat forward running a hand over her eyes, trying to focus on the person who had woken her yet wishing she were back in her dream with Damon. His handsome, familiar blue eyes met her sea green ones.

Cameron Night. Cam was now officially her brother-in-law, given that she had married his brother just the night before.

"Cam?"

"You were calling out Damon's name in your sleep."

Lilliana pushed her long, black hair off her shoulders. "Where are we?"

"Just about to land in Darwin, Australia. I thought I would give you a few minutes to freshen up. The paparazzi will be waiting to snap you up as soon as you step out, love." He pulled her to her feet and pointed to the small bathroom.

"Thanks Cam," she stepped around him and closed herself in the bathroom. It took her a couple of minutes to wash her face, put on a light dusting of mineral foundation with a hint of blush, eye shadow, mascara, and lipstick. She ran the brush through her long tresses, letting it fall in a silky wave down her back. A squirt of perfume, a dash of deodorant and she was fresh again.

Leaning closer to the mirror now, she inspected her face, feeling lost, having left behind everyone she loved and everything she knew for the past nine and a half years. Her home. She squeezed her eyes shut as a sharp pain knifed through her at the thought of being away from her Damon. Separated once again. This was for the greater good.

This, she knew was to protect all the people she had left behind from the threat of a Bioweapon attack that had been issued by the Ex Diplomat, Reid, a narcissistic millionaire, turned terrorist and Leader of one of the most despicable underground organisations. He had kidnapped and murdered more people than the Officials could account for, as well as wreaking havoc upon several major cities worldwide, and their innocent civilians.

His son, David Reid who had recently been held at the Louisiana's Given in the Black Ops unit for the past six months, was on board this very jet, in a secluded cabin section separate to Lilliana, due to their hostile relationship.

Having received the threat over 24 hours ago, Johnson, Head Crime investigator of the Louisiana's Given establishment, had released David Reid into the hands of the undercover unit to make contact with his father, and then take the team along with him to infiltrate the compound under the guise of David's security men.

Johnson's team had surgically implanted a chip in David's eyes that would transmit all images and audio back to the Given for Johnson and Damon to view 24/7. This program was called The Guardian.

A microchip bomb had also been implanted inside David's skull that would be detonated if he attempted to put Lilliana or the team in any danger.

Reid Senior had demanded Lilliana be released from the Given, along with his son. This worked in perfectly with a project Lilliana had initiated and which required her physical presence in the outside world for a short time.

Lilliana's Dark Angel campaign had begun to raise money in order to build safe houses for those affected by crime; these houses would offer counselling, protection, and support until the victims were ready to get back on their feet. Lilliana had several photo shoots and interviews, along with a gala night planned to raise awareness and funds for the safe houses to flourish. The modelling, she could handle; it was the combination of being in the outside world again and everything so unknown to her that was out of her control, that it made her feel apprehensive.

She reflected on the years Damon had been away, working undercover; how he had committed himself to his role, to the extent of marrying the diabolical enemy Felicia Reid, who was as disgusting as her father and as psychotic as her brother. Some things did run in families.

Lilliana took a deep breath and opened the door. Stepping out she realised she had not left everyone she loved back home. There were Eric, Marcus, Fox, and Cam all sitting together, watching her as she closed the door behind her.

"That's better," Fox, her stunning redheaded friend smiled. "Now you look the part."

Lilliana sat beside Eric who patted the seat beside him. "We're landing in ten minutes."

Lilliana nodded, her eyes moving behind Cam and Fox to look at the eight men selected to protect and serve. Marcus had been her team leader since she was just sixteen, and when she had first entered the Given's Main House. His brother, Rocco, flashed her his trustworthy smile. Desmond, Rider, William, Rodney, Daniel, Lincoln, and Max sat silently looking at her. They were a formidable team in both appearance and based on their prestigious resumes.

"Lilliana?" Eric gently squeezed her arm; he had been trying to get her attention.

"Sorry, what?" Lilliana glanced at Eric, avoiding Cam's concerned look.

"Your wedding ring; we need to put it in the vault. We were going to leave it behind, but Damon insisted you wear it for as long as you were able."

"Okay, I understand." Lilliana lifted her hand, glancing at the ring that had been on her finger for less than twenty-four hours.

Cam reached across and took her hand gently, pulling the ring from her finger and placing it in Eric's hand, who immediately got up to put it in the vault.

Cam squeezed Lilliana's hand gently. "You okay?"

She met his gaze steadily and forced a smile. "Don't stress about me Cam, I'm fine. How could I not be with you here?"

"So true, darling; just breathe when those doors open so you don't pass out." Eric sat back down as the jet hit the tarmac and lurched forward before coming to a smooth stop.

"Unit Eight, be ready." Cam instructed. The unit stood as one to attention and nodded at Cam.

Rocco tapped Marcus's shoulder. "Eyes open from here on out, Brother."

"No worries Rocco, I've got this." Marcus nodded to his older brother, feeling a sense of pride wash over him. He had known for years that Rocco had led many a team throughout the world on complicated missions and had rescued plenty of innocents and put some real garbage away.

To have been asked to help protect not only Lilliana, Fox, and Cam, but to be close to his brother and part of the action made Marcus feel very blessed right this second, as well as having Eric alongside him.

The team exited through the doors of the jet and down the flight of steps, forming a small line either side for the group.

Fox and Cam went first, followed by Eric, Lilliana, and Marcus. Lilliana took a deep breath and was grateful when Eric linked his arm through hers. She looked up at him as they stepped out into a sea of flashing cameras.

"I'm glad you're here Eric, thank you."

"No need to thank me, Lilliana." He smiled quickly before turning his attention to the crowd, eyes scanning and surveying the grounds for any trouble.

Lilliana couldn't believe what she was seeing. People were waving and screaming out both Fox's and her name, Dark Angel. It was a very intense twenty minutes. A news camera was filming, and Cam and Fox were now being interviewed as they made their way towards a long Hummer limousine. A large, black jeep was parked behind it, which Unit Eight would take, following them in procession. In the meantime, they made two lines either side of the limousine awaiting the girls, along with Cam, Marcus, and Eric.

Cam, more comfortable with the press, answered every question smoothly in his charming manner. Fox also did her part, playing the part of a famous model who had been used to being in the limelight of both worlds for well over a decade.

Once the reporters turned their attention to Lilliana, Cam stepped into the vehicle. Fox remained with her arm slung around Lilliana's shoulder, showing a united front. Lilliana expressed her excitement and enthusiasm about her new project to help many and thanked the Australian public for making her and her team feel so welcome. She made a point of mentioning she had visited Australia once as a child and so looked forward to being in this part of the world again. Both she and Fox smiled, flashing their best angles towards the photographers, willing to answer all their questions gracefully.

Marcus took Fox's arm as Eric took Lilliana's, and together they led the girls to the vehicle once the session had ended. As soon as their behinds hit the seat, the vehicle took off quickly. Lilliana let out a sigh and looked at Fox, who let out a laugh, exclaiming, "That was fabulous!"

Lilliana smiled at her, understanding how she felt. She was thrilled to have had this platform for her campaign, as it gave her the opportunity to share their story with millions. The more people who knew, the more may be willing to come along and volunteer services or donate the extra funds that were required to begin and maintain the safe houses.

"Enjoy that little bit of stardom did we, Foxy?" Cam raised an eyebrow.

Lilliana hid a smile, loving the way Cam reminded her of her beloved Damon at times.

"Well why not? We don't feel it so much where we live, Cameron." Fox raised a sexy eyebrow back, running her fingers through her luscious red locks.

Cam nodded. "Just sit back and enjoy the ride; we should arrive near Jabiru in an hour." As he finished the sentence, Lilliana felt herself thrust back against her seat as the vehicle burst with excess speed and rocketed forward. Cam smiled and closed his eyes, enjoying the feeling of leaving his stomach behind. Lilliana tried to look out the window, but everything was rushing by in a dark blur.

"Where's Reid?" Lilliana asked no one in particular. Marcus answered.

"He has a task to complete himself if he wants to keep his head. He'll wait till the crowd disperses, contact our team on the ground and get a message to his father that he has been released, then make his way to Kakadu National Park where our unit will intercept him at a specific location."

Lilliana nodded slowly as she looked back towards the window.

Cam opened his eyes a fraction to look across at his new sister. He could imagine how she felt right now. He himself, had left behind the woman he loved, adored, and had known since she was two years old. Josephine, with her beautiful smiley brown eyes and kind heart. His wife, and one of Lilliana's dearest friends. And Lilliana finding herself once again separated from the man she loved with all her being.

Her eyes met his and he smiled slowly, offering her a look they both understood. We can do this! she thought. Lilliana returned his smile before letting her head fall back against the headrest. Looking across at Eric, she hoped the next few hours would run smoothly without any disturbances.

***

Once the vehicles stopped, they stepped out under a Southern sky full of stars; the scent of gum leaves and peppercorn trees pleasantly perfumed the warm, muggy air. Crickets and cicadas called out a greeting as the group walked towards four large tents, with several smaller ones scattered around. Tiny, solar lights were strung around the outline of each tent, emitting soft light amongst the nearby trees. Lilliana noticed that the earth under her feet was dry, warm, and red, and the tranquility of her surroundings soothed her immediately.

"Tents, really? I heard we were staying in some crocodile shaped hotel?" Fox was not as impressed as Lilliana.

"Gagudja? Maybe thirty-two years ago." Cam indicated for Rocco and his team to put their bags in the tents. "After the outbreak in 2020, this entire section of the Territory has been abandoned. I'm amazed there's still wildlife around."

"Outbreak?" Fox looked stricken.

Cam smiled. "Not to worry love, there is no virus lingering here now. Right, let's get settled in, have a feed and a good night's sleep. We are up early in the morning people, and we have a long trip out into the middle of Kakadu. Ladies, we will be doing a photo shoot in the Yellow Water Billabong, then we'll head back to Darwin for your publicity interviews. So, it's going to be a busy twenty-four hours."

"And then where?" Lilliana asked.

"New York," Cam said as he was about to step into one of the larger tents; at the same time a tall figure stepped out, bringing a smile to all their faces.

Tim was one of the Given's lead photographers who travelled the globe to snap the interesting individuals of the world.

"Well, hello my lambs." He smiled at Lilliana and Fox.

Fox laughed as she threw herself into Tim's arms. "Darling, it is so very brilliant to see you!" she kissed him on the mouth with a big smooch smack. Tim smiled down at Fox, before turning his attention to Lilliana.

"Hello Angel, how are you holding up?" He opened his arms for her to step into. Lilliana did so, wrapping her arms around his waist.

"It's good to see you, Tim."

He kissed her cheek, patting her gently on the back. "Well, I am the lead photographer for your campaign; Damon had me organised pronto. Luckily, I've just completed a shoot in Tasmania, so I was really close by in this beautiful big land Down Under. It's going to be a fabulous shoot tomorrow."

She smiled up at him. She had done her first shoot with him when she was just sixteen and had always felt comfortable with his effortless charm. "I'll certainly do my part to make your job easy."

"As always." He stepped back and nodded hello to Eric who had been standing behind Lilliana the entire time.

Lilliana turned to look at Eric. "Why don't you go and freshen up Eric, get something to eat?"

"I will when you do, Doc." Eric liked calling Lilliana by her nickname.

"Eric!" Cam called out. "Just Lilliana when we are out here, buddy."

"Yes Sir," Eric answered.

Lilliana walked into the larger tent. Once inside, she shook her head in wonder. The dome roof of the tent was supported by a large and beautifully stained, carved tree trunk. The tent had real timber walls with shelves running along their length, lit with candles, and in the centre of the room was a sturdy round table that had been set up with a feast for twenty people. Lilliana's stomach rumbled. She couldn't remember the last time she had eaten.

Marcus and Rocco helped themselves to a cold drink and were talking quietly. Daniel and Ryder had taken point outside the door and the rest of the unit were on patrol. Fox had poured a long glass of water and handed it to Lilliana, before pouring herself a glass of wine and helping herself to food. Cam too, started to pile up a plate, as he asked Tim about the location for the following day.

It all sounded lovely to Lilliana. The thought of doing an actual shoot off the Given's land excited her. She sat down at the table and started helping herself to some cold chicken and salad. Placing it in a wrap full of seeds, she threw some basil in it and was happy to see Eric join her.

"That looks good," he said and sat beside her, reaching for a freshly brewed coffee. She pushed her plate across to him, smiling as she began making another for herself.

"Thanks," he took a large mouthful of food. "Awesome."

"You're welcome," she said as she finished making hers and they ate in appreciative silence.

"It's all clear Mr Night, Sir." Lincoln reported as he stepped into the tent.

"Thanks Lincoln," he nodded over to Rocco. "I want you and your men to eat and chill for a bit."

"We are on it Sir, we'll rotate our shifts till morning; Marcus and I, along with Will and Lincoln will be on first watch. Don't worry Sir, we have this under control."

"Trust me Rocco, I'm not worried; I know you and your men are the best, I just want you to eat. It makes me feel better."

Rocco grinned. "Yes Sir," he said. He walked over and sat beside Fox, who was delighted to have some more male company. It wasn't long before the room was filled with their entire, cheerful group.

Lilliana enjoyed listening to Tim and Rocco entertaining the group, having them in fits of laughter as they shared tales, experiences, and mishaps from traveling around the globe. Once Rocco's team joined in the conversation, they shared tales of poverty and sadness, due to the ghastly corrupt and polluted minds that they had encountered during missions, and the feeling in the tent turned grim. Lilliana felt very tired suddenly and pushed herself up from the table.

"Where am I sleeping?"

Cam stood and walked over to her, putting his arm about her waist, and leading her out of the tent.

"Goodnight, Miss," Rocco and his team called out.

"Goodnight," she called over her shoulder, noticing Eric right behind her. "It's all right Eric, you can stay." Lilliana didn't want to pull him away from a relaxing night with his new team.

He paid her no attention and continued following her and Cam, who led her to one of the smaller tents. A cosy looking, single bed was draped in a mosquito net positioned in the centre of the tent, with her overnight bag sitting at the end. Tucked in the corner of the tent was a small bathroom and toilet.

"Now, Tiger Lilly; I want you to relax and sleep. Can you do that for me?" Cam kissed the top of her head as he gently stroked her arm.

"I can try," she said looking up at him. "Will I have the opportunity to speak to Damon?"

He looked down at her, understanding how desperately she wanted to talk to his brother. He shook his head slowly. "Not at the moment baby."

Lilliana nodded begrudgingly and walked over to the bed, unzipping her bag and pulling out her toiletries and sleepwear.

"Make sure you sleep too, Cam. Goodnight," she said and disappeared into the small bathroom.

"Good night sweetheart. Eric." Cam then left the tent to say goodnight to the rest of the team.

"Goodnight Sir," Eric called after him as he positioned himself near the entrance of Lilliana's door.

Lilliana enjoyed the hot shower, brushed her teeth and tied her hair back. Slipping her knee length cotton nightdress on, she stepped out and walked over to her bed.

"Eric, are you going to stand there all night, or are you going to go to your own tent and get some sleep?"

Eric turned to face her, his eyes scanning her beautifully sculptured face, her neat, firm and curvaceous body. She watched him appraise her, raising a suggestive eyebrow. She noticed that he didn't look tired whatsoever. His handsome face looked fresh and alert. He stood, hands on the gun at his front, legs spread hip length apart, ready for action.

"Lilliana, I don't sleep when you are my number one priority."

"You don't sleep?"

"Not at all. Nurse Rachael and Dr Ryan have me on awake meds. I don't need any sleep. Damon chose me for this role, and I don't intend to let him down. Whatever I say and do will be to totally protect you."

Lilliana sighed as she sank into the middle of the bed, pulling the covers up to her waist. "Eric, I'm so grateful you took this role. I really am. But I don't want you to get hurt; you're my friend and if anything happened to you because of me…" she trailed off.

"Nothing's going to happen to me, Lilliana; now go to sleep, ease your mind and let your thoughts go."

Lilliana laughed. It was something she had said many times to him when she had taken him into hypnotherapy to ease so much abuse he had suffered as a child. He grinned back at her and pointed to her pillow. She let herself fall back onto the soft bedding and forced her eyes shut.

"I guess that makes you my therapist now, huh Eric?"

"I'll be whatever you need me to be, Lilliana. Now, go to sleep."

She let out a small sigh and let her mind wander to her husband. The man who could knock the breath out of her with a particular look. Any look, really. Damon's dark blue eyes could see through most people's darkest thoughts. He had hair as black as night that framed a face chiseled by the gods. Tall dark and handsome did not even cut it. On the outside, Damon Night was a mouth-watering specimen, but inside, he was all heart. Kind, loving and patient, he gave so much of himself to so many in need.

Lilliana rolled over and buried her face in her pillow, forcing her tears not to spill. Yes, she missed the man she loved with all her being. But she would see him again, and soon. This would all be over in a matter of weeks, surely—then she would be back home with him and the remainder of her family.

CHAPTER 2

Sleep did come, but it was not an easy, deep, peaceful sleep. Lilliana's dreams were disturbed by an eerie figure, lurking and getting closer to her by the minute with slow, jerky movements. She would run the run that dreamers do; frustratingly slow, sluggish, and lost as the mysterious figure kept gaining on her with each step that she tried to take, her heart feeling like it would explode out of her chest with every panicked breath.

The figure approached, raising its massive arm. She saw the glint of the razor-sharp surgical knife grasped in its ham-like fist as it slashed down towards her. She was unable to move in the murky, bog like fog, but she raised her arms, screaming as the knife slashed through her flesh, her nerve ends on fire as blood flowed thickly.

"Lilliana, wake up—you're dreaming." The hand that gently rubbed her shoulder in the land of awake was plunging her with the surgical knife in her dream world.

She jerked upwards slapping Eric's hand away, her body shaky.

Just a dream she thought, trying to pull herself together and rubbing her shoulder that ached at the thought of being mutilated.

"Sorry," she mumbled, pushing the waterfall of hair off her

shoulders.

"It's alright, go have a shower, wash it away." Eric walked back towards the entrance, taking a plate of food that was handed to him through the door.

After showering and joining the others for breakfast, Lilliana did feel a little better, her mood lighter with the morning banter and the freshness of the air that the Australian Outback offered. After everyone had finished breakfast and packed up their belongings, Cam indicated they follow him. "Right, this way." He carried a large backpack, as did Tim and Unit Eight as he led them on a hike through the vibrant countryside for a good forty minutes. The earth was a brilliant red, giving the green plants a stunning backdrop. Birds called out to each other, warning of the intruders. By the time they'd arrived at the river, they were each covered in a thin veil of sweat. A sturdy boat sat in clear water, its waves gently slapping at its sides.

"Russell," Cam smiled. "Always reliable."

"Is that safe?" Fox raised an eyebrow, gesturing to the corroded looking pier that the boat was tied to. Marcus walked onto the pier and jumped up and down a couple of times.

"Safe enough."

Rodney helped Fox into the boat as Lilliana and the remainder of the team got themselves comfortable on the spacious raft. Within minutes they were speeding along the water, watching waterfalls cascade over the sides of the land, flushing cool jets of spray along the red walls of the earth.

"Serenity," Fox sighed as she leaned over the side of the boat to drop her arm in the cool water. As she did, Ryder snapped out his hand quick as a striking snake and jerked Fox back into her seat. Her head whipped around.

"Problem?" she asked coolly, rubbing her wrist once he'd released her.

"Not for me—but almost for you," he warned, pointing a finger towards the water. They all turned to look. They had all seen alligators, they were impressive enough, but the Australian saltwater crocodile was a thing of majestic beauty. Like the ancient royal beasts of the past, it glided through the water, skillfully navigating its way, looking for its next meal.

"Wow," Fox breathed. "Thanks!"

"Sure," Ryder looked away, and like his team members focused on their surroundings.

"It's a saltwater croc; has to be over seven meters long, easily!" Cam exclaimed. "Did you know," he continued enthusiastically, "salt and freshwater crocodiles can live in both fresh and saltwater?"

Lilliana and Eric exchanged a smile.

It wasn't too long before the gorges fell away revealing open waters and the wetlands thick with green, lush vegetation. Large knotted white trees reached for the sky with gnarly limbs, covered in leafy foliage.

The boat was soon surround by thick patches of the most breathtaking water lilies. Their leaves were bigger than dinner plates with flowers stunning shades of pinks, yellows and white.

"What is this place?" Fox asked Cam, as William shut the boat's engine off. There were many birds calling, frogs croaking and other strange animal noises that could be heard amongst the swamp.

"This is the Yellow Water Paperback swamp and the location for today's shoot." Tim indicated to a cluster of thick white trunks with beautiful foliage spilling down. The stunning backdrop beheld other ghostly white trunks and nothing but miles of clear blue waters with bursts of water lilies everywhere.

"Okay Tim, set up and do your thing." Cam nodded.

Rocco and Marcus were handing out water containers whilst Lincoln, Daniel and Max continued surveying the area. Ryder flipped open a small computer and hit a switch and a hologram appeared of their location. "All clear," he said quietly for his team to hear.

"Right; let's do this, Lilliana," Tim smiled as he began setting up his gear. "Fox, if you wouldn't mind getting Lilliana ready."

"No problem," Fox stood and crossed over to Lilliana. She dropped a small cube on the ground near their feet and pressed into the middle of it. In a flash the two of them were surrounded by four walls, blocking them from their group. The sky and branches showed through the open roof above them.

"Whoa," Lilliana exclaimed. "Neat."

"Yes, very neat, now strip."

"And put on what?" Lilliana pulled her jeans off and yanked her tee shirt over her head. She had stripped naked in front of Fox many times over the years for photo shoots and assignments. Doing it in the middle of a boat, surrounded by a hologram wall with ten plus men on the other side was not the slightest bit uncomfortable for Lilliana.

Fox thrust her hand through one of the walls, making it look as though her hand had been cut off. "Cam," she called out. "Wardrobe, make up."

Within seconds Cam had pushed a bag into Fox's hand.

"Here we go," she handed Lilliana a handful of deep red silk. "This will look sensational with your black hair, Lilly dear."

"It's beautiful," Lilliana gasped and pulled it over her head. "Are you doing a shoot here also?"

"No, both you and I will be doing a large one in New York; the pictures taken today will be sent ahead. Tim will get a copy to Pier and by the time we rock up to the centre of fashion, The Big Apple, your face will be plastered everywhere, from Down Under." Once Fox was satisfied that Lilliana was in the dress, she clicked the hologram wall off and sat Lilliana down to do her make up in the natural light.

Lilliana relaxed under the sun's rays as they spilled through the canopied trees, listening to the different bird calls. Within minutes Fox had transformed Lilliana from an elegant, natural beauty into a sensual swamp goddess. Lilliana's brooding dark eyes contrasted with red lips, long red painted fingernails and black hair falling silkily around her shoulders in curls.

"Well done as always, Fox," Cam nodded in approval.

"Where am I supposed to stand?" Lilliana asked Cam and Tim.

"We are going to do dry shots first; I'll get you to stand in that clump of trees over there, Lilly, and then we'll do the wet shots where I'll lay you on top of the water amongst the flowers," Tim said gesturing to the trees.

"You mean this water here, where a giant crocodile swam not far from us?" Lilliana pointed to the water, a horrified look on her face.

"You'll be safe darling, look—" Cam walked over to Ryder and got him to snap on his heat radar. The hologram flashed open, revealing themselves on the grid, their body heat presence indicated in red, while small fish, birds and wildlife lay on the far outskirts of the swamp's banks, and snakes showed up in blue.

"That is going to be on while I'm in there, right?"

Cam tapped her chin. "Of course, darling! Can you imagine my life from here on out if I let anything happen to you?" He raised an eyebrow, a mock look of pain on his face.

Lilliana laughed, nodding. "Yeah okay, that makes me feel much better."

"Right Lilly, we are going to place you over there amongst the trees. You will appear to be rising from the swamp, and your feet will be submerged ankle deep, hands either side of the trunks. We'll do a few close ups, others distant. Serious, sultry, you know the drill." Tim smiled.

Lilliana nodded. There she was, standing alone in the middle of the swamp, her feet balanced on a slippery tree trunk in the gloriously cool water. The air had such a sweet scent; it reminded her of days past when, as a child, she and her dear friend Jessica had spent hours in the swamps of Louisiana.

She let her mind drift to those days. They were carefree and exhilarating, where a day painting and exploring the bayous made bonding with a new friend an adventure. How blessed she had been to form such a tight bond with lovely Jessica. It was that bond that helped her remain strong when the two girls had been abducted at fifteen, to be abused and tormented for three months of their young lives. It was three months of hell before Orlando, Jessica's now boyfriend, had helped them murder their captives as they fended for themselves. Escaping the evil clutches, they had then been delivered into the hands of The Given. And here we are, Lilliana thought to herself; almost ten years later and never a dull moment.

An hour later after striking many different poses and angles, Lilliana dried off and pulled her jeans and tee shirt on as Fox pulled out wrapped sandwiches from a bag.

"Who made those?" Lilliana asked.

"Russell's crew," Cam answered for Fox. "His men set up our meals last night, organised breakfast and sent lunch. They are the only other ones who know our current location."

"Where is the Australian's Given Facility?" Lilliana asked Cam as she thanked Fox for her salad roll.

"Not far," he said, before sinking his teeth into a delicious roll with chicken, herbs, and salad. "Being such an big country they have a facility being built in Glenormiston South, plus the one here in the Northern Territory, and Brisbane."

"Maybe I'll be able to do a safe house in those areas too?" Lilliana asked; she was excited about the thought of being able to help so many. Cam was about to reply when Ryder cut in.

"We have heat coming up ahead," he said, trying not to sound alarming.

Unit Eight were on immediate alert. Eric stood in front of Lilliana as Marcus stood near Fox. Lilliana's head swivelled around to where Ryder was staring intently along the banks, his gun and the others pointed in the direction of the approaching figure.

"Relax." Cam sighed with relief. "It's just Reid."

"I think *relax* is the wrong word to use, Cameron," Fox scoffed.

David Reid stepped out from between the trees. He was effortlessly tall and blonde, with the palest blue eyes. His lean, strong frame looked relaxed, as always, whether he was being interrogated or tortured; no matter what situation Lilliana had seen him in, he always appeared cool and in control, even when he wasn't. He instantly made her blood run cold.

"Breathe Lilliana," Cam whispered for her ears only. "He can't hurt you. Desmond, let's pick him up."

"Yes Sir." Desmond turned the boat around and headed over to pick up Reid.

Lilliana put the rest of her roll into the plastic wrap; it was impossible to swallow another bite. She looked up as Eric pushed a water bottle in her hands.

"Thanks," she took a grateful swallow.

"Well that prick will need to bullet proof everything whilst I'm around." Fox snarled.

"We need him—everyone chill, please." Cam ran his hand through his hair, a gesture Lilliana had seen his brother do often enough when stressed.

"Show time," she heard him mutter to himself, as David stepped on board. She watched him as he was led down the opposite end to her, and Eric stood in front, blocking Reid from her view.

"Let's go," Cam signalled.

Desmond got the boat in gear and they flew across the water, back to where they came from hours earlier. Lilliana kept her eyes on the clear water and picturesque surroundings. She took a few deep breathes and composed herself before they got off the boat. She knew The Guardian was activated to the establishments network back home.

She did not want Damon to worry about her. She would appear relaxed and calm and dedicated to this mission.

She glanced over at Tim, who was working furiously away at his computer, editing and sending the photographs to Pier in America.

"Right everyone," Cam stepped out of the boat onto the pier, pulling Fox up beside him. "I want us in the vehicles and in Darwin ASAP, so let's move. David, Rocco, Marcus and Eric—I'll need you with me and Lilliana, let's go."

Lilliana met David's eyes for the first time.

He smiled coolly. "Hello Angel."

"David." The sun that beat down on her skin did nothing to remove the chill in her bones. Eric took her arm and moved her along.

It was going to be a long day.

***

The jet flew at cruising altitude just hours after they had left Darwin. Lilliana sat beside Eric, who was playing a game on some new gadget. Cam was beside David with Rocco, and Marcus questioning him about the progress he had made with his connections in New York. David said that he had made contact with all the appropriate individuals in order to send a message to his father that he had been released, and that the Given establishment had complied to all his demands.

Tim and Fox were discussing the latest technology in camera equipment, and what he hoped for in the modelling shoots once they reached New York. Fox was excited to meet the people who had been following her career for years, and with all the extra press that had been following Lilliana's Dark Angel campaign, she secretly hoped her brother had been watching and would attempt to make contact with her.

Lilliana thought back to the press conference in Darwin; the people had been so friendly and enthusiastic, excited to hear what she had planned to do with her campaign. She had met several families and been photographed with many children who had been thrilled to get both her and Fox's autograph. It had all been so rewarding to be able to reach out to the people and offer them hope. She just couldn't wait to get started and begin the process to help those that needed it the most. She stood up and was about to walk past Eric when his hand shot out, grabbing her wrist. He smiled as her head whipped down to look at him.

"Sorry, just want to know where you are going."

"Bathroom." She sighed as he stood. "Eric, it's ten seats away."

She glanced at the back of David's head and shrugged. "Ryder is on him."

"Nevertheless, after you." Eric waited for her to walk past then followed her to the bathroom.

She shut the door gently on him then she opened it again, looking up at him. "Can you get my bag please, Eric? I really need a shower."

"Sure." He turned to walk down the aircraft's aisle, and, retrieving her bag, bought it back to her. "Enjoy."

"Thanks." She smiled as she closed the door once more.

Stripping and stepping under the blissful hot spray, Lilliana scrubbed and lathered every inch before relaxing in the warmth, allowing the conditioner to soak into her hair.

"Hey Lilly, can I come in?" Fox called out.

"Yeah sure."

Fox shut the door behind her after quickly slipping into the room.

"How are you doing?"

"I'm fine, you?"

"Loving it! It is so awesome to be out and about! I mean, I have not left our grounds in over fifteen years! My God, I can't wait for New York! Darwin was just a small taste of the fame we have coming my friend." She stepped closer. "Lilly, I have to tell you something," she said, glancing behind her, all conspirator-like, lowering her voice as she leaned towards her friend. "I've got a feeling I'm going to see my brother!"

"Oh Fox, how wonderful." Lilliana rinsed the swampy water from her hair and shut the shower off. "But how?" She dried herself and slipped a blue sundress over her head. It floated about her knees and sat prettily on her shoulders with thin straps. Slipping on low blue heels, she began brushing her hair, before braiding it over one shoulder.

"Well, he'll just come to me of course, what with all the publicity Johnson's men have organised with Tim and the Officials; he'll know where I'm going to be before I do! It will be perfect, I never thought I'd have this opportunity to see him again, and now because of you, I will!" Fox was beaming as she stripped off and stepped into the shower.

"You'll have to be careful Fox—you'll need to keep him safe. With our situation, and Reid Senior probably watching our every move, don't let it be known who he really is to you." She slipped blue feathered earrings into her ears, and around her neck she placed a long silver chain with a heavy glass ball that hung between her breasts.

It was a noticeably young, fresh look. Sexy and clean. Just what Tim had requested for the cameras which would greet them on their arrival.

"I will be careful, Lilly." Fox looked closely at her friend. "Tell me truthfully; how you are?"

"I miss Damon so much it feels like there is a rock in my chest! My arms ache at the thought of not being able to wrap them around him. If it weren't for the fact that we are going to be doing some real good, not just with my campaign, but hopefully by putting that bastard Reid away, well, I wouldn't be here. I think I'd be curled up in the foetal position, waiting for him to pick me up." She shrugged, realising how incredibly crestfallen she felt.

"Oh Lilliana," Fox stepped out of the shower and grabbed a towel and flung it around herself before pulling the younger woman into her arms. "You beautiful, sad girl—it will all be alright, you'll see him again, sooner than you think. You are one of the strongest women I know, and the depth of your missing him will pass as we get busier." She kissed her cheek before looking her in the eye. "We will be home before you know it, and you and Damon will have many, long years in each other's arms. Trust me. Redheads never lie!"

Lilliana laughed, raising an eyebrow. "Really, never heard that one before!"

"Yeah? Well, I just made it up, go with it." Fox shrugged, dropped the towel and stepped back into the shower spray. "I don't suppose you'd tell Rocco I dropped the soap and pulled a back muscle?"

Lilliana smiled and shook her head in wonder. "I can do anything for you."

"Better not, head of the team and all." Fox sighed as she lathered herself up.

Lilliana smiled, closing the door behind her and found Eric sitting there, waiting to walk her back to her seat. As she walked by David's seat, she looked him dead in the eye and flashed a beautiful smile. It was for Damon, her guardian Angel, looking at her from within this demon.

***

Thousands of miles away Damon leaned his hip against his desk and smiled at the screen. He had paused the live video feed just as Lilliana had walked past David and smiled at him. Damon automatically knew she meant that smile for him. Two screens floated in the air, side by side above his desk. This one, the paused screen, while the other continued playing the live video feed. Nothing too exciting to see at this stage, he thought, just Reid watching Cam and occasionally flicking through a magazine. Damon poured a coffee as a knock sounded on his office door.

"Come in," he said, taking a mouthful of the strong coffee.

Johnson strode in, tall and handsome in a rugged sort of way, his sandy blonde hair falling over honest eyes. Loyal and dependable, he was always ready for action and always had an intelligent plan at the ready when danger threatened.

"How's it going?" he nodded his thanks as Damon passed him a coffee.

"It all seems to be falling into place. Did you get the last twenty-four-hour feed on Reid?" Damon walked around to his desk and sat.

"Yes, my team and I watched it live. I have spoken to our men in New York; apparently Reid Senior is pleased that we have met with his terms. The attacks have been called off, but we have scouts located all around our perimeters. If an unauthorised flight comes anywhere near us, we'll take it out of the sky."

"Excellent."

Johnson studied the younger man over the brim of his cup. "How are you holding up, Damon?"

Damon smiled slowly. "I won't lie; I miss her dreadfully. She should be here with me, but I know she is in good hands. Cam, Eric, and Marcus won't let anything happen to her, or Fox. If things go accordingly, she should be back here soon enough."

"Let's hope so." Johnson nodded to Lilliana, frozen, smiling prettily into the camera. "At least she knows you can see her through The Guardian."

"Yes, it gives us an advantage, that's for sure. Reid's phone call to his father's men was guarded, but he knows he can't slip up or we'll end him."

"It's a bonus alright," Johnson placed his empty cup down on the tray. "I'll get back upstairs, second surveillance with be starting soon."

"Yes, as soon as they touch down, thanks Johnson."

"No problem." Johnson walked out the door as Josephine burst through. "Hello Johnson," she smiled.

"Mrs Night," he nodded and continued on his way up to Black Ops.

"Damon." Josephine walked over to the man who had always been her brother, even before she had married his. He stood and walked around his desk, opening his arms for the woman that he had known since she was just two years old. She slipped her arms around him and dropped her head on his chest.

"How are you sweetheart, got all the orders finished?" He kissed the top of her soft, wavy, honey brown curls.

"Yes, Rupert and I have been flat out since six this morning," she smiled up at him. "New seedlings, fruits and veg are finished and our crop rotations complete. The order is ready for pick-up first thing in the morning. We are blessed with an extraordinary team."

"There is no doubt about that," he squeezed her gently before offering her a cup of tea.

She shook her head. "No thanks, the girls and I are having a girl's night in—wine and plenty of it." She sighed looking at Lilliana's face then back at Damon. "I know; I miss her too."

He looked down at her. "We make a fine pair, don't we?"

"Oh yeah, no doubt about that," Josephine smiled.

"You have always been a positive ray of sunshine in my life, Josephine. I am glad that in all of this, if I have to suffer without my heart by my side, I still have you."

"Oh Damon. I will do all that I can for you, as you constantly do everything you can, for others. Three days till Christmas, and we can put on our smiles and get through this, together?"

"Yes, I believe we can. You go and have a good night, sweetheart."

"I'll be at the meeting as soon as I can after my delivery in the morning," she called out as she headed towards the door.

"I'd rather you see the footage after Johnson and I have viewed it, Josephine."

She stopped in her tracks and turned to face him. "Why Damon? Cam is my husband; Lilliana is my best friend; I think I should be able to view it live with you both."

He sighed inwardly, folding his arms over his firm chest. His dark head dropped to look at the floor for a moment, before lifting his glorious dark eyes in the direction of his sister.

"Josephine," he began quietly. "We've talked about this; the reason I do not want you to view the live feeds is because we have no control from here on, in terms of what happens. I do not want you to witness anything ugly that may occur."

"Such as?" She folded her arms, not wanting to have a standoff with the one man in the entire world that she had loved and respected since she was two-years-old.

"Anything violent, anything before the team can act. It's just as a precaution. Please love, I have so much to deal with, let me spare you any discomfort. Trust me; if anything happens to our group, anything at all, you'll be the first to know. But until then let Johnson and I view things first, then you can enjoy it afterwards knowing nothing bad has happened."

She watched his handsome face closely before walking over to gently stroke his cheek. "Sorry Damon, of course I understand—you want to protect me and I love you for that. I'll look forward to seeing the footage when you're comfortable with it." She leaned up on tiptoes and kissed his cheek. "Goodnight."

"Goodnight sweetheart."

As she left, Damon ran a hand through his hair, picking up his phone on the second ring. Glancing at his watch, he listened to the voice on the other end urgently explaining a crisis requiring his immediate attention. At that moment he was grateful to oversee a facility that never left him bored; there was always a situation that needed to be dealt with. Time away from Lilliana was time best spent being flat out and occupied.

✳✳✳

Driving from the airport through the city, Lilliana saw hundreds of billboards with many beautiful faces selling sports items, jewellery, cosmetics, and a variety of things the world seemed to need. Her own face had been amongst them. It had been surreal, seeing her face splashed around the city like that.

To think: her photographs, her time, would contribute to setting up safe houses for the young people of the world who would need a soft place to fall. The thought of helping so many filled her with such satisfaction. The first few weeks in New York were a hectic blur of campaign building, photoshoots and volunteering in a city that needed more healing hands than they could count. Lilliana and Fox had been assigned a flood of shoots with individual companies. Perfume, lingerie, shoes, cosmetics, and fashion. It was an eye opener for both of them to see how the modelling world operated on the outside.

Tim was highly admired within the agencies and Lilliana was learning a great deal from him as she watched him deal with the most highly demanding personalities, with professional decorum. She was thrilled, too, to have had the chance to work alongside several charity organisations that wanted to support her with her campaign.

They had celebrated a very quiet Christmas morning with the team, before venturing out to meet and volunteer with Christopher's, Goth-Kitchen-Heads, simply known as the G-heads, where they spent forty-eight hours serving meals to the homeless and getting to know many families that had been through hell in a world that couldn't seem to maintain decency to all.

The G-heads ran their organisation successfully, due in large part to the two million Damon had sent them a few months ago. Along with continuous supplies of fresh fruits, vegetables, and soils from The Given's Horticultural Department, they were able to plant their own vegetable gardens and small rotation crops to maintain healthy and fresh foods for those in need all year round. It was so good to see that the work her friends did back home benefitted so many outside their walls.

Lilliana also filmed a commercial for her Dark Angel Campaign, advocating her desire to help serve and protect the innocents of the world, explaining what she was all about. It was elegant and informative and gave many families and lost souls hope.

When Tim and Cam played the commercial for her to see, Lilliana was shocked and happily surprised to see how the message of help and hope was sincerely conveyed. Also, not having watched any sort of television for ten years, it was interesting to see herself move across a commercial screen for the whole world to see.

The hotel they were staying in had forty-seven levels. Fox was impressed as she lay her eyes on the building, all glass and steel, expensively designed with an appreciation for architectural balance, both new and old. The foyer was sophisticated and welcoming, and the bar and dining areas were lush, affording its patrons both privacy for meetings and spacious areas to socialise. The elevators had thick, clear glass walls that whisked one up to their floor in seconds.

Lilliana's room was large and cosy. Polished wooden floors were scattered with lush Persian rugs, and a four-poster bed with massive columns supporting silky gauze that floated down around the bed like a protective shield. At the foot of the bed lay a colourful Montego chaise covered in decorative pillows coloured in orange, purple and red silks. The artwork on the walls included a Buddha, temples, and sunsets, giving the entire room a Mediterranean feel. The bathroom was exotic and sleek; white marble covered the floor and walls, and sitting around the room were enormous sculptured hands made of coloured glass, each delicately holding a tall, white candle, its rays flickering light across the generous clawfoot bath, which sat in the middle of the room, filled with scented, lukewarm water. The shower and toilet sat privately behind a tall screen of lilac coloured glass. Lilliana fantasised it would be a beautiful bathroom to share with Damon.

Fox's room, meanwhile, was sleek and modern with all the latest technology at her disposal, which suited her perfectly. Cam had chosen the rooms that he thought both women would be most comfortable in. The rooms which housed him, and the Unit Eight team were on either side of the women, with Reid placed with Unit Eight.

The team had taken several tours to view the properties around the United States where Lilliana's safe houses would be built and set up; Unit Eight were always lurking protectively in the background while Eric remained constantly by her side, along with Cam and Fox. They had day trips all over the continental U.S: trips and flights from Canada to Alaska, Washington to Mexico, Guatemala to Costa Rica. They even had a week in South America, with two photo shoots in

Brazil and Argentina.

The structures of the buildings would be made with Bio bricks and randomly placed bluestone, creating an elegant, old-world appeal reminiscent of churches in days gone by. The interiors would be modern and spacious, with thick black steel beams, glass and featured river stoned walls creating dividers to medical, kitchen, lounge, office, and smaller separate bedrooms. The floors were to be a polished concrete, warmed by hydronic solar heating, offering up blues, greens, and a rainbow of colours, sparkling as the sun reflected down through the stained-glass roof.

The windows were designed to have had planter boxes full of colours and sweet scents, and all views from inside the buildings would look out to courtyards of flowers and water features, with plenty of seating, surrounded by archways with hanging wisteria, offering a feeling of serenity and calmness—all of these were of course Rupert's creations. Colourful azaleas would pop with a subtle scent and imbue a feeling of welcome and warmth. Urns and small pots of poppies and tulips would be placed on pedestals around the buildings adding a spill of colour to every corner.

In each archway above the doorway there would be no cross, but in its place hung a symbol of angel wings enveloping the small figure of a child, offering the promise of protection and safety. There would be several buildings built in each country where a Given Facility existed. The Officials had been extremely helpful in regard to acquiring vacant lands to begin building, or purchasing existing properties that were deemed structurally damaged, and therefore needed bulldozing. It was all happening quite quickly according to Ryder, who in the past had worked for the Officials before he went undercover; he was impressed with the speed, efficiency and influence that Lilliana's project was having on them.

Back in New York, Lilliana took the opportunity to catch up on a few hours' sleep before showering and slipping on a pair of jeans and a tee shirt before Eric walked her to Fox's room. He told her about an interesting movie he had watched while she had slept, as they waited for Fox to open the door. Lilliana had to smile at his enthused tone;

she was glad he had at least some downtime to himself whilst on this mission.

Fox buzzed the door open and they walked in to see her sitting in a pod-like chair that seemed to be suspended in mid-air. The red

haired beauty was lounging back with a glass of champagne. She had ended a phone call by clicking off a see-through screen and flicking it away, just as one would a pesky house fly. It seemed to disappear into thin air.

"Lilly, what are you wearing to this event tonight?" She asked, sliding off the chair and walking over to the bar to refill her glass. She held up the bottle of champagne. "Want one?"

"No thanks." Lilliana walked over to the large window to look out over the city; she could see all bright lights, tall buildings, and busy, clean streets below.

Fox sipped from her glass as she joined her friend. "I saw the Officials take down a group of teenagers last night after a street brawl that got way out of hand. The Officials shot them with nasty little dart guns and loaded them into a van. I wonder where they were taking them?"

"Some facility to help rid them of their growing violent ways I'm sure. Ryder was telling me of these hypnotherapy centres that have been running for the past eight years to rid society of signs of violence, impurities and such."

"Ah, society; was there any real hope that human beings could just get along and live peacefully?"

"Mmm...you wouldn't think that it would all be so hard, would you?"

"I don't know, when are they going to realise that some people simply should not procreate, just to raise the poor kids with shitty standards and pass them off as fucked up adults, only to start the entire process all over again? Let us just say, I don't have a lot of positive thoughts towards how the Officials handle society." Fox sat her glass down and walked over to the bed where a slim black strapless dress sat, with spiky heels and elegant, white gold jewellery.

"So, again, what are you wearing tonight?"

Lilliana turned, running her hands over her face. "I don't know, whatever Cam puts me in I guess; I wouldn't care if it was a potato sack. Do you think I really have to be there? I'm exhausted and could sleep for a month—all these side projects, along with the campaign set up have been going non-stop."

Fox turned her full attention towards Lilliana, noticing her tired eyes, and exhausted expression. She knew the cost of smiling and being upbeat all the time, presenting a professional face around the clock, when inside, you just wanted to run back to your place of safety and close down. She sighed.

"I'm afraid you do have to go, love—there will be many people coming tonight who have great influence in powerful organisations and that will contribute to your campaign, assist in running things when you go back home. I will be with you every second, okay? Come on, it will be fun."

Lilliana smiled, "You could make watching paint dry, fun."

"Well, I don't know about that, but we will have a roomful of vibrant individuals to connect with."

A knock came at the door, and Fox checked the ID panel. Eric stood waiting. Fox buzzed him in.

"Ladies, Cam needs us in his room, pronto."

"Alright then, let's get this show on the road." Fox followed Eric and Lilliana out, a small ball of concern growing in the pit of her stomach as the unknown lay ahead this night.

***

Thousands of miles away, Damon sat with Johnson, Brett, and the team, watching the scene through David's eyes. The impending meeting was putting Damon on edge as he paced his office. He didn't know how Lilliana would react to this part of the operation that had been designed solely for her protection.

Johnson watched Damon, thinking he looked more like a caged panther than a man leading an undercover operation from thousands of miles away.

"It will be fine, Damon, they've got a handle on it; Cam won't let anything happen to her."

"He is only human, Johnson." Damon stopped in front of the screen, folding his arms across his chest, looking on at his brother and the team and hoping they could hold it all together when their plan finally went into action.

CHAPTER 3

Cam, Unit Eight and David were all in the room waiting for Lilliana to arrive. Marcus handed Lilliana a cup of tea after she greeted the team, deliberately ignoring David. Cam placed his arm around her shoulder, smiling down at her.

"Hi."

"Hi yourself," she said, feeling comforted by him. She allowed herself to relax a little as she sipped the hot tea. Being near him made her miss Josephine and Damon, but she forced herself to push the pain away.

"Righto; now that we are all gathered David has an update to share with us."

Lilliana turned her eyes to the man she loathed, not only because he had witnessed the evil, vile deeds done to Jessica and herself when they were teenagers, but for every sordid crime he had been a part of.

He was an unpredictable, sinister individual; it shocked Lilliana for the fact that everyone else in the room seemed at ease working alongside him, in order to reel his father in. Even with that knowledge, it did nothing to calm the battle of butterflies that were gearing for war in her stomach.

David Reid sat back in a large leather chair wearing a charcoal grey suit with a bright red tie, rolling the stem of a wine glass between his fingers, all the while watching Lilliana.

"Get on with it, Reid." Eric snapped, not liking the way he was watching Lilliana so closely, and with such familiarity.

"Of course," David smiled ever so politely, after taking a mouthful of the red liquid. He glanced around the room as he spoke, looking each person in the eye.

"Tonight's the night. My father will be watching, and when the time comes, I will place myself and Lilliana in his men's hands, along with my new team." He saluted his glass to Eric, Marcus and Unit Eight. "We will vacate the premises peacefully and go with them. No doubt in little time, with your marvellous tracking technology, your surveillance team back in Louisiana will locate us at my father's main compound. As long as my father gets what he wants—which of course, is me—with the added bonus," he nodded, and gestured towards Lilliana. "It should all work out quite well, don't you think?"

"Well if it doesn't, it's literally your head." Fox looked pleased at the thought.

David stared at her with pale eyes.

Ryder addressed Cam. "All our gear is set up; William and Daniel met with Reid's men eight hours ago and confirmed the meet for tonight. It looks like it will be a quick extraction, we don't anticipate any problems."

"Good," Cam said, and rubbed Lilliana's arm before walking over to the fireplace, gazing into the flames. He turned around to face David.

"It is up to you to make sure no harm comes to Lilliana; and it's in your best interest that your father is gentle with her. If he comes up with any evil scheme to hurt her or use her in any way, we will not only end you, but your sister."

Cam's eyes darkened, hoping David could understand how serious he was in this moment.

"Yes, I have had this lecture from your brother before we left; I'm aware he has the power to blow my head off at any time with this little device he inserted," he said, pointing to his eye. "My father will of course attempt to get a rise out of our good doctor here, but I will not allow him to actually hurt her, I have given my word. But I do believe Mr Johnson's proposal is the best course of action to keep her safe."

"And what proposal is *that*?" Fox said, ignoring David, addressing Cam. David jumped right in, replying gleefully.

"For Lilliana to pose as my wife."

"What!" Lilliana could not contain her outburst, feeling revulsed at the mere thought.

"Think about it logically; my father will not lay a finger on you if he believes you are mine."

Lilliana swung her head around to look at Cam; she was intelligent enough to know that in some ways this proposal made sense, but she prayed there was another way.

"Lilly," he started softly. "Johnson's right, it's practically foolproof. There is no way Reid will hurt you if he thinks you are his beloved son's wife."

Lilliana glanced around the room.

Eric stood with arms folded, not looking impressed. Fox looked stunned and was uncharacteristically silent. All of Unit Eight's expressions were carefully blank, staring at Lilliana like they had the first time they had met her. Like she was bait.

Regrettably, she turned her gaze toward David. "Do not think for one second that you can put your hands on me."

"Well, of course I'll have to when we are in public; I will put on a good show of being your loving husband—and if you want to fool my father you'd be wise to do the same." He eyed her coolly.

"Yeah, alright Reid, relax!" Eric couldn't help himself. "Bastard!" He hissed under his breath.

"I'd say, cocky much?" Fox scoffed.

David opened his mouth to speak; he had an arrogant and menacing look on his face; but before he could let slip another comment, Cam stepped in, hands raised.

"Calm down, this isn't helping our already precarious situation." He glanced at Fox, then Eric before turning to David. "And you just behave yourself—don't push it Reid, that is a warning." David nodded once, before slowly raising his wine glass to his lips.

Lilliana glanced down at her tea; it had quickly lost its comforting appeal. She placed it on the coffee table, gently tapping her finger on the fine china. She thought of Damon and laughed out loud before she could stop herself. She glanced up noticing all eyes on her and shook her head.

"Sorry, it's just the irony of this situation. Damon married Felicia and now I'll be pretending to be married to David; you couldn't read about this in the most twisted novel." She ran her hands over her face and placed her hands on her hips. All for the greater good, she thought.

"Sure, I can pretend to be his loving wife, Cam—if it gets me safely back to Damon and helps put an end to one of history's most vile criminals."

Cam walked over to her and put his arms around her, dropping his chin on top of her head. She closed her eyes against his chest and let out a shaky breath.

"Can you do this?" He whispered quietly close to her ear.

She nodded her head. She'd basically agreed to do whatever it took when she left her home. Anything to bring down the house of Reid.

"Am I going with Lilly when they come to take her?" Fox sounded nervous.

"No," Lilliana shook her head, turning to Fox. "I am not having you anywhere near that man, no way."

"I tend to agree with the good doctor." David drained his wine and stood.

"Sorry Fox," Cam smiled at her, "I'll need you here with me anyway, we have a few more projects for you."

Fox looked worried for her friend, yet relieved for her own personal reasons. Tonight, was the night her brother was going to slip into the crowd. Tonight, she would be able to put her arms around him, after so many years of being apart. Cam looked around the room at Marcus, Eric and Unit Eight.

"This is it. Stay alert, stay alive and good luck. I'll see you downstairs in an hour."

Marcus walked over to Cam and shook his hand. "Everything will be fine, Cam."

They exchanged a smile as Cam squeezed his hand. "Thanks Marcus."

Marcus nodded and headed over to the door where his brother was waiting for him. They were going to have a private meeting before they gathered downstairs. Ryder had walked David out and into their room. Cam clapped a hand on Eric's shoulder before he left the room.

"I'll walk Lilly back to her room; you'll escort her downstairs for the event. If we don't get the chance later Eric, let me say thank you. Be careful once you're at Reid's compound, we have no idea how things are going to pan out once you are all there. I know he's familiar with a few of our men and will trust the rest of you believing you're David's men, but be careful all the same."

"Yes Sir," Eric looked down at Lilliana. "I'll be with you, every step of the way. I'm not going to let anyone hurt you."

Lilliana looked up into his warm, caring eyes. She reached out and touched his arm. "I know Eric," she smiled and he nodded and quickly exited the room.

Once everyone had gone, Cam and Lilliana were alone. Cam let out a deep breath and ran his hands through his hair.

"Well little sister, this is it," he placed his hands on his hips looking down at her.

"It certainly looks like it," she agreed. "Cam, if anything happens to me, please tell Damon he saved me."

Cam shook his head. "Don't…"

"Cam, please."

"Nothing will happen. Eric won't let a thing happen to you and David does not want to lose his head."

"Cameron. Please, just tell Damon how much I love him, that he is everything to me."

Cam smiled down at her. "I will Angel, the next time I talk to him, and you can tell him to his face when you see him. Deal?"

Lilliana smiled back. "Deal. Let my girls know how much I love them too."

"Of course; now, before we get you freshened up, changed and extra stunning, there's one thing we need to do." He walked over to a drawer and pulled out a small box. Flipping it open, he pulled out a large diamond ring, surrounded by crimson rubies. He walked back to her and placed the ring on her finger.

"David agreed this was something he would put on his wife's finger."

Lilliana cringed. "Yes, it certainly looks like it." She ran a finger over the large stone, thinking of the classy, elegant ring Damon had placed on her finger when he'd declared his deep, overwhelming love for her. She looked up at Cam.

"Here we go then."

"Yep, it's showtime." He offered his arm, and together they walked out towards her room, to prepare for the night ahead.

***

Fox helped Lilliana transform herself into a dark and seductive chess piece for the gala event. She slid into a tight, short red dress with thin straps, showcasing her curvaceous body. She sported heels red and high, with a tip so sharp that it could slice an ice block in half with one tap. Lilliana's long, black hair hung down her back in silky waves, and her nails were painted red to match her dress. Whatever unpredictable world she was entering into, she felt she'd have a rather good handle on it. She had been through another kind of hell herself and had heard plenty of others tell their disturbing stories of the horrific tragedies they had endured in the world they lived in.

This thought alone made her feel stronger and more determined to succeed at her task.

Lilliana knew she was about to star in a role alongside a cast that had some of the most gruesome lifestyle addictions. She would certainly do her best to pull off this act if it meant putting the scum away for good. When Eric greeted her at the door he was taken aback.

"Wow, breathtaking."

She smiled and took his offered arm, appreciating how handsome he looked himself, dressed in a smart black suit.

"I just let Fox do her thing, have her way with me," she shrugged as they stepped into the elevator to whisk them downstairs.

"You look smashing yourself, Eric." Their eyes met steadily, and he offered her a slow smile. She could see he was nervous and squeezed his arm reassuringly.

"You're going to be alright; we all are. I don't want anything to happen to you. Don't put yourself in danger for me, Eric."

"But that's exactly what I'm here for, Lilly. Here we go," he whispered as the elevator came to a stop and its doors opened.

Together they stepped out into a room of soft chandelier lighting and candles, and where the sweet tinkering of piano music and flowing conversations greeted them. The air was scented with flowers that filled crystal vases, and delicious aromas wafted from the serving trays carried by waiters to the party crowd. As Lilliana and Eric walked, cameras started clicking away, discretely snapping them from different angles. They crossed over the foyer and entered the large function room, and Eric escorted her straight to Cam, who was talking to Fox and Tim.

"Stunning." Cam kissed her cheek and took her arm from Eric. Eric took a bottle of water from a waiter and put his back towards Lilliana, his eyes to the crowd. Sipping his water, he glanced around the room, making eye contact with Unit Eight. All were in their places, keeping Lilliana and Fox in the centre of their vision.

"You look very handsome yourself, Cam. Hello Tim," she said, kissing his cheek.

"Hello Love. It's going to be one hell of a party. Are you ready?"

She thanked Fox for a glass of champagne and smiled at Tim. "Guess I'll have to be," she took a large mouthful, finished it off and placed the empty glass on a passing waiter's tray and grabbed another.

"That's the spirit," Fox saluted her, knowing her insides must have been churning.

"Ready for introductions, Lilly? We have a lot of enthusiastic people wanting to meet you. I have already been told that there is a company that wants to donate a quarter of a million to your safe houses in Australia and Ireland, and possibly other areas in Europe."

"Seriously?" Lilliana shook her head in wonder. "I'm blown away by the level of generosity— I'll have to make sure to show my appreciation... I am just so nervous, Cam; trying to act normal and relaxed right now feels almost impossible," she whispered to him.

"Just act your way through it, love; according to Rocco's intel, Reid won't be making a move for a few hours yet. Come on, there is someone dying to meet you."

As they made their way across the room to the man Cam most wanted Lilliana to meet, they were stopped constantly for introductions and conversation. One hour turned into two, with so many people wanting to talk to Lilliana and congratulate her on her wonderful campaign which had already generated four million dollars, a combined effort spanning several separate organisations as well as the Heads of other Given establishments. With all the generosity and positive comments, plus the champagne, Lilliana's head was reeling. As they continued along their way, a tall sandy haired man approached Lilliana. He was handsome and clean cut, with an eccentric quality about him. There was something about his eyes that she found familiar, soothing.

"Hello Lilliana, you haven't changed a bit." His voice was warm and smooth.

Who was this man? It clicked in a flash, and a flood of warm memories washed over her. She could see him; a kind man cooking pots of crawfish, teaching her how to paint, while listening to his grandmother's favourite artist, Harry Connick Jnr. Feelings of being surrounded by laughter, kindness, generosity, and a sense of welcome. Stephan; her dear friend Jessica's brother.

She burst into laughter at the sight of him and threw her arms around his neck, feeling tears of happiness lodge in her throat.

"Stephan," she whispered against his neck, "Jessica is doing so well, she's happy, and in love and a successful Team Leader. Everybody adores her, and she teaches art too," she pulled back from his arms to smile up at him.

"Then that's two of you who are happy and successful," he wiped a tear from her cheek with his thumb. "Give her all my love will you, and look after each other for me. Tell her I'm doing well and that I think of her every day," he gripped her hands and dropped a kiss on her cheek.

"I will, I promise. It was so good to see you Stephan," she squeezed his hands as he smiled at Cam, then turned away.

By the time they arrived on the other side of the room, the man that had been watching Lilliana with interest was intrigued not only by her beauty, but her seemingly honest, genuine appreciation of people's reactions to her. She was both kind and sincere with her responses and freely thanking people she had never met before. Her reaction to the last man was touching. She was just beautiful. Everything his good friend had told him about her, appeared to be accurate. By the time she reached him her cheeks were flushed and she was laughing at something Cam whispered to her. Cam opened his arm and made his introduction.

"Lilliana, let me introduce to you; this is Damon's dear friend and Head of the Australian Given, Russell Meek; Russell, this is Lilliana."

Lilliana recognised the name immediately as a friend Damon talked about fondly. Her heart quivered, she smiled as she shook Russell's hand. This man was another connection to Damon.

"Hello Russell, it's so lovely to finally meet you. We were just recently in Australia; we thought we might see you in Darwin."

He took her small, soft hand and shook it before raising it to his lips.

"I was close by. It is a real pleasure to meet you; I have watched your progress over the years as a Given, Lilliana. You have done so well, and by the way things are going, you will continue doing so. I have to tell you, it makes me and many others in my position happy to see one such as yourself, do so much for others."

"Lilliana has been helpful to others for quite a while now, Russell." Cam thanked a waiter as he took a plate of salmon and crispy duck sushi from the tray. "At least inside our establishment. But to be able to reach outside our walls and help many others well—that's something the Officials should have thought about years ago." Cam popped a delectable, bite sized piece of sushi in his mouth and offered the plate to Lilliana, who shook her head. "You need to put something in your stomach, Lilly."

Russell watched as she popped a mouthful in and chewed, looking at Cam as if to say, *happy now?* He could see that they were extremely comfortable with each other. It was something that would certainly give Damon comfort, he thought.

Cam nodded, "Better."

Lilliana realised how nervous he looked, himself. He was in such a difficult position. Missing his wife, his brother, home and now facing a dangerous situation with Lilliana herself.

"Cameron," she wrapped her arms around his waist and looked up at him. "It's all going to be fine; I promise. We will bring him down, all of us, together. Relax, nothing bad is going to happen."

He bent down and kissed the tip of her nose.

"Is that the champagne talking?" Fox stepped up from behind them.

"It may very well be," Lilliana smiled at her friend and slipped her arm around her waist. Fox placed her arm around Lilliana's shoulder and turned on the charm for Russell.

"Hello there."

He smiled back at the attractive redhead. "Hello yourself." They slipped into easy conversation as Eric stepped forward.

"They're here," he said quietly, resting his hand on the small of Lilliana's back, trying to offer her some comfort.

Fox turned around and glanced behind Lilliana. Over at the bar, David stood sipping a glass of Remy Martin cognac. She had to admit, even though she thought him psychotic, he was a very handsome man. She was nervous for Lilliana and hoped her young friend could handle this man, let alone his evil bastard of a father. If only she was going with them.

But her brother would be here in an hour and she was beyond excited at the prospect of seeing him. She only hoped that Lilliana would still be here to meet him. She quickly hugged her friend, whispering in her ear.

"Love you, Lilly. Be careful, be clever." She kissed her cheek before walking back into the crowd to mingle and blend.

Russell smiled down at her. "We'll meet again Lilliana; I wish you well."

"Thank you Russell, it was so nice meeting you." She swallowed the nervous lump forming in her throat and forced a sweet smile.

Cam kissed her cheek. "You'll be safe, we'll be watching," he whispered, close to her ear while nodding to Eric. He turned to Russell, who wanted to introduce a member of the South African Given. Eric gently guided her arm through his and led her through the crowd towards David; their roles were about to begin.

"Just breathe," Eric said quietly.

"Yes Sir," she whispered, and turned on her best fake smile as he led her towards the bar.

***

Damon watched through David's eye as Lilliana walked towards him. He could see how nervous she was. To a stranger she appeared confident, not knowing that when she ran a hand over the back of her neck, she was revealing a sign of her unease. It was knowing her for ten years and watching her grow from a traumatised teenager into a confident, caring twenty-six-year-old that gave him such insight into her insecurities. Just watching her walk towards David had Damon's heart thumping in his chest. He wanted her here, safe with him, in his arms.

"Here we go," a voice said quietly behind him.

"Indeed," he replied to Johnson. The door opened and Josephine stepped into the room.

"I am not going anywhere, Damon, so please don't ask me to leave," she sat on the arm of his chair, watching the screen anxiously with him. "It's going to be fine; it is all going to be fine." She placed her hand on his shoulder as much to comfort him, as herself.

Christopher was in the room pouring tea and coffee and refreshing the lemonade jug. "Josephine," he said quietly, "There's soup and toasted sandwiches. If you need anything else, just buzz Sandy."

Josephine smiled at him, tearing her eyes off Lilliana's face for a split second to acknowledge her friend. "Thank you—can you let Allie know that contact is being made? I'll fill you all in tonight."

"No worries, good luck," Christopher said to the room.

Damon thanked him without taking his eyes off his beautiful wife's face. His gut was clenched, and he forced his fists open to smooth his damp palms over his jeans.

Johnson pushed a coffee into his hands. "Thanks." He sipped at the hot liquid, grateful for the burning sensation as it slid down his throat. He imagined Lilliana's throat was on fire, too.

***

It was. She forced another swallow and smiled at David. His father could be watching right now. This was it. Time to prove herself one hundred percent in love with David, her husband for the sake of this ploy.

"David," she moved forward and offered him her cheek, trying to ignore the fact that he actually smelled divine. Whatever he was wearing was the scent of seduction. His red tie matched her dress.

"Hello lovely," he breathed her in. "You look smashing as usual." His lips brushed over her cheek before cupping the back of her neck gently, yet firmly holding her in place. "Daddy's watching," he whispered, looking into her eyes, before leaning forward and claiming her lips as his.

She gasped and tried to pull back. It was a knee-jerk reaction. It took her a full five seconds before she closed her eyes and relaxed as much as she could into the fake kiss. Thankfully, it was short and clean. He smiled down at her and released her. "Good girl."

She smiled sweetly at him and brushed a finger along his lapel. "Don't push it sugar," she said sweetly. "My Darling can blow your head off any time."

He nodded, still smiling, "Play nice, or no one will get what they want, little lady."

She looked away and tapped a red nail on the bar. "I know," she said quietly, "I'm just nervous," she glanced back at him.

He looked at her while he sipped his drink. "I know how hard this must be for you. I know I am disgusting to you; but we can make this work you and me, make it work to our advantage."

Lilliana nodded, looking away.

"Are you ready to go?"

David's eyes met Eric's over the top of her head. He nodded. "We are."

Eric resisted the urge to ask Lilliana if she was alright.

She took the drink David passed to her and had a mouthful as her eyes scanned the room. Marcus and Unit Eight watched from their positions. Her eyes met Fox's. Her friend smiled across the room while dazzling a handful of Tim's associates.

Cam was watching as he chatted to Russell and he ran a hand over his face, waving his fingers to her. She smiled as she turned to place her empty glass on the bar, hoping it sent a message of calm to Cam.

David took her elbow. This was it. The fact that Damon was with her through The Guardian was of small comfort, but a comfort, nevertheless. She could feel Eric at her back as David led her through the crowd of people towards a side door. Unit Eight, along with Reid's men, filed in behind them and they exited the building.

Once they stepped out into the chilly night air, a long white limousine was waiting by the curb, and a black four-wheel drive behind it. David guided Lilliana into the back of the limousine and nodded for Eric to join Unit Eight in the other vehicle.

Eric looked over his shoulder at Lilliana as he followed his Unit. She was alone with the enemy for this part of the trip, but he believed she could pull it off.

Lilliana sank down into the plush leather seat, taking a quick look around. There was a black glass panel blocking her view from the rest of the vehicle, while attached to the top was a small black dome, and a red light on in the centre. Lilliana presumed it was a camera. David slid in beside her placing his hand on the soft flesh of her thigh where her dress rode up. His long, white fingers looked odd and out of place on her firm, tanned thigh. His fingers were so different from Damon's fingers. She forced herself to relax when he began stroking her back and forth as the car sped forward. She wondered if David's father was watching, so she placed her hand on top of David's in an attempt to stop him stroking her, and smiled up at him in a manner that warned him to stop what he was doing.

He moved closer to her and brushed his lips over hers.

She forced herself not to freeze. "Where are we going?"

"I'm not sure, gorgeous—wherever Father takes us." As the windows were blacked out, he had nowhere else to look but at her. Not that that was a difficult feat. "Your campaign seems to be thriving already, well done."

"Thank you," she murmured, preferring to keep her eyes on his fingers rather than meet with his cool blue eyes. Being alone with him in such close proximity with his fingers stroking her flesh made her feel a combination of anxiety and revulsion.

His eyes followed hers and she froze. "Relax," he said, moving up against her ear.

Lilliana was trying to relax but knowing that Damon could see what David was doing to her leg made the situation almost unbearable.

***

Damon was gripping the arms of the chair back in his office; he quickly got up and paced the room. Johnson sighed inwardly; he did not envy Damon in his position right now.

"Sleazy bastard," Josephine hissed out between her teeth. "Can't you zap him or something?"

Damon looked across at her and let out a pained laugh.

Her eyes met his from across the room and she offered him a soft, compassionate smile.

"What I wouldn't give to zap him right now, Josephine. But we have a little way to go just yet." He turned his attention back to the screen and then to the door, as a knock sounded.

Johnson checked his watch. "That will be Rachael." He kissed her as she walked in, her hands full with a small tray containing two syringes.

"Oh, I didn't realise Josephine was here," Rachael said, looking at Damon. "Do we need another syringe, Sir?"

"No, Josephine needs to get on with the day to day running of things here."

Josephine understood that Damon and Johnson were to be

injected with a top grade 'awake' serum that would keep them alert and functioning for seventy-two to ninety-six hours. Johnson's head security, Brett, who was upstairs in the Black Ops division, was also being administered with the serum as he ran the team upstairs.

Damon stood still as Rachael rubbed his arm with an antiseptic before jabbing him. He gave no reaction, his eyes ever watchful on his beloved's face.

***

"Ah, here we are." David stepped out of the limousine as it stopped, and he held his hand out for Lilliana to take. As she stepped out, she glanced around expecting to see a building of some sort. Instead, she found that they were at a small, secluded airstrip.

A silver jet was waiting with lights on, engine going. "Let's be quick, shall we." David hurried her towards the stairs leading up. Lilliana glanced behind her and noticed Unit Eight were close behind. It gave her relief to see friendly, familiar faces. With them were two large men dressed in black suits and dark shades. She noticed they were not plain sunglasses as flickering green lights illuminated over the lens.

She couldn't have known that they could penetrate through metal and contained heat sensors. Once all were seated the jet took off at such speed it almost made Lilliana ill.

Concern filled Eric's face as he noticed Lilliana's discomfort. He reached across and took her wrist. "Are you alright?"

She nodded quietly. "Too much excitement and champagne I'm afraid," she said, forcing a smile.

"We have such good security, don't we darling?" David looked Eric in the eye as he put his arm around Lilliana and pulled her close to rub his large, pale hand up and down her arm.

Lilliana could feel her anxiety building; being so close to David, his smell, the feel of his body pressed hard up against hers, along with the probability of Reid senior watching, was all leading up to a not-so-good moment, she was sure of it.

"I think I'm going to be sick," she whispered.

Eric quickly got to his feet and reached down to scoop her around the waist and pull her up. "I've got this Sir," he forced himself to sound respectful, in case Reid senior was listening.

"Good, thank you Eric." David noted the pain on Lilliana's face before Eric quickly rushed her to the bathroom and locked the door behind them.

She vomited till there was nothing left. Eric held her hair. She washed her face, rinsed her mouth, and leaned her forehead against the cold mirror, water droplets dripping down her face, hands gripping the sink as she closed her eyes and willed the greasy feeling in her stomach to cease.

"Lilly?" Eric dropped her hair and handed her a hand towel.

She opened her eyes and took it from him, wiping the cold droplets from her skin. Sighing, she turned to face him, leaning her back against the sink. "I'm okay Eric," she said, her eyes lifting to his.

He could see the tears in them now, not knowing if they were due to her vomiting or the pile of emotions crashing down upon her.

"You know, Damon has given me quite a lot of free range with you," he said, looking down at her.

"Such as?" She had no idea where he was going with this.

"Such as, if I think you are struggling, I can make it easier for you."

"How are you going to do that Eric?" She pushed her hair back, turning to drop the washer in the sink. As she turned back to face him, she had time only to let out a small gasp, seeing what Eric was about to do. He pricked her quickly in the arm with a sleek silver needle.

She was out in a second.

Eric carried her back to David explaining that Lilliana wasn't great with air travel and tucked her in the seat opposite David so he could lay her down. He covered her with a soft blanket and popped her head on a pillow.

He was sure Damon would approve.

***

Damon did approve. He observed all their movements through The Guardian, watching as David flicked through a magazine, chatted to security, poured drinks, and constantly looked over at Lilliana. Damon was thankful to Eric for sparing Lilliana any more stress; this tranquilliser would at least give her a few hours peace.

Johnson was flicking his fingers over a screen. "It looks like they're heading to South America."

"Thank God it's not Italy." Josephine took a huge bite out of her roast pumpkin and zucchini sandwich, catching a dollop of mustard with her finger as it made an exit from the corner of her mouth.

Damon gazed at her, raising an eyebrow.

Josephine shrugged and tried to chew quickly and swallow so she could explain. "She says that's one place she'd love to have a romantic getaway with you. If they took her there... well, it would ruin it for her."

Damon poured a cup of rich, pea and ham soup down his throat, before grabbing half a toasted sandwich. Taking a big mouthful, he crossed over to another set of screens. Tapping the console, he noted that Fox's signal indicated she was not with the rest of the group in New York. He picked up the phone and rang his hotel where they had all stayed. After a few rings and two connections later, Damon was talking to Cam.

"Cameron, why is Fox not with you or Tim?"

Josephine dropped her sandwich and sat down on the chair; eyes glued to Damon. She missed her man so much it hurt.

"She's fine Damon, she's safe," Cam replied. "How's Lilliana and our crew?"

"Up in the air, looks like they are landing in Manaus." Damon nodded his thanks to Johnson as he tapped on the screen for Damon to see the location. "So far so good."

"Great. Fox has met up with her brother; I allowed her time to catch up with him, spend a few days bonding. In the meantime, I have met with the Official's delegates. Several of Lilliana's safe houses have begun development. Three have been completed. I know Lilliana wanted to interview the staff herself, but if you could somehow get Allie to me then I think the two of us can make a good start on filling the positions. We have thousands of applicants to interview already." Cam said and waited.

"That sounds doable—I will talk to Allie immediately. Maybe

I can send her and Christopher to you. I know he would absolutely love to catch up with his G-heads. And I believe Lilliana, all things considered, would appreciate both your and Allie's judgment on who would best fit those roles. I'm sure she would want the positions filled as soon as possible so the completed buildings can open up and start serving those in need." Damon was watching Josephine's eager expression as he listened to Cam's reply.

They talked for a few minutes more whilst Damon filled Cam in on how the establishment was running whilst he was away. He told him Lilliana's brother, Scott, was doing extremely well and helping Jessica teach in her art classes. He had already finished portraits on a handful of the new Given that had recently arrived, and they were exceptional.

"How are you dealing, Brother?" Cam asked, once business was out of the way.

"Probably the same as you are," Damon answered dryly.

"I don't think so; I know my wife is safe and happy with you. Your wife is involved in a mission that is not only dangerous and unpredictable, but out of your reach. So, I will ask you again. How are you dealing?"

Damon appreciated his brother's concern. He missed Cam. Having the two most important people in his life be away left him with a dull ache in his chest.

"I'm surviving. I do know of one particular sweetheart who would love a quick chat with you. Take care, Cam. Talk soon," Damon said, passing the phone to Josephine.

"You too," Cam replied.

Damon left them alone to allow for a private conversation and turned back to Johnson who was chatting on speaker to his team upstairs. He clicked off and turned to Damon.

"They landed in Manaus and have headed east. I hope Lilliana can speak Portuguese?"

"Yes, a little, she can speak Italian and French fluently." Damon poured a coffee. David's screen had gone blank as he had been blindfolded when they were escorted off the jet.

The tracking beacon was indicating red hot on the map. Lilliana and all of Unit Eight, along with Marcus' and Eric's signals were all strong, indicating they remained together as a group.

So far, all was going well. If they could just mark Reid, find out what other locations he had and take him down once and for all. They had been so close in the past. But he always managed to stay just out of reach. And his reach in the underground, was far and foul.

Reid's slave labour trade profited into the millions every year, extending from child labour, which included farming and drug labs. Not to mention prostitution. Men, women, and children. Whatever the cliental demanded, Reid supplied them all. It was big business.

He ran fantasy worlds in which the client could carry out whatever fantasy he or she desired, from hunting an innocent down in the jungle, or taking their time to stalk and murder. Their fantasies allowed them to act out on any desire from torture to rape to murder and snuff films.

Reid even had labs set up where one could perform operations, say, be a plastic surgeon, or simply mutilate their victim. It could be a victim that Reid had supplied, or the client's boss, husband, or wife. Whatever the client wished to act upon, they could. Organ thievery, sex trafficking, terrorism, assassination, the list seemed endless. Reid was a man with an army of thousands that needed to be put down, and that was what Damon and his team of eight hundred undercover Units worldwide were going to do.

CHAPTER 4

Lilliana woke in a strange bed. The air was so humid it was hard to pull any air into her lungs. She sat up and glanced around, rubbing a hand over her eyes. The room was large, with plenty of light coming in through the open windows and door, which led out onto a balcony. Simple yet expensive and tasteful furnishings decorated the room and a ceiling fan circulated warm air down on her.

She jumped suddenly as a figure moved towards her from the open balcony. She relaxed when she saw it was Eric.

He held out his hand and took hers, squeezing gently. "How are you?"

"Fine," she nodded, "thirsty." She squeezed his hand back, releasing it as he went to pour her a water from the decanter. She got off the bed as he passed her the glass, and, thanking him, she walked to the balcony.

Lilliana took a large mouthful of cold water as she looked out in surprised delight. It was a jungle out there. The largest trees, wrapped with thick vines, seemed to touch the sky. A kaleidoscope of blooms broke the tenebrocity of endless green as they lay scattered throughout the jungle, searching for the light.

The property itself was neat, trim, and landscaped with every plant and blade of grass positioned meticulously.

Men with guns standing on guard broke the serenity of the grounds below, bringing Lilliana back to her current reality as to why she was in this paradise in the first place. She recognised Rocco laughing with one of the men, slapping him on the back in a mate-like fashion. He glanced up and met Lilliana's eyes for a second. He nodded to her and turned his attention back to the man he was chatting to. The other man looked up at her and began making thrusting motions with his hips, kissing his fingers toward her before cracking himself up, turning back to Rocco as he puffed away on a cigar.

"Jesus," Eric shook his head and walked over to the water decanter.

"I didn't think people smoked anymore?" Lilliana drained her glass.

"It sure is rare to see." Eric poured a water. "We can speak freely in here, Lilly; I've scanned the room for any listening devices, and it doesn't appear that the room is bugged. Why don't you have a shower? I've been told to take you downstairs to meet your father-in-law once you've freshened up."

She looked at him and groaned. "This is going to be tough. To go down there and not only act like a woman in love to a man I would rather knock out, and be all, 'hello-daddy-like' to another I'd like to see exterminated," she shook her head. "I don't know how I'm going to do this."

"Well, I could knock you out again and tell them you're still sleeping?" Eric reached into his pocket.

"No," she held up a hand. "Don't worry, I can do this. I just don't want to. I'll suck it up. Now, bathroom?"

Eric walked past her towards the far end of the room and stopped in front of a wall made of small frosted glass panels. He pushed the one in the centre and the bulky door of frosted glass swung open.

Lilliana raised an eyebrow and walked over to him. Poking her head inside, she took in the beautiful room. Sunken bath beside a window that swung open to let in the humid air, surrounded with ferns and large-leafed exotic plants in pots. The shower burst out of the wall like a waterfall surrounded by crystal and black rocks, the water falling beneath a shelf to the lush green land beneath them. Twin sinks ran along the opposite wall, where a ceiling to floor mirror reflected the entire room.

Lilliana stood there looking around, feeling tired and a little sad. She wrapped her arms around her waist and looking out into the lush wilderness, allowing her eyes to cloud over without focus.

She wanted Damon.

She felt Eric's arms wrap around her instead as he pulled her back against his chest, dropping his head onto her soft head of hair. "It's all right, take a moment."

She placed her hands along his arms and let herself relax into him. "Thank the stars you are here Eric." She patted his arm and shook her melancholy mood off. "Right then, let's do this."

"David left orders for me to tell you that your clothes are in the wardrobe. Perfume, jewellery. He expects you to dress up for his father."

"Wonderful, I guess that means I'll look like a prostitute for my visit here," she shook her head.

Eric grinned. "At least you'll be a classy looking prostitute. I'll wait outside; no one will enter. Unless David comes up to see what's taking so long." He pulled a face as he backed out of the bathroom.

"Thanks Eric."

He saluted her and smiled as the door swung shut, leaving her to shower underneath the hot waterfall of water.

Using the lush cleansing cremes and conditioners, Lilliana scrubbed the past few hours away. Once she felt relaxed and assured enough that she would not internally explode, she rinsed, dried, and dressed in a beautiful silky white strapless dress that fell in soft waves to her knees. Slipping on white heels, she tied her hair up high with a thick white scarf, so it fell in soft, wet curls down her back. She did her makeup sexy, soft, nothing too dramatic. A squirt of perfume and a quick jewellery check. She was sure David would be happy enough; at least happy enough to make the necessary introductions to his father and ensure that things ran smoothly.

She stepped out of the room to find Eric standing by the door, alert and at attention. He turned to her, his eyes appraising her figure. "God, you are beautiful," he said softly.

"I recall you saying the very same thing to me when we were teenagers." She smiled, remembering that unfortunate time when they were anything but friends. It wasn't a good memory for her. His eyes too, darkened at the unpleasant memory of that time in his life when he'd been young, confused, and angry—and had forced himself on her.

"Yep, you wanted to take me out if I remember correctly."

"I did." She replied shortly. "I certainly tried my hardest to." She smiled.

"Yes. Yes, you did." He chuckled, though in reality it had ended painfully for him.

"Well, I intended this compliment to be strictly platonic." He smiled.

"Thanks Eric," she took a deep breath.

"Mrs Reid, let me escort you below," he announced in a formal tone and turned on his heel to walk them briskly towards the elevator.

"No stairs?"

He shook his head as he punched in the button for the ground floor. They were whisked down in seconds and stepped out into an enormous round foyer that had several corridors leading off into various directions. Large pillars reached up to the ceiling, four levels high, and beautifully crafted sculptures in black marble were standing tall beside each corridor's entrance, along with an armed guard: two of them being Ryder and William.

Maids were dressed neatly in short white uniforms, carrying trays of linen and what looked to be medical equipment.

Eric made eye contact with their two team members as he led Lilliana down a wide stone corridor towards the back of the building. As they drew closer to their destination, Lilliana could hear laughter. She took a deep breath and relaxed her shoulders.

"Good luck," Eric whispered as he stepped aside so she could walk past him and into the room. Pushing his own nerves aside for this first meeting, he kept his eyes on Lilliana and appreciated her elegant femininity. He hoped Ex-Diplomat Reid would do the same. Lilliana appreciated the design of the room as she walked in, admiring the way the sun streamed in from all angles under the enormous glass dome ceiling. The tall trees outside sheltered parts of the room from the hot sun, and a waterfall flowing on the opposite side gave a cool feel to the open room. A large round, white leather settee sat in the centre, near a beautifully crafted wooden table varnished to a shiny gloss, reflecting the trees above.

Decanters of many shapes and sizes filled with wine, liqueurs and aged Scotch Whiskey sat on a side table, along with crystal goblets.

The room held many strange and disturbing sculptures; a row of slaves, all in solid iron, linked by a gold chain several feet long around their throats; eight feet tall, there were eleven slaves in total with a figure standing in front of them cracking a whip. If that wasn't disturbing enough, one sculpture made Lilliana uncomfortable. A water feature, six feet in height, carved out of bone, in the shape of a vagina. Blood-red water flowing out and along the sides, and in the centre, a young boy trying to claw his way out with long, sharp black nails, and an evil snarl on his face; his eyes painted in such a way that no matter where one stood in the room, his eyes seemed to follow.

Jesus Christ, she thought to herself—she did not want to know what made this man tick. She swallowed hard, looking away from the bloody flow.

"Ah, here she is, my beauty." David pushed himself away from the wall where he'd been leaning and strolled towards her. "Sleep well, love?" He reached his arms out and slid them around her waist, drawing her towards him.

"I did, thank you," she looked up at him in anticipation and forced her eyes to smile. She ran her tongue over her bottom lip and parted her lips as his drew closer. The contact was as unpleasant as she anticipated. She did her best, trying to block out the image of the trickling blood water feature and swept her hands along his arms to stroke his neck.

David drew back looking into her eyes and smiled. He was

impressed. He thought he might milk it some more. His hands framed her face and pulled her towards him again. This kiss was deep, fast and hot. His tongue swept into her mouth and he gasped as she bit his lip.

He laughed, watching her. "My little wild cat," he murmured. "Father, let me introduce you to my darling wife, Lilliana." He put his arm around her waist and led her towards the settee.

The tall man stood. He seemed everything Lilliana feared he would be. Handsome, no doubt, in an eerie kind of way. That was something that seemed to run in their family. Dressed well, distinguished looking, he carried himself with such an air of confidence. It was his eyes that cut through her. They were so cold they sent a chill over every inch of her body.

Gregory Reid placed his hands loosely in his slacks pockets as he watched the breathtaking woman walk towards him. Her face was enough to make a man lust and cry. It was hard to imagine she could be even more beautiful in life than on the billboards and magazines. He'd seen her before she first began appearing around the globe. Her body was curvaceous, strong and firm. He smiled inwardly, thinking about how she was every man's, boy's, and probably even some women's, wet dream. He remembered her well from the Snuff Film Simon Grey had sold him. A film that had ended quite differently from the way Simon intended. Instead of the two young girls being raped and killed, it was Simon and his men that met a nasty death. Simon had his son to thank for that. Sons. He looked over at David. His son was an incredibly lucky man indeed.

"Lilliana, what a pleasure, finally." He smiled as she stepped towards him. He pulled his hands out of his pockets and extended them towards her.

Do it, she told herself. She relaxed and gave him a beautiful smile and placed her hands on his arms and tipped her head back to look up into his eyes.

"Mr Reid, how lovely to meet you. David's told me so much about you," she said, accepting his kiss. His lips were cool and dry on her cheek.

"Has he? Name one thing," he gently stroked her arm and held her in place. His fingers swept down to take her wrist. Lilliana knew he was feeling for her pulse and she smiled easily.

"Well, he's told me what an avid hunter you are, and what a brilliant father you were to David and Felicia growing up." She was up to date with most things, Reid. She was ready for any question.

"And how old was David when I made him watch his first orgy?"

Lilliana's smile faded. "Eight," she said quietly.

"You don't approve?" His cool eyes watched her swallow.

"Father, come now." David sat down, reaching his hand out for Lilliana to join him. "You know Lilliana has been through a rough time herself, what with Simon Grey taking her as a child. Lilliana is a bit old fashioned when it comes to orgies and such. Aren't you, darling?"

Gregory stroked a finger over her wrist before letting go.

Lilliana fought the urge to rub off his touch but gave him a quick smile and nodded as she turned toward David.

"I only have one man I'd like to be touched by," she said, thinking only of Damon as she sat next to David, crossing her legs as his arm slid around her shoulders.

"Well, I guess there's nothing wrong with being old fashioned."

Gregory poured three glasses of wine and handed one to his son and one to Lilliana. Picking up his glass, he saluted the young couple.

"Congratulations on your marriage. Tell me, how did you two meet?" He asked, placing himself down on the other side of the settee, crossing an ankle over his knee.

Lilliana took a slow sip, hoping David would field the questions.

"It was almost love at first sight. When I was first interrogated in regard to several of your locations, it was Lilliana they sent in to talk to me," he said, beaming down at her and letting his hand slide down her thick, silky ponytail. He gave her a subtle look that told her to get with the program.

Lilliana placed her hand on his lap, between his knee and groin, letting her thumb gently stroke his pant leg, all the while sipping her wine and glancing across at Gregory. He, however, was watching her with intense interest.

"Yes, I recall those raids. Thank you, David; I needed to clean house. It was a shame though; I'd been enjoying those children. Well, I enjoyed most of them before I was extracted." He took a slow mouthful, watching for Lilliana's reaction.

She stilled, but only for a second. Then she watched him back, grateful he could not read her mind.

"Well, after the first interrogation there were others, and every time she came to visit me, I fell more and more under her spell." David looked down at her as he spoke. A man in love. She looked up at him. He was as good at acting as she seemed to be.

"So, it looks like my threat of attacking the establishment allowed you two to truly be together. How interesting, considering it was both of you I wanted released. And do you intend for Lilliana to be a part of our family business, David?"

"Well, that's up to her, Father," he cupped her chin and tilted her head back, leaning down. "She's far too precious to upset; if she doesn't want to, I will not force her." His kiss was soft and almost sweet.

Lilliana closed her eyes and allowed him to take them where they needed to go for the sake of fooling his father.

"I see." And he did. He had the most fabulous plan running through his head that he almost laughed out loud with the sheer delight of it.

"Well Lilliana, my home is now your home. If you do wander around, please make sure it is with your man out there," he indicated to where Eric stood on guard at the door. "Or David. This is not only my home; I do run a couple of my business ventures from here, and I wouldn't want you frightened if you ran into something you may deem, shall we say, unpleasant?"

"Thank you Mr. Reid," she stood as he walked towards her.

"Please, call me Father," he bent and brushed his lips across hers.

She almost balked but met his eyes steadily. "Thank you, Father."

He bowed slightly, nodded to David, and walked briskly from the room.

David stood and said very quietly near her ear. "I can see you fitting in here so well, Lilliana. It's a shame."

She turned to look at him and whispered. "Don't delude yourself."

Making sure Gregory was out of sight, she firmly wiped the back of her hand across her lips where they still tingled in disgust from the unpleasant touch of Gregory's mangey lips.

David shrugged. "Just saying; come, let us walk outside before lunch. You must be starving after sleeping for so long." He took her arm and linked it through his and lead her out into the humid air. Eric stayed close behind and took time to survey the area. The hunting grounds led from a large iron gate deep into the Amazon and Reid's other enterprises were placed around the compound, all guarded by heavy artillery.

Lilliana appreciated the gardens. It was a beautiful area. She looked across and saw a building up ahead with a large glass dome roof, like the waterfall room where she had met Gregory.

"What's that building?"

He smiled down at her. "That's the medical laboratory. Would you like to see it?"

She glanced behind at Eric, who gave her a quick nod. "Yes."

"Excellent," he guided her towards the front entrance where two guards stood. "Hello, gents."

"Hello Mr. Reid, it is good to see you again."

"Thanks. I'm wanting to take my wife on a tour. Any action today?"

"There should be plenty enough Sir, we have nine in today." He looked Lilliana over, wondering if she had any idea what she was in for. He glanced back at David, not wanting to look too long at his employer's lovely wife.

"Wonderful. Shall we?" He put his arm around her as the guard punched in a code and the large metal door swung open.

"Eric, would you mind waiting out here? Get a coffee. Have a chat," David said casually. It was less of a suggestion and more of an order even if it didn't seem like it.

"Yes Sir." Eric nodded, respectively. He watched Lilliana disappear until the large door swung shut behind them; nodding to the two guards, he turned on his heel to go chat to Marcus and Rocco, whom he saw walking their way.

Inside the medical laboratory Lilliana's nostrils were assaulted by a strong, hospital grade disinfectant. The tiled floors were black and white marble, cold and sterile. Lilliana's heels clicked as they walked down the wide, long corridor.

A door slid open as they walked by; inside a very pretty woman in a clingy white nurse's uniform stepped out carrying a tray of bloody towels and instruments. Lilliana peeked in as they walked past to see a doctor wiping his bloody hands on his starch white apron as another nurse was handing him a glass of scotch. The smell in the room was horrendous. David walked her on as the sound of screaming came from up ahead.

"Don't they use anesthetic here?"

He laughed, shaking his head. "Aren't you sweet. Don't you know what this place is, Lilliana?"

She shrugged, not answering. All she knew was that she really didn't want a tour after all. At least Johnson and Damon would be receiving plenty of intel through The Guardian.

"Come," he led her up a flight of stairs and they came across a viewing room.

"They can't see us, you understand. This is set up for the client who wants to see a loved one suffer but does not want to inflict the pain themselves. We had a wife brought in recently who had had an affair. Her husband stood here and watched as they tortured her, cut off her lover's private appendage then inserted it inside her and melted her flesh together with a blow torch. Funny what love can make you do."

"Hardly funny. Definitely not love." Lilliana muttered. She watched as a young man and woman were pushed into the room. The woman, who not much older than Lilliana herself, was sobbing, begging the guard to please let her go. The young man had a stony look on his face and said nothing. They strapped the young woman down onto a cot then hung the man by his handcuffs to a hook hanging from the ceiling, a large white tub waiting under him.

The guards made sure they were secured before leaving, pulling the door firmly shut behind them.

"Tourists, by the looks," David said, more to himself.

A short time after an older man entered, along with a nurse who helped him out of his clothes and into a lab coat, passing him a wickedly sharp looking surgical instrument.

"Oh no," Lilliana took a step back away from the view, deciding she wanted no part of this.

David's chest blocked her exit. His hands went either side of her, hanging onto the rail along the wall. "Father may pop in and see us on tour, Lilly. Be a good girl and watch."

She folded her arms and closed her eyes, stepping closer to the rail so his chest wasn't against her back. He didn't need to know she wasn't watching.

"Open up, princess; I want you to see. Come on, now."

She turned her head to see David leaning around, watching her.

"What's the point of me watching, David? It doesn't help us with anything. Aren't you frightened you'll lose your head?"

"Now why would my son lose his head just because he wants you to watch?" Gregory's cool voice interrupted them.

Lilliana couldn't help herself and she jumped.

David chuckled. They turned to see Gregory leaning against the door frame, his arm around the shoulders of a very pretty blonde woman. Her face was simply exquisite. Long, strawberry-blonde hair floated around her shoulders in a shiny halo. Her body was slim, and firm and she was dressed elegantly in a fresh blue sundress with flat ballet slippers.

Lilliana looked from Gregory to the young woman thinking she looked far to fresh and innocent to be tucked under the arm of such a perverted demon. It really does take all types, she thought.

"Not to worry, Father." David stroked Lilliana's arm. "I'm just trying to toughen my baby up; she constantly threatens to take off my head, don't you, sweet thing?" He ran a hand along her smooth, soft throat before dipping his head for a long slow kiss. Lilliana shut her eyes, not wanting Damon to see her suffer any more than she was.

"Well now, I thought I'd come and join you. This client loves a blood bath. It's good to see he gets his money's worth. Interesting what people will do." Gregory pulled the blonde young woman over to where David and Lilliana stood.

They all turned to see the client slicing the knife slowly and meticulously along the woman's veins in her arms, then along her thighs, before sliding his fingers into her deep wounds, closing his eyes and moaning in pleasure as his fingers slid around in her warm blood, as she screamed in pain.

Lilliana felt the strong urge to vomit. She closed her eyes briefly and turned her head to the side.

David was watching her with zero emotion. Lilliana looked up at him. Did she just see a flicker of regret flash across his face?

It was gone in a second though, as he turned his head back to the show.

Below, the woman began sobbing. "Why are you doing this? What have we ever done to you?"

"Always the same boring questions. You have done nothing, dear girl. Now shush, while I play with your boyfriend."

He walked over to the male. The nurse had finished cutting his clothes away. He thrashed, screamed and cursed, as his girlfriend sobbed weakly, blood dripping from all the deep cuts.

The nurse simply smiled and got on with her job. She stepped back, waiting for the client's next order. She handed him another blade and he sliced the man's back open in a quick slash. When the blood started to flow, the client pressed his naked chest to the man's bloodied back and wrapped his arms around his torso, rubbing himself into the blood as the young man screamed and cursed.

"Get you're fucking hands off me, you sick fuck or I will kill you!"

"Leave him alone, you monster!" the woman begged; her voice soft as she felt her life slipping away.

"It's alright, Baby, we'll be alright," the man said, trying to soothe his partner, pain filling his soul.

The client threw his head back and laughed before running the knife along the man's chest and viciously cutting behind his ankles. Blood continued to pool into the tub. The client sliced deep into the man's thighs then plunged the knife into his chest and stomach again and again. The man screamed for a few minutes, crying weakly and dribbling on himself before he stilled completely, death at his door.

Lilliana closed her eyes, unable to view the vile act.

David allowed her to look away; he could see how pale she was. Just then Gregory asked Lilliana if she knew the benefits of a blood bath.

Lilliana opened her eyes and saw the client laying naked in a large tub full of blood, whilst the nurse wheeled in a trolley with champagne and lunch. Both bodies had been discarded on a belt beside the wall, slowly moving along towards a black-deposit-door at the back of the room, their cadavers twisted at gruesome, odd angles.

Just twenty minutes ago they were breathing, living humans, Lilliana thought to herself, and now sadly, they looked like nothing. Just slabs of meat.

"Do not fret, nothing goes to waste here; they'll make a grand meal for our jungle pets." Gregory sounded proud.

Lilliana looked away from the macabre scene. "David," she whispered. "I'm sorry, but I feel quite ill."

"Of course darling. Father, we'll see you at lunch." He put his arm around her waist and escorted her downstairs while Gregory stood in the background and looked on.

Lilliana's departure couldn't have come soon enough as soon as she was outside, she pitched her body over a clump of grass and dry heaved. There had been nothing in her stomach since she'd been sick on the jet, bar the small glass of wine she had had with Gregory and David earlier. Liquid was the only thing that came out along with desperate heaving sounds, leaving her feeling dizzy and weak.

"What's happened?" Eric called, as he knelt beside Lilliana on the grass.

"Fragile," was all David said, looking down at the usually strong, beautiful woman.

He'd remembered a time when she had attacked him, had thrust a sharp earring under his chin, breaking skin, drawing blood, and leaving a scar. He touched the rough, raised surface on his flesh as he looked down at Lilliana. Where was that little hell cat now, he thought?

"Bloody hell," Eric whispered as he scooped her up. "I'll take her in to freshen up, maybe she needs to sleep."

"No," David inspected his nails. "Father is expecting us for lunch. Take her up to change, then if you would, Eric, bring her down to the lake room for lunch."

Eric stared at him, then, not wanting to step out of line in front of the other guards, turned with Lilliana in his arms and strode off to the house.

"Eric," Lilliana muttered, sounding pitiful even to her own ears. "I can walk, put me down."

"No." Eric continued carrying her, storming towards the house.

Lilliana felt so weak that she didn't struggle. She closed her eyes and tried to block out the images that swam before her eyelids. She immediately opened them and wiggled out of Eric's arms. Landing on her feet, she held onto one of his arms for support.

"Sorry Eric," Lilliana said, shaking her head. "I can't do this," she whispered.

"Yes you can, Lilly. Just breathe, Okay?"

She took in a clean, fresh gulp of air.

Eric nodded and led her towards her room to rinse her mouth and rest for a few minutes, because he knew he had to be strong for her for when they went back into the lion's den.

CHAPTER 5

Damon had to visit the hospital to meet four new Given that had recently arrived. He had time to have a chat with Rachael and Billy concerning a healing centre they were building. He had three staff meetings with the HD, the Watchers, and all head Team Leaders.

Then he would take a quick trip to the psych ward to have a meeting with Hillary and Richard, followed by a visit to the stables.

He'd had to hold an assembly with the Given before a two-hour conference call. He'd seen Christopher and Allie off on the Given's jet to New York, then had a bite to eat between a quick hot shower and a change of clothes before meeting back up with Johnson to see what had been happening. On his way down to his office he saw a lone figure leaning against the wall, a portfolio tucked under his arm. It was Lilliana's younger brother, Scott. His handsome young face was staring out the window, watching a group of Given get ready for their afternoon run. Damon casually looked around and was relieved to see Scott's watcher, Alan, close by. He nodded his head hello before turning his attention back to Scott.

"Hello Sir," he leaned off the wall when he spotted Damon walking towards him.

"Scott," he smiled. "How are you today?"

"Good thanks, Sir. I finished my class and spent an hour out in the garden drawing some of Rupert's finest blooms. He's asked if I can do them on a larger scale so he can place them around the lab. Brighten up the place some more."

Damon nodded as he placed his hands in his pockets. He felt a connection to the boy, looking into those familiar sea green eyes.

"How are you feeling in general, Scott?"

Scott looked down at his feet and shrugged. "Fine." He looked up into the taller man's eyes. He hoped he could be like Damon when he was older. Just standing the way he did, with his hands in his pockets, he exuded such a relaxed, yet confident air. Damon was such a cool guy and he had done so much for him since his sister had been away. God, he missed his sister right now.

"How's Lilliana, Sir?" He said, his voice low.

Damon smiled, placing a hand on Scott's shoulder. He was pleased to feel that Scott wasn't so skinny anymore. Since he had been out of the Psych ward Scott had been working out twice a day, running, or walking and spending time in the gym. He also had a love for horse riding after Damon had given him lessons. They had ridden together twice a week, for the past several weeks.

"Your sister is doing fine, and hopefully will be home soon."

"How soon, Sir?"

Damon sighed and ran a hand through his hair. "A week, maybe two."

Scott nodded, not wanting to add to the man's burden. He forced cheer and smiled. "That will be cool, thanks Sir. Have a good afternoon." He turned to go.

"You too." Damon headed into his office, relieved to shut the door behind him. He'd hoped it would just be him and Johnson. But he saw Josephine sitting on the couch, a handful of tissues in her lap and tears falling down her face. She was on the phone crying to Cam. Johnson stood, arms folded, a grim expression of rage on his face.

What the hell I have missed? Damon thought to himself.

Josephine looked up at him and handed over the phone. He walked over and took it gently from her. She stood and walked out of the room.

"Hello."

"Damon, it's Cam. How are you?"

"Fine, what's going on?"

"Johnson will fill you in. Josephine saw something that upset her. I've tried to tell her not to watch what's going on at the compound, but she insists. She just couldn't handle what she saw today, and she's scared for Lilliana. Please talk to her, Damon. If we can get Lilly and the unit out of there sooner rather than later, I think we need to. Let's bust this bastard wide open."

"Okay Cam, I'll sort things out this end and see what's going on. I know our men have gathered useful Intel on several of Reid's other facilities. It's been beyond helpful having Unit Eight work so closely with Reid before. We're getting closer. Christopher and Allie will be with you tonight; settle them in, give them a week, and soon as you're done, head back here."

"We'll be back sooner if we can wrap things up. Talk soon, Brother."

"Bye Cam." Damon hung up and turned to Johnson.

"What have I missed?"

Johnson turned to the coffee machine and poured them both a coffee. Handing it to Damon he asked him to sit. He re-wound the live feed and showed him the activity he had missed in the medical laboratory.

Damon had watched the replay, and he felt himself becoming ill. Stark white face, fists clenched at his sides, his eyes blazed with fury. He swallowed a lump and closed his eyes for a brief moment, pinching the bridge of his nose. His poor Lilliana, and those poor victims. He started pacing, feeling Johnson's eyes on him. He turned to look at the man he had always respected.

"Okay, what are we waiting for? We have Reid's home location, or a major one out of what, thirty? We can go in hard now. Ryder, Rocco, and William have all communicated that they have several other teams already in position in eleven major facilities of Reid's. We can take him now, and whatever happens after that, the other facilities will fall."

Johnson nodded. "It's good in theory, but I think you'd be interested in one more thing," Johnson said, turning back to play another file Damon had missed while he had been working on Establishment matters. They watched David sitting with his father in an office, surrounded by the latest technology and walls lined with hunting trophies; panthers, leopards, bears and other beautiful creatures that had also met their end too soon. As if that wasn't disturbing enough, there were also several human heads on display.

The two men sat back drinking and David listened as Gregory spoke about a main event he was hosting that would provide entertainment for the wealthy and disturbed and make them millions. As Damon listened to the Reid men discuss the entertainment for the upcoming event, his blood ran cold. He turned to Johnson.

"We cannot let this happen."

"Damon. The men that will come to this event are the biggest names in politics, the entertainment industry, not to mention the underworld. This is a rare opportunity that we have, to get inside and finally take down some of the big players. Organisations that have created indestructible chaos. I think Lilliana would agree with me and want to go ahead with this part of the mission. She will not be harmed, Damon."

Damon shook his head and ran his hands over his face. "Maybe not physically, but mentally." He hung his head, looking down at the ground. "It's killing me, having her in this position, and not being able to protect her. I sent her out there to protect everyone in here." He raised his head and looked out the window.

"And you yourself have been in some despicable situations to save many. I ask you this. Do you think Lilliana would want to be here, safe with you, if it meant sacrificing hundreds of thousands of lives?" Johnson put his coffee down and looked at the man.

Damon looked back at him, square in the eye. "Point taken. It still doesn't take away the fact that in this situation I cannot protect the woman I love."

"I understand your point and your pain. But the one woman you can help right now is your sister. I can imagine Josephine will be beside herself. Give yourself an hour, Damon. Ride Beast get some fresh air. This will all be here when you get back. I've got it covered."

Damon clapped his friend on the shoulder as he strode towards the door. "I'll take Josephine for a quick walk. I'll be back soon." He was determined to put that sweet smile back on Josephine's face.

Johnson sighed, his eyes returning to the screen, tapping on it to catch it back up to the live feed.

***

Lilliana sat on her heels by the toilet, not quite sure if she wanted to be sick again or simply pass out to escape the horror of this assignment. After twenty minutes, she pushed herself shakily to her feet and stepped, fully clothed, into the shower. Leaning against the wall, she let her eyes drift out to the sea of green beyond the window.

"Lilliana, are you alright?" David called out.

She didn't answer. She did not want to speak to him, or him to her. Ignoring him was best for them both.

"Lilliana?" He waited a handful of minutes before entering the bathroom.

She did not react. She simply stared out the window. Pretended he was not there, that he would go away, she thought to herself. He was just bloody lucky she had clothes on, otherwise she'd let him have it!

David devoured an eyeful of the beautifully lush, sad woman. Black hair hanging over her shoulders, her white dress plastered to her figure as the hot water pulsed over every inch of her. Her face looked so pale. He frowned as it occurred to him that he was concerned for her. This was not good.

"You are late for lunch," he accused.

She slowly brought herself to focus on him, bringing her arms up across her chest.

"Do you seriously think I can eat after what I just saw?" she said incredulously, swallowing the tears that threatened to burst. It felt like a red-hot lump of coal was stuck in her throat. She looked back out the window. "Can you please just get out?"

Lilliana jumped a little as he was quick to move there beside her. His hand stretched out and flicked the shower off. She didn't move; she just remained there, against the wall. He stepped into her, bending his head close to hers. Lilliana felt his pale blue eyes casually drift over her as he traced a long finger along her collar bone before collecting a handful of her hair and squeezing out the excess water. She pushed his chest hard, thumping him with her fist.

"Don't bloody touch me!" She wanted to punch him in the face.

He could see that she was about to punch him as she pulled her arm back, fist bunched in readiness, so he firmly grabbed her wrist, shaking his head and placing his lips a whisper's breath from hers. "Hurry up, " he said. "Father's waiting." Then he dropped her wrist, turned and walked from the room without another word.

She leaned her head against the wall and silently swore, allowing angry tears to fall as she tried desperately to block out the scene playing over and over in her head. Closing her eyes, she let out a shaky breath, trying to collect herself. Lilliana gasped; her eyes flew open as strong, firm arms scooped her close.

"Lilly."

Eric. She relaxed. "I'm alright."

He squeezed her gently before leading her into the middle of the room. Handing her a big fluffy towel, he nodded before stepping out of the bathroom.

"It must have been awful." He spoke through the door.

"Beyond." She replied, stripping off and drying herself, then her hair, before wrapping the towel around her, stepping into the bedroom.

She walked over and plonked down on a plush chair.

"When you went in, the two guards said they actually felt sorry for you. Mind you, it didn't stop them from betting whether you'd come out crying or throwing up." Eric passed her a water.

"Nice," she shook her head, taking the glass and enjoying a refreshing swallow. "Thanks."

"Welcome. While you were busy with Psycho One and Psycho Two, I did a bit of hunting around, spoke with Rocco; he has become good buddies with a few of the guards over the past eighteen months.

There's a village not far from here—five hundred or so men, women, and children. They use them in the hunting games. Just pluck them out and throw them in the jungle." He shook his head and walked over to the balcony. "I tell you now, Lilly; I have often scratched my head at the term, 'to be human.' But these people, I don't know; they are just too much. If I could take them all out, I would." He kept his back to her.

"And I would help you. No questions asked."

"Listen, you better get changed; if we don't hurry, he'll be back up here looking for you." He kept his back to her.

Lilliana walked over to the wardrobe and selected a soft cotton, butter yellow sundress with low matching heels. She felt completely comfortable slipping the dress on with Eric in the room. His presence offered her much comfort. She thought of Damon then, and could not stop the ball of pain growing in her chest, along with the feelings of helplessness, given what she had just witnessed. She leaned onto the bed, squeezing her eyes shut in an effort to stop the persistent images flashing through her mind, unable to stop the small cry of fury as it escaped her lips.

Eric walked over, pulled her up and turned her to face him, brushing away the tear that fell from her eyes. "You miss him, don't you?" He asked.

Lilliana looked up into Eric's dear face and squeezed his strong upper arms. "Desperately; and after what I just witnessed I need to be near him." She wiped her tears away and took a deep breath. "I really am okay; I just miss our people and being here amongst all of this..." she said, looking around and shaking her head.

Eric nodded. "I totally get it. I certainly have discovered the true meaning of pure evil in the short amount of time we have been here. Just remember one thing, Lilly; to help you get through each demented, unpredictable moment, we are here to take Reid down for good. That's it, then we will be on our way home, pronto."

She nodded, appreciating the mini pep-talk. "You're right. I can do this."

"I know you can," Eric said without hesitation.

Damon had certainly selected the perfect person to be by her side through all of this. "I love you like a brother you know, Eric."

He smiled down at her. "I know, and I love you. Now, let's go do this."

Lilliana forced a quick smile before heading into the bathroom to freshen up her face, and together they walked down to the lake room.

***

Eric followed Lilliana as they walked along a thick, polished marble hallway that formed into steps, set inches above a thin channel of water that opened out into a wide and flowing stream full of exotic plants. Stepping up the pavers, water flowed behind them like a small waterfall until they landed on a large disc of white marble, which seemed to float on a pool of water, surrounded by tall plants and works of art in glass and stunning coloured tiles reflecting light and water, giving the entire surroundings a feeling of beauty and peace.

Peace. Not in this lifetime, Lilliana thought to herself. As they approached the table, set with an elaborate looking feast, she felt Eric stiffen beside her. Lilliana followed his gaze and then she understood what had taken hold of him.

The beautiful blonde woman that had been with Gregory in the medical laboratory now sat beside him, looking into the water where a giant, lazy fish swam by. She popped a strawberry into her mouth. It appeared more a robotic movement than a matter of need. She was absolutely the most stunning woman Lilliana had ever seen in her life.

The woman's eyes wandered to Lilliana and Eric and Lilliana could see the unwanted attraction immediately as soon as the woman's eyes connected with Eric's.

It almost made her smile before she felt David and Gregory's eyes slide towards her.

"Darling, come," David held out his hand.

Eric quickly turned on his heel and walked back the way they'd come.

"Oh Eric—don't wander too far, I may need you in a little while."

David took Lilliana's hand and pulled her down on the seat beside him.

"Yes, Sir." Eric stood to the side, feeling the woman's eyes on him. He was trying to pull himself together; he had never reacted to any woman the way he had to her based on one single look. Even in his younger years with his attraction to Lilliana, he had simply put that down to lust.

Drinks were poured and lunch was served. Gregory and David discussed the market, business, and some latest death game they were both pleased about as the profits worldwide soared into the millions. Lilliana pushed her food around the plate with a fork, occasionally reaching for an iced tea to wash down the sick feeling that kept trying to crawl up her throat.

"Is something wrong, Lilliana?" Gregory asked, slicing open a large log of roasted meat as assorted herbs and nuts spewed out onto the plate. Lilliana had to look away and force herself not to think of the young man's intestines spewing out of his body. She held the cool glass up to her lips and shook her head. Then she felt her hand shake and feeling self conscious, placed it in her lap, out of Gregory's view.

"Lilliana, tell me one thing you absolutely love about my son," Gregory demanded.

She could feel David's fingers running up and down along her back. He leaned down and dropped a kiss on her temple. She forced a smile knowing it did not reach her eyes, but it was all she could manage.

"His clever mind, his humour," she uttered, but she could see the doubt sweeping across Gregory's face. She turned to David. This would have to be good. She smiled sweetly at him, almost begging him for help. She traced her finger along his jaw, down his throat.

"And his good looks, of course."

"Not his money?"

"Hardly. I have plenty of my own," she quickly retorted and kissed David's chin before leaning back, picking up her iced tea.

"And what would you do for your husband? Would you do anything to please him? For example, Eric," he turned his attention to the younger man.

Eric walked towards the table. *This ought to be interesting*, he thought to himself. He glanced at Lilliana before turning his attention to Gregory.

"Yes Sir."

"Undo your shirt."

Lilliana immediately felt nervous. She glanced at David. He made out as if he were kissing her neck; holding her in place, he pushed his lips near her ear and whispered, "Relax; whatever happens, relax."

Lilliana turned her attention back to Gregory. "Now, Nadia my darling, please pick up your knife and make handsome Eric here, bleed a little."

Lilliana went to move forward but David tightened his grip around her wrist, stopping her.

Eric's eyes met Lilliana's; he shook his head slightly before turning his gaze back to Nadia as she slowly picked up the sharp knife and pushed herself up from the table.

He watched her as she walked slowly towards him. He unbuttoned his shirt, seeing her pretty, bright eyes looking downcast. She stopped in front of him and looked back over her shoulder at Gregory.

"Be a love," he asked quietly.

Eric could see her swallow as her eyes lifted to his; a sheen of tears filled them, and she blinked quickly to clear them. She smelt divine, he thought, and he swore he felt a pull of electricity shoot straight from her to him. She mouthed the word 'sorry' before running the blade quickly along his firm, sculpted chest. He gasped in pain, holding his palm to the deep cut as blood seeped slowly under his fingers.

Gregory commanded again. "Again, Nadia—then lick the blood from him."

Eric frowned down at the beautiful Nadia as she looked up at him. He dropped his arm so she could do what was bid of her. She quickly drew the knife along him once again, careful not to slice his open wound, before bending her head to run her tongue along a line of blood. The sharp pain of his wound, paired with her warm, soft tongue sent him spinning. He almost laughed but couldn't because the pain was so intense.

"Enough," David said on behalf of Lilliana. He could see her shaking and didn't know how far his father would go.

Gregory began clapping as he walked over to Nadia. He cupped her chin. "My beautiful, obedient girl." He slowly bent and directly in front of Eric, kissed the young woman passionately, as though they were in seclusion. She kissed him back and elicited a moan. Once Gregory had finished, he stood straight and looked at Eric. "Go to the nurse's station, get yourself cleaned up. We have stitching serum. That will be healed in a jiffy, lad."

Eric pulled his eyes away from Nadia and nodded. "Yes, Sir." He glanced across at an ill-looking Lilliana and quickly turned on his heel, running out and down the steps.

Gregory turned to Lilliana. "Now *that*, is love. To have your wishes be obeyed by your lover one hundred percent, without question—that's what I call love. Loyalty at its finest."

Lilliana had to look away from Gregory's arrogant face, only to see Nadia wipe her fingers across her lips. A cloud of sadness seemed to fall over the girl when Gregory wasn't looking at her. Lilliana felt a pang of sorrow for her.

✱✱✱

The screen was paused on Nadia as Damon stood, arms folded staring at the stunning lady. Twenty minutes earlier he had sent Johnson to find Orlando.

"Afternoon Damon," Orlando said walking into Damon's office. "How's everything?"

"Up and down. How have you been? Is that new group behaving now?" Damon handed Orlando a cold glass of iced lemonade.

He smiled as he took a mouthful of the freshly squeezed lemons. "Yes Sir, Jessica and I have them under control. They respond positively to Scott when Jess has him doing art with them. She is brilliant—but Scott, well he's just something else."

"His talent is phenomenal, no doubt." Damon nodded, agreeing. He looked at Orlando closely. How far he had come since arriving, all those years ago. He had been through a different kind of hell himself.

His mother, then his sister, sold to the highest bidder by his own father. Abused himself by his own father, who had involved him in illicit acts, one of them which included kidnapping Jessica and Lilliana over a decade ago.

Watching Orlando now, Damon felt proud of him. They had all come such a long way. Not all those that arrived here, healed. Some did not survive; suicide, though it was rare, did happen occasionally. Sometimes, even the brilliant support and healing programs they had couldn't help those with broken minds. Those that did go on to heal and overcome such devastation thrived, and went on to become strong leaders, and help many others in turn.

Orlando looked around the room. He had fallen in love with Jessica here, getting to know her as he did in their compulsory group therapies. It was such a spacious, warm environment. Glancing up, he noticed the screens, and froze when his eyes fell on the beautiful blonde woman. Damon watched Orlando carefully. He was right, he thought. It was his sister.

"Sir, how can this be? That's my Nadia. I know it is." Orlando had paled and almost dropped the glass as he went to place it on the table.

Damon walked over and placed his hand on Orlando's back. Looking him in the eyes, he said softly, "The evidence you found regarding Nadia's death—it was all a hoax, Orlando. She is alive and has been with Gregory Reid all this time."

Orlando's legs gave way and he sank to his knees. "How can this be?"

Damon turned to the door and met his friend's eyes. "Johnson, can we get Jessica in here please. ASAP."

Johnson nodded and was gone in a flash to fetch Jessica.

"We can't imagine what she had to endure, Orlando, to stay alive. To serve a purpose." Damon sat on the arm of the chair.

Johnson arrived back with Jessica.

Damon smiled as she comforted Orlando, and he quickly briefed her about what had happened.

Jessica looked worried but smiled and ran a hand through Orlando's hair.

"This is great news, Baby; when we extract Lilliana we can bring Nadia here—can't we, Sir?" She looked across at Damon. She still couldn't believe this handsome man with the intimidating eyes was her dear friend's husband.

He stood, arms folded and nodded slowly. "Of course."

"See," Jessica hugged Orlando and helped him to his feet.

"Are you both alright to get on with your groups?"

"Yes, thank you Damon. I'll be fine. It's just a shock, is all—thinking her dead all this time. Now, to have to think what she must have suffered. It's almost worse."

"I understand, but, if we can get her back here—and I promise you, we will do everything to make that happen—we will help her in every way possible."

Orlando reached out and clasped Damon's hand. "Thanks so much, Sir."

"You're welcome. If you need anything at any time you know where to find me." He nodded at Jessica as she smiled over her shoulder at him as she left with Orlando.

Johnson shook his head. "I need a coffee."

"Make that two. You think you know complicated, and then a web like this appears."

Johnson poured the coffee and turned to the screen as they resumed the live feed to see what the spider was getting up to next.

***

"Tomorrow, dear daughter, you are going to show me how committed you are to my son and this family—and if you can't prove your commitment I do believe I will be greatly disappointed, perhaps to the tune of some hazardous misfortune befalling someone close to you." Gregory's cool voice washed over her as he wiped Eric's blood from his mouth that had lingered there, off Nadia's lips.

Nadia sat still, looking down into her lap, her silky mane fluttering in the breeze.

Lilliana had to push down not only the urge to puke again, but the temptation of spitting out a nasty insult that she knew would get her nowhere.

"Father, don't upset my sweet girl, she has a tender heart, that's all." David rubbed her arm up and down, trying to hide the fact that

Lilliana was shaking.

Gregory plucked up his glass and drank quickly. "What do you think of slavery, Lilliana?" he asked, watching for her reaction over the crystal rim.

"It's despicable that it still happens in this day and age." She folded her arms and resisted the urge to push David away as he pulled her closer to his side.

"Tell me, then—what do you think of men who beat their wives till they are black and blue? That gamble all their money away till there is not even a stale crust left to feed their children?"

"Domestic violence has to stop. Those that beat their partners need to be dealt with—permanently. Those that gamble to the detriment of their families need support and therapy to stop." Lilliana wished this conversation could just be over so she could go and hide in her room until the next hell-filled episode.

"I do believe you, and I can agree mostly on this. You see, I am the cure of cancer in our society. The cancer being the ultimate evil of men. I hunt these men, and in some cases women too—and I place them in my business. Yes, in some circumstances, they work till they drop dead—but I do believe that is their deserved punishment for hurting their loved ones."

Lilliana raised an eyebrow. "Thirty years ago, there were over thirty million people used in the slave industry. It's gotten worse. And it will get worse still if people like you don't stop."

"You think I should just let the evil filth walk this earth and continue, guilt free?" Gregory placed his glass on the table and leaned forward. "Because the system has worked so well now, hasn't it. For hundreds of years, humans and their flawed system just keep failing us. What I do, I put to good use. I'm simply cleaning the streets of the vermin that brings society down, the ill minds." He leaned back, placing his arm around Nadia's shoulder.

"Yes, but not all you harm are guilty, are they? You hurt the innocent too, the children that society try to protect. The mentally ill need our help—not people like you making judgment calls as to who needs to be taken out. What do you say about the thousands, millions even, that you have murdered?" Lilliana shook her head. Why was she even bothering to argue with this man?

"Overpopulation. That's what I say. Even where you were sent as a child, they had an answer for that, didn't they? Isn't it true you were sterilised on arrival at The Given? You cannot have children. That's certainly one solution to our world in crisis. Another is the plague, and better yet, for others' entertainment, me." It was obvious to Lilliana that Gregory was done; he was shutting down their conversation.

Good, she thought; she was sick of it, all of it, and having to interact with him on any level for longer than necessary.

"It really must distress you both, not being able to create our next line of Reid's. Fear not, I have a wedding gift for you. This afternoon I have my own personal doctor coming in to inject your body with some magical little virus that will get your clock ticking again, and by tomorrow my son, you may impregnate your wife and make me a proud grandfather."

"Wonderful, Father." David forced his cheer while wondering if, at any moment his head would be blown off by Damon. Damon would not be happy with this.

"But, we are not in a hurry, are we my love? You know, Father, we really are enjoying things with just the two of us at the moment."

"Ah yes, lustful young love. I understand. Well, off you both go, tuck yourselves away for the afternoon. I've got some work to do. Nadia dear, go and see if the young man you sliced open is alright." He tapped her chin and nipped at her lips.

"Yes Gregory," she stood and quickly left.

Gregory turned his gaze to Lilliana. "You know, I really am enjoying having you here with us," he walked over and bent down to drop a kiss on her hair, before turning to walk off in the opposite direction to Nadia. He seemed to walk across the water as he took the steps down and away from her before disappearing.

As soon as he was out of sight. Lilliana pushed herself away from David and began walking back the way she had come earlier with Eric.

David's cool long fingers circled around her wrist and he smiled down at her, even as she looked up frowning.

"You have such a sexy scowl."

"Hardly," she seethed inside, wanting to scream at Gregory. *Bastard.* To degrade the mental mind in front of her!

Once they entered the room Lilliana snatched her hand back, pulling it out of his grasp as she walked over to the balcony, kicking off her shoes as she did.

"What's got your tail in a twist, love?" David threw himself on the bed, placing his hands behind his head. He was a man relaxed in his own castle, enjoying the view of this incredibly attractive woman. If only she was really his. He nearly chuckled but stopped as she turned to stare at him.

Lilliana folded her arms, raising her eyebrows.

"What?"

"Your father really believes he is helping the world, doesn't he? I mean, those poor people out there, the children, the innocent, the mentally ill; they need help, not some deluded sociopath killing them or using them for his own evil, money making schemes." She shook her head.

"Everyone who does wrong in this world has some sort of illness. Tell me, Lilliana: if you had the chance to put all wife beaters, paedophiles, serial killers, psychopaths into a room and shoot them, would you?"

"No."

"Liar."

"I deal with people who have done wrong, serious wrong, in order to survive, save themselves, or a loved one. I've had my own issues with mental illness and have some friends with mental illness."

"Some friends? Oh, so you're a 'picky' mental illness person. You like some, yet you don't like others?"

"That's not fair; don't twist my words. Some don't harm others; some have no control over their actions."

"But yet *you* decide who gets into your club. You decide who deserves kindness and who deserves your harsh judgment."

"No. Yes. You're complicating it. I'm not talking about a person with anxiety disorders or depression or bipolar—those who are innocent, harmless. I'm talking about personality disorders, like your father. He is a premeditated destructive sociopath. It's those like him that need to go."

"Okay so let's say for example, if you had the choice to kill my father, Simon Grey, or me. Would you?"

Lilliana sat down tucking her legs under her, looking out to the jungle of green. "Your father, yes."

"Ah, at last, honesty."

"He needs to be gone from this earth after all his wrongdoings," she shrugged, non-apologetically.

"Simon Grey?"

Lilliana looked at him. "Simon Grey is dead, not because of me, but for everything evil he did to his son and his family."

"And what about me, Lilliana?"

She turned her eyes towards him, thinking. "It's debatable, given your previous crimes, but you have done a good thing in coming here and helping us take down your father. That has to count for something."

"Thanks, that means a lot coming from you." He closed his eyes.

She sighed and stood up. "David, could you go to your own room so I can get some sleep? I'm beat."

He snorted. "Get over it. This room is ours, for all pretences. I don't want to lose my head so there's your guarantee—I won't touch you." He moved to the left side, keeping his eyes shut.

Lilliana walked over and sank onto the soft bed and lay down on her side with her back to him. It felt awful to be sharing a bed with any man other than Damon. She quietly let out a deep breath and closed her eyes, shuffling the pillow around till it was comfortable, trying to block out all the mayhem of the past few hours. She was finally moving into a calm, sleepy headspace when David spoke again.

"Do you remember the last time you questioned me? When you thrust your earring into my flesh?"

Lilliana remembered the moment all too clearly. Not only because it terrified her, but because it was the night, she and Damon had become lovers. She remained quiet, hoping he'd think her asleep and shut up himself. She wasn't that lucky.

"I'll never forget how much I wanted to plunge into you, over and over again, to take you right there on that cold, sterile floor. To own you." He felt the bed shift as she launched herself across the room.

He sat up on his elbows and looked across at her as she stood over by the balcony, arms tightly folded across her chest, a guarded look on her face.

"Relax Lilliana, and you too Damon," he said for Damon's ears to hear. "I just want you to know, that was then, this is now—and I'll do everything I can to make this mission a success."

"Why bring it up then?"

"Because I want a fresh start, a different life for me and for my sister. I see what you do for those you love, and I want that life. You have to understand, Lilliana—our father conditioned us from the day we were born. It was the only life we knew. What we saw, what we did..." he trailed off.

"You're lucky I don't have a say in what happens to your sister, because as far as I'm concerned her crimes are unforgivable. And as for you—for a start, you raped and murdered our own mother."

"It's more complicated than that. My father ordered me to. He had six men on my sister, two of them raped her before I had the guts to do what he asked of me. Even when Felicia was crying, screaming, begging me not to kill our mother. What choice did I have?"

"You kept your mother's eyes in a jar."

"Yes, to remind me she was always watching. Making me accountable for any wrong I was doing, any bad decisions I was making."

Lilliana leaned against the wall. What his life must have been like. What she had seen today was just a tiny sliver of the things he must have had to endure over the years.

"I'm just trying to say to you that I will not let anything happen to you while we are here. No matter what, I will protect you with all that I have. And yes, it may freak you out, but I do want you. That at least should reassure you that I will not let my father do any wrong by you. If I can somehow come back to your Given, be useful, and make

a change. Make up for the things I have done? This is what I want."
Lilliana detected that his voice held a note of sadness.

She nodded. "I'm sure Damon will do everything he can to help you once you have helped us, David."

"Yes, he seems to be a very honorable man. Now, you look exhausted. Come, sleep." He patted the bed beside him.

Lilliana hesitantly returned to the bed, sinking into the soft sheets. Closing her eyes, she tried to relax and after a few minutes she drifted off into the sick and twisted dream world of Gregory Reid.

CHAPTER 6

Eric was just leaving the nurse's station after having had the stitching serum applied. It had fascinated him, watching the deep cut disappear as his skin gelled back together. Walking out of the room, looking down as he buttoned up his shirt, he slammed into a small, soft figure.

Nadia almost fell, but Eric's strong, steady hands held her firmly upright.

"Whoops," he said apologetically, though once she looked like she could stand upright he quickly released her, taking a step back. Standing so close to her, touching her, was another kind of torture. Her scent was vanilla mixed with sandalwood, a heady mix that was both innocent and seductive.

"I'm sorry," she said, her gaze lingering on his naked chest, unable to break away. Her eyes rose to meet his, holding him in place. It was if she could see into his soul.

"I truly wouldn't have hurt you; I knew Gregory would send you down here to get fixed up. He was just proving a point to Lilliana."

"And that makes it okay, does it?" Eric could see the impact, the harshness of his words had on her.

She stilled, looked down at her feet, nodded and took off in the direction she had come.

Eric cursed under his breath, finished buttoning up his shirt and followed her. She had disappeared around the corner and up another pathway lined with the evergreen jungle.

He spotted Daniel. "Mate, have you seen a little blonde walk this way?"

Daniel pointed down to where several paths branched off. "Be on guard, Eric; something big is happening in the next fortnight, I overheard Max chatting with Reid's men."

Eric nodded. "I'll keep my ears to the ground."

Daniel nodded and continued along his way as Eric quickly headed down the path after Nadia.

He walked for several minutes wondering where she had disappeared to and questioned himself as to why he felt the need to comfort her, when she was the one who had cut him. Just when he needed his counsellor to talk to, she was busy elsewhere. Eric stopped short when he saw her there, leaning against the large enclosure which had been built around the jungle; she was watching several jaguars lying about, lazily cleaning themselves and basking in the hot sun. One of the majestic cats was pushing up against the fence, leaning into Nadia's hand as she was giving the feline a good rub behind the ears. He heard her talking softly to the beautiful creature, purring soft words of love and endearment in her sweetest voice. As the animal sensed Eric, it growled deep in its throat.

"Careful," Eric said softly, but firmly. "I'd get my hand out of there if I were you."

Nadia pulled her hand out and turned to Eric, looking so small and pretty beside the large wildcat.

"She is the last creature around here that would hurt me," she said, holding her head up and folding her slim arms across her chest.

They stood quietly there for a few moments, sizing the other up, both very curious about their strong attraction to the other.

She appreciated his strong jawline and bone structure, his beautiful tanned skin that made his large, almond coloured eyes stand out. Her gaze drifted to his lips of their own accord. They were the most kissable lips she had ever seen on a man. Firm and full, they seemed to hint at a hidden smile hidden just there, even when there wasn't one. They both felt the tug as her eyes remained on his. It took everything in him to stand still and not walk over to her and crush his mouth against hers.

Nadia quickly looked away and pushed her hand through her hair.

Eric saw how the sun made her strands sparkle like pink champagne, soft and silky. Her eyes looked back at him, warily.

She forced a relaxed pose, but he could see she was quivering, ready to run. What was it about her that made him want to sweep her up into the safety of his arms and take her away from this place?

"Are you enjoying your stay here?" she said, hoping to fill the bizarre silence that seemed to stretch on endlessly between them.

"Well, despite the stunning location and charming personalities, not at all." He didn't feel the need to pretend with her.

She almost laughed at his bluntness and a smile lit up her entire face, turning Nadia from something beautiful into something absolutely breathtaking. Tucking a piece of flyaway hair behind her ear as she turned, she reached up to pluck a vibrant orange bloom that hung from an overhead vine.

It was then that Eric spotted a strange scar on the side of her neck.

He marched over to her and cupped her chin, tilting her head to the side so he could get a good look at the mark.

"What are you doing?" she demanded, trying to pull away from him.

"Keep still," impatience filled his voice as his gentle hands swept her hair aside to run his fingers over the scarred letter R; he cringed, feeling the raised skin.

My God, Eric thought; *the bastard has branded her*! He stroked the side of her neck one last time before he moved his hand away and took a step back. "Sorry," he all but whispered, feeling like he was apologising for more than just invading her personal space.

She felt embarrassed that he had seen her mark and rubbed her hand over her neck where it still tingled from his touch. She had to get away from his curious eyes and unwanted sympathy; but before she could take two steps away, his hand shot out and grabbed her arm, holding her still just inches from him. She looked up into his eyes, a frown marring her beautiful features.

"What?" she said, feeling uncomfortable as her heart raced. She should not be feeling any attraction to this man. It was dangerous for them both. She jerked her arm, trying to free it from his grasp, but he didn't budge an inch; Eric just stood there as solid as a rock and she could feel the heave of his chest rise and fall against hers. Before she knew it, he had slammed her up against him, dipping his head and claiming her lips as his.

Eric only wanted one taste, just one. He could feel her stiffen and begin to protest, but as he sank deeper into the kiss and parted his lips, he heard her moan softly as her lips willingly parted in response to his. Her smell, the taste of her. It was almost too much. It ended too soon as she sprang away from him and then they just stood there like that, several feet apart, her arms across her chest, breathing heavily, not unlike the wildcats behind her, always wary of the stranger at bay.

He held still; not wanting to frighten her.

She burst around him with such speed that he didn't know someone so small and fragile looking could possess, and in seconds she was out of his sight.

He exhaled, shaking his head. What the hell was he thinking? Eric had to wonder what Lilliana would say about this. He quickly stormed off in the direction of her room, hoping she was doing alright with David.

***

Back in New York, Cam was busy taking Christopher and Allie around to visit with Christopher's old acquaintances, the G-heads. Christopher was ecstatic to see old faces that had survived hard times, and it was a real treat for Allie to meet people from his past that he still held such a deep connection with.

They spent six days with the generous, vivacious group, helping to serve thousands of meals to people in such need. It filled both their souls with pure happiness, being together and helping so many.

Cam and Allie had spent several days interviewing candidates for the positions for Lilliana's safe houses. They were both impressed and blown away by how many experienced people were suitable for the positions, and how many sought to be a part of her campaign. They hired some of the most brilliantly dedicated and capable people for the roles, and they knew Lilliana would be pleased with the selections.

Fox completed every scheduled photo shoot set up by Tim and had been thrilled to have the chance to introduce her brother, Levi to their group.

As their time drew to a close, Fox and Levi spent as much time together as they could discussing the past and filling each other in on so many tales that had occurred the past fifteen years they'd been apart. The final night before they were due to fly back home, Fox had begged Cam to allow her to go out into the city with Levi; she was grateful when Cam gave her permission and Fox in turn promised to be at the air strip on time the following morning.

***

The air was sweltering, making it difficult to breathe. Her hearing had become muffled by an unpleasant humming growing persistently louder.

Lilliana felt sweat uncomfortably sliding down her skin. It was the kind of sleek, hot, and heavy sweat that made her feel gritty all over. She went to move her hand to wipe it off but discovered both hands were tied to the bedhead. Her eyes flew open in panic and her heartbeat quickened as she realised she wasn't tied to the bed at all but to a stake hammered into the earth. She blinked, gasping as it came to her that it wasn't sweat, she was trying to blink out of her eyes, but blood.

Lilliana jerked on the restraints, glancing around the pit as her hearing returned. She felt a sense of horror and dread build inside her as the persistent humming disappeared to reveal the faint sound of pitiful moaning and crying. Bloodied, mutilated bodies, withering in pain and trying to escape their tomb were now climbing over her, sightless, scratching at her flesh as they searched for an escape. In that split second as another body was thrown amongst the heap, Lilliana thought she was going to lose her mind. Long red hair flowing behind a pale body thumped lifelessly against Lilliana's legs, one arm twisted at a disturbingly odd angle behind its head, its eye sockets now nothing more than gaping black holes. Fox.

Lilliana tried to suppress her frightened sobs; the stench in the air was unbearably foul as sharp nails scraped across her skin desperately trying to take hold, but the blood was making it too slippery to get a firm grip. She desperately tugged again at the restraints, shifting her body, trying to remove the heavy weight of Fox's lifeless form and the male behind her who was trying to use her as a prop to get out of the pit. His fingers wrapped around her neck, squeezing the air from her as he pulled himself up against her, his face glaringly angry.

David, and the mechanical eye that housed The Guardian feed, was hanging out of his eye socket by a thread. His breath was hot as he screamed into her face.

"This is all your fault! Yours alone! We are all dead because of you! Because of *you*!"

Lilliana gasped, and bombarded with emotions, struggled against him, screaming at him to stop. She prayed she would rather pass out when a sharp slap across her face bought her out of the macabre dream.

She slapped at the hands in front of her sobbing as she came to, and sat upright, scrambling backwards until her back hit the headboard. Lilliana drew her knees up to her chest and wrapped her arms around them, trying to calm herself down by taking deep breaths. Lifting a hand to her throbbing cheek, she felt unwanted tears begin to fall and quickly brushed them away.

"I'm truly sorry Lilliana, I did not want to strike you—but I could not bring you out of your nightmare." David walked into the bathroom and returned with a cold, wet cloth. He held it out to her, and she thanked him, taking it to her stinging cheek.

He nodded and stepped back with a concerned look on his face.

Lilliana shook her head; she was so relieved it had only been a dream. It almost made her want to laugh, but the sickening images were still with her. "It's alright David, it's probably the aftershock from what I saw at the medical lab."

He folded his arms, unsure of her state of health. "It's been a hell of a day for you; maybe you need Eric to jab you with one of his knockout needles?"

"Absolutely not," she snapped before adding in a gentler tone, "I'm fine."

David nodded though he remained unconvinced as a knock came at the door. It swung open and Eric strode in. David frowned at him.

"It would be unfortunate if you walked in and we were not decent."

"Yeah, unfortunate for you, maybe." Eric grinned at Lilliana, before noticing her red cheek as she lowered the cloth. "What the hell?" he quickly walked over to her as she stood up.

"I'm fine Eric. I was having a nightmare; it was the only way David could snap me out of it."

"Bloody hell! Must have been a good one. Surprised he's still got his head though." He looked over at David, wondering what Damon would have thought about the whole scene. "I just ran into your father on my way here. He had about twenty men with him. Clients I presume. Anyway, he wanted me to tell you that you are both going hunting with him tomorrow; as for tonight, Lilly and Nadia are to have a girl's night."

"Alright," David nodded, and walked to the serving stand to pour himself and Lilliana a cold beverage. He took a long mouthful as he turned to Lilliana and passed her a glass full of mint and lemon water. She finished it off in two large swallows.

"I'll get changed in the bathroom. If you come in this time David it won't be pleasant for you."

David held up his hands. "Never again will I trespass on your privacy. I'm off to see what Father is up to," he said and strolled out of the room.

"Who's *he*, and what has he done with the real David Reid?" Eric raised an eyebrow.

Lilliana smiled as she walked to the closet, pulling out the first thing she saw. "I think *he* has seen the light. Hopefully, it's not too late for him." She crossed to the bathroom and opened the door.

"Why don't you try to get some real sleep, Eric? I'll look out for you."

"You always have." He sat on a chair and nestled back into the pillows. A frown crossed his face as he thought of Nadia and a mix of confused feelings swamped him.

"What is it?" She leaned against the door frame looking down at him.

"Nothing."

"Eric, I know you—and I know it is not nothing. Talk to me."

He glanced up as he ran a hand through his hair, and, crossing an ankle over his knee he pushed his black boot off, reaching for the other to pull off. He shrugged. "I kissed Nadia."

"Oh no, Eric." Lilliana felt for him immediately. It was a dangerously sticky situation. "You can't have feelings for that woman, it's too complicated—for her, and for you. Reid would kill you." Lilliana was worried. She threw the clothes into the bathroom before crossing to Eric and kneeling at his feet, placed her hands on his knees, trying to offer him some sort of comfort.

He looked down at her. "It's not like I planned for it to happen, Lilly. It just did. It was like I couldn't help myself. I needed to touch her. Taste her." He shook his head and looked away. "Saying it out loud probably makes me sound like an out of control teenager, huh."

"Hardly that; you're just a normal man with a man's desires. What was her reaction?"

He grinned before he could stop himself. The male ego, she thought, smiling inwardly.

"Let's just say, she *responded*." He shrugged looking back at her. "I knew it was wrong; it won't happen again. Mind you, here's a bit of interesting info—Reid has branded her."

"Branded her? As in, what they used to do to animals when it was legal?" Lilliana stood, thinking of how much pain Nadia would have endured. "Where?"

He tapped a finger behind his ear against the side of his neck.

"Ouch, poor thing. That man is one sick bastard." Lilliana shook her head. "I dread to think about this hunting business tomorrow;

what will it entail? Maybe you can help me fake a sickie, Eric?"

"I'll do whatever you need. Now go freshen up and change. You want to look fresh and pretty for your girl's night." Eric closed his eyes and dropped his head back onto the soft cushion to try to relax, but he was always on guard, always on the ready in case anything untoward were to happen.

Lilliana entered the large bathroom, shutting the door behind her and walked towards the large open window. Leaning on the sill, she looked out upon the sea of green and escaped into a daydream of being back home with Damon and her friends. It was a busy but simple, happy life and she missed it with all her heart.

"It won't be long, Damon," she whispered, before turning to pick up the soft, black skirt and dark purple singlet top with sparkly black sequins in the pattern of a butterfly. Her black waves hung down her back, and she wore low black heels. A handful of bracelets, swinging hoop earrings, a dash of perfume and light makeup and she almost felt human and ready to face whatever the coming hours were to bring.

***

Eric escorted Lilliana down to a spacious open plan room; the jungle's trees were almost kissing the inside of the room. The mosaic floor was a jewel of colours, adding to the festive vibe along with oversized, coloured pillows thrown across white, backless couches. The artwork along the walls were paintings of the Amazon's spectacular rainforests, birds, and wildlife. It was the first room Lilliana had been in besides her room that did not give her the total creeps.

"Oh, hello." Nadia stepped off an unseen pad near the closest tree and entered the room. She smiled at Lilliana. "Thanks for joining me, would you like a cocktail?"

"Sure, that would be lovely." Lilliana knew she should keep a clear head, but surely one cocktail wouldn't hurt. She walked into the centre of the room as Nadia turned to mix and pour the drinks. "This is a beautiful space."

"Thank you; it's the only room in the entire house I got to have a say in decorating." Nadia turned, smiling, and handed Lilliana a round frosted glass with sugar around the rim.

"Thank you. Mmm, that's yummy." Lilliana said after a mouthful. She heard a chuckle behind her; it was Eric standing on guard by the door.

"Problem?"

"Yeah," he snickered. "A full-grown woman saying 'yummy.'"

"Get over it," she called back sweetly.

Nadia took a mouthful of her drink, envious and curious about the playful banter between the two of them. The sound of his voice sent shivers down her spine. Speaking of yummy she thought, eyeing the man candy up and down.

Lilliana turned her attention back to Nadia. "Sorry about that."

Nadia waved her hand and sat. "Please, sit, tell me about yourself."

"Well, there's probably not much to tell that you don't already know." Lilliana sat on the comfortable seat, as she sank down, the chair seemed to hug and support her lower back as though it was designed just for her.

"I had a good childhood, but after a tragic incident I was sent to The Given in Louisiana. I found I loved modelling and, well, here I am today. Happy in love and loving what I do." What else could she say?

"And I hear you are putting your skills to good use, setting up safe houses for the less fortunate around the globe. Congratulations, that must be a wonderful feeling knowing you are helping so many."

"It sure is." Lilliana was enjoying her drink and finished it before she knew it. She wasn't usually a lush drinker, but it tasted so good. Nadia got up to pour her another.

"Thanks."

"You're welcome."

"Tell me about yourself, Nadia."

"Aright. Well, I had a great childhood, my mother was an angel. So sweet, generous, and kind. She was beautiful inside and out. My father could never take his eyes off her; even at mealtimes, I remember his eyes barely left hers, even as he ate. He was always focused on her." She smiled sadly. "Then one day my mother disappeared, simply vanished from our lives. I thank the stars my brother and I were so close, otherwise I don't think I would have survived the pain of losing her. He was always there for me, as I was for him." She sighed.

"I was at school one particular day when the Officials came to collect me, saying my brother and father had been murdered, massacred beyond recognition, leaving me all alone." She was silent for a few moments, swallowing the lump that grew in her throat at the memory. "I cannot even begin to describe the devastation I felt at that moment."

As Lilliana listened to Nadia's story she became very still. She knew she had heard this story before, only many of the details were vastly different. She felt a slow chill run through her body. She stood and walked over to Nadia.

"How did you end up here with Gregory? You are so much younger than he is."

Nadia turned and smiled. "Yes I am, but love has no age barriers." Lilliana wanted to believe her, but it looked to her as though Nadia was forcing her cheer. "Gregory saved my life; it was he who came to the Officials and made an exceptionally large donation to take me in. I don't clearly remember those first few years I was with Gregory. I was depressed, disconnected. But what I do remember was that Gregory was always kind to me; he was caring, generous. I received the highest education, travelled the world many times over, and experienced so much because of the lifestyle I have with him. I sometimes question how fortunate I am. I adore him."

Lilliana thought Nadia was speaking a little too loudly and it sounded like she was trying to convince herself more than trying to convince Lilliana of her deep adoration for Gregory Reid.

"Do you ever question what he does? The business he runs?" Lilliana felt this a safe enough question; she was after all now married to the son of the Reid Empire.

Nadia looked away and said nothing for a few moments; Lilliana noticed then that her lips moved but no sound could be heard. She moved closer, thinking she had caught Nadia muttering, "Always, always."

Lilliana became certain in this moment that this was in fact Orlando's sister, Nadia. She quickly turned on her heel and walked over to Eric. Making sure no one was about she leaned on tiptoe up to his ear, pressing her lips against his lobe, being careful not to be picked up by any sound-tracking devices along the corridor. She whispered, "I think Nadia is Orlando's sister."

Eric jerked backwards and stared down at her.

She nodded at Eric again, for emphasis.

Eric remembered all too well the sad, sorry tale of Orlando's sister in one of the first group therapy sessions he had shared with Lilliana, back in the day. A tale of the little beauty she had been, and that her father had sold her to Diplomat Reid for a fortune to be used, prostituted, punished, and tortured. He also remembered another part of the story; that she had been killed. Obviously, it had all been a set up, but thank the stars that Orlando had, at the time, thought his sister dead all those years ago, or else Lilliana and Jessica may not have been saved. He shook his head.

"What a bloody world," he muttered as Lilliana stepped away from Eric and went back into the room.

"Nadia, it's such a beautiful afternoon; shall we go for a walk?"

Nadia looked over at Lilliana and finished her drink. "Of course, have you had a tree top walk yet?"

"No, but it sounds perfect."

Nadia smiled. "It is, come." she placed her glass on a side table and turned towards the outdoor jungle beyond the room. Stepping out, her foot landing on a large pad, she disappeared into the thick green arms of the trees.

Lilliana followed, unsure at first, but once her foot stepped out, it encountered one large green disc, then another and another. They were set amongst the trees like floating steps, all spaced perfectly and large enough for one to be comfortable crossing.

As they walked, the green jungle swallowed them up, shielding them from eyes below. The canopy above sheltered them from the soft rain that began to fall.

They continued along for some time, and Lilliana found herself becoming more and more relaxed, enjoying the fresh air and the call of birds. Then they heard a scream in the distance. Feral. She froze.

Where were they going?

Nadia had turned back until she stood in front of Lilliana. "It's all right, it's a cougar, he can't get us here, they are deep in the jungle. Come, we are nearly there." She set off again at an easy pace.

Lilliana considered slipping off her heels but didn't want them to drop on anyone's head below; she was grateful they were only low heels.

"Here we are," Nadia said a few minutes later. She stepped onto a square platform, reaching for Lilliana's hand. "It's safe."

Lilliana took Nadia's hand and allowed herself to be pulled onto the clear shelf as both her feet made contact, they travelled slowly to the jungle floor. Lilliana was dazzled by the beauty of the jungle; the atmosphere was damp, warm and inviting. There were bursts of colour everywhere amongst the tall, green leafy plants and moss-covered ground. A hot spring bubbled welcomingly, surrounded by smooth, flat rocks that were staggered into comfortable seating.

"This area was designed just for me. You can't see it, but there is a force field that runs around this area, protecting me from any wandering hunters or jungle predators." Nadia pulled her silky dress over her head, leaving her standing in white bra and knickers. Lilliana thought if Eric could see her now, he would no doubt have had a heart attack and dropped dead on the spot.

"Come in, have a swim."

Lilliana slipped out of her shoes and pulled her skirt down, tugging the singlet top over her head. Stepping into the water, she appreciated the smooth surface of the large, black and butterscotch coloured stones. Sitting beside Nadia, she exhaled in pleasure.

Nadia smiled. "It's good, isn't it?"

"It's heaven." Lilliana felt herself fully relax for the first time since she'd arrived at the compound. "Does Gregory do a lot of this sort of thing for you?"

Nadia's smile tightened slightly. "Yes and no." She reached over to a distinctive butterscotch rock nestled between two black rocks and ran her hand over it: the top slid open, revealing a full bar with ice. She pulled out two bottles of mixed vodka and passed Lilliana one after popping the top.

"Thanks." She didn't know if she would be able to walk back along the tree pads if she had another, but wanted Nadia to talk, so she sipped slowly.

Nadia swallowed the entire bottle before dropping it into a waste section near the bar. Reaching for another she popped it open, then closed the bar again. She focused on Lilliana as she sank further into the warm, soothing water and floated there for a few moments, before starting softly.

"I know you. I've watched you, along with Gregory. That's how I know my brother Orlando is not really dead. That it was he who killed our father and set you and that other girl free. I watched it all, along with Gregory, David, and Felicia. Gregory thinks I was too drugged to remember. There is so much he thinks I've been oblivious to. But it's safer for me for him to keep thinking that way. Gregory has wanted to get his hands on you since I can remember. When David was sent to your Given, Gregory put a plan in motion to have him released. When he saw via the headlines that you were planning to set up your safe houses, he knew that threatening chemical warfare against your establishment was the perfect way to get your Head Heir's attention and have you removed, along with David."

Lilliana had to push down her anxiety and take a sip of the vodka mixer.

"Why didn't Gregory ask for Felicia's release?"

"He was ashamed of Felicia and her failings. Falling for an undercover operative crippled many of his blood drug labs. He lost billions in those raids."

That undercover operative was Damon. Lilliana forced herself not to think of him and focused on Nadia. "How can one man with so much money care if he loses a few billion here or there?" She shook her head.

"He is a greedy man, Lilliana — and that makes him very dangerous." she said with a sad smile. "Money and power are all that matter to him."

"Not love?"

"He wouldn't know what love is. I do. Even though it was years ago, I felt it for my mother, my brother. I can see that you and David do not love each other, although he is in lust with you." She smirked. "I'd like to know the real story there one day, not your cover story. After all, I've just exposed myself to you."

"Cover story?" Lilliana thought it best to play innocent, protect herself. She didn't know this girl well enough yet.

"I can detect a bullshit cover story when I see it," she smiled, unapologetically, and, seeing Lilliana pale she added, "It's okay, Gregory won't catch on for the simple fact he is star struck with you, and feels like he has won, having you so close to his clutches."

Lilliana cringed inwardly at the thought of being anywhere near his clutches. Nadia continued.

"One day I'd like to hear the entire, and no doubt interesting, story."

Lilliana saluted her with her bottle. "Then one day, you shall." She waved her hand around at where they were sitting. "It's obviously safe to talk out here?"

Nadia nodded before moving closer to Lilliana, whispering. "I don't know exactly how to ask you this, or even if it's possible. When you leave, will you please take me with you?" Tears clogged her throat and she suddenly had to look away, embarrassed.

What pain and suffering she must have had to endure all these years, Lilliana thought; having to lie beside a man she knew that deep down had lied to her about her brother and father. Lilliana reached out and grabbed Nadia's hand.

"Nadia, of course we'll take you with us; I'm sure Eric is already working on a plan."

His name brought Nadia's eyes back to Lilliana's. "You seem close to him. Friends?"

"Yes," she smiled. "We are." Lilliana slipped a little deeper under the water. "We weren't always."

"Sounds like another story there."

"There's always a back story. Your father took me, and another young girl and we went through months of pure hell. Then there was

Orlando. He too, played his part in taking us; but I always knew there was a kindness to him. He used to whisper to us when he knew the camera's recorders couldn't pick up what he was saying. Always kind words, firm but kind. Always reassuring us, telling us not to give up, to do whatever they told us to do so we wouldn't be punished more. We were still scared of him at the time, of course; but he became our saviour in the end and we were sent to the same Given—that's where I met Eric."

Nadia wiped a tear away. "I saw what they did to you both, it was beyond deplorable."

"Yes. Yes, it was." Lilliana nodded, mentally shutting out images from the past, locking them into a place where they couldn't escape. She leaned her head against a smooth rock and thought about how blessed she had been with everything that had occurred since.

"In situations like ours, you can either reach for the helping hand that offers hope, or you can slide into the darkness and continue being a victim. I chose to live the best I could with the life that was given to me. I've made wonderful friends that have become my family, and I have a fabulous role where I help many every single day. I've fallen in love." She smiled then, thinking only of Damon. "I am one of the lucky ones."

"Lucky man. When did you first meet David?"

"Well, I had the unpleasant task of interrogating David when he was sent to us; I had to retrieve information from him regarding Gregory's criminal activity." She made air quotations with her fingers on the word *activity* for want of a better word.

"Long story short, from Gregory's threat, to my campaign along with David's release—my superiors thought it would be safer for me if David and I were to play the happy couple." She held up her hand showing off David's large, glistening ring.

Nadia nodded. "Yes, smart move. Gregory would do horrible things to you if you weren't his precious son's wife—you'd be in danger."

Lilliana shivered. "I'm supposed to go hunting tomorrow. Prove myself somehow. I don't know why."

Nadia placed her empty bottle in the bin and took Lilliana's half empty bottle. "Be smart, be brave—and whatever he wants you to do Lilliana, just do it. It's not worth the struggle, trust me."

"What you said about Gregory, back at the house. I can't imagine how exhausting it must be for you, living in this pretend world. You must be a nervous wreck?"

Nadia stepped out of the water and walked over to a thick tree trunk. Pushing on a knot in the wood caused a door to open revealing a tiny room where thick towels hung. Reaching for one, she wrapped it around herself, then passed another to Lilliana as she got out of the water.

"There are days where I wish it would all just be over."

"Did you ever try to leave?"

Nadia slowly shook her head. "No. I've seen what he does to people who try to leave. He has eyes everywhere. I'm strong enough to play the part though, for a while longer at least."

"What do you think he would do to you Nadia, if he knew how you truly felt?"

Nadia simply stared at Lilliana. The silence was more unsettling than any answer she could give.

"Poor you," Lilliana whispered. "It must be hell?"

Nadia let go a laugh. "I know this will sound so wrong to you, but Gregory knows how to please a woman. He prides himself on it. It is the only thing that makes being his prisoner tolerable." Nadia turned bright red at being so candid.

"You don't have to be ashamed of that fact, Nadia. You have been with him since you were young, most likely conditioned in many ways. It's natural you would feel some sort of loyalty to him."

Nadia looked at Lilliana. "Loyalty is a strong word. Self-preservation may be closer to the truth. I can tell you this, Lilliana; if I don't get away from this situation soon my soul will perish and die."

"It says a lot about your strength of character that you have lasted this long."

"I don't know about that, but thank you. Your kindness is very refreshing. Whenever Felicia visited us here, she would do everything in her power to cause me pain and put me in uncomfortable situations. She created trouble for me with Gregory. She was always unbalanced, unkind."

"I know someone very similar," Lilliana said, thinking of Natalie in the back of her mind.

"When Gregory talked about you coming here, I was so excited. I know it was wrong to want you to come here, considering the dangers it would pose for you, but I've been so curious about you. When I saw you this morning in the medical lab, I could finally understand Gregory's obsession with you. And now here you are, the Dark Angel he has been talking about for years."

Lilliana squeezed Nadia's outstretched hand. She couldn't believe all that hell had really happened in just one short day. Now here she was, opening herself up and trusting Nadia with dangerous secrets that were sure to put herself and her people in immediate danger if Gregory were to find out. Her gut instinct was strong though; she knew she could trust Nadia. She pushed it all down and smiled.

"Jessica is going to love you."

"Jessica? The other girl Father and Orlando took?"

"Yes."

"Well, I look forward to meeting her." Nadia led the way back to the glass lift that would carry them back up through the jungle canopy; it was a safe place where they could speak freely and share more insight on Orlando and who he was now.

Nadia felt such longing in the pit of her stomach, hopeful that Lilliana would be the key to releasing her from this prison.

CHAPTER 7

"What do you mean, you've lost her?" Damon faced his brother, a dark frown marring his handsome features. He was thrilled to have his brother finally home safely, but the news of Fox missing came as a devastating blow.

"She was desperate to spend her last night with Levi; her tracker signalled the locations she said she was visiting and she was to meet us back at the airport the following morning, where Tim had planned to do a quick photo shoot of her and Levi. Her tracking device indicated she was at the airstrip with Tim. Only, when we walked into the room where their signals had led us to believe they'd be, their trackers were sitting in a pool of blood: no Fox, no Tim."

"Oh no," Josephine whispered, fearful. She wrapped her arms around her husband's waist, peering sadly up at him.

Cam looked down into her beautiful big brown eyes. "It's alright, love, we will find them." His hand stroked her hair lovingly, relishing touching her. It had been too many months since he'd been able to look upon her sweet face. He dropped a kiss on her lips, keeping it short in front of Damon. He knew how much his brother was missing Lilliana.

"It's going to be alright; I have a tracking crew back in New York tracing their last steps. We should be able to locate them, or whoever took them," Johnson added, running his fingers over his keypad. "I'll head upstairs Damon, see where we're at."

"Thanks Johnson," he watched Johnson leave the room as he addressed his brother. "Cam, why don't you take a couple of hours to take care of your wife, enjoy some quiet time." He smiled at Josephine.

"Thanks brother." Cam walked over and pulled Damon into a hug, before adding, "She'll be home soon."

Damon hugged him back hard. "I know," he said, releasing Cam as a knock sounded at the door. "Come in."

"Damon, is now a good time to talk to you about the safe houses?" Allie asked, entering the room. Her blue hair fell softly to her shoulders, bangs framing her pretty, pixie-like face.

"Allie, we'll have to postpone our meeting; I'm sorry, I have a million things to do before another meeting. I'll buzz you if I get through it all sooner."

"Sure thing, Sir."

Once the door closed and he was left alone, Damon raised his face to the ceiling, stretching his neck and back and shut his eyes for a moment to mentally prepare himself for the demanding hours that lay ahead.

∗∗∗

The heat of the day was overwhelming, making it difficult to breathe. Lilliana pushed away the uncomfortable similarities of her nightmare the day before to the feeling of this day. Sweat trickled down her back and between her breasts; her hair, tied in a high ponytail gave her neck small relief from the humidity of the day. She wore flat brown boots and a short sleeved, knee length brown dress, with a thick belt around her waist. Hunters attire, David had told her.

She couldn't suppress her growing anxiety as another gunshot blasted into the air, sending birds screeching across the sky. They had been out in the jungle for over an hour, hunters branching off here and there with their guides and assorted weapons. It became increasingly eerie, and paradoxical, hearing the hunter's laughter off in the distance, in parallel to the screams of the hunted.

"Are you alright Lilliana?" Gregory asked in a tone that clearly implied he didn't care either way. He thrived, seeing her growing more nervous by the minute.

"I'm fine, this just isn't my thing," *Or clearly anyone else's, who wasn't a psychopath,* she thought, trying to play it down. She wiped her sweaty palms down against the stiff fabric of her dress trying to conceal her nervousness.

David thread his fingers through hers, squeezing them once, trying to control her nerves.

"Perhaps I'll take Lilliana back now, Father; have a swim or a massage," he said, pulling her towards him, kissing her quickly.

"What do you think, honey?"

Lilliana pulled back from his kiss and ran her fingers through his hair.

"Now that sounds like a much better way to spend the day," she smiled, hoping Gregory would let them go.

"Not just yet son—you know I have issues with people who haven't proven themselves to me. I want Lilliana to show me how much she loves you, and that she wants to be a part of our family."

"And how would you like me to do that, Gregory?" Lilliana's tone wasn't sweet now. She knew she was failing at being the precious, obedient daughter in law in this moment.

"Dear Lilliana, I told you to call me Father."

She grit her teeth and forced herself to use a sweet, calm tone. "Father, what will you have me do?"

He walked behind her and placed his arm over her shoulder, pointing to a blue figure darting amongst the green of the jungle that was trying to hide from the hunters.

"I want you to kill one of your own sex and bring me her heart. You have one hour to do this."

"Seriously?" she asked quietly.

"Deadly," he whispered against her ear, flicking his tongue into her lobe.

She jerked away from Gregory, moving closer to David as she wiped out Gregory's saliva with her finger. The man was beyond gross. Looking up at David she whispered, "This is insane."

He nodded. "It is, but you can do it."

"Like hell I can!" She hissed quietly. "Firstly, I am *not* taking an innocent life!"

David looked at her with sympathy; she clearly didn't understand the gravity of her situation. "You *must* do this. Try to remember that they are as good as dead anyway; if you don't do it, another hunter will, there is no saving these people."

"Do you think that little pep talk makes me feel better, makes this all alright?"

He shrugged, reaching for her hand.

"And secondly, I am NOT going to cut out another woman's heart!" Lilliana jerked her hand away, turning to face Gregory. She was about to tell him to go to hell when the words faded from her lips; she felt the blood drain from her face.

Fox, who was naked and painted blue from head to toe, stepped out onto the trail, struggling between two of Gregory's guards as they manhandled her dragging her towards Gregory.

"No!" Lilliana whispered in fright. She stepped forward to reach out to her friend when a strong hand clamped firmly around her arm.

She looked up into Gregory's calm face.

"Here is the deal, my darling daughter. You do what I have asked, or I will place your pretty little friend here in the hunting arena."

Lilliana didn't struggle from Gregory's grip; she didn't want to give him the satisfaction. But internally she was flipping out. Could this really be happening? Her beautiful friend, Fox's crystal-clear blue eyes were filled with fright, staring straight back at her.

"Are you alright?" Stupid question, Lilliana realised, but she had to ask.

"I'm fine, Lilly; don't worry about me. This is like a resort, a walk in the park." she forced a brave smile for Lilliana. The guard pulled back his fist and slammed it into her stomach, making her gasp in pain.

"Don't hurt her!" Lilliana yelled, her own fists clenched by her sides, quaking with rage as she watched Fox double over, gasping for breath.

Gregory walked over to Fox and helped her stand upright, running a hand over her face. "Such a sexy little piece," he drooled sickly stepping up against her as the guards held her in place. He ran his hands up and down her body, taking slow pleasure in touching her private areas in a leisurely fashion, stroking and cupping her. He leaned down and took her mouth.

Lilliana froze, fearful for Fox. She knew her friend well, and, knowing her temper, prayed that Fox would not lash out and make the situation worse for herself.

David stepped around Lilliana. "Really, Father; do you think hurting Lilliana's friend is going to cement your relationship with her?"

"Enough, let's get this hunting going, so we can move onto other things the day has to offer."

Gregory ran his thumb over Fox's trembling lower lip, enjoying the fact that she was filled with fear. Her eyes weren't as fearful as he would have liked, though. Silly girl. But that would come. He turned his attention back to Lilliana, enjoying the fact that she looked both furious and frightened. He couldn't contain the burst of delight that emanated from him. Oh, how he *loved* days like this!

Lilliana looked away from him, trying to block out the evil sounding laugh as a masked guard stepped from the trees and marched towards her, a large bowie knife in hand. Liliana swallowed hard as he came to an abrupt halt in front of her, roughly pushing the knife through the gap in her belt.

"Don't stab yourself," he warned. Lilliana immediately recognised it was Rocco's voice. He slipped back into the shadows of the trees.

"We'll be watching you the entire hunt; Little Red Riding Hood here will get a knife of another sort thrust inside her if you don't do what I have asked." Gregory said, gesturing to Fox as her red tresses fell down over her face.

Lilliana was unable to mask the look of disgust and fear she felt as she stared back at him. He was repulsive.

"Go, little girl. Time is ticking." He snapped.

David pulled Lilliana into a hug, pretending to kiss her neck as he whispered urgently. "Your target is dead anyway, just do it and get back." He released her, amazed again that Damon hadn't blown his head off already.

With one last backward glance, Lilliana's eyes met with Fox's.

"Just another day in paradise, Lilly," Fox whispered.

Lilliana nodded to her friend. "I'll see you soon." Turning, she disappeared into the thick, dense jungle green.

***

The symphony of gunshots and laughter that came from the hunters far away, mixed with screams of despair from the hunted, echoed throughout the jungle.

Lilliana could hear the sound of blood pumping in her ears with every step she took as she moved closer to committing her vile act. She swallowed down the lump of bile that formed in her throat. How the hell could they be laughing? She swatted at a large insect and pushed a giant leaf out of her way. She could not believe the situation she was in right at this moment. How the hell could she live with herself if she did this? If she killed an innocent human?

A life for a life, Lilliana; think of Fox, just think of Fox, she thought as she battled with a cluster of green vines blocking her path. Grabbing the heavy knife that Rocco had thrust into her belt, she slashed at the vines and stepped through them, returning the knife to her belt when she was done. She squealed as her body suddenly slammed into a large man dressed in a hunter's uniform.

She jerked backwards.

He laughed as he grabbed her upper arms, holding her steady when she looked like she was about to topple over.

"Sorry little darling." He released her, stepping back. "Quiet now, there's a bunch of them gathered up ahead trying to hide under a small waterfall. We've set explosives; they'll go off shortly, and the explosion will send them running like cockroaches. You'll have your pick of targets." He winked as though he was giving her the best news ever.

She considered using her knife on him, but she knew he was too large and would overpower her in a second. Plus, this entire hunting arena was monitored, and Gregory would no doubt be watching. Lilliana nodded, as if this were just what she wanted to hear. As he disappeared into the trees, she shook her head, wondering what was wrong with people. She already knew the answer to that. So much. Too much.

Lilliana walked on for a few minutes before spotting thirty or so figures, all hunched under a small waterfall. She saw their terrified eyes peering out, whispering soft murmurs of comfort to each other, both young and old. Bodies were marked by gender; males were painted red, females, blue.

Lilliana froze. Surely they could hear her heart beating wildly like a drum pounding repeatedly. *It's time, it's time* she thought. She felt a shockwave of thunder move through her as the explosive went off, blasting her backwards five feet. She squeezed her eyes shut as her hair blew all around her. She staggered backwards, covering her ears as the explosion shook her to her core.

She braced herself against the trunk of a tree as bodies flew around her, seemingly in slow motion. She shook her head, keeping her eyes closed. Please, make it stop, make it *all* stop! she begged to a higher being. The sounds of the hunted were more animal than human, and she forced herself to open her eyes again. She saw painted bodies scrambling about, desperately searching for a place to hide from the hunters. Seeing their eyes filled with terror broke her heart; Lilliana remembered the feeling of fear, knew it well, of what it felt like to be utterly terrified. To not feel so human.

A young boy slammed into her as he tried to escape, his eyes filled with distrust. He froze, breathing heavily.

She wanted to cry for him, for them all. "Climb high," she whispered in his native tongue.

He blinked once before spinning around and ran back through thick foliage and out of sight. She prayed he would make it to the highest tree and hide till this was all over, that he could somehow escape to safety.

She had only a moment to think of the boy before her vision was once again filled with horror. Twenty feet away a lovely young woman had fallen to the ground screaming as an arrow pierced her leg. She had no chance of getting up to save herself before a large man fell upon her, intending to rape her. Her screams for help soon became pitiful sobs.

Lilliana's eyes clouded over in a red haze of fury. She strode forward without thinking, hand reaching for her knife. She stepped behind him and without so much as a moment's thought reached around his neck and slit his throat.

Blood spurted over the young woman, who was now crying softly.

Images of the past came back to haunt Lilliana; it was a scene not so different from this one where she had had to cut into men's flesh and made them bleed. She shook the memories away as one would an annoying mosquito and pushed the bleeding corpse off the young woman. Kneeling, she saw the woman's look of disgust, and remembered she was wearing the attire of a hunter.

"It's alright," Lilliana assured the woman in her native Portuguese tongue, hoping to calm her a little. "I'm going to help you." She tried to think of how she could fulfil her promise on that statement as she watched the woman shake in utter distress.

"Why?" the woman screamed back at Lilliana in her native tongue, repeatedly asking, "Why? Why?"

"I don't know! I'm sorry, I don't know!" Lilliana said desperately, along with the distraught female. She wanted to put her arms around her, offer her comfort, reach out to stroke her smooth, dark cheek, when suddenly everything became eerily distorted.

Lilliana blinked hard, thinking that with everything she had witnessed, it must have affected her vision. But, no—once she regained her focus, she saw the woman's eyebrows slide down her face as she slowly melted into a blob of skin and eyeballs.

Lilliana jumped up and leapt backwards, staring in horror at the woman. The woman's screams were beyond anything she had ever heard. What was worse, when she screamed, her skin seemed to melt in strips from top lip to bottom, like thin straps off spaghetti smiling along her teeth.

Lilliana's stomach lurched as male laughter came from behind her and made her whip around. She stared as the hunter strode towards her on his stocky legs.

"Sorry," he held up a hand. "Didn't mean to frighten you. Just wanted to test this out." His voice held a note of, 'I was born with a silver spoon up my crack,' quality.

He is apologising for frightening me, she thought, *but he isn't sorry he just melted the flesh of another person?* She could not wrap her head around the decency aspect of things just yet. It was all too much.

Cradled in his arms was a gun-like device called 'The Melter'. David had told her about this new type of hunting technology. It could melt the skin, fur, and scale off any prey. At this point she was relieved it had not melted her own skin.

He winked at Lilliana as he began walking backwards before vanishing into the jungle. Once he was out of her sight, she looked down at the woman, her skin still painfully, stretching, melting in front of her eyes. Lilliana knew there was only one thing for her to do and it was the one thing Gregory wanted her to do. She jumped again as another gunshot sound rippled through the air sending another burst of uneasy nerves inside her.

She shook her head as she pulled out the sharp and bloodied knife and knelt, careful not to rest her knees too close to the woman's melting skin. She quickly ran through her options, wanting to put the poor woman out of her misery in the quickest, kindest way possible. She didn't have long to think about it, and, taking a deep breath, along with a quick prayer, she ran the knife along the woman's throat, slitting it in an instant with the sharp blade, before opening her palm and letting go the bloody knife as it fell with a thump into the dirt of the jungle floor.

Her head fell back, and she looked up at the bright blue sky above, taking in the deep, green leaves of the jungle set against the blue like a painting. It was picture perfect. Would anything feel perfect again? She wondered. Thoughts of Jessica, Allie, and Josephine trickled into her numb mind, and then, God help her, came thoughts of Damon and their beautiful life together. She forced her train of thought to stop right there.

She was here in part to protect those she loved, and right now she had a job to do, and that was to protect Fox. She wondered how much time had passed since Gregory's ultimatum, and tired, she reached for the knife, grasping it tightly in both hands, feeling all her muscles tense with what she was about to do. Taking a deep breath, she plunged the knife down, cringing as it pierced the woman's flesh, hitting bone. Jerking it out, she plunged it in again and again, repeatedly into the woman's chest. It made her feel sick.

After creating a gaping hole Lilliana dropped the knife, watching as the blood slid slowly along the open wound, covering the woman's flesh and pooling on the ground to make patterns in the dirt.

Lilliana covered her face, trying to block out what she had done; tears welled in her eyes and slowly started to fall. She shook her head, feeling as if she was having an out of body experience, knowing what had to come next. She took another long exhalation, and, holding her breath slipped her fingers into the jagged slashes, feeling around for the heart muscle as the splintered bones scraped her fingers, cutting the back of her hands. She plunged deeper, reaching for the organ Gregory wanted.

In that moment Lilliana heard nothing; the world had gone totally silent.

Feelings of hysteria began building inside her as her fingers connected with the organ, and she gripped hard and pulled with all her might. She did not hear herself screaming as she fell backwards, the heart in her hands. She got to her feet, sobbing, and looking down at the carcass of the dead woman.

"Forgive me," was all she whispered.

Lilliana staggered in the direction she had come; another couple of gunshots went firing in the distance. She ran as fast as her feet would carry her through the jungle, holding the warm dead heart in both hands, hoping to reach Fox before the hour was up. If not, she would gladly end her own life right then and there.

***

Damon swallowed hard, his hands clenched behind the back of his neck as a grim expression covered his face and he stared at the screen. The Guardian's footage showed Lilliana as she burst, running from the jungle, covered in blood, sweat and tears, screaming, "I've done it, where is she? I've done it!"

"It's alright Lilliana," David called out, "Father has taken Fox inside, he has been watching from the filming room. Most hunters like to take a copy of their hunting adventures home with them." David said then winced at his own verbal dribble as Lilliana fell to her knees, paler than he had ever seen her. As if she was in any state to hear about what his father had been up to for his clients, he thought.

"God, sorry, I'm an idiot," he apologised, quickly walking over to her and pulling her to her feet scooping her up. The heart fell from her hands dropping with a wet splat into her lap.

David headed back towards the house, hearing Lilliana's desperate cries as she repeated in despair, "I killed her, I killed her."

"It's alright Lilliana, it's going to be alright," David said. In truth, although he hoped she would be, he wasn't fully convinced by his own words, because if he knew is father like he did, there was so much more to come.

***

Damon turned to Johnson and the room full of men; all were unsettled by what they had just viewed.

Cam's arms folded tightly across his chest, a pained expression on his face.

"Do we risk it all, and move sooner rather than later?"

Johnson shook his head. "From the intel we have been receiving, this event Reid has planned since Lilliana walked through his door, is an opportunity we cannot pass up on. It's been confirmed—there has been movement in the Underground and many of the syndicates we've been trying to pin down will be attending."

Damon was silent; he was taking it all in, and though he appeared calm on the outside, on the inside he was full of rage and despair. Not being able to hold and support the woman he loved or extract her from such a dangerous and precarious situation was almost more than he could bear.

"I don't know," Cam rubbed his hands over his face. "Damon, this should be your call. Do we go in now, get Fox and Lilly out of there?"

"This goes above what I wanted, Cam. We have got Reid, and the enormity of that in itself, goes without saying. But this could be our chance to take down some of the vilest names in crime our globe has seen in decades. We have no choice; we have to wait." Damon nodded to Johnson.

"I agree. Everything is in place for us to make our move in a fortnight's time. Lilliana knew the risks and would not want to put the entire operation in jeopardy just to save herself from unpleasant tasks. In fact, I think she'd be furious if we pulled her out now." All heads nodded in agreement.

"Alright then; let's start preparing, gentlemen." Damon was grateful for the strong team around him. It was his confidence in them, and the team that was with Lilliana right now, that made getting through all this uncertainty, bearable.

***

Eric stepped forward, relieved to finally see Lilliana come out of the jungle, but upon seeing what was sitting in her lap he was about to lose it. He calmed himself quickly as a maid approached, holding a tray out to David. Eric snatched the heart from Lilliana's lap and slapped it down onto the tray. The maid nodded and left.

"Give her to me." Eric's voice clipped.

David nodded as Eric took her up into his arms, turning towards the house.

"Eric," David said quietly, making sure to look casual in front of the cameras. "If you still have some of that concoction you can give to her to make the coming hours bearable, please do."

Eric's face was grim, but he nodded as he and David took separate paths into the house. Reaching her room and pushing the door open with his foot, he carried Lilliana to the bathroom. Eric sat her down gently on the seat near the window and she covered her face with her hands.

Eric turned the taps on to fill the tub. "Have a shower, rinse that blood away; it will make you feel better"

"But I killed her Eric, I killed her." Lilliana whispered weakly.

He knelt, gently taking her hands in his, looking up at her face. Even with all the blood, dirt, sweat and tears; it did nothing to take away her sweet beauty. He desperately wished Damon were here, or Allie. Someone, anyone who would know the right thing to say.

"Lilly, look at me." She squeezed her eyes shut and shook her head.

"He melted her skin, she was in so much pain… then I stabbed her, over and over. I did that. Me!"

The despair in her voice was too much; Eric knew he had to snap her out of it.

"Lilliana, you knew walking in that this assignment would be precarious. We are dealing with the world of Reid. You did what you had to do, to save your friend." He stood, pulling her to her feet.

"Now, I need you to go and rinse off and soak in this tub. Can you do that for me, Doc?" His affectionate nickname always softened her, and he knew it would have the desired effect.

She looked up at him. "Yes, Eric."

He dropped an air kiss near her cheek. "Good. Now get cleaned up so I can kiss you for good." A knock at the door sounded, and as Eric walked backwards to answer it, he looked at her again, pointing to the shower and closed the door behind him.

Lilliana pulled the filthy dress off and ran the water so hot. She scrubbed until her skin was pink and raw; the detox soap washing off the blood stains made her feel clean again. She knew everything Eric had said made sense; but the horror of what she had just done was making her feel like a nervous wreck. The image of the woman's bloody, melted flesh flashed before her again and again. She doubled over, vomiting up her horrors.

***

Eric opened the door to a vision of Nadia dressed in a green top with black jeans, silky blonde hair floating about her shoulders, framing her ever-so-delicate face. In her arms she was holding a tray of soup, bread, and fresh fruit. She looked at Eric guardedly.

"Hello."

"Hi," he said, looking her up and down slowly. "Can I help you?"

He did not like the fact that as soon as she was near, he wanted to put his hands on her, to claim her, protect her. This beautiful woman that Reid had mentally abused for years needed him. Lilliana had shared all she had learnt about Nadia with him the night before. It seemed that she was a good and decent person trapped in a madman's world.

"David sent me; he thought I could help Lilliana. Give her some company?" He stepped back into the room, closing the door behind her.

"That was unusually thoughtful of him. We are free to speak here; I had the bugs frozen. I check hourly."

She smiled at him. "That is excellent. It is so rare to be able to speak freely without any repercussions."

His heart felt sorry for her and for the life she must be leading behind Reid's doors. Their eyes connected, each appreciating the other in the moment. The sound of vomiting from the bathroom interrupted them.

Nadia quickly dropped the tray onto a side table and moved to the bathroom door, hand up ready to push it open, when Eric grabbed her arm, stopping her.

Nadia looked up at him as he shook his head. "Wait," he said quietly. "Lilly, are you alright?" He could feel the soft skin of Nadia's wrist under his fingertips. He frowned, releasing her. He did not want to think about how soft she would be all over, while inside the bathroom his friend was so ill.

"Lilly; Nadia's here, can I send her in to you?"

"Please," came Lilliana's small reply.

"Be gentle with her," Eric said softly as he looked down into Nadia's large, clear eyes.

"Of course," she nodded and went into the bathroom. Nadia entered the bathroom; she shut off the water and pulled Lilliana to her feet. "Can you make it to the tub?"

"Yes," Lilliana nodded. "Sorry to be such a nuisance," she said as she stumbled shakily to the deep hot tub, grateful for Nadia's help.

"Don't apologise. I can only imagine what Gregory made you do today. Let me give you a head massage, that will help with the tension."

"You are kind, Nadia, considering what you have been through too. Most people would have become their environment over time."

Lilliana closed her eyes as Nadia grabbed a handful of creamy hair treatment and started massaging her scalp.

"I have fought every single day to never to become a product of this environment. Is it strange that somehow, I knew you would be the key, the one to release me from this prison? Saying it aloud does sound insane, doesn't it though?"

"No," Lilliana whispered. "That's destiny."

"How's it going in there?" Eric called out; his voice laced with concern.

"Come in Eric," Lilliana called.

He opened the door to see Nadia gently massaging Lilliana's head. He was relieved to see Lilliana was not crying and was thankful that she had stopped vomiting.

Lilliana could see Eric's concern, and forced a smile for him. "Eric, do you think you could get me a cup of herbal tea?"

"Of course, give me a minute, I'll buzz the staff. Anything for you, Nadia?"

Nadia looked shocked that he thought to ask her. "The same, thank you."

Lilliana smiled inwardly at how cute they were together. Obviously, they were attracted to each other, but clearly, they were unsure what to do about it. And rightly so.

Once Eric left, Nadia's hands slipped under the water to Lilliana's shoulders and she massaged her with skilled hands.

"Oh Nadia, that is wonderful; but please, don't feel you have to. Just come and sit with me."

"It's alright, I enjoy massage. I've been told by politicians, celebrities even Given Directors' that I am the best they've had."

"I agree with them," Lilliana said, but she had to ask, "Do you know Russell Meek, at the Australian Given?" she prayed for the answer she desired.

"No, Gregory has no association with him; they run a straight organisation in Australia, much like your Given."

Lilliana felt relieved; she knew Russell was one of the good guys. Like Damon.

Damon. She pitched forward, covering her mouth.

"Lilly, are you alright?" Nadia started to become worried as Lilliana's breathing became increasingly shallow and rapid. She had seen panic attacks before. She reached out to Lilliana's neck and began to rub soothingly, hoping it would have some effect.

Lilliana took a deep breath, trying herself to get ahead of the oncoming panic attack. Stop it, she hissed to herself. You cannot think of Damon. When she felt her breathing evened out, she took a steady breath before replying.

"My heart feels sick. Sick. I'm sad, devastated. Being here, enduring Reid's demented world." She shook her head. "I knew what I was getting into, coming here. And even knowing, even being as prepared as I could be for whatever was to come, I wasn't prepared enough."

"Your Director, Damon Night, tell me about him. I have seen him in so many magazines, and of course Given campaigns. I have to say, he is devilishly handsome. Tell me, what is he like? Nadia asked as she continued massaging Lilliana.

Of course, Nadia would want to know about Damon. It would be his decision as to whether she would be able to have a permanent home with them. If only she could tell her that Damon was her husband. Assure her all would be well. Although she did trust Nadia, she had to think of herself right now, and the position she would put herself, or David in if the truth somehow found its way back to Gregory.

"His heart knows no harshness, unless of course you are one of the bad guys. He is firm, fun, and gentle, generous and the absolute best person for his role. Our Given are certainly incredibly lucky to have him as our leader."

"And he is not married? He sounds like every girl's dream catch."

"Mmm." Lilliana bit her tongue, adding, "Sure does."

"Where can I get me one of those?"

"I'll put an order in for you." Lilliana said, thinking of Eric.

"Ladies," Eric called from the doorway.

"Come in."

Eric walked in carrying the tray Nadia had bought with her, plus a pot of herbal tea and cups. Sitting it on a side table, he poured the tea and passed them one each before sitting on the open window seat himself, facing half in, half out of the room.

"Thanks, Eric," Lilliana carefully sipped the hot, soothing liquid.

"Thank you," Nadia said softly, sitting opposite Eric and facing Lilliana. She could feel him watching her as he addressed Lilliana.

"How are you feeling?"

Lilliana leaned her head back against the side of the spa. "Better."

"Can you eat?"

"No, please, you have it, Eric. The thought of eating anything…" she shook her head, unable to finish the sentence. "Tea is all I need."

"Sweet," he scooped up the soup and tucked into it, breaking off a chunk of bread and dipping into the thick broth. Lilliana focused on her tea.

"There's a lot of big people coming in over the next fortnight," Nadia said, looking at Lilliana, then across to Eric.

He put down the empty bowl and snatched up a piece of fruit. After taking a big bite, chewing, and swallowing, his eyes returned to Nadia.

"Do you know what they're planning?"

"Not all of it. Enough to know that you must be careful."

"We will be we're prepared for anything," Eric nodded and looked over at Lilliana. A small beep could be heard from inside his jacket. He reached in and pulled out an earpiece and placed it inside his ear, clicking it on.

"Marcus—what's up?" Eric nodded as he listened, giving Nadia a chance to really look at him. His face was a chiseled sculpture of male beauty. Sharp, clean, defined. His eyes swung to hers, causing her to blush and look away.

Lilliana laughed inwardly. If only she could get up and leave, she would love to leave these want-to-be lovebirds alone.

Eric pulled the earpiece out, inserting it back into his jacket. "Lilly, we need to get you ready. David asked me to tell you, it's heart time. Fox has been placed in the torture room. If we are not there in five…" He did not need to end the sentence for Lilliana to grasp his meaning.

"What the *hell?*" Lilliana gasped. "A torture room? Why am I not surprised? We have to hurry!"

Eric stood and reached for a thick towel, handing it to Nadia. "I'll escort you as soon as you're ready." He watched as the small piece of relaxation that had seeped into Lilliana the last few minutes, completely vanished.

Once Nadia had Lilliana's hair dry and brushed, she followed her into the bedroom. Nadia pulled out a white dress and turned to Lilliana.

"No, not white. Is there black?"

"Yes, but it's long sleeved."

"That's perfect," Lilliana said, taking it from Nadia and pulling it over her head and stepping into the tall black heels.

"It's too hot for long sleeves, Lilly," Nadia said quietly.

"It's fine, I need to be covered in his presence."

Nadia nodded, understanding.

"I'm ready Eric."

Eric turned and walked over to her, placing his hands on her shoulders. "You are going to be alright; so is Fox. Let's just get through the next phase, okay?"

Lilliana nodded.

"Now, listen up. I've got some good stuff on me that can help make the next hour seem dreamlike, more 'bearable' if you know what I mean."

"No Eric; thanks, but no. I need a clear head for whatever Gregory has in mind."

"Are you sure? It was David's idea, and he knows what they have planned. For him to suggest it makes me think it would be better for you if you let me give you something."

"Eric, I love you, but no. I need to be alert for Fox." She patted his cheek. "Let's get moving."

CHAPTER 8

When Lilliana and Nadia entered the large room, it looked more like the setup for a decadent dining experience than a torture chamber.

A long table set with roses, crystal ware and candles sat under an open window. In the centre of the room, a smaller table was placed between two wing-backed chairs facing each other. A lid covered a pewter serving dish that sat on the tabletop; Lilliana immediately noticed there was a strange odour permeating from it.

In one of the chairs sat Fox, dressed in a green, off the shoulder ball gown.

Lilliana rushed to her side and leaned down, putting her arms around her friend.

"Fox, are you alright? I promise you—I will get you out of here." Lilliana realised she sounded desperate, even to her own ears.

Fox remained stiff in the chair, her arms limp, hands resting in her lap.

Lilliana cupped her friend's pale face, looking into her eyes. She whispered, "What have they done to you?"

Fox's eyes welled with tears. "They've injected a serum that paralyses my body. I couldn't move if my life depended on it, Lilly." She looked terrified even as she said it trapped in her own body as she was.

Her eyes shifted behind Lilliana as ten men walked in dressed in black from head to toe, with reflective glass masks covering their faces. They stood to attention, evenly spaced around the room.

"Ah wonderful; I see everyone is here and on time." Gregory briskly entered the room clapping his hands together, as if announcing the start of a meeting. "Nadia, my love, would you like to take a seat, some lunch perhaps?" He gestured to the elegantly laid out table as wait staff entered, filling it with succulent dishes, pouring champagne before leaving again.

"Yes, I will have lunch, maybe Lilliana can sit with me?"

He smiled down at her fondly, catching her lips in a deep kiss.

Eric, who was standing behind them both, was unaware his hands had balled into fists.

"Easy soldier," David whispered, as he walked by to stand beside Lilliana.

"You go sit, Nadia; Lilliana will be dining over here," Gregory pointed to the covered dish that sat between Fox and the empty chair.

Nadia shot Lilliana a concerned look as she moved to the dining table and sat down, reaching for a champagne glass to wash away the foul taste of unease creeping into her throat.

Lilliana looked back at Nadia as she sat opposite Fox, meeting her new friend's worried look.

Gregory casually strolled over to Fox, placing his long, pale fingers around her throat. He squeezed slowly, feeling a thrill rush through him as terror filled her eyes.

Fox tried to look bored as his face came close to hers, finding the peculiar, ice cold way that he watched her, more terrifying than the feeling of her air supply being cut off.

"*Enough!*" Lilliana yelled. "I'll do whatever you bloody well want me to do—just leave my friend alone!"

"Ah, of course my dear, sweet daughter, loyalty will get you everywhere. If it's given to the right person." Gregory stroked Fox's throat before he turned to stand in front of Lilliana.

Fox, grateful to Lilliana for coming to her defence, gulped in a lungful of air.

Gregory's face was forever a mask of calmness and authority, his voice steely.

"We will all be having lunch over there," he swept his hand over to where Nadia was seated. "*You* are dining here." He gestured to the covered dish. "You will eat every morsel under that lid, without question. Prove your loyalty to your family, and, if you cannot, your friend will suffer the consequences. And I do mean, *suffer*."

"She is my *family*." Lilliana shot back.

"Not today she's not. Injector, enter," he called.

His voice was so cold it sent icy needles of fear through Lilliana as she looked sadly across at Fox.

Fox closed her eyes.

The Injector entered, carrying a long vial filled with a toxic looking green liquid, and where a wickedly long needle glistened at its sharpest end. Lilliana's eyes narrowed; her mouth hung open. What was this?

"What you are looking at here, for those of you uneducated in biological weapons and parasitology, is our latest concoction of microorganisms. Once injected, they make their way through the blood stream, absorbing the blood. As they grow, they form a razor like skin that slices through tissue, muscle, bone—and eventually exits out of the host organism's flesh." He sounded entirely too impressed with himself as he said it. Lilliana thought she was going to convulse.

"I have to say, I have quite enjoyed watching people sit so calmly, feeling nothing at first, before the worst kind of pain imaginable hits them. Hours of severe agony builds from within, culminating in a torturous death." He shook his head in wonder. "Quite gruesome, amazing really."

Lilliana shot to her feet. "You are *not* injecting that into my friend," she said fiercely.

"Not if you do what's asked." Gregory watched as David quickly walked over to Lilliana and placed an arm protectively around her shoulder. Quietly, he coached her.

"It won't be so bad darling, just sit; we will all eat lunch and your dear friend Fox will be allowed to go free and join you on your holiday here, won't she Father?"

Gregory shrugged, "Of course, Son! Absolutely!"

Lilliana looked across nervously at Eric, before reluctantly sitting again.

Gregory looked like a happy child on Christmas morning, about to present the best gift imaginable as he gleefully lifted the lid from the dish.

Lilliana's heart thumped uncomfortably in her chest; her breath froze momentarily as she stared at the contents. The heart she had pulled from the woman's chest was sliced into mouth sized pieces, scattered with micro herbs as if to make it somehow more palatable.

Nadia gasped.

David highly anticipated Damon blowing his head off any second now.

Eric stepped forward, wanting to put an end to it all immediately.

The Injector stepped closer to Fox. Lilliana and Fox stared at each other in horror.

Gregory laughed delightedly as he walked over to the main table and sat down, smiling, and asking Nadia to pass him a champagne glass.

"It's all very simple, Lilliana dear; eat, and your friend will be free."

The room was silent, as if someone had pressed a mute button. Lilliana blinked as David's words filled into her ears.

"Don't chew, just swallow," he suggested helpfully, as his father flagged him over to join him at the table.

Lilliana stared at the organ she was supposed to eat. As if it were that simple.

The sound of knives and forks scraping against fine china filled the room as Nadia, David and Gregory began to eat; the look on Fox's face broke Lilliana from her trance-like stare.

With a keen glint in his eye, Lilliana looked as the injector stood close to her friend, at the ready to inject the foul liquid into her, and Lilliana spun into auto pilot. Reaching for the small fork, she stabbed a piece of the heart and before she could think about it, placed it into her mouth and swallowed. It tasted slippery and wet. Like an oyster.

That was not so bad, she thought to herself. *My God, I think I can actually do this.* She stabbed at another piece, and as the delicious aromas drifted across from the dining table, she imagined herself eating something warm, roasted, and delectable.

She placed a second piece into her mouth and faltered for a second as the image of herself, plunging the knife into the dead woman's chest flooded her mind. A life for a life, she thought, and focused on the task at hand.

Unfortunately, the second piece was larger, and needed chewing; it was a bit rubbery and Lilliana tried not to think about what the slimy coating could be.

Fox saw her friend hesitate, as Lilliana squeezed her eyes shut, and concentrated on swallowing the mouthful. It quickly came back up, and Lilliana clamped a hand over her mouth to force it back down, eyes watering, heart racing. You can do this—you must do this, she chanted to herself. She stabbed another mouthful, her hand shaking as she placed it in her mouth again, looking at Fox.

"You can do this Lilly," she said quietly, willing it to be true. She watched as Lilliana struggled with her third mouthful, with at least six more to go.

Lilliana choked the next mouthful down, then turned to face Gregory. "Would it be too much to ask for a glass of water?"

"Oh darling girl, but of course." Gregory smiled, and snapped his fingers to Eric.

Eric strode to the table and quickly filled a glass with water, placing it into Lilliana's unsteady hand.

"Thanks," she whispered before taking a large, grateful mouthful.

Eric nodded before stepping away, and David crossed over to rub her back.

"Good job, Lilliana," he said, hoping she could finish the rest; he had seen the effects this particular pathogen took on a human, and it wasn't pretty. Lilliana looked up at him, keeping her nasty comments to herself, before draining the glass; turning, she thumped it down near the dish and stabbed another piece of heart.

Taking a deep breath, Lilliana closed her eyes and swallowed again, then, dropping the fork, she selected the next piece with her fingers, bringing it to her mouth out of sheer belligerence.

It was a mistake, not using the fork. The slimy coating, along with her finger slipping into an artery became the undoing of her on her mission. Her eyes flew open as she pitched forward. The combination of water sloshing around in her belly and the images of the jungle hunt, plus every mouthful she had consumed, came rushing back up, and she fell to her hands and knees, vomiting all over the plush carpet. She did not have a moment to compose herself, as Fox's scream had her lunging to her feet.

"Wait, stop!"

But it was too late; the injector had already inserted the needle into Fox's arm, his eyes on Gregory as he awaited instructions. Gregory indicated a drop, and so a drop was injected, and the scream that tore from Fox's lungs pierced Lilliana's heart.

"*Stop.* Please, I can do this!" Lilliana turned, eyes blazing towards Gregory. She ran the back of her hand along her mouth.

"David?" She pleaded.

"Father, come now, Lilliana is doing the best job she can. You can finish, can't you darling?" he walked over and ran a hand over her hair.

She nodded quietly, looking away. She did not want Damon to see her in such a state. She prayed Cam would keep Josephine away from seeing any of this footage too.

"Well, the trouble is, now you have less than a whole heart on your plate—and you can't simply suck up the mess in front of you, can you? So, I guess you'll have to eat the next thing on the menu. Can you do that?" He raised a pale, cool eyebrow.

Lilliana nodded as she looked away from Gregory to Fox. Her dear friend was sweating profusely now, her eyes streaming tears. That one drop evidently was enough to start a slow, torturous attack.

"I'm so sorry Fox; I'll stop this now, I promise." Her throat caught and she swallowed her own tears. She would not indulge them when her friend was suffering.

The plate of heart was removed, and a new dish was placed in front of her. Lilliana almost wanted to vomit again, and inwardly kicked herself, wishing with all her might that she had been able to eat the rest of the heart.

Nadia gasped. "Gregory, you cannot be serious—this is ridiculous, you know she loves David, she shouldn't have to prove this to you anymore. This has to stop right this instant."

Lilliana paled, looking at Fox; behind them stood Eric, who was also pale but visibly furious.

"Oh, come on Father, enough! I'm taking Lilliana to our room." David went to get up from his chair, but one single word from Gregory stopped him in his tracks.

"Trust." Gregory stared into his son's eyes.

David swallowed.

It was the first time Lilliana had ever seen him look truly frightened.

She could not know that many years ago, Gregory had said that exact same word to his wife before he had made David rape and murder her.

This was not just a simple, endearing word, but a code.

David walked briskly over to Lilliana and grabbed her by the arm, pulling her close to him. He whispered sharply into her ear.

"We are all dead if you do not do this. All of us. Dead."

Lilliana could not have paled anymore, yet she did. She turned ghostly white. Her eyes slowly met his.

"I see," she whispered, swallowing. How the hell was she going to do this?

David gently swept his hand over her cheek. "Please Lilliana," he implored quietly. "Don't think, just do." He stepped back.

She slowly turned her attention to the next plate. Just looking at it made her stomach churn. Her hand shook as she reached to pick up the first piece. *Don't think, just do, don't think, just do,* she chanted over and over in her head.

"Lilly," Fox whispered, desperate to support her friend even as pain began to slowly, torturously build within her.

Lilliana nodded across to her friend, assuring her that, no matter what, she would do this; and she knew from the pained look in Fox's eyes, she had to hurry.

The woman's face that had melted before her in the jungle, was now cut into bite sized pieces, staring up at her through jelly eyes resembling runny egg yolks.

She swallowed as she slowly reached for a piece.

Saying a silent prayer to the angels, she quickly picked up a floppy piece of flesh and, raising her eyes to the ceiling where an ornate chandelier hung, popped it into her mouth. Blocking out all thoughts, Lilliana swallowed. Blindly reaching for the next piece, she did the same; over and over again she swallowed.

Unbeknownst to her, tears poured down her face as each mouthful burned her throat. The fifth mouthful nearly came back up as she registered that it was hair brushing against her gum; a piece getting caught between her teeth.

"David," she groaned.

She really wanted to call out for Eric but knew she couldn't, not with Gregory looking on.

David rubbed her back. "Keep going sweetheart, nearly finished." He brushed her hair away from her face.

She felt a small hand squeeze her arm. Nadia forced a smile and nodded. "You can do this Lilliana," she whispered. "You have to."

"What fabulous support! See, dear Lilliana," Gregory exclaimed in happiness. "This is what family do. Continue!"

She ignored the madman and focused on swallowing the next piece, quick chew, swallow. Last piece, chew, do not think about it, and swallow. It lodged in her throat. One hand clamped around her mouth while the other was pinching her nostrils tightly, even as her body heaved automatically. She jerked away from David's touch, wanting to concentrate on just keeping it all down.

Nadia held a glass of water out to her. "Just drink; here's a fresh, cleansing mouthful of sweet rainwater."

Nadia had such a way with words as she tried to distract Lilliana's mind away from the filth that was not wanting to stay inside her.

She closed her eyes and nodded, accepting the water as Nadia pushed the glass into her shaky fingers, helping her raise it to her lips. She took a mouthful and swallowed, the water pushing down the unwanted mass. Her eyes watered, but she nodded at Nadia, whispering, "Thank you."

Nadia turned her pretty eyes to Gregory. "Is that the end of it, then?"

He seemed entirely too happy.

"It is definitely the end. Well done Lilliana, well done." Turning, he nodded to one of the guards and pointed to Fox. "Give her a shot of the anti-toxin." He smiled at Lilliana. "This shot will counteract the damage that is being done. Better hurry, though." He slapped the guard's back as he walked past and scooped Fox up in his arms, before quickly exiting the room.

Gregory's eyes met David's, and he held his son's gaze for several moments before turning and casually leaving the room. Nadia looked up at David too, who seemed unusually anxious, before rubbing Lilliana's arm. Lilliana was frozen to the spot, too afraid to move an inch in case she threw up again. She wanted to throw up; just not here, not in front of the room full of guards.

Eric wasted no time and walked over to Lilliana; placing his arm around her waist, he began leading her out of the room. "It's alright Lilly, nearly over."

David sighed and shook his head at Nadia as they followed Eric. "Never a dull moment around here, hey?"

Nadia shook her head. "Unfortunately, no."

***

Fifteen minutes later Fox was holding her hands to her face, tears slipping through her fingers. The nurse picked up the tray and left the room, leaving Fox alone with the guard.

She had been injected twice; first, with an anti-paralysis serum, then with the anti-toxin serum. The unbearable pain was only just starting to leave her body, and she was shaking uncontrollably. She pushed her hand through her tumbled mass of flaming red hair and stared hatefully at the guard.

"How can you people work for an insane man like Reid?" she spat.

The guard walked to the door, pressing the red lock on, slowly turning towards her. Fox's heart froze. What the hell was going to happen next in this freak show of a place? She mustered up what little courage she could find.

"If you even try to put your hands on me, I will rip your throat out with my teeth," she hissed.

The guard removed his helmet, which reflected Fox's tear stained, frightened face, and when she saw who was beneath it, she collapsed onto the floor in fresh tears.

"Hey, it's alright now. I've got you." Marcus bent and scooped Fox off the floor, holding her close to his chest and rocking her. "It's all going to be alright; no one is going to lay a hand on you again. Trust me."

Fox pushed her face against his chest, arms clinging around his neck and sobbed like she had never sobbed before as waves of relief washed over her.

***

Johnson had had a few disagreements with Cam over the years, especially after Cam's and Damon's father had died and Cam had been a lost, grieving teenager. But for the past decade, and especially the past five years that Damon had been away working undercover, he and Cam had enjoyed a smooth and productive working relationship.

The fact that Cam had pushed for the footage of Lilliana's operation to be viewed by staff and their Given, had been a bitter pill for Johnson to swallow.

Cam's argument was that he believed everyone in the establishment should be aware of the lengths one of their own would selflessly go to in order to protect them all. Loyalty. Love. Family.

And so, given Johnson's disapproval, it was voted upon by the major head of staff that the least offensive footage be shown in the main assembly hall for all Given to view when their rosters allowed.

A select group had been allocated a private room for a separate viewing of all that Lilliana and the team were going through. Senior staffers plus Allie, Josephine, Jessica, Christopher and Orlando,

Rupert, Leon, Rachael, and Billy were permitted to attend.

It shook everyone to their core to see what their loved ones were dealing with whilst they themselves were safely protected within the walls of the Given.

Damon had also agreed that this group should see all the footage The Guardian accessed once they hit Reid's domain; Dr Hillary, too, reasoned that the more their people understood what Lilliana and the team had been through, the more they would be able to support them on their return home.

Scott begged Damon to give him access to the private viewings, but there was no way in hell Damon was going to let that happen. He knew Lilliana would not be able to offer Scott her strength when she returned if she knew he had witnessed her falling so far.

CHAPTER 9

Lilliana held up her hand, shaking her head to say no as Eric started to follow her into the bathroom.

He nodded, sliding the door shut after her; but not before he heard the vomiting start up again. He turned and leaned his back against the door as he listened to Lilliana purge the forced meal. He leaned forward, dropping his hands on his knees and closed his eyes. Poor Lilliana.

David poured himself a stiff drink from the bar, remaining unusually quiet as he walked out onto the balcony, watching Nadia as she paced the room anxiously.

"Are you alright?" Eric asked as he walked over to answer the knock at the door.

Nadia didn't answer him; instead, she watched the maid pass Eric a tray through the doorway filled with iced water, vodka, and lemon slices.

He kicked the door shut and sat the tray down, squeezing a lemon into a glass of iced water. *He's so... efficient,* Nadia thought; Eric was always precise, not one movement was ever wasted. Her gaze followed a trail of lemon juice that had escaped his fingers and was sliding along the back of his hand.

He crossed over to her, handing her the glass, and watched her watching him as he raised his hand to his lips to suck off the juice.

Nadia flushed and turned away to raise the cool lemon drink to her suddenly very parched lips.

David rolled his eyes and poured the remainder of the drink down his throat before getting up to pour another. He took a mouthful, then pointed to the bathroom.

"Should someone go in there?"

Eric had to pull his gaze away from Nadia to address David.

"Not if someone doesn't want a punch in the face," Eric responded.

"Christ man, ease up, I was simply asking."

Eric was about to respond when his communicator vibrated in his vest pocket. He swore under his breath as he checked the message.

"What is it?" Nadia said, placing her empty glass down and crossing over to Eric.

"A complication." He shoved the communicator back into his pocket after sending a quick reply. He pointed to David. "Do not go anywhere."

David simply raised an eyebrow.

Eric turned and knocked sharply on the bathroom door. As it slid open, he stepped backwards into the room, keeping his back to Lilliana, his eyes on Nadia before closing the door between them.

"Lilliana?" he addressed her quietly, keeping his back to her.

She did not answer.

"Lilly?" He said again after a moment's silence. He slowly turned around to face her.

Lilly sat under the hot waterfall, forehead dropped against raised knees, her arms hugging her legs tightly, shielding her privates from view. Her hair hung around her like a dripping wet curtain.

Eric kept his eyes on her head, blocking out her nakedness as he walked over and knelt under the spray, gently placing a hand on her shoulder.

"I'm sorry to disturb you, Lilliana. I have some bad news."

She raised her head slowly, water raining over her face. Her eyes had lost their shine; hallow grooves sat deeply beneath them. The heat of the shower did nothing to improve upon her paleness. She looked at him, unblinkingly, waiting. He hesitated, not wanting to burden her further.

"What is it Eric?"

He paused, unsure as to how she would react after everything she had already endured. "It was Marcus who carried Fox out of the torture room. She told him that when Reid's men abducted her, they also took Tim and her brother, Levi."

"Oh my God, no! Is she alright?"

Eric nodded quickly, "Physically she's going to be fine; she was injected with an anti-toxin and a repair serum. She told Marcus that they're holding Tim and Levi at the medical lab and are using them in a main event that Reid is holding in a fortnight's time."

Lilliana closed her eyes, leaning her head back against the shower wall. This nightmare they had entered was growing more horrific by the day. Her thoughts began a slow burn of fury and rage towards Gregory Reid. People's lives simply seemed beyond insignificant to him. As though people were merely commodities, so replaceable, so… nothing. She shook her head, trying to clear the quiet hum that was building in her ears. Her rage was nearing explosive. Fox, now Tim and poor Levi. She had to do something.

Shocking Eric, she stood up in front of him stark naked, screaming out, "*David!*"

David stepped inside as the bathroom door slid open, his eyes delighting in the flash of Lilliana's smooth, wet body before Eric quickly blocked her from his view.

"*Lilliana,*" Eric hissed between his teeth, not allowing her to take another step around him towards David.

David, however, leaned against the tub, enjoying the live nude show as Nadia stepped in the doorway.

"Is everything alright?" she too, was shocked to see Lilliana naked, and struggling to get out of Eric's grip. It was clear that Lilliana was trying to get to David and Eric was doing everything in his power to stop her.

"Nadia, get me a towel, please." Eric sounded frustrated as Nadia quickly grabbed for a towel. Lilliana was still trying to get by Eric; cursing under his breath Eric had no choice but to lift her a foot off the ground. It was the only way to stop her from attempting to get to David.

"Lilly, you are *naked*," he forcefully reminded her.

She stopped fighting him then, emotionally exhausted, she dropped her forehead against his chest, giving up the fight and feeling the soft towel cover her back as Nadia wrapped it around her shoulders.

Eric nodded his thanks to Nadia as he placed Lilliana back on her feet, wrapping the towel further around her, covering her body. He rubbed her back up and down before tucking her under his shoulder and leading her into the bedroom and toward the bed.

"No, I need to do something about Fox, Levi, and Tim! I can't just get into bed like nothing has happened!"

Eric nodded his thanks again to Nadia as she handed him a towel. He began quickly wiping down his leather jacket.

"Lilliana, Fox is safe; she'll be with you soon enough. The team's working on a way to get her out of here. As for Tim and Levi, Unit Eight are keeping a close eye on them. You have had one hell of a day and you need to rest, and if I need to inject you with something to make that happen. I will." His glared down at her.

She could see he meant every word. "That's not fair, Eric."

"I'm sorry, it's the way it's going to be. Will you do this Lilly, for me?"

She was silent for a moment but could see the strain this mission was having on Eric also. "Okay." She said quietly.

"Good." He nodded to Nadia who lifted the covers for Lilliana to slide under, before sitting next to her, to dry Lilliana's dripping hair with a smaller towel.

David stood at the end of the bed, drink in hand. "Are you alright?"

Lilliana shot him a dark look. "Is that a trick question?"

He shrugged. "Not if you don't want it to be."

"Your father," Lilliana shook her head frustrated. She had plenty to say about his father but right now she was at a loss for words. Speechless.

Eric passed Lilliana an iced water. She took a sip, wincing as it went down.

"Sore?"

She nodded. Her throat had taken a beating this day. Taking another small sip, she passed the glass back to Eric.

"Thanks, Nadia." she smiled as Nadia finished drying her hair.

"What do you know about this main event?" Eric asked David.

"I know a lot of big players have paid an exorbitant amount to come to this, while others come to actively participate, and plenty more have paid to view the live stream that will be going out to the underworld. Father has made mention that the event will be featuring a favourite from past recordings, and he has been inundated with requests from players who want in on that. Who knows what else will take place?"

"Well right now that's your job to find out. Get your father talking. Get the information that Damon and Johnson need to make the arrests and necessary culling's." Eric pushed his hand through his hair, feeling as weary as Lilliana looked. Two more weeks. If they could just hang in for a little while longer, they could be a part in taking down the absolute filth of the earth that had impacted millions in the worst kind of ways. He just needed to stay alert and focused. Keep Lilliana, Nadia, and Fox safe.

Eric walked briskly into the bathroom and removed a small pouch from his vest pocket. Pulling out a vial of awake serum, he injected it, feeling an immediate rush of energy spread throughout his entire body.

Popping the empty vial in the bin, he put the pouch back into his vest pocket and returned to the bedroom, his eyes zeroing in on Nadia. What he would like to do to her, with this sweet burst of energy.

Nadia met his heated gaze the moment he stepped into the room and caught the meaning of the glint in his eyes. Her face flushed crimson. Their attraction was palpable. A longing unlike anything she had ever felt, swept through her. It was insane to even think she could have him without putting either of their lives at risk. She forced herself to look away, her desire for him that strong.

"Can you bring Fox here, Eric?"

"I don't see why not."

"I'll see how she is and bring her up if she is fully healed."

"Thanks Nadia," Lilliana reached for her hand, squeezing it gently. She couldn't remember ever feeling as exhausted in her whole life.

"You need sleep, dear." David poured another drink.

Lilliana nodded, feeling like she could sleep forever.

"I'll go with you, Nadia." Eric followed her towards the door, before turning around and jabbing a finger in David's direction. "Look out for her. I mean it."

"Of course." David raised an eyebrow, slightly insulted that Eric would suggest otherwise.

"Sleep if you can Lilly, I won't be long."

Lilliana offered Eric a small smile before he disappeared out the door, leaving her alone with David.

"Do you want some water?"

"Please."

He poured and handed her a glass filled with sliced lemons.

"Thanks." She took a long swallow, hoping the icy water with healing lemon would work its magic and sooth away her stressed, swollen throat.

David slowly sipped from his glass, eyes not leaving her.

"What?" Lilliana said blankly.

"You. What you did today. You are amazingly strong. I would never have thought after first meeting you, that you could have endured all that and still have fight in you."

"We do what we must for the people we love."

"Yes, I believe you would. What would you do for your Damon, I wonder?"

"I'd die for him," Lilliana said simply.

"We don't want that. Sleep now."

She passed him her empty glass and slid down under the covers, pulling them up around her face. Closing her eyes, she tried to relax her body and calm the train wreck of images in her mind by doing a breathing technique for relaxation and mindfulness called pattern interrupt. Her Grandmother, Danielle, had taught her as a young girl and she used it successfully on her Given.

Taking a deep breath in, focusing on nothing but her breathing, she counted four seconds, holding her breath for four seconds before exhaling to the count of eight seconds. She repeated the process twice, feeling her mind relax as she began to breathe normally again.

Finally she could feel herself slowly beginning to relax, her muscles unwind, her body grow warm and heavy, as she let her exhausted mind drift towards sleep; what she couldn't control were the unwanted nightmares that seemed to have become a permanent resident since she had been on Reid property.

David stood at the end of the bed watching over her. If she were his, and he'd had to endure watching his wife go through all that without being able to help her, as Damon had just done, he truly believed he would have gone out of his mind. "I'll look out for her," he said aloud, hoping Damon would hear his good intentions.

***

Damon heard. Loud and clear. He felt ill watching the past twenty-four hours of Lilliana's footage. There was a rage building inside of him unlike any rage he had ever known, which said a great deal considering all he had endured and witnessed during his time undercover. He simply wanted Gregory Reid put in a cell, and to have a solid week alone with him, torture him before ending him.

He shook his head, taking a deep breath to steady himself, before going up to speak to Johnson and the team regarding his role in the next fortnight.

***

Eric followed Nadia down the corridor towards the lift. He couldn't help that his eyes were drawn to the small backside that swayed as she briskly walked along. *Probably fit right in my palms*, he thought, then cursed his male, lustful side, trying to shut it down. *Don't be a pig*, he chastised himself, before slamming right into her as she stopped abruptly in the middle of the corridor. Her soft, small body smelt like paradise.

A maid had just walked out of a room and blocked Nadia's path with her cleaning trolley.

"So sorry, Ms Nadia."

"It's alright Hilda," Nadia smiled kindly at the frazzled maid, who quickly excused herself and pushed her cart along, disappearing around a corner.

Eric looked into the empty room, and without thinking, he grabbed Nadia's arm, and pulled her in close, closing the door behind them.

"What are you doing?" Nadia looked up into his dark almond eyes, just as any thought of what they shouldn't do disappeared instantly as he stepped towards her, hands reaching for her hips and pulling her against his hard frame.

"I'm so sorry about this," he whispered, before his mouth took hers in a long, hungry kiss.

The heat of him, his hardness, set Nadia's insides ablaze. Filled with lustful thoughts, her fingers automatically ran through his hair, gripping the back of his neck, pulling him closer to her as his kiss deepened.

Nadia's soft moan drove Eric crazy as he ran his hands over her back and down, cupping her backside, that did in fact, fit perfectly in his large hands. He picked her up effortlessly, his tongue mating with hers as she wrapped her legs around his waist, moving against him.

He was set to explode with every movement she made, pushing herself against him. Her hands reached in to push off his vest, even as a small vibrating sound started going off inside his jacket, causing their lips to part. Their breathing heavy, eyes glued to each other, she reluctantly unwrapped her legs from around his waist. He lowered her gently until her feet hit the floor, tasting her kiss on his lips.

She watched the pink of his tongue flicker out as she ran her hands through her hair, wishing she could have another taste of his lips. Her heart was beating wildly, while her insides were flowing molten lava.

He reached in and checked the message. "Shit," he whispered.

"What is it?"

"Nothing that need worry you. Let's get Fox." Nadia nodded, looking hurt that he wouldn't confide in her.

She turned to open the door, but he grabbed her wrist; stopping her, he turned her around.

"Nadia, I don't want to hurt you."

"Then don't."

He sighed as her pretty eyes lifted to his, lips swollen pink from their kiss. "I wasn't expecting you," he said quietly.

She nodded. "I know."

"We can't do this again."

"I know."

"It's too dangerous," he said and ran a finger along her soft cheek.

This time it was she who stopped him, taking hold of his wrist, and moving it away from her skin.

"I want you more than I've ever wanted anyone, but I won't put you in harm's way. While you're here, do not touch me again."

"I understand, and I'm sorry."

"Don't be sorry. I liked it. I want you, just not here."

He bent down so their eyes were level and said softly, "Yes Ma'am."

Nadia laughed, shaking her head, and wondering at the many layers of Eric, hoping she would have the opportunity in this life to explore them.

***

Lilliana opened her eyes; they felt heavy from disturbed dreams and an unnaturally long slumber. She eyed David and Eric suspiciously as she ran a hand over her face. David immediately pointed a finger towards Eric, who just sighed.

"I jabbed you after you continued screaming in your sleep. I thought you deserved to be knocked out for a few days after what you went through." Eric shrugged. "I won't apologise for it."

Lilliana sat upright in the bed. She privately wished she could be knocked out for the entire duration of their stay.

"It worked out well actually, darling," David smiled. "Father wanted you to participate in some unsavoury activities and was most disappointed that you couldn't join in. I told him you had a severe case of food poisoning, and under the circumstances he seemed inclined to believe me." He sounded quite proud of himself.

"Can you never call her darling again? It's just plain wrong."

Lilliana's head shot in the direction of the balcony where a sexy, smooth and familiar voice floated in. Fox.

Lilliana felt tears of love fill her eyes. She leapt from the bed and threw her arms around her dear Fox. The two friends hugged long and hard and were silent for a moment before Lilliana drew back to look upon Fox's face.

"Are you alright?"

"I will be," Fox nodded, "when we get the hell out of this hell hole." Fox smiled at Lilliana. "Someone has been wanting to say hi, come in Marcus," she called.

Marcus stepped into the room, dressed in full Reid guard gear. Lilliana had to admit, it suited him. He crossed over to her and pulled her into a hug. "Lilliana, I am so sorry for everything you have had to face on this mission." He shook his head. "Your strength and willpower to protect your loved ones has always been something to admire, but seeing you in action…" he trailed off, swallowing down the emotional lump in his throat. As her Team Leader, he had always been proud of her as he had watched her grow and become a valued asset to their establishment. Seeing her suffer in order to protect Fox the other day had made him beyond proud.

"Thanks Marcus," she squeezed his arm.

"This will all be over in eleven days, right?" Fox folded her arms, looking at Eric.

Eric walked over to the bar and poured an iced water. David joined him and poured a scotch. Fox snapped her fingers until she caught David's attention, then held out her hand, an eyebrow raised, waiting expectantly.

"Your Highness," David mock bowed as he passed the glass to Fox.

Lilliana sat on the balcony seat, grateful as the sun warmed her skin, and smiled at Eric as he passed her an iced tea.

"Right," Eric addressed them as they each got settled with a beverage. "The next eleven days we want you to keep a very low profile, Lilly. David—it is up to you to convince your father you are enjoying quality, alone time with Lilliana. If you've got any business to attend to with him, make sure Lilliana has plans with Nadia first so he can't conjure up something twisted."

David nodded. "It shouldn't be too difficult to keep her away from him now that he's had his fun with her, although she will need to make a daily appearance, breakfast or lunch." He nodded.

"What about Fox?" Lilliana asked. "How do we keep her out of harm's way?"

"Good question." Fox tipped the scotch down her throat, hating the nervous feeling that had surrounded her since arriving in this nightmare of a place.

"I've told Father she is off limits as your friend. He seemed more than happy to oblige." David raised a glass towards Fox, saluting her safety.

"Don't expect a thank you," Fox snapped.

"Oh believe me, Sugar, I wouldn't dream of it."

"Call me 'Sugar' again and Damon won't have a chance to blow your head off, because I'll…" Fox did not get a chance to finish as Eric interrupted her in a frustrated tone.

"Enough! Don't start any bullshit you two, we've got more important things to focus on." He shook his head and looked at Lilliana. Stress marred his features.

"What about Levi? Tim?" Fox asked. "We need to get them out of here."

Eric nodded, folding his arms. "Yeah, it's something else we are working on; David, what can you do to get them out of here safely?"

David ran a hand along his jawline, thinking. "I'm sure I can come up with something, just give me time."

Fox looked at David, not wanting to beg him to save her brother. Her eyes filled with concern as she looked at Lilliana.

"We need to save Levi, Lilly."

Lilliana nodded. "We will do everything we can, right David?"

David nodded, wishing he could be certain he had the power to intervene. "I promise I will do everything in my power to help both Tim and your brother."

Fox nodded.

"Can I talk to Eric alone please?" Lilliana addressed the room.

"I'll take Fox to Nadia's room," Marcus reached over and squeezed Lilliana's hand. "Stay strong, Lilly; not much longer."

Lilliana got to her feet and hugged Fox, whispering, "The team won't let anything happen to you. I'll see you a bit later, we'll get Nadia to take us to her private pool in the jungle."

"Sounds good." Fox kissed her cheek before following Marcus out of the room.

"I'll head off, have a meeting with dear old Dad about our guest list, which I'm sure your Guardian will enjoy hearing," David said, referring to the ever present Damon, who was always watching their moves. The door closed behind him leaving Eric and Lilliana alone.

"You look tired. Have you actually slept, or are you still pumping that awake serum into your system?"

Eric thought he heard a hint of disapproval in her tone. "No, I've not slept. I can't Lilly, not in this place."

"You have to. Even if you just have a few hours, please Eric?"

He sighed at her worried expression and kicked off his boots and went about removing his jacket along with all the guard paraphernalia.

"Right, I'll sleep on one condition; that you do not leave this room. At all, without waking me first." He pulled his black t-shirt over his head, as he pointed to the pack Rachael had put together for the team. "I'll knock myself out, but if you need me, hit me up with the blue vial." He pointed to his heart. "Right here. Can you do that?"

"Of course," Lilliana nodded, relieved he was actually going to sleep. She put out of her mind how long the needle was and was certain she wouldn't have to use it.

A knock sounded at the door before opening, and Nadia froze at the sight of a practically naked Eric. Her eyes swept over the firm abs that looked beautifully sculpted above a narrow, lean waist. She desperately wanted to run her fingers over his body. And those thighs. My God! She blinked, feeling her cheeks redden as her eyes lifted to meet his.

"Maybe I'll just go and get something to eat..." Lilliana wished she could vanish and give them some space. Watching them devour each other with lustful eyes made her miss Damon even more. She truly hoped that a relationship between them was possible.

"You're not going anywhere," Eric quipped, painfully aware that Lilliana wanted to give him time with Nadia. He wanted that too. But now was not the time, and this was not the place for any indulgences. He snatched up Rachael's pouch of meds and strode to the bed, throwing back the covers and getting in. He looked across at Nadia. "She's not to leave this room whilst I'm sleeping—not under any circumstances."

"I understand." Nadia nodded.

Lilliana almost felt sorry for Nadia then, for the way Eric barked out the order.

He sighed as he pulled out the sleep serum and slammed it into his thigh before tossing the needle near the pouch and lying down. He looked at Lilliana.

"Don't let me down."

"Eric, I won't, I promise; now just go to..." She smiled as she realised he was out cold before she could finish. "Thank God for small favours." She grinned at Nadia. "Are you okay?"

"Of course. I've been bitten by less appealing creatures." Her eyes drifted back to the sleeping male, his breathing regulated and heavy.

"He really is a sweetheart, isn't he?"

"He is." Lilliana stretched, feeling stiff after days spent in bed recovering. She was grateful for Rachael's concoctions that had kept her hydrated and fed while she had been knocked out. She never thought she would be able to eat again after what she had been forced to eat the other day, but her stomach did finally rumble for some real food now.

Nadia laughed, hearing it. "Why don't I go sort out some food for you?"

"That would be wonderful. Marcus took Fox to your room; I'd hate for her to run into Gregory."

"I'll get one of your team to bring up the food for you, and I'll take care of Fox. Why don't you shower?"

Lilliana smiled in appreciation. "Thank you. I want Eric to get at least eight hours sleep. Do you think you can find something for me to read?"

"Absolutely. Have a nice shower, there'll be lunch and a book waiting for you and I'll make sure you get to go for a long walk once Eric's awake."

"Sounds perfect."

Nadia headed towards the door. "See you later then."

"See you." Lilliana sighed once she was alone. Looking at Eric sprawled in the bed, she felt happy that at least he was getting some real rest. He had been working around the clock for weeks on end now. Eleven days. They could all do this. They were so close to the finish line. She walked into the bathroom and stripped off, running the shower to a just warm temperature. Closing her eyes, she raised her face to the stream and whispered to herself.

"Not long Damon, my love. Not long now."

***

The team spent the next eleven days with one priority in mind; making sure Lilliana and Fox avoided Gregory whenever possible. David suggested that breakfast was the best meal to have with his father due to his preoccupation leading up to the event. It worked out well as Gregory's schedule was overflowing and he barely had time to make Lilliana uncomfortable. In fact, he seemed to be going out of his way to calm her nerves by barely saying no more than ten words to her a day.

His politeness and the knowing glint in his eye made Lilliana just as uncomfortable as when he was grilling her; but she played along, smiling, and nodding and leaving the breakfast area as soon as possible. They took long walks in the jungle in the mornings; then quick, secretive meetings with the team in the afternoons to recap any updates. Afterwards, they spent time swimming in Nadia's jungle pool followed by a movie or reading. When the day finally rolled around for the main event, the entire team felt relieved. They were so close to the finish line.

Lilliana felt uneasy as she dressed for the event. Gregory had delivered a dress to the room and insisted she wear it for the night. Reluctantly she thanked him; though once she saw what it was, she refused to wear it. She went to her closet to select another dress, only then to discover that all her clothes had been removed when she had gone for her afternoon swim.

"I don't have a good feeling about this, Eric." Lilliana stepped out of the bathroom wearing the dress Gregory had insisted upon.

"Jesus, Lilliana! You look gorgeous." Eric shook his head. "What's wrong with it?"

Eric had no idea that the dress she was being made to wear was identical to the white leather dress she and Jessica had been wearing the night they were to be slaughtered almost eleven years ago.

She shook her head again and repeated herself. "I've just got a really bad feeling about this night."

Eric crossed to her and hugged her hard. "You're going to be okay; you will not be unprotected, trust me. Now, finish up and let us get this bloody show on the road so we can get these bastards and get home."

She nodded and went back into the bathroom to finish her make up. Once she was done, she turned to head back out to Eric, when a crash from the bedroom sounded. Running out, she saw Eric on the floor, surrounded by broken glass where he had connected with the decanter trolley.

"Eric!" Lilliana cried as she knelt beside him, shaking his shoulder, and patting his face. "Eric, please wake up!" She coughed suddenly and felt a wave of chemicals burn her throat and seep into her lungs as she took a deep breath. The last thing she thought of before she collapsed on top of Eric was, *we were so close…*

CHAPTER 10

A swarm of angry bees buzzed against Lilliana's eardrums. Black and white spots danced furiously against her eyelids. Her hands throbbed painfully, bound tightly together the restraints cutting into her wrists. The feeling of cold metal pressed against her back, chilling her to the bone.

Please, let this be a dream—this cannot be happening.

But God help her, it was.

She blinked her eyes open; the eerie buzzing sound turned to cheering, clapping and laughter as her hearing returned. The sight before her made her stomach churn in despair. Fear danced along her spine. She swallowed the bile that threatened to rise as her heartbeat accelerated dangerously close to that of a panic attack. Taking a steadying breath, she looked around, wondering where Eric, Unit Eight, Fox or David were.

Lilliana found she was standing in the middle of a large arena, tied back to back with another body. Lilliana twisted her head as far as she could to see behind her and briefly glimpsed long blonde hair covering the person's face, head dropped forward and unconscious. It wasn't Nadia. Her eyes flew forward, frantically searching the crowd.

The audience wrapped itself around the raised stage and Gregory was walking towards her, laughing, clapping as he turned in a full circle, drinking in the applause from the hundreds of guests around the room. He was soaking up their energy like a sponge soaking up blood from a horrendous crime scene.

Dressed in a black tuxedo, he looked the welcoming host as his gold cuff links sparkled under the stage lights. He clapped towards the left and Lilliana followed his direction to see a platform slowly being lowered through an opening on the stage. The platform held two figures who bowed to the applauding audience, holding glistening knives, dripping in gore; five bloody corpses lay in macabre positions at their feet.

The applause continued as several other platforms, holding entertainment for the most perverted of minds, were being raised up.

Beautiful women and men were being paraded and sold to the highest bidder. Like cattle at a market.

Young girls and boys, eerily enough, were not crying. Lilliana presumed they had been drugged due to their slack expressions and lack of fear. She stared in disgust as a man took hold of a young boy's arm and pulled him onto his lap. She forced her eyes away, not wanting to see the poor boy suffer when there was nothing, she could do about it. No matter where Lilliana looked, there was no escaping the unsavoury activities that were on show for the sick human's enjoyment.

Just how long had she been out of it? Her insides began quivering, and before long she was freezing cold and shivering uncontrollably. She knew she was going into shock. Her breathing became shallow as she glanced nervously around the crowded arena, trying to pull herself together. If she was in this position, it was because the Team needed her to be. They must have been waiting for something specific before stepping in. *That's it*, she thought; *they need to time this right, I'm going to be fine. I'm safe and all these victims will be saved soon enough. Please, let it be so.*

She looked about to see lustful, greedy eyes stare up at her as well as the other attractions on the stage as Gregory approached her.

He stopped a hair's breath away and smiled.

"Well, well, my beautiful daughter, I hope you're ready for a night to remember."

"Thank God I am no daughter of yours," she spat back in disgust.

He threw his head back laughing, then stopped suddenly, bending down so his eyes were directly level with hers. She really wished he hadn't. His unfeeling, dead eyes bore into hers. He ran his fingers slowly across the bare skin of her throat. She cringed as his grip tightened, before forcing a vile kiss upon her lips. Lilliana jerked her head to the side and away from his touch.

"Get the hell off me!" she hissed with hatred.

"Your discomfort is only just beginning," Gregory smiled eerily. "So many people have been waiting for this night. You wouldn't believe how much money they were willing to part with just to spend a minute in your company; I'll never be able to spend it all in two lifetimes!" He threw back his head and laughed again.

"Where's David?" She asked. Surely, he'd be doing something to help shut this all down.

"Why he has a centre seat, love. Unfortunately, he was a little unimpressed with your role in tonight's show; but he'll appreciate my creativity in the end." Gregory smiled coolly, saluting David.

Lilliana looked into the crowd to where Gregory pointed, shocked to see David, sitting looking like a wax mannequin, staring expressionlessly back at her.

"What have you done to him?" Fear caught in her throat.

"Just a bit of harmless freeze serum; I didn't want him to miss any of the fun." His eyes returned to hers. "But for now, Lilliana, the show must go on." There was no hint of a smile as he stared at her silently for several moments, before turning to address the crowd.

Gregory raised both hands and stood still, waiting for the arena to fall silent, before speaking into the microphone handed to him.

"My esteemed Ladies and Gentlemen, tonight is the finale to a highly entertaining series many of you have adored watching for years." Lilliana watched as he waved a hand in the air and she felt the blood drain from her face.

Around the arena were a hundred giant monitors lit up to play the final scene of her and Jessica's childhood. The gruesome night that was to end their imprisonment and their lives. The night Orlando had saved them and helped them escape their torment and anguish, before they were all rescued and delivered to the Given in Louisiana. It was the image of she and Jessica tied back to back on a large steel cross, surrounded by desperate, leering men who had wanted nothing more than to inflict the cruellest of acts upon the two girls. The images filled Lilliana now with sadness and fury.

Tears slowly fell from her eyes as she looked on at her dear friend, remembering their night of terror. So much trauma had been blocked out over the years as she concentrated instead on helping others.

The audience was filled with fans and buyers of the series, and they went wild in their excitement. Lilliana wanted to scream at them all to shut the hell up, but she knew that would only waste her energy. Whatever gas had been used to knock both she and Eric out had left her feeling sick and lethargic.

"It's time for you to partake in your prize! For those who paid the gold ticket fee, please come and enjoy the deliciousness that is The Given's Dark Angel! For the highest bidder of ten million dollars, you will get to have an hour alone to do whatever you like with her, only making sure you leave breath in her body," He chuckled delightfully before continuing. "After that, she will be joining all bidders on stage for her grand finale and the end of our show tonight. Bidding starts now! Do come see me or my lovely assistants and we will take care of you. Enjoy!" Gregory raised both his arms to the thunderous and deafening applause of the crowd.

Lilliana swallowed nervously, her arms aching. She squeezed her fingers together, trying to pump some feeling back into her numb hands, feeling the wetness of blood. Her fingers brushed against the person bound behind her, which startled her for a moment as the person began to wake, moaning.

"Hey," Lilliana soothed the woman. "It's okay, everything's going to be alright."

The person struggled against her restraints, crying softly.

"Lilliana?"

Oh my God, Lilliana's heartbeat with horror. "Fox?"

"What the hell," Fox tugged against the restraints with all her might, crying out as they cut into her wrists.

"Don't fight it Fox, struggling will give them what they want. We're going to get out of this, I promise you. Just take a deep breath."

Fox tried to do what Lilliana was asking and took a deep breath. Never in her life had she been so frightened. Tears of terror continued to fall, and she took comfort as Lilliana's bloody fingers gripped hers, squeezing her reassuringly.

"Oh Lilly, if we live to get out of this," she whispered.

"We will, sweetie. We will." Lilliana sounded determined, despite her own fear. She looked at David, who had not moved an inch. She prayed Damon was not watching this through The Guardian; prayed none of those she loved could see her here now.

Glancing around the crowd, Lilliana tried to locate her team. She was shocked and saddened as she recognised many faces in the crowd. Some who had been big donators at her Dark Angel safe-house campaign in New York were here. Politicians, high ranking Officials, Religious Leaders. And here they were, laughing and partaking in the illegal activities. It made her blood boil. Her stomach rolled and she prayed that their efforts would not be wasted here tonight. That Damon, Johnson, and the Team were ready to end this.

Her eyes were drawn back to Gregory, who laughed and chatted with his guests, taking their bids.

Champagne and Scotch were being consumed in ridiculously large quantities and she watched as many of the guests were taking their winning bids off to private rooms around the arena where they could have their way with their victims. She froze as she saw the set of blue eyes that were so similar to those of the man she loved. They belonged to a man she wished never to see again.

Seth Night. Damon and Cameron's Uncle.

His smile was like ice, smooth and cold. A predator waiting to claim his prey. She looked away, her breathing shallow. It was no real surprise to see him here. Her eyes fell on Nadia, who was tucked under Gregory's arm while he laughed and talked to a group of men. Nadia turned her head at that moment, her eyes meeting Lilliana's. She looked pale beneath her beautiful make up. An angel amongst devils.

Gregory's eyes turned back to her at that moment and he cleared his throat as he prepared to announce the commencement of the event in a raised voice.

"It's time."

Lilliana's breathing rapidly accelerated as several men stood to approach her and Fox; hearing Fox whimper broke her heart.

One by one they had their minute's worth of pleasure with her, before moving on to Fox. They were certainly trying to get their money's worth. Some kissed her, and one enthusiastic man bit her lip. Blood trickled, but that didn't put the others off from kissing her. Some stroked her hair, whispering what they'd do to their wives while thinking about her, taking photographs with her. Others simply held her face, staring into her eyes. It went on and on.

As Lilliana's energy to fight began to wane, Fox's fight seemed to return as she cursed and bit anyone who came near her. Lilliana struggled to avoid the foul touches of the participants, but eventually exhaustion got the better of her and she ceased to fight. Instead, she closed her eyes, blocking them all out as best she could for the following hour. A painful slap across her face brought her back to reality and she gasped in shock.

"I paid to look into your eyes, Beautiful; the least you could do is open them for me." Seth's voice slid over her like a wet slug.

She stared hatefully at him, the blood in her veins turning to ice as he stepped closer, cupping her face.

"Don't," She hissed, exhausted, waiting for him to strike her again.

He did not. He simply placed both hands around her throat, stroking her neck up and down. "Such soft flesh," he said, mesmerised by the softness of her skin. Slowly he bent down towards her lips, a mere breath between them.

Lilliana turned her head before his kiss could meet with her lips. She'd rather another slap than his set of lips ever touching hers.

This time she got one. A huge and heavy slap straight to her cheekbone. Her face stung. She glared hatefully at Damon's uncle.

"Don't you know? I'm the highest bidder. You're mine for an hour."

"Then you'd better keep me tied up, because I will rip your throat out if you touch me again," Lilliana said with as much venom as she could muster. Exhaustion stole some of the heat from her intent, which disappointed her somewhat.

"Mmm, I cannot wait to go one or two rounds with you. In fact, I'm hoping to see your claws come out." He said loudly as Gregory approached.

"Our little wildcat isn't causing you too much grief yet, is she Seth?"

"None that I can't handle," Seth smiled.

"Get your man to take her to the Presidential suite and enjoy your hour. Just remember, we need life left in her for the finale, my good man."

"Of course," Seth clicked to his guard who approached Lilliana from behind, cutting her binds, freeing her of her restraints.

She tucked her hands protectively under her chin, willing them to feel again so she could use them.

"Get away from her," Fox screamed as another guard approached her, cutting her binds too.

Fox's eyes met Lilliana's, and a shared look of fear flashed between them as Fox was dragged away. "Lilly," she called before being jerked off the stage, the blonde wig falling down around her.

Lilliana wanted to cry for her friend, but she didn't have a moment more to consider Fox's predicament, for Seth reached out a hand towards her face. She hastily stepped away from him, colliding against the guard's solid chest. Strong hands came up to hold her still as she struggled.

"I'm not going to hurt you, Lilliana," Seth reached out again after sucking his finger to wipe dried blood off her chin.

She jerked back and gasped in pain as her head collided with the guard's chin. She hoped it had hurt him as much as it hurt her. Seth grabbed her arm and marched her beside him, the guard on their heels.

Lilliana could hear Gregory's booming laughter; it was a sound she hoped never to hear again. She attempted to pull her arm free of Seth's hold, but it was useless. She was too weak physically and mentally in the moment to fight anyone. She watched as a young man was being led into a private room by a couple of guards. She had no idea it was Fox's brother Levi but felt sorry for him all the same.

Seth led her towards a door and into a pristine white room where an assortment of torture and pleasure instruments hung along a wall beside a high table with restraints. He released her arm as the guard closed the door behind them, pressing a panel on his tactical helmet and proceeded to give instructions that she could not hear.

Lilliana quickly stepped away from Seth and the guard and put the table between them, watching them closely, waiting for their next move. She was frustrated with herself for feeling so lightheaded and lacking energy. She needed her wits about her if she was going to escape this nightmare.

Seth appeared relaxed, placing his hands in his pockets, just watching her squirm. He took a step towards her and smiled when he saw alarm replace panic on her face. He was enjoying this pre-match way too much.

"Relax, Beautiful, I said I wasn't going to hurt you. And I meant it." He walked briskly around the table and reached for her arms. She pushed against his chest, leaving bloody handprints on his crisp white jacket.

"Don't, just don't." Lilliana was not going to plead, but she felt she was close to doing just that as she struggled to get out of his clutches. Outside she could hear the continued celebrations of people laughing and cheering; panic starting to set in as it all became too much.

A sudden movement to her left side startled her as the tall figure in black approached. Her throat tightened in fear as she believed the guard was now here to restrain her in order for Seth to have his way with her.

Her eyes widened in fear. "Please," she shook her head. "Please don't…" Her throat tightened. *NO*, she shouted to herself. *Do. Not. Cry.*

She glared up at Seth, who nodded towards the guard. Turning her head, she followed his gaze, watching as the guard pressed the panel again on his helmet, giving another command.

"It's time. Be ready to move in one minute." He removed the helmet, tossed it onto the table as he stepped towards her.

She stopped struggling against Seth.

Lilliana's vision blurred again as tears streamed freely down her face.

Seth released her.

Her knees gave way; she had no control now. Her body was completely beyond her control, and she sank towards the ground.

Eyes she had been longing to see suddenly swept her up in a look filled with longing and fury.

His strong, firm arms dove down to catch her, and he pulled her gently, into his chest.

She knew these hands, this chest.

Damon glared at his Uncle. "Slapping her wasn't part of our deal."

"Come now, dear boy; if I didn't play the part of a sadistic creep, Gregory would have caught on in a second. Don't hold it against me, I got her out of harm's way, didn't I?"

Damon kissed Lilliana's head. Her arms wrapped themselves tightly around his waist; her face pressed against his chest. Lilliana's stunned silence and shock overtook her bodily movements and she began shaking uncontrollably. What she had been through!

"It's time." Damon nodded to Seth.

Seth forced a tight smile and drawing out a tiny gas applicator from his pocket, fitted it into his nostrils.

Holding Lilliana close, Damon released one arm around her and pulled out his gas applicator and did the same.

A few things happened simultaneously; the laughter and conversations that had flooded the arena suddenly ceased as though someone had hit a mute button. The sound of heavy thuds could be heard as hundreds of bodies hit the deck from wherever they had been standing or sitting, leaving an eerie silence in the air. Then came the parade of thunderous footsteps flooding the arena as it filled with the Officials and Undercover Operatives.

Damon looked down at Lilliana. She was out cold. Whatever drugs had been in her system along with the knockout serum that had been pumped through the arena's air ducts, had sent her into a deep sleep. Damon was grateful for the fact that she would not have to see any more of it.

"Eric—locate me now," Damon said into his communicator.

"Yes Sir."

Damon stepped out of the room holding Lilliana gently, watching as the teams moved efficiently with military grace, placing the criminals and victims into separate sections where they would be held or released.

The victims would be injected with a gentle, low grade serum and be returned to their families, or seek assistance from the Officials to get their lives back in order.

The Officials held up glass screens to the fallen faces, revealing the identity and details specific to each individual. The screen flashed red to alert the authorities if the fallen were amongst the names they'd spent years searching for. Seeing the number of screens flashing red around the arena filled Damon with relief. It had been a momentous operation, and it looked like it had paid off.

Eric approached Damon, carrying the shape of a slim body in his arms.

Damon nodded to Eric and asked, "Nadia?"

Eric nodded, then glanced at Lilliana. "Is she alright?"

"Time will tell. Can you wake Nadia? I want Lilliana to remain under and I need you to take her."

Eric nodded. "Of course, Sir." He knelt, balancing Nadia on his knee as he pulled out a slim needle. Injecting it into Nadia's arm, it took only seconds before the awake serum took full effect and her eyelids began to flutter open.

Her eyes met with Eric's. "What happened?" Nadia asked groggily, raising a hand to push her hair away from her face. A healthy colour flooded her cheeks. Eric was holding her so close and Nadia thought he smeltled divine.

Eric stood, keeping his arms around her until he was a certain she wouldn't fall.

"We used the knockout serum once Lilliana and Fox were out of harm's way. Seth helped get her away, then we had the orders to drop it all."

Nadia turned away from Eric and stepped towards Damon, a frown crossing over her lovely features as she looked on at Lilliana.

Damon appreciated Nadia's softness and felt her instant concern for the love of his life.

"Nadia, I'm Damon. It's nice to finally meet you; Orlando has told me a lot about you."

Her eyes lifted to his. She also had heard plenty about the famous Night Brothers and their success running one of the world's most prestigious Given Establishments. And here one of them stood before her; Damon Night, holding Lilliana in a way that Nadia sensed he was more than just her director.

"It's so nice to meet you, Mr Night; can I help you with Lilliana?"

Damon smiled over Nadia's head towards Eric.

"That would be great, Nadia; you can go with Eric. Take Lilliana to the jet, Marcus is waiting outside for you. Fox and Levi are with him. Just keep her sedated until you get her home to Rachael, and she will attend to her directly—and Josephine and the girls are all set to take care of her and Fox too."

Nadia nodded, as Damon spoke to Eric.

"I shouldn't be more than a day behind you once we sort through all this here. Cam and Johnson will need your report once you've settled in and rested for a bit." Damon looked down at Lilliana and felt a rush of protectiveness wash over him. Could he really part with her again?

Her silky hair hung around her like a curtain. He dropped a gentle kiss on her forehead before passing her over to Eric.

"Don't worry Sir, she's going to be fine; the worst is behind us now."

"Thank you," Damon nodded as Eric turned to go. He watched as Nadia slipped her hand into Lilliana's and they moved away from the chaos of the arena. He suddenly had an unnerving sense of déjà vu.

Once they were out of his line of vision, Damon turned to give his full attention to the grave matters at hand.

CHAPTER 11

Lilliana opened her eyes to sunshine and serenity, her appreciation for it all the more magnified after the hell she had just experienced. She could feel the sun's rays coming through the window, and then even warmer was the soothing sound of Josephine's voice as she read to Lilliana about her favourite topic: gardening.

"Jose."

That was all Josephine needed to hear before she dropped the book down and leapt off the window seat, laughing.

"You're awake!"

Lilliana pushed herself up, reaching for Josephine who threw herself onto the bed and into her friend's arms.

Laughter soon turned to tears. Tears of relief, tears of joy, just to be able to comfort her friend. They clung to each other for several minutes and only drew apart once their tears slowed. A bright smile broke out on both their faces.

"You are an absolute hero my friend," Josephine said and wiped Lilliana's tears away before slipping off the bed to reach for the water pitcher.

"Definitely not," she smiled her thanks as Josephine handed her a glass of water.

"Yes, you are, Lilly. I've seen what you went through, what you did to save Fox. I saw pretty much everything."

Lilliana froze as she was about to take a sip from her glass.

"Oh no," she whispered. "Please tell me you didn't." For any of her friends to witness what she had endured the past few weeks filled her with sadness and dread.

"You're home safe. That's all that matters, you just need to…" but Josephine didn't get a chance to finish as the door opened, and once the new arrivals saw that Lilliana was awake their intended quiet entry turned into a stampede, and hysterical laughter filled the room, before turning to tears. Josephine saved the glass of water as Allie and Jessica threw themselves onto the bed, either side of Lilliana.

"Thank God your home, girl!" Allie squeezed her before leaning back, allowing Jessica room to kiss and hug their friend.

"Oh Lilliana, are you alright?" Kind-hearted, soft spoken Jessica clung to Lilliana's hands.

"I certainly am now."

Jessica shook her head. "I am so sorry for everything you've been through," a look of utter sadness crossed her face.

Lilliana felt her pain as they both reflected on their past. "It's alright Jess, I'm home now and I'm not going anywhere again." She wanted to see her friend smile. "I've a special message for you." She hugged Jessica again and dropped a kiss on her cheek. "Guess who that's from? Here's a clue; he is a good-looking artist that makes the best pot of crawfish this side of the globe."

"Stephan?" Tears flowed again as Jessica became overwhelmed with gratitude that Lilliana had spoken with her brother.

"He's doing so well, Jess; he's kicking goals in the art world and apart from missing you, he is very happy." She smiled at her three dearest friends, and they quietly sat back and looked at each other for several moments.

"How are you feeling?" Allie asked cautiously.

"Ecstatic to be home."

"You've been out cold for three days. Detoxed, and pumped full of good serums. Racheal and Leon should be here shortly." Allie looked towards the door as it opened. "Speak of the devil."

Leon walked in ahead of Rachael and smiled brightly when he saw Lilliana sitting upright, looking relaxed, surrounded by her friends.

"It is so good to see you, Lilly."

"You too Leon. Hello Rachael."

Rachael grinned and dropped a kiss on Lilliana's cheek. "Are you feeling okay?"

"Better than okay. Thanks for taking care of me while I was… out."

"You are so welcome. Now, I know the detox bath cleans you up physically, but why don't you have a shower and a walk out in the sunshine? There's going to be an assembly in a couple of hours' time to celebrate you, Fox and the Team returning safely. But until then, I think some fresh air will do you well," Rachael said, nodding.

Lilliana smiled. "I feel like I've been away for years, not months."

"Which is why you need to take some time for you, before you're swamped by everyone who has missed you."

"Where's Damon?"

"In an urgent meeting. He has been sitting with you the past few days Lilly, but an emergency popped up."

Lilliana nodded. She was home with Damon and those she loved. There was some kind of comfort in that it was business as usual. She felt a burst of energy and threw the covers back. "Shower and a walk. Who's with me?"

"We are, well, at least for the walk," Jessica smiled.

"We'll wait for you in the library, Lilly." Allie followed Leon towards the door.

"I'll wait here for you; I'll just pop out and make a tea." Josephine had promised Damon she'd keep an eye on Lilliana and would not leave her side until Damon was with her again. She walked out into Damon and Lilliana's kitchenette and poured a tea, beyond grateful that Lilliana seemed to be okay.

***

Within two hours of waking, Lilliana felt every bit of tension that she'd carried with her the past weeks fade as she basked in the sunshine and laughter of her friends as they walked in the fields beyond the stables.

Everyone was trying to get a word in as they entertained her with stories of what had been happening while she had been away. Her sides were aching from laughter as Allie reenacted Dr Richard filling in for her.

"I mean, seriously, you cannot make this stuff up," Allie shook her head.

"He's a character, that's for sure." Lilliana laughed.

"That is so polite of you to say. I can see you've had a break from him." Allie scoffed.

"I'm glad it was you and not me stuck with him in sessions, I don't think I could have survived him."

The other girls looked at each other, knowing what Lilliana had been through; they knew she could survive any situation thrown at her.

"How's Scott been, Jess?" she asked, knowing Jessica had been working closely with him in her art groups.

"Apart from missing you, he's been doing… fairly well." She flushed, a tell-tale sign that she wasn't telling the whole truth.

"Jessica, what is it?"

"He had a tiny hiccup, but nothing to worry about."

"Hiccup?"

"He didn't appreciate the fact that Damon wouldn't permit him to view all the footage regarding your mission and went on a hunger strike."

"Oh no. Well, I don't really appreciate that any of you witnessed what Fox and I went through, you all didn't need to suffer." She shook her head. "What happened next?"

"Damon had to threaten him with being force fed if he didn't start eating normally," Josephine piped in.

"How long did he stop eating for?"

"A week undetected, then another four days when Orlando noticed his weight loss." Jessica shook her head.

"His Watcher, Alan, got demoted for not noticing or reporting him not eating." Allie said. "He has Finn Watching him part time now."

"Now that I'm back, I can help take care of him. I can't wait to see him."

"And you've met Orlando's sister? What's she like?" Jessica sounded nervous.

"She's lovely, considering all she's been through."

"Yes, I attended her with Hillary for her first psych evaluation," Allie nodded. "She is going to be held in the psych ward for another week, and it will be up to Damon and Johnson if she clears for Main House. There's been talk she could benefit the Black Ops division."

"She would have a lot of information that could assist in other operations for sure," Lilliana nodded. "But I do worry that she has been through so much already, and if she does get a pass to Main House, I think a position in HBR would be better for her mental health." Lilliana was referring to the Health Beauty and Rejuvenation centre that Fox ran on the tenth floor.

They stopped by the oak trees where the therapy swings hung, and each of them sat down in a swing and rocked to and fro.

Lilliana sighed, feeling an overwhelming sense of ease fill her soul. She was home, safe and she never wanted to leave again. Looking over Josephine's shoulder, her heart stopped momentarily before it began to beat crazily in her chest.

"Damon," she whispered, feeling butterflies dance against her rib cage as she saw two tall figures approach from the tree line. The other girls turned their heads to see Damon and Cam walking towards them. Lilliana slid from the swing as her eyes locked with the darkest of blues.

Damon stopped walking, and Cam's conversation halted as he saw his brother's eyes land upon the love of his life.

This will be good, Cam thought as he grinned across at Josephine. She returned her lover's smile before Lilliana broke into a run and flew through the trees towards Damon.

Damon watched her beautiful face fill with glee, her dark hair flailed behind her like a silken cape and her white dress flowing as her legs bounded towards him. He then broke out in five long strides as she launched herself into his waiting arms.

"Damon," she cried with glee.

"Lilliana," he whispered and rained kisses all over her hair, hands clinging around her waist, holding her off the ground. "Baby," he said and kissed her cheek slowly letting her slide down his body. They both felt the magnetic effect of being so close. Desire trickled through their loins, pulsing.

Her feet touched the ground and she tilted her head back, lost in his glorious, intense look. An ocean of blue swallowed her sea green gaze and as his head bent down to meet to hers, she was oblivious to all but him.

Their kiss was smoldering, intense and desperate as their lips rushed to meet the other's.

Her hands swept behind his neck, pulling him close as his hands tangled in her silky locks, tilting her head on the perfect angle to deepen their kiss. She melted into his kiss as his tongue swept to mate with hers and she could have cried for the intensity of their passion. After several moments Damon pulled back to gaze upon her face.

He looked so serious as he gently brushed her hair back before dropping a sweet kiss upon her lips, and then another before a…

"Ahem," was dropped behind them.

He smiled hungrily down at Lilliana, causing her breath to hitch and her checks to flush. If only they were alone right now. Damon dropped one more kiss on her lips before stepping back.

"Well, I don't want to intrude but we do have an assembly, and I have a sister to greet!"

Lilliana turned to Cam, and a beautiful smile spread across her face as he swooped her up and spun her around in a circle. She burst out laughing as his foot hit uneven ground, causing them to stumble.

"Whoa there," Josephine called out to her husband. "We've just got her back in one piece, let's keep it that way." She walked up beside Damon and popped her arm about his waist. He smiled down at her, and she was so relieved to see the tension gone from his features.

"She's home," she whispered gratefully to him.

He squeezed her waist, before turning his gaze back to his wife, watching as Cam and Lilliana quickly caught up. Jessica and Allie joined them.

"We'll head off and meet you at the assembly," Allie play punched Damon in the arm. "Good to see you smiling again, Sir."

Jessica turned bright red at Allie's playful banter with Damon. She had always considered him an imposing figure; not unkind or unfriendly, just a presence that made her feel less inclined to call him anything but Mr Night, or Sir.

"It's so good to have everyone safely back," he smiled again, but a darkness churned within him. They'd lost one of their friends along the way, and he knew it would destroy Lilliana's happiness when she found out.

Damon felt a small hand clasp his. "Shall we go then, Mr Night?" A kiss brushed his check.

He smiled and returned the kiss, "We shall, Mrs Night."

As the others began walking back towards Main House Lilliana stopped in front of him and reached up to caress his face as she stared silently at him.

He simply nodded. "I know, Angel, I know."

"I don't ever wanted to be apart from you again Damon, from this day forward. Ever."

His arms wrapped around her waist as he pulled her close, dropping his face into the groove of her neck, breathing her in. She pushed her lips against his neck and kissed him, silent tears of relief and joy trickling from her eyes.

"I completely agree, love." He kissed her forehead and pulled back to look at her, a frown marred his handsome features. He gently kissed her tears away. "My beautiful brave girl, it's going to be alright now. Whatever we need to do, to help you heal from your trauma Lilliana, we will do it."

"I'm fine, Damon," she said and stood on tiptoe, brushing her lips across his. It was a feathery light kiss, soft and full of love. "I promise you, I'm fine."

He shook his head. "I'm going to be keeping my eye on you, Miss

Resilience."

"I hope it's a very *close* eye." She raised an eyebrow and ran a finger across his lips.

He grinned at her playfulness. "You better believe it."

"Lovebirds!"

They looked towards Cam where he stood in the distance, cupping his hands around his mouth. "Assembly!" He waved his arm before heading off at a jog.

"That's our cue," Damon kissed her again before clasping her hand tightly in his, and they quickly set off for assembly.

***

Lilliana felt a tiny bit out of place, and exposed, sitting up on the stage as the assembly gathered. She usually sat tucked away with her friends in the crowd.

Looking out over the entire Given establishment faces, she felt so much love in her heart. Allie sat with Christopher, who was beside Jessica and Orlando. Josephine sat beside her co-worker and super star inventor of drought tolerant plants, Rupert, and his boyfriend, Luke. There were her colleagues from the psych ward, Shelley, Jaycee, and Brad, along with Billy from the hospital with Dr Ryan and Leon. She smiled when she saw Thomas salute her, and she felt tears of joy threaten when her eyes fell on Scott.

Scott was staring back at her with a happy grin plastered across his face. Lilliana was happy to see, that, even though he was still thin, he had a healthy-looking tan and glow about him.

She swallowed and looked across at Damon who had his head bent low, listening and in deep conversation with the ever-serious Johnson.

By the stars, she thought to herself. *How I have missed that handsome man.*

Damon caught her eye in that moment and placed his hand on Johnson's shoulder before walking across to where she sat.

"Are you doing okay, Baby?" His hand stroked her check. "Is this too much for you?"

"No," she took his wrist and squeezed it reassuringly. "It's just there are so many people I want to hug and say hello to."

"You'll get your chance, sweetheart." He smiled down at her, before whispering, "I so want to kiss you right now."

She beamed back at him. "I know, me too."

He straightened as Fox joined them on the stage and swept Lilliana up in her arms. "My darling friend! It's good to see you."

"Fox," Lilliana hugged her hard, before releasing her. "How are you? Is Levi okay?"

"I'm great Sugar, I've been well looked after. And Levi has been returned safely home to our Aunt." Fox looked at Damon and raised an eyebrow. "Does she know yet?"

"Know what?" Lilliana looked from Fox to Damon, and watched his handsome face darken.

"Fox, please take your seat," He looked down at Lilliana. "Baby, I..."

"Damon, It's time." Johnson interrupted as Cam took his seat alongside Unit Eight.

Damon sighed and rubbed Lilliana's arm indicating she take her seat, before joining Johnson at the front of the stage.

Lilliana sat, feeling a niggle of alarm creep along her spine. What hadn't she been told? Damon's velvety voice cut into her thoughts as he addressed the assembly.

"As you all know, Lilliana and Fox embarked on an imperative mission recently, for a number of reasons. The first was to protect our home and everyone in it. The second was to set up safe houses for those less fortunate outside these walls in order for them to heal after abuse and be given opportunities to thrive in a world that is, as most of you aware, often difficult to survive in without a helping hand. And thirdly, and most importantly, was taking down an Underworld Lord, along with hundreds of his associates." Damon's speech was cut short as the audience erupted in a roar of cheering and clapping.

Lilliana forced herself to embrace the goodwill instead of fearing the sounds that had terrified her only days ago. Damon noticed her pale slightly and he held his hands up to cease the noise.

"Yes, we are all extremely proud of Lilliana and Fox for their sacrifice and bravery, and we are beyond grateful to the Team, Unit

Eight, for their remarkable efforts in protecting our people." He turned, nodding to Unit Eight, who looked almost unrecognisable to Lilliana as they sat in casual clothes and not their black, tactical guards' uniforms. She caught Eric's eye, and he winked cheekily. She smiled before turning her gaze back to Damon, but not before noticing that Fox and Marcus were holding hands as they sat beside each other.

"I know many of you will have questions for Lilliana and Fox, but please note that they have survived an incredibly difficult experience. I do not want anyone asking them questions regarding the footage you have viewed about their experience at the Reid compound."

Lilliana cringed inwardly, wondering who had had the bright idea to share the deplorable footage in the first place.

"If they wish to open up and share with you, then that is an entirely different matter, but I will not have anyone disrespecting their healing time with invading questions. I hope I am understood."

His gaze swept over the audience, followed by a collective silence as those who had viewed the footage nodded quietly, filled with admiration and respect for Lilliana and Fox.

"There's going to be a celebration get together in common room three at four this afternoon for anyone who wants to come along. Until then, let us resume our classes and work for the day. Thank you."

He turned and walked over to Lilliana and, taking her hand, pulled her to her feet. "Do you want to see Scott now?"

"I want more than anything to be alone with you, but I would love to say a quick hello, yes."

Damon nodded. "I'll get him to come up to our room; we'll head out the back way." They left through the rear door that lead up through the secluded labyrinth of passageways, down to the hospital and psych wards, and up to the Black Ops section to Damon and Cam's levels. Lilliana loved feeling her hand nestled in his strong grip as they walked silently to their rooms. Once they stepped in, Damon kissed her hand before letting go, and walked along the polished floorboards towards his desk at the end of the long, open lounge to make the call to have Scott come up for a visit.

Lilliana looked about her, feeling a rush of happiness. She truly was home. Being surrounded by Damon's bookcases that overflowed with years of their Given's rich history, photographs filled with sentimental pride from past to present. The large, open fireplace mantel, which held photographs that warmed her heart. She turned to watch Damon as he hung up from the call.

He faced her, leaning back against his desk, eyes hungrily watching her. "I can't tell you how happy it makes me, having you home again, safe, Lilliana."

She sighed as his eyes swept over her from head to toe and back again. Whenever he looked at her like that, it made her want to launch herself at him, rip his clothes off and consume every inch of him. But Scott would be here any minute. She nodded, and simply replied. "I know."

He started walking towards her, slowly. How could he have gotten more irresistibly handsome in the time she had been away? And why did she feel nervous?

"Lilliana." He stopped in front of her and gently took her hands. "It's okay, we can take this as slow as you need. You've been through so much and you know I would never do anything to hurt you. Please tell me you know that?"

"Oh Damon," she raised his hands to her lips, eyes on his, and kissed his knuckles. "You never have to tell me that. You're my guardian angel. My knight in shining armor."

She tilted her head back and whispered, "But if you don't kiss me right now, I think I will die wanting."

Damon didn't need to be asked twice. His hands swept through her glorious silken hair and he tilted her head so he could kiss her deeply. Her hands clung to his wrists for support, as a wave of lustful dizziness stole her breath. His tongue danced with hers as he deepened the kiss to heights that had her seeing stars. She almost wanted to laugh, it felt so sublimely good.

A knock came at the door. "Finally," she whispered against his lips, causing laughter to erupt from him.

"There she is, my vixen. Come on then, let's get this greeting out of the way, so I can have my way with you, wife."

"Gladly," she watched as he walked to the door and opened it for Scott.

Scott burst through like an energetic gelding wearing the biggest smile across his face as he ran towards Lilliana. She laughed as he swept her up, amazed at his strength, despite his lean frame.

"Who are you and what have you done with my brother?"

He put her down and they stood back, grinning at each other. "All in a few month's work really," he flexed a bicep proudly. "Weights, archery and swimming three times a week."

She laughed, "You look wonderful Scott, happy." She didn't want to lecture him just yet about his hunger strike episode.

"I am—especially now that you're home safe. Are you okay?" He quickly looked over his shoulder at Damon. "Am I allowed to ask that, Sir?"

"Of course you can, Scott." Lilliana answered for Damon, taking hold of her brother's hands. "You can ask me anything, just not right now," she smiled, watching Damon fold his arms.

"Just give me a bit of time. I'm more interested in how you are. How's your artwork coming along?"

"It's been fantastic, I've been helping Jessica and have completed several entry portraits for new arrivals."

"Your talent amazes me every time I see one of your drawings, Scott," Damon said, walking over and placing his hand on Scott's shoulder.

"Maybe you'd like to give Lilliana her Christmas present now?"

Scott nodded and pointed to Damon and Lilliana's bedroom area, "Is it still where we put it?"

"It is," Damon nodded as Scott took off, before turning his eyes back to Lilliana. He smiled and ran a finger along her check. She grabbed his hand, turning it to kiss along his wrist, eyes penetrating his. He ran a hand along her hair, letting it fall through his fingers. She smiled and planted a kiss against his lips. He wanted more in that moment, but Scott returned carrying a parcel that was almost the height of Lilliana.

"You left the day after you got married and just before Christmas, so I thought this was the perfect gift to say Congratulations and Merry Christmas." Scott placed the parcel gently on the couch.

"Scott, that's so lovely of you." Lilliana walked over and took a corner of the wrapping paper, before tearing it down, gasping in surprise when she saw it revealed the most intricate black and white portrait of Damon holding her at their wedding. The only colour Scott had put in it, were of her piercing green eyes staring lovingly up into Damon's intense blue ones. The detailed patterns in her dress were flawless, the creaminess of her skin glowed and her black hair glistened along with the stars and the moon Scott had weaved into the background. Damon looked like every woman's dream. Tall, strong, and handsome as he looked down at Lilliana adoringly.

Lilliana could see the love Scott had poured into this piece of work, framed in a gilded black and gold frame. She looked at her brother and shook her head.

"This is the most beautiful present I have ever received. Thank you." She flung her arms around him and hugged him tight.

Scott put his arms around her. "You're welcome, I'm just so happy you're home and that we can spend time together."

Lilliana nodded as Scott stepped back and they watched as Damon picked up the portrait and place it in the middle of the mantel piece.

"Perfect," Lilliana smiled.

"Well Scott, we'll see you this afternoon at four. Until then, I think you've got Official Law?"

"Yep. I mean, yes Sir," he grinned at Lilliana.

"See you later Scott," she smiled as he walked towards the door. "And thank you."

He waved before the door closed behind him, leaving them alone at last.

Lilliana turned to smile at Damon, and her smile froze as she met with the intensity of his stare.

"You, me, now." He strode towards her and reached for her waist, drawing her against the hardness of his torso.

"Yes please," she managed to get out before his lips assaulted hers in the most immensely pleasurable way. She felt molten waves of desire build with each taste of Damon's lips, each thrust of his tongue as it skillfully mated with hers, sliding in and out across her lips, before plunging in to claim her again, showing her what he wanted to do to her all over. She felt weak, hot, and heavy, and before long she was throbbing below. She felt slick between her legs with every taste of his lips. His hands crushed her lovingly, holding her close, moulding her to every inch of him.

She could feel his swollen shaft against the sheerness of her dress, and she rubbed against him, almost in tears with desire. "I can't wait Damon, I want you right now," she whispered against his lips.

Damon didn't need to be told twice. He scooped her effortlessly in his arms and continued kissing her as he strode towards the bedroom. He sat her on the bed, and tore his shirt off, before reaching to unbuckle his belt, losing the remainder of his garments.

Lilliana knelt on the bed, her eyes not leaving his as she pulled her dress off, breathing heavily in anticipation of their union. He halted her hands as she went to remove her bra, shaking his head and seeing her silk knickers slick with her wanting juices, he reached slowly towards her, and gently cupped her between her legs, stroking back and forth as he watched her eyes fill with desire.

Her panting told him she was close to coming as she rubbed against his hand, before she quickly pushed it away, reaching for him. He moaned with pleasure as she wrapped her small hand around his hot, thick shaft and stroked him, dipping her finger against his sensitive head.

"No you don't," he ground out, before reaching behind her to unclip her bra, setting her full breasts free. He hooked his arm around her waist as he lifted her back and settled her against the pillows, laying across her. His fingers stroked her smooth skin, cupping her firm breasts, before lowering his head to take a plump nipple into his mouth.

She gasped as the pull of his lips set her loins on fire, and she grasped his buttocks, drawing him against her as she placed a leg high around his waist, opening herself up to him.

"Lilliana," he whispered, his lips leaving her breasts to capture hers in a deep kiss, as he guided the tip of his erection to her moist entrance; his finger swirled over her swollen bud gently and firmly before thrusting up, finally giving them both what they'd been longing for.

They rocked together, all the while kissing and pouring their love into the other as their rhythm increased, taking them closer to euphoria.

Lilliana arched her hips as the delicious, lustful wave they rode peaked to dizzying heights.

Damon placed a hand under her rounded bottom, raising her higher as he slammed into her a final time, hitting her centre deep and hard, sending her into a spiral of repeated glory. She arched against him as she cried out, clinging to his chiseled back, her orgasm overwhelming her.

He kissed along her neck, her check, chin, ear and back to her lips in the sweetest, longest kiss until their breathing returned to normal.

He eased back, stroking her hair away from her face and stared at her for the longest time, unwilling to break the magic of the moment.

Lilliana smiled softly, enjoying being adored by such a delicious male specimen. *If we could be like this forever*, she thought, *then I would die happy.*

Damon kissed her lips again before leaning back to watch her.

She ran a finger back and forth over his jawbone.

"I think it's fair to say that we could happily remain in this position for a week," Damon said, grinning.

"Two weeks," She leaned into him and planted a trail of kisses along his jawline and then his throat. He sighed as his lips collided with hers, and they both sank deeper into the other. He rolled her onto her side, pulling her leg over his hip, and ever so gently he slid inside her warmth again. The rocked together, building up to another electrifying moment, before sliding over the edge into erotic bliss.

Arms wrapped tightly around the other they lay still, absorbing each other's pulse rates for several minutes in silence.

"I missed you so much," her whisper broke the silence.

"And I, you, love. There wasn't a moment you weren't in my

thoughts. Not one. I'm so proud of you, baby. You were so strong." His hand brushed over her back.

Lilliana lay there, peacefully silent for a few minutes.

"Are you okay, darling?" She nodded contentedly against his chest.

He kissed her hair against the side of her face before sitting up, pulling her with him.

"We have so much to discuss, but I don't want to rush you. You have an evaluation with Richard and Hillary tomorrow." He saw a look of alarm darken her stunning features that only moments before, had looked peaceful. "I'll be with you darling, do not be afraid. I won't let Richard go hard on you." He cupped her chin to get a read on her eyes.

Lilliana nodded. "I understand, really I do. I just thought I'd have more time."

"It's protocol, sweetheart—the sooner it's done, the better, then you can slowly go about your routine and get back to normal."

She forced a smile. "Of course."

He kissed her before getting off the bed. "For now, how about a relaxing float in the tub, before your get together?"

Lilliana took Damon's extended hand. "Anything sounds perfect, as long as I'm with you."

***

The common room was full of merry makers wanting to catch up with both Fox and Lilliana and the chance to see Unit Eight up close and personal. The atmosphere was bright and bubbly and the conversations diverse as laughter spilled out across the room. Trays of canapés and champagne were shared amongst the crowd as waiters moved about busily, circulating the hors d'oeuvres.

Damon squeezed Lilliana's hand as they stood in the entrance way. "Are you ready, Baby?"

She smiled up at him, "As I'll ever be."

Damon led her in, and in no time, she was swamped by familiar, loving faces, all wanting to know how she was, and if there was anything they could do for her. Many wanted to know when she was going to resume her position as their therapist again, saying how much they'd missed her. She felt lucky enough to have had ten minutes with Allie, Josephine and Jessica and a lovely conversation with Johnson and Rachael, before being swept away by Rupert and Luke, who wanted to kiss and congratulate her on all her efforts.

Two hours after arriving, Lilliana was listening to Sophia, a very sassy blonde young lady who had once publicly urinated in one of their group sessions, justifying her actions by saying that 'Having to listen to everyone's, 'bullshit' was just like being in the toilet anyway.'

"Dr Richard just isn't *you*—and I swear to God, he has major issues, and if I have to hear him say the word, 'latrine' one more time…"

Lilliana had to suppress her laugh as she squeezed Sophia's shoulder.

"I'll be back very soon, Sophia, I promise. Don't worry about Dr Richard; I'm sure he did his best considering the workload of his own schedule."

"Thanks, Miss."

Lilliana watched her walk off, sighing quietly.

"So—happy to be back in the land of the tormented?" Eric said, coming up behind her.

She turned, smiling, "Oh Eric, it's good to see you." She reached up and hugged him hard. "And it is beyond good that we are all back. How are you?"

Eric nodded as he released her, grabbing two champagnes off a nearby tray, and, handing her one and clinking his glass to hers, took a mouthful before saying, "I'm doing okay. Had my evaluation this morning with Dr Spock and Clair. Interesting."

"What was?"

"My restraint not to rip out Richard's vocal cord after everything we've been through."

"Oh dear, was it *that* bad?"

"Well, when he made mention of me taking every opportunity to see you naked? Yeah, I got pissed." Eric referred to The Guardian's ever recording eye that captured the bathroom scene.

"He never makes things easy. I'm supposed to have my evaluation in the morning. Can't say I'm looking forward to it."

"Well, you can handle him, Doc, no doubt about that."

She smiled up at him as she finished her champagne. "We shall see."

"Speaking of seeing people, have you seen Nadia yet, heard what's happening with her?"

"No; I was hoping to see her tonight once I finish here."

"I just want to make sure she's comfortable, not locked up like an animal. She doesn't deserve to feel like a criminal after everything she's been through."

"Of course, Eric—I'm sure she is being treated very well. She'll be put through the same process we were when we first came. Don't worry, she'll be fine, Okay?" Eric nodded, looking over her head as Marcus and Fox approached.

"This conversation is looking a little too serious for a celebration get together," Fox said, putting her arm around Lilliana's shoulder. Eric and Marcus shared a knowing look. They'd all formed such a tight bond after working on this major operation.

"Unit Eight want to spend a bit of time with you Lilly, before they take their leave. Are you up for that?"

"Of course, lead the way." She was more than happy to give her thanks and say farewell to the Team that had worked so diligently and had spent so many of their months—some even years—focused on the case of taking Reid down, let alone doing their all to keep Lilliana safe. It may have been their day job, but their dedication impressed her no end.

Damon wandered around the room enjoying the lively conversations. Everyone was so elated to have their people back with them safely. He kept his eye on Lilliana throughout the afternoon, making sure she was okay, catching her eye and sharing a knowing look every now and again. She seemed to relax being surrounded by their friends and colleagues, along with some of the Given that Lilliana treated.

Watching her in conversation with Unit Eight filled Damon with pride, and he felt such respect for his beautiful wife. She never ceased to amaze him with her genuine interest in all those around her, no matter what she was feeling internally. He did dread her evaluation session with Richard the next day, as he too remembered how thorough and invasive Richard's questions had been for him when he had returned from five years undercover. He sighed.

"Are you alright, Sir?" Rachael asked as she and Johnson approached him.

"I am, it's just been emotionally exhausting."

"Understandably so," she sympathised.

Damon smiled gently at her, always thorough in her role as head nurse.

Johnson put his arm around Rachael. "You'll need a good sleep tonight Damon, we've got a massive day tomorrow."

"Don't I know it. After Lilliana's evaluation we have a team of Officials arriving for the first meeting. We've got decisions to make regarding the three Reid's, along with forty or so others taken from the raid. The Officials refused to end many of them on the night, which frustrates me to no end."

"I know, but if they say they can use them for intel regarding other leads, we'll listen. Give them a chance to plead their case. After that, we can make the decision ourselves to end them." Johnson checked his watch. "I've got to head upstairs before I call it a night. I'll see you at eight am, right?"

"You will. Goodnight." Damon smiled at Rachael as Johnson led her from the room at the same time feeling an arm slide around his waist. His heart welled with love as Lilliana stood on tiptoe and embraced him.

"Ready to call it a night?"

"I am. I'm about to fall asleep on my feet," she smiled. "It has been so wonderful seeing everyone, though."

"I'm glad, Baby; before we head up, I've got something for you. Come." He took her hand and led her from the room and down the wide corridor, past the dining rooms where many of the Given and staff were finishing up their meals for the night. They walked past the library and across the open foyer where two decadent, winding staircases led to the rooms above as they continued across to Damon's office. He opened the door and led her inside.

She looked about the space of the room, and almost cried at the joy of being back. She knew her emotions were close to overwhelming her, so she took a deep, steadying breath and watched as Damon walked over to his desk to grab something from his drawer.

"I remember my first group in this room as if it were yesterday," Lilliana mused.

He stopped in front of her and ran a finger under her chin. "As do I. What a journey we've been on since." He smiled, leaning in for a sweet kiss. "I've got something for you," Damon said and took her left hand, sliding her wedding ring back onto her finger.

Lilliana's face lit up as she stared at the stunning emerald sitting in its elegant setting. "Oh, I have missed this!" she smiled, beaming at him, offering her lips for another kiss.

"You've been so brave, my sweet girl."

"Not really," she shrugged. "We do what we must, for the people we love—don't we?" She wrapped her arms around his neck and dropped her head against his shoulder.

"We do, love. We do." His arms bound tightly around her waist and he breathed her in. He didn't know when the best time was to tell her of their sad news. She was exhausted already and had an early start with her evaluation. For the first time in a long time, Damon felt lost with what the right thing to do was.

"Damon. Tell me," Lilliana said, interrupting his thoughts.

"Tell you what?"

"Whatever it is that is causing you stress. I've seen it on your face since Fox asked you at assembly if I knew anything yet. Please," she leaned back so she could look up into his face. "Just rip the band aid off and tell me. I can handle it."

He sighed, running a hand up and down her back. "Tim is dead. Reid had him slaughtered before the main event."

Lilliana gasped, covering her checks with her hands as tears filled her eyes. "Oh, Damon, I thought the Team were protecting him."

"They were, darling, they did the best they could, but it was out of their control." Regret filled his voice.

"Oh no, Tim, poor Tim," She ended on a whisper, before sobs

overtook her. Once she started, she couldn't stop because every vile encounter she'd witnessed at the Reid compound came back to knock her over, flood her like a tsunami. Every shocking thing she'd done sent deep feelings of remorse through her core. She fell against Damon, sobbing as his arms wrapped round her, holding her tightly.

He swallowed the lump in his throat as her body shook. As devastated as he felt seeing her break down, he was glad at least she was finally releasing pent up emotions.

He held her until she was spent, kissing her hair all the while whispering, "I'm so sorry, my darling. So sorry."

He took her up to their room, washed away her tears and tucked her into bed, feeling guilty as he inserted the needle into the soft flesh of her arm, hearing her gasp quietly before the knockout serum did its work. He sighed and sat down on the bed beside her, tucking the blankets up to her chin before getting ready for bed himself.

CHAPTER 12

Lilliana stopped in front of the evaluation room situated in the Black Ops level and took a deep breath, raising her hand to knock on the door. Damon had left a note on her pillow before leaving for an earlier, unscheduled conference call with Russel Meek, apologising and promising to meet her there.

Taking a deep breath, she finally knocked on the door. It swung open to reveal Johnson, Dr Richard, Clair, and Damon already there, waiting. Her heart lifted at the sight of Damon as he walked over to her, greeting her with a sweeping kiss.

"How are you, sweetheart? Did you sleep alright?" He asked, his voice filled with concern.

"Yes, with help from my husband and his good intentions," she smiled, letting him know she wasn't upset that he had injected her without her permission.

He dropped his head close to her ear and whispered. "Sorry baby, I knew you were exhausted and devastated about Tim. I honestly just wanted to help."

"I know," she said, squeezing his hand before turning to her interrogators.

"Hello Richard, Clair." Lilliana hadn't seen either of them since her return. She offered Johnson a smile, which he gladly returned.

"It's nice to see you, Lilliana," Clair crossed over and shook her hand.

"You too Clair, I hope you've been well." She turned to Richard.

"How are you, Richard?"

Richard was sitting at the panel table, tablet at the ready. She could see a list of questions that looked a mile long. She remembered her first evaluation when she had come to the Given over a decade ago that had been held in Damon's hospital office. Surely she could handle anything Richard thought to throw at her now.

"I'm well, thank you."

Richard reached for a narrow container and took out an extracting syringe before crossing over to her. Peering down over horn-rimmed glasses, he held out his hand for her arm. "I am going to remove your tracking chip."

She nodded, offering her arm out for him to take and forced herself not to cringe at his cool touch as his long fingers wrapped around her wrist, turning her arm over to place the syringe close to where the chip had been inserted.

"This may hurt a little."

Lilliana sucked in her breath as he pushed the metal tip into her arm to extract the chip, forcing its way through her arm, towards the pull of the syringe. Removing the chip hurt more than it had going in.

"Done," Richard said simply, turning away to deposit it in a nearby bin.

"Thanks," Lilliana said rubbing her arm before walking over and sitting opposite the panel table. A monitor was set up to record the session, which she had fully expected. Damon, Clair, and Johnson took their seats beside Richard, and the session began.

"Lilliana," Johnson started, "We have an advantage here that may make this entire procedure more bearable for you, for the fact that we have witnessed all that happened and all that you endured, thanks to The Guardian's recordings. Let me also add that we are beyond grateful for everything you did so selflessly, and, thanks to you and the Team, we have detained and captured many of the wanted perpetrators that have slipped under the radar for years; to finally have these criminals in custody, to remove them from society, has been a more successful ending than we ever thought possible."

Lilliana nodded, crossing her legs and placing her hands in her lap, glad she had dressed in jeans, ballet slippers and a tee shirt. Comfort for an uncomfortable situation. "Thanks Johnson." Her eyes swept over them, stopping at Damon. He was sitting back in his seat with his arms folded, an uncertain look on his face. She knew he was nervous for her.

"Let's do this," she smiled back at Richard. "Fire away."

After two hours in, she wished she'd used a better phrase, as Richard seemed to take her literally. She expected the questioning to be uncomfortable, and at times, invasive; but once again, in typical Richard style, he seemed to enjoy her unease a little too much.

She ignored her discomfort and focused on answering the assault of questions honestly and thoroughly regarding what she had witnessed and experienced, holding her emotions in check. With each question, she was visually transported back to each horrid experience; she had to force herself to block out the images that threatened to melt her calm exterior as fury and sadness waited to engulf her.

Damon watched silently, wanting to comfort her, shield her from Richard's questions. When she looked his way, he prayed she could feel the love he was sending her.

Richard questioned her regarding how she felt Marcus and Eric had performed with Unit Eight, along with Nadia's trustworthiness. Lilliana couldn't praise Eric and Marcus's efforts highly enough and stated that she thought Nadia to be very trustworthy.

"What's your relationship with Eric?" Richard asked, tilting his head. "It seemed to be a very close one on many occasions?"

Lilliana knew that was coming. "I guess I'd want to feel close to the man who was protecting me with his life. Makes you realise what a great job he did, doesn't it?" She shot back, unblinking.

"What are your views on David Reid, regarding his future?" Clair asked.

"I know he came to us as a very fractured and unstable individual with an appalling criminal background, and if you asked me that question six months ago I would have said to eliminate him, no questions asked. But since then I believe he has proven his loyalty. The mission would not have been a success if it weren't for David Reid. There is no way we would have gotten that close to obtaining Gregory Reid, as well as all of his connections who have created God only knows how much chaos, debauchery and destruction over the past decades."

"Will you go against the Official Law and their verdict that David Reid does not deserve or earned the right to enter a Given facility?"

"I certainly don't want to go against the Officials in any way, but I will support David Reid and speak up for his case; I do believe he deserves the chance for entry into any Given facility, and I also believe that he may in fact benefit from what we have to offer. I think at times our laws need to be more flexible in certain cases."

"What about his sister, Felicia Reid?" Richard raised an eyebrow.

Felicia Reid; Damon's undercover wife. They had created a life together before Richard had made Lilliana assist him in aborting the baby. Lilliana swallowed and glanced at Damon, who stared silently back at her, eyes unblinking, fingers resting on his lips.

Lilliana looked away before answering. "No, she doesn't deserve a second chance."

"Is that personal?"

"It's my opinion." Lilliana shifted uncomfortably in her seat. Surely this would be over soon?

Richard continued taking notes on her every answer.

"Do you hold any resentment towards your Team or your husband for not extracting you sooner from Reid's clutches?" Richard used his middle finger to push his glasses up onto the bridge of his nose as he continued to stare at her.

"Resentment?"

"Yes, resentment."

"What, for doing their job? Hardly."

"I'm simply trying to ascertain if you have any pent-up anger towards the establishment for not only placing you in such a position, but for not rescuing you sooner, therefore eliminating some of the trauma you would have experienced."

"No one placed me in any position I didn't want to be in. I did what I did to protect our home and the people in it—and of course, Fox. The only person I feel resentment towards is Gregory Reid, but I believe he'll get what's coming to him, in due time." Damon looked across at his wife; he could hear frustration and fatigue in her voice.

"Damon and the Team extracted me at the right time to enable this mission to be the success that it was. Patience is the epitome of strength and time is the strongest of warriors. It takes fortitude to stand still in the face of your enemy; and I think it is a sign of weakness or cowardice, if you will, to move when you should not."

"Tolstoy—War and Peace," Johnson smiled.

Lilliana nodded. "If we'd moved too early, I honestly believe we would not have been so successful in our mission. Timing is everything."

"I think we are done here." Damon slid his chair back, nodding to the panel. "If you're satisfied, Johnson?"

"I am." Johnson stood.

"I still have a few other questions that need answering," Richard looked at Damon.

*Of course he does...*Lilliana sighed inwardly.

"No. We're done, I think we've covered everything of importance Richard." Damon moved around the table and reached for Lilliana. She gratefully took his warm, large hand as he pulled her to her feet.

"Lilliana," Clair stood. "You'll need to have therapy once a day for the next fortnight. An hour with Richard or Hillary, just to decompress. You've experienced a lot of trauma and some things may pop up and become difficult to handle, along with your workload."

"Hillary and I have already discussed this; my schedule is free to slot Lilliana in," Richard confirmed.

Great, Lilliana thought as she nodded in agreement.

"Any questions, Lilliana?" Johnson asked kindly.

"When can I resume my role?"

"Let's give you the fortnight to settle back in, take some time for yourself, along with therapy," Clair answered.

Lilliana nodded. "Is Nadia going to be released into Main House?"

Damon squeezed her fingers. "That's something Johnson and I will discuss in due course, darling. She is still undergoing evaluation."

"Can I see her?"

"You may," Damon said, smiling down at her, "Once Hillary and Richard feel it's the right time for Nadia." He watched as a small frown appeared. He would not see her unhappy.

"How does a ride sound?" Damon suggested, trying to sound upbeat.

"It sounds like paradise," she smiled up at him.

"Let's go then."

Damon led her from the room and down through the secluded passageways to their rooms to change for an hour-long ride before he had to return to business as usual.

***

The fortnight passed in a blur of activities, starting with an early morning run. Lilliana chose a different running group each morning, giving her the opportunity to connect with many of those she had missed in the past months.

Her run was followed by a horse ride with Damon before his day stole him away from her. His schedule was always full to the brim with his duties as Director, but given the extra meetings with the Officials and conference calls with other Given establishments around the globe, any spare time was stretched thin, so Lilliana felt blessed she had at least one solid hour with him during the day.

After her ride, she spent time watching Scott assisting Jessica in her art classes before visiting Rachael and Billy down in the hospital; then if time allowed, she'd sneak into her and Allie's office for an impromptu visit and say hello to anyone who was there at the time.

Lilliana was pleased to be invited to sit in on one relaxed staff meeting and be updated about the safe houses' success so far.

Eric waited for her by the front door every day after lunch to walk her to the horticultural department. It may have only been a twenty-minute walk, but they both enjoyed their time together, each checking in with the other, making sure they were both doing okay.

She then spent an hour or so with Josephine in the elaborate hot house, pulling weeds or potting plants, discussing life and laughing over the day-to-day gossip until they were hoarse. Cam walked her back for her therapy session, and they discussed future modelling assignments that would further benefit her safe houses that were supporting thousands already. Afterwards they both fell silent as their thoughts turned to Tim, which made them heartsick.

After therapy, Lilliana went up to visit Fox in HBR for a de-stress massage. Like her time with Eric, Lilliana enjoyed her session with Fox as it gave them both a chance to support the other.

Marcus collected her from HBR, giving himself a few moments with Fox. It lightened Lilliana's heart to see their relationship blossoming, especially after their horrific time with Reid.

Marcus would then walk Lilliana down to the library where Scott would wait for her, and together they'd have a leisurely one hour walk outside before Scott returned her to Damon's office in the late afternoon.

She was not oblivious to the support Damon had orchestrated around her day in order for her to feel protected and safe, and she loved him deeply for it. She could finally admit to herself how exhausted she was, feeling drained every afternoon due to keeping busy, recovering, and the biggest culprit; the nightmares that stole her solid sleep away, leaving her waking more tired than when she'd gone to bed the night before.

"I'll see you later, Sis," Scott saluted as he walked backwards, his Watcher, Finn, waiting for him by the foyer's large, decorative fishpond.

"See you," she smiled, thrilled that he had settled into a happy life here with them all.

"Hey Lilly," Orlando strolled up to her, hands in his pockets.

"Orlando, how are you?"

"Good. Damon is taking me down to visit with Nadia."

"How is she going? Did you tell her hello from me yesterday?"

"I did. She said she can't wait for the month's evaluation to be up so she can catch up with you and meet Jessica." He had a twinkle in his eye. "She certainly does ask a lot of questions about Eric."

Lilliana tried to hide her smile but couldn't. "Does big brother disapprove of a possible relationship?"

"Nah," he shook his head as the office door opened. "As long as she's happy."

Lilliana nodded as she turned to Damon, and her heartbeat quickened. Dressed in a black tee shirt and jeans that outlined every perfect muscle had her salivating. *My stars*, she thought. *He is all mine.* He caught her look and smiled, reaching for her hand.

"Orlando, just give me a moment will you—there's something I need to discuss with Lilliana before we head down."

It was Orlando's turn to hide a smile as he nodded. "Yes Sir, I'll just wait over there." He took off towards the hospital stairs as Damon tugged Lilliana into his office, shutting the door behind them. The look on his face was that of a hungry wolf wanting to devour his prey. Lilliana smiled softly as she wrapped her arms around his neck, pressing her body close to his.

"I've missed you," she whispered, loving the way his head slowly lowered to hers. She licked her lips in anticipation.

His eyes left hers, watching the top of her pink tongue and he placed his hands on her hips, drawing her in, moulding her to him, loving the feel of her soft curves as they pressed up against his hardness. Bringing his hand up behind her neck, he gently took a handful of her silky, long locks and tugged her head backwards, before swooping down, collecting her waiting lips in a deep kiss that left them both wanting more. Lilliana brushed her fingers through his hair, sighing contentedly as their kiss lingered. Both wishing they could take it further, but a knock at the door interrupted the fire that was igniting between them.

Damon let out a long sigh as he leaned his forehead against hers, running his hands up and down her back, frustrated. He moved in, claiming her lips softly again for one final kiss.

"Damon—" Cam's voice interrupted their moment from the other side of the door. Lilliana smiled up at Damon as he whispered a curse.

"What was that, Sir?" she chuckled.

"Never mind," he kissed her brow gently, before turning to open the door.

"Cameron," he raised an eyebrow in response to his brother's cheeky grin.

"Now I'm wishing I'd taken care of the incident in Black Ops myself, but your expertise is required, brother." He looked at Lilliana, "Sorry to interrupt, darling."

"That's okay, Damon was…" she didn't have a chance to make something creative up before Brett, Johnson's right-hand man, entered.

"Sir, we need you to come right now, Gregory Reid is creating a…a problem." Lilliana sensed Brett was being evasive about the situation.

Damon nodded, dropping a quick kiss against her pale cheek at the mention of Gregory's name.

"Cam, can you take Orlando down to see Nadia?"

"That's why I'm here."

"Sweetheart, I'll see you tonight."

Lilliana nodded.

"Lilly, Josephine and the girls are taking you on a picnic tea, to celebrate your fortnight's retreat ending, and before your workload resumes."

"Lovely," she watched as Damon disappeared with Brett.

Cam took her hand, kissing it. "It's all going to work out for the best, Sugar Plum." He smiled down at her, referring to Reid Senior.

"I know, I just can't wait for him to be no longer consuming our air."

"Agreed. But until then, off you go; Christopher said to hurry so that your goodies don't go cold. They're in the west wing garden." He took off quickly, collecting a patient Orlando, before disappearing down the hospital stairs, out of view.

Lilliana forced Gregory Reid from her mind and set off to the garden to her friends.

****

The picnic blanket was spread out under a waterfall of Jasmine, the scent perfuming the air around them as the stars began to twinkle in the darkening sky. Platters held an assortment of sandwich fillers, roasted vegetables, crumbed parmesan schnitzels and thinly baked focaccia breads had everyone eating in appreciative silence.

"Christopher, that was amazing, thank you." Lilliana nursed her third flower wine, a new concoction made by Rupert.

"You're welcome," he rubbed Allie's shoulder as the brisk air made her shiver. "I've got to head back in, finish service." He kissed Allie's check. "Leave all this; I'll send the crew in to clean up after you're all done."

"You are a champ, Christopher," Josephine said and reached for a strawberry. "Thank you for your service."

"Of course, Mrs Night," he grinned before getting to his feet. "See you all later."

Allie smiled as she watched him leave. "He is so hot."

Josephine laughed, "That's one way to sum up our multi-talented Christopher."

"He was amazing out there," Allie said, shaking her head. "Watching him, working alongside him, seeing how he and his Goth Kitchen Heads worked so hard feeding the community, supporting so many people. He impresses me always. I feel extremely lucky to have had that opportunity."

"And while you were at it, your advice and guidance in selecting the perfect staff for the safe houses was such an enormous benefit, Allie. The reports coming in so far have been incredibly rewarding. I can't thank you enough for all the work you did with Cam."

"I think you've done more than enough to say thank you to me, Lilly," Allie smiled gently at her friend, who had been looking tired since she'd returned.

"Are you ready to come back to work tomorrow, or do you need more time?"

Lilliana could detect the note of concern in her friend's voice and rushed to reassure her.

"I am more than ready to come back; I think it will actually help me feel more settled, fulfilling my role. Caring for our people again."

"Just don't overdo it, Lilly," Jessica reached for her hand. "If you need more time, take it."

"I'm fine sweetie, truly."

"How's Orlando getting along with Nadia?" Josephine asked Jessica.

"I have never seen him so happy; he absolutely raves about her. I can't wait till she enters Main House, although I am nervous to meet her."

"Don't be, Jess, she is going to love you."

"Lilliana," Fox called as she approached their group.

"Hey Foxy-Loxy," Josephine smiled. "Join us for Rupert's new concoction. Flower wine. It gives a nice, natural little buzz!"

"No thanks, Cam wants a quick chat with you Lilly, along with Natalie and I."

"Oh?" The one person Lilliana had happily not seen since her return a fortnight ago, was Natalie. Their relationship had never been an easy one, even from the very beginning in their first group therapy session together. For whatever reason, Natalie had always treated Lilliana like a nemesis.

"Don't worry, Sugar, I won't let Natalie put her claws in you. I've got your back, girl." Fox would destroy anyone who upset Lilliana in any way, shape of form, since her friend had gone through hell in order to protect her.

"What's it about?" Allie asked, getting to her feet and pulling Lilliana up with her.

"Just a chat regarding a commercial that's scheduled for the end of the month."

Lilliana nodded, reaching out a hand towards Jessica and Josephine to pull them up as well before heading inside, grateful for the hour of peace, and hoping Natalie would be on her best behaviour.

***

A fortnight later, despite the recurring nightmares, Lilliana was beginning to feel like herself again. Being back in her familiar routine of work, plus the comfort of being in her and Allie's healing space gave her all the care and support she needed. She was also able to assist others and offer her care, support, and advice to the new Given, and it helped her feel in control, feel useful again. It gave her a sense that all was right in the world. She had just finished her last session for the afternoon and was walking Eddie, who had manic depressive disorder, to the door when Eric walked in, looking frustrated.

"Thanks Lilliana, I'll see you next week," Eddie said leaving, looking shyly past Eric as he left. All the younger boys had always thought of Eric as formidable in his role as Watcher. But now, after seeing the Guardian's footage of him undercover, they were in even more awe. Lilliana smiled watching Eddie's checks turn pink as he flew out the room.

"What it must feel like to be a hero."

Eric shook his head, stuffing his hands into his jeans pockets.

"Hardly."

"You look like there's something on your mind?"

"Nadia entered Main House today and I was wondering if you'd seen her?"

"No, I haven't been out today, I've had back to back sessions, along with two groups. It's been flat out since I've been back, which has actually been great."

"Nightmares stopped?"

Lilliana shook her head, "They will, though, when they've run their course."

"Always the voice of reason." He smiled at her fondly.

Allie's glass partition slid open as her private session with Natalie ended. She winked at Lilliana as she walked Natalie to the door. Natalie stopped in front of Eric, looking him up and down. Lilliana cringed, praying she would just leave.

"I haven't had the chance to thank you properly," Natalie said, walking her greasy paws seductively up Eric's chest.

He grabbed her wrist gently, glaring down at her. "Thank me for what?" He dropped her wrist, stepping back.

"Well, for protecting our Lilliana, of course!" She drooled, smirking over her shoulder towards Lilliana. Lilliana thought she looked like she was about to add something crass, but thankfully they were interrupted as Cam walked in the room.

"Hello all, Lilliana, Eric, Damon would like to see you both in his office right now. Natalie, I do believe you're taking an afternoon class at the range? Marcus is waiting for you." He referred to the new group of Given, having their first archery session.

"Later," Natalie blew Eric a kiss as she sauntered out.

"Always not a pleasure," Eric mumbled as he turned and headed towards Damon's office, with Cam and Lilliana in tow.

"I'll see you later, Allie," Lilliana called over her shoulder as Allie waved, heading in the opposite direction to the psych ward.

Stepping into Damon's office several minutes later, Eric felt his pulse rate quicken as he spotted Nadia sitting opposite Damon. She looked sleek and delicate dressed in a white jumpsuit, her strawberry blonde hair sweeping the top of her smooth, creamy shoulders. He stood there as Lilliana and Cam walked in ahead of him.

"Hello Eric, darling." Damon got up and met Lilliana as she went to him for a kiss. He placed his arm around her shoulder, worrying over the tiredness in her eyes. Her dreams were not allowing either of them a good night sleep of late.

"How are you, sweetheart?" He asked quietly as Cam poured Eric a coffee.

"I'm great," she hugged him hard, dropping a quick kiss against his lips. Oh how she would have loved to linger on those lips. She smiled up into his eyes, before turning towards Nadia.

"So today was the big day." She crossed over and hugged her. "How was it?" Nadia hugged her back, and thanked Cam as he passed her a latte.

"Overwhelming, but exciting. After all those evaluations and never-ending questions, it's great to be out and to see you all again."

"I'm glad. How was your tour with Fox in the HBR?"

"Amazing! I've travelled the world and have seen some gorgeous spa retreats, but this is one of the most beautiful I have ever seen." Nadia smiled and turned to Damon. "I can't thank you enough, Mr Night, for allowing me to take on a role there."

"Of course, Nadia, and please call me Damon."

Nadia nodded, still feeling a little nervous around Lilliana's husband. He was the definition of a strong, beautiful man who held his position of power with great respect. Speaking of which, her eyes finally met Eric's, and it was her turn to swallow.

He stood there casually, sipping from his coffee cup and listening to Cam, his eyes fully on her.

"Over to you, Damon?" Cam sat on the arm of a chair, facing Eric and Nadia.

Lilliana sat on the chair beside Cam looking across at Damon, waiting to see why they'd been summoned. Not that she minded, every opportunity to be with him made her heart sing.

"As of now Eric, I need you to remain beside Nadia throughout her day. Obviously when she is working in the HBR, you can go about your day with Sam, who is needing less one-on-one time with you now."

Eric nodded. "Sam has come a long way the past eight months and he won't need a Watcher at all before long."

"Yes," Damon agreed, "the treatments and therapy along with his improved attitude have been wonderful to say the least."

Eric nodded, looking over at Nadia. "I'm presuming my role with Nadia will not be as a Watcher?"

"That's right. It will be as a Guardian. As most of our establishment saw the footage that took place at the compound, so many see Nadia now as the woman who was sleeping with the enemy," Damon said, looking at Nadia apologetically, before continuing. "We just want to make sure that, going forward, Nadia's transition to Main House is as smooth as possible."

Eric nodded. "Won't be a problem."

"I know—you have my complete trust in this assignment, Eric; I still haven't been able to thank you enough for protecting Lilliana the way you did, all those months you were away. Your dedication to our family has not been lost on me."

Eric smiled at Damon, before reaching over and knocking Lilliana's arm in a friendly gesture. "She wasn't too much trouble Sir...

when she was behaving herself, that is."

Lilliana shook her head, smiling at Nadia. "Feel free to give him hell for me."

Nadia looked at Eric, unsure how she felt about having to be by his side until Damon deemed it otherwise. One part of her was absolutely thrilled: the other part, terrified. How would she be able to keep her hands off him?

He looked down at her, before addressing Damon. "Where to now?"

Damon checked his watch, "Why don't you take Nadia for a stroll around the stables before dinner?" Eric nodded as Nadia got up, placing her empty cup on the tea trolley.

"Thank you so much Mr Night… Damon." She turned to Cam. "And for my tour today, Mr… Cam," She smiled.

Cam returned her smile as a knock sounded at the door and Josephine breezed in. "Hello, my loves," she wrapped her arms around Cam's waist, as he dropped a kiss into her hair.

"Have you come to collect me for our HD meeting?"

"I have, Rupert is waiting patiently. He is bouncing off the walls with excitement regarding the interview tomorrow."

"He should be, with his latest invention, the silver-lining. He is certainly the man of the hour. What this could mean for the drought afflicted regions around the globe will be phenomenal. He could be looking at a Nobel Prize."

Damon folded his arms, leaning back against his desk. "It's been an absolute pleasure watching him over the years. His passion about protecting and preserving nature has never waned."

Josephine nodded. "It warms the cockles of one's heart, doesn't it?" She tucked her hand in Cam's.

"Lilliana, make sure you get a good sleep tonight love, it's a big shoot tomorrow."

"Okay."

"I'm serious, Sugar Plum. Damon," he addressed his brother. "Make sure she sleeps."

"Yes Cameron." Damon didn't need his brother telling him what his wife needed. He may have to use the knock-out serum on her again tonight, as he had wanted to use on her for the past month, only she had refused.

He sighed quietly as Josephine pecked Lilliana on the check before waltzing out with Cam towards their meeting.

"Shall we?" Eric asked Nadia.

Nadia stood, smiling at Damon and Lilliana, then followed Eric out the door as Damon's phone rang.

He hit the glass panel, bringing up Johnson. "Is it time?"

"Yes, bring Lilliana."

Damon looked across at Lilliana before replying. "Is it really necessary?"

"I'm afraid so."

"We'll be there shortly."

Lilliana felt a flutter of unease in her belly as she watched Damon tap the screen closed, before slowly turning to face her.

"What is it?"

"Reid has a Bioweapon that is set to dispel a virus into the atmosphere in 24 hours. The disease will disperse, not to kill, but cause deformity and inflict the most agonising of pain. He usually resets the timer once a month, but since he has been under arrest..." Damon trailed off and Lilliana paled.

"Sorry darling, but he won't disclose the location of the weapon or the code to dismantle it to anyone, but you."

"What is it with the Reid men wanting to tell me things?" She grew worried and pushed long, silky strands of hair behind her ear as she looked at Damon.

He crossed to her and slipped his arms around her waist, rubbing one hand up and down her back, as her forehead dropped against his chest. She took a slow, deep breath, inhaling as much of him in as she could to calm her racing heart.

"Damon," she whispered.

"Yes, love?"

"I will speak to him and do whatever it is I have to. But then I want you to take me up to our room. I want to eat dinner with you, sit on our balcony with a glass of wine, and simply be alone." She tipped her head back so she could look into his eyes. "And then I want to take you to our bed and ravish you."

Damon's eyes glistened. "That will not be a problem my love." His lips slid over hers, promising her what was to come later after dealing with the grisly business of Reid.

CHAPTER 13

Nadia and Eric walked for an hour in comfortable silence. They'd just visited the stables, where Nadia had met Thomas and Edward. Thomas had filled her in regarding the running of the stables and assured her that, outside of her working hours at the HBR and any other activities Damon may have rostered on for her, she was more than welcome to come and spend time with the horses or go for a ride. She had been thrilled, and as they approached the trees leading into the forest, she told Eric what a friendly man Thomas had been.

"Yes, he's a good sort."

Nadia took a deep breath and held the air in her lungs before slowly releasing it. "It's so beautiful here," she whispered.

He watched her walk towards a low hanging swing and sit down, feet gently swaying her back and forth as her head rested against the thick rope.

"How old where you when you came here?"

"Seventeen."

"What did your life look like before all of this?" She watched as his eyes darkened.

He wandered over to a swing opposite her and sat. Apart from Lilliana and the group sessions of his youth, he had never really spoken to anyone about his time before he came to the Louisiana's Given. He really didn't want to start now.

"You're right," he answered instead. "It is beautiful here."

So, she thought; *he doesn't want to answer that question.* She'd come back to that. "It's so quiet, no cries from big cats." She looked as far as her eyes could see. Nothing but trees for miles.

"Do you miss it? Your jungle?"

She closed her eyes, tipping her head back to listen to the birds calling goodnight as twilight eased between the forest's branches. "No. It was a prison."

He was about to reply when a group walked through the trees towards them. He stood. Nadia noticed how watchful his eyes were, how ready and alert he was for anything untoward to occur. He was so impressive. It was Marcus and Natalie with the group of Given who had finished their archery session and were heading back to get ready for dinner.

"G'day Eric, Nadia," Marcus smiled, stopping in front of her.

"How'd you enjoy the tour today?"

"It was great, busy."

"It always is. The tour is a gentle indication of how busy the day-to-day running of this place is. Natalie, gang," he smiled at the younger Given. "This is Nadia. Some of you have Orlando as your Team Leader." A few of the youth nodded. "Well, this is Orlando's little sister, so make sure when you see her around to say hello." He smiled, before nodding to Eric. "Better head back. See you later."

"See you."

Natalie stood a moment longer looking at Nadia, before trailing behind Marcus and the class. Eric waited till they were out of his line of vision before sitting back on the swing, relaxing a little. Nadia stared at him, feeling restless. She had felt a sexual tension grow in the pit of her stomach since the moment she had laid eyes on him. He was an enigma wrapped up in a sexy scowl and she wanted to feel his hard body against hers again. She didn't know what the protocol should be here, but they were both adults and for the moment, they were completely alone.

He watched her watching him, and the fire that had been building since his return home began to flicker again as she stood and took a step towards him.

"You won't want to stay out too late tonight—you'll need a good sleep, like Marcus said, the routine is pretty hectic, especially in the first few weeks when you're getting used to things."

"I'm sure I'll be fine," she said softly as she stood before him. The darkening trees behind her gave her the look of a wood nymph, tiny and bright in her jumpsuit. She reached a hand towards his face and brushed his silky fringe out of eyes that darkened with lust.

"We should head back," he said, though his voice wasn't as firm as he would have liked.

She put her hands above his on the ropes of the swing, then slid one leg over his hip, then the other until she was straddling him, daring him to stop her, and quietly praying he wouldn't.

His breath caught as he felt the warmth of her core through her sheer jumpsuit. She sighed as she felt the swollen bulge in his jeans press hard against her pulsing warmth.

"Nadia," he warned quietly as her hands let go of the rope to slide around his shoulders. "We shouldn't, not now, not while I'm your Guardian."

Her eyes met his as she drew closer to his lips, whispering, "I'm as safe as I can be, this close to you." Her lips brushed his gently, back, and forth, begging him to kiss her back.

He did, hungrily; and she moaned as his lips parted hers, his tongue gently greeting hers, before she sucked on him, making him see stars.

His hands grabbed her hips as she began rocking against him, sliding her pulsating bud and wet core against his rock-hard shaft.

He kissed her deeply as he held her firmly down against him, and she continued sliding back and forth against him repeatedly, hoping she would come soon before he lost his mind.

Her fingers slid into the thickness of his hair and she angled herself as she ground down hard, rubbing against his bulge, feeling greedy, feeling hot. She couldn't stop herself.

He kissed her unlike any other man had ever kissed her, his tongue swirling with hers as she rubbed against him one last time, crying out in release against his lips.

He felt her sweet cries as she lay against his chest, breathing heavily. He kissed the top of her head, forcing himself to think of Natalie, hoping that would deflate his erection. It took time, but it worked. Nadia's voice came out muffled as she said something against his chest.

"Sorry, come again?"

She lifted her head to look at him, as a small smile played against her lips.

"Next time I will, with you."

"No, what I meant to say was 'sorry, I didn't catch what you said.'" He felt a deep flush creep up his neck, feeling very out of control, which was unlike him.

Her fingers played with his hair near his collar. "I said—I'm slightly mortified."

"There's no need to be, Nadia. I think it's fair to say that we've wanted each other since the first moment we laid eyes on each other."

"I know, but…" She didn't know how to put it all into words, the feelings she had for him. Feelings she had never experienced in her life. Nor had she ever had the opportunity to in a world that had moulded her to be someone else in a place where she never did fit, no matter how hard she tried to act the part, in order to survive.

No one would ever truly know, the pain and torment she had suffered at the hands of Gregory Reid.

Feeling safe in Eric's arms, she finally felt like she belonged somewhere, and she was thrilled that, after being introduced to so many people here, she would now be considered family.

It was all so overwhelming.

Nadia climbed off Eric's lap, turned, and ran off into the darkness of the trees.

Eric sat and cursed under his breath. He knew every inch of the property like the back of his hand and wasn't worried about losing her. But he was worried about her hurting herself, running off into the pitch-black forest like that. The stream that led to the lake wasn't deep, but if she fell into it, she could get injured.

He sighed, slipped off the swing and set off into a jog, heading in the direction she had left. After a few minutes, he arrived at a clearing, stopped, and, turning slowly in a circle, he listened to the forest speaking to him. He could hear a soft and quiet weeping interspersed between the calls of an owl.

"Nadia, please," he said quietly. "Just follow my voice. Let me get you back to the house for dinner." He waited a moment before continuing. "Everything is going to be alright, Nadia, I promise you."

Nadia rubbed her hands over her face and getting up, pushed off the tree trunk she had stumbled against. She knew without a doubt she could trust Eric. It wasn't really him she was worried about; it was just her jumble of emotions.

"I'm sorry," she said quietly, walking towards him in the clearing. "I… I am just honestly so overwhelmed. The feelings I have for you… on top of coming here… seeing Orlando after all these years, not wanting him to be disappointed in me… the thought of people hating me because of Gregory…" She shook her head, wringing her hands together.

He crossed to her, taking her hands in his and looked down at her sweet face, understanding how overwhelmed she must be.

"Nadia. I know it's a lot, you don't have to explain. But you do have to stay close to me. Please do not run off again, especially when you don't know where you are going. Deal?"

"Deal." She forced a smile, taking a steady breath.

Eric cupped her chin and leaned down to capture her lips in a soul shattering kiss that had them both ready to rip each other's clothes off, then and there. Eric quickly pulled back, holding her to him.

"Sorry," he muttered over the top of her head. "I think we both have to figure out some boundaries. I have never been so unprofessional. Mind you," he chuckled as he led her back through the tree towards the house, "I have only had the boys and Lilliana to watch over up until now."

"Well, I can see how this may be a challenge for us both, then."

He saw the smile crossing her lips, and tucking her arm through his he said, "I've always thrived on a good challenge." *God give me strength though,* he whispered to himself.

***

Lilliana stared at Gregory Reid, waiting for him to give her the location and code for the Bioweapon device so it could be automatically shut down. It pained her having to look upon the face of the man who had put her through pure hell. Damon and Johnson waited in the opposite room, watching through a one-way mirror.

"So, technically, you're not really my daughter in-law? Well, never mind; I shall always consider you mine."

"You can consider whatever you like. I've been told you want to give me a code and location to shut off your Bioweapon?"

"Yes, that is correct. Once I have it in official writing that both David and Felicia will remain here, under this establishment's protection."

Lilliana's eyes almost popped out of her head with yet another one of his ridiculous demands, but she nodded calmly to assuage the madman.

"Absolutely; we were pardoning David anyway, so I'm sure Mr Night will agree to it and get the Officials on board with the idea, just as soon as the code and location is handed over." How would he know she was lying? She'd promise him the moon to get what they needed. Once they had it, he'd be none the wiser and safely locked up here before his termination.

"No, I require the pardons for my children first before I give you what you need. And I suggest you hurry, because according to my calculations, you have less than twenty minutes."

"Just give me a moment," Lilliana said and walked out the door as Brett opened it for her. Damon was waiting outside, and he took her into the room with Johnson.

"What do we do?" Lilliana asked Johnson, who was just ending his call.

"Paul has been working with Clair since you all returned. His position with the Officials is high enough that he can wrangle up the documents to show Reid. He is on his way here now."

"What are your thoughts on honouring any document we sign?" Damon folded his arms, a concerned look on his face. There was no way in hell he was going to allow Felicia to walk around free as a bird with his people.

"Paul will answer that."

Just then Paul walked in carrying a clear glass tablet that had a call on waiting to the Officials Head Office.

"Hi—I came as quick as I could; how much time do we have?"

"Long enough we hope," Johnson answered.

"Right, my boss is waiting, I've apprised him of the situation." Paul tapped the screen and laid the tablet on the table as a hologram appeared before them all and Paul's boss, Mason, looked back at them.

"Hello all, I believe we have a decision to make. What are your thoughts, Mr Night?"

"There is no way in hell I want Felicia Reid walking around amongst my people, not after everything she has done. I can't agree to this." Deep down though, he knew he had to; he just didn't want to. He felt Lilliana's small hand rub his back as they all faced Mason, awaiting the Official Laws decision.

"I understand the position you are in Mr Night, but unfortunately this decision goes above even your great standing as director of your establishment. If we sign this contract—and it looks like we must— it will be up to Paul and yourself to honour it. Otherwise, serious consequences will ensue."

Lilliana was numb as she tried to digest what was being discussed; the possibility that Felicia Reid would be free to walk amongst them at the Given. It was inconceivable.

"Of course I will honour whatever order is handed down, Sir. But I will tell you right now, and this part is not up for debate—Felicia Reid will have an assigned Watcher on her, 24/7. She will not be allowed the luxuries that our Given are privileged to receive…" Damon would have continued, but Mason held up his hand, stopping him.

"Mr Night, I agree with you, but right now we don't have time to list off all the rules you'd like to put in place for this woman. The countdown is on; Paul, I'll send the contract through immediately, and I'll need yours, Mr Night's, and Mr Reid's signature's ASAP, so we can shut this thing down."

Paul nodded.

"Furthermore, Mr Night, we will need to have a discussion first thing tomorrow regarding another matter; but for now, let's get this done."

Damon was about to ask a question, but Mason interrupted.

"We'll be checking Miss Reid's progress monthly. Paul, you will continue your position with the Black Ops division and continue your interrogations with the remainder of the prisoners. Good work." Then he clicked off and the screen went black for a moment before an agreement document appeared, along with three thumb spaces for Paul's, Damon's, and Reid's scanned print signatures.

Paul stepped forward and pressed his thumb into the space provided before turning to Damon, who looked over at Johnson.

Johnson shook his head. "What choice do we have?"

Damon stepped forward and placed his thumb in the space provided, watching as his name and a photograph of himself appeared next to his print. He picked up the tablet and turned to his wife, who looked like she was about to be sick.

"Lilliana, are you alright to take this in for Reid's print?"

She nodded, taking the glass panel. "Of course."

Johnson followed her out of the room with a small disabling device for Reid to program his details in, in order to stop the countdown and shut off the Bioweapon.

Lilliana was quietly seething as she entered the room and seeing the pleased look on Gregory's face as she handed him the document to sign made her feel sick. She watched as he read over it before placing his print down, then he handed it back over to Lilliana as Johnson passed him the disabling device.

"Why should we trust that you won't spread another virus?"

"It's simple, really. In the past, when I have spread a virus, I have been able to inoculate myself and those I deem worthy before releasing chemical parasites into the world. Unfortunately, being your guest, this past month, has prevented me from taking my usual precautions." He began typing in a code and instructions as he spoke, his fingers moving hurriedly as the countdown loomed. Johnson folded his arms, feeling disgust for the man before him, but he wore a professionally calm expression, dedicated to his code of ethics.

"There, it's done—" Reid handed Johnson the device as the door opened and two guards entered to retrieve Gregory and return him to his cell.

He smiled at Lilliana as he was escorted past her. "Always a pleasure, Dear; I'll be seeing you soon."

"Not if I can help it," Lilliana mumbled under her breath as he disappeared from sight.

"Come on, let's get you out of here." Johnson indicated she walk ahead of him, before heading up to his office to call the Team out to the permanently disable the device at its location.

Lilliana saw Damon waiting for her. She stopped walking for a moment just to take him in. He was leaning against the wall, arms folded as a tired look overshadowed his gloriously handsome face. He listened as Brett filled him in on details that needed to be covered for tomorrow morning's meeting. He nodded, clapping Brett on the back as he finished.

"I'll see you then, Sir." Brett smiled before leaving to catch up to Johnson.

Damon turned; his eyes connected with Lilliana's as a small smile spread across his lips. "Ready?"

"Oh yes," she said held out her hand for him to take; he moved in to kiss her cheek, before walking hand in hand out of Black Ops and up to their rooms for some well-deserved quality time alone.

***

Damon woke to Lilliana crying and thrashing about under the covers before her cries turned into a blood curdling scream. He switched on the lights, calling them to dim as he sat up, and reached over to stroke his wife's face. As soon as his hand touched her damp cheek, Lilliana bolted upright, swiping his hand away, yelling, "Don't touch me!"

She backed away from him, breathing heavily as she pushed herself up against the oak headboard, not seeing who was in front of her.

Damon reached for a tee shirt and pulling it on, quietly assured her.

"Lilliana, it's Damon."

Lilliana rubbed her hands over her face, pushing her hair back over her shoulders and forced herself to steady her breath.

"I'm sorry, Damon; I'm so sorry," she whispered, her eyes meeting his as he passed her a glass of water and stroked her face.

"Don't, Baby. Don't apologise to me. You've been to hell and back."

"I just need these nightmares to stop, for both our sakes. I'm so sorry; I don't think I've given you one peaceful night's sleep since I've been back."

Damon pulled her into his arms, dropping his chin on top of her silky head. "We need to do something to change that, Baby, and soon. I can't handle seeing you so devastated. I think you might want to start those hypnotherapy sessions that Richard suggested."

"You're right, I've just been so busy and, well, stubborn I guess," she said and rubbed her face against his chest. "I'll talk to Richard tomorrow after the commercial shoot, I promise."

"I'm going to hold you to that," Damon dropped a kiss on her head as he got up and disappeared into the lounge.

Lilliana slid down under the warm blankets, tucking them up to her chin, when Damon returned, holding a small syringe.

"Is that what I think it is?" She asked, referring to the knock-out serum.

"Just a small dose, sweetheart. It will give you a few decent hours of solid sleep."

Lilliana smiled up at him. "I love you, Damon Night."

"And I love you. Now, sleep." He injected the serum into her arm, watching her beautiful green eyes flutter shut until she was asleep.

He sat there watching over her, thinking of the conversations they had had regarding Felicia, her release, and what it would mean. They were both concerned about the of impacts having her in their lives again; but, in the end, as always, they came together as a team to support each other with whatever was going to happen, going forward.

If there was one thing the past decade had taught them it was that, if they had each other's love and trust, they could face any challenge and survive.

CHAPTER 14

The assignment for the commercial was done in two parts. Both were to be filmed in the HBR. The client was a world class company unlike any other of its kind, and had partnered up with Rupert and his scientists, to develop the next level organic, herbal rejuvenation creams called 'New Beginnings.'

The first shoot was to film Fox dressed in a sheer black dress that flowed about her ankles as she walked barefoot through the HBR's lavish rooms. All the windows and doors to the balconies were open allowing the sunlight to spill in in abundance, the breeze catching the long, sheer drapes, creating a sultry feel as they danced into the room, swirling romantically.

Fox looked like a goddess as she held up a black, glass vial containing the product, whispering into the camera, "New Beginnings," before approaching Natalie, who mirrored Fox in the same dress, but in white. Natalie was sitting comfortably in one of their chairs, the product on her face while holding a white glass vial and looking serenely into the camera as she whispered, "New Beginnings," before the director yelled, "Cut."

"Great job—just beautiful," Pier called out. "Next frame, I want

Lilliana entering from the balcony." He nodded to Cam before turning to address the producer.

Fox had been a little stiff for the first half hour of filming, but between Cam and the producer's wit, they had her laughing in between takes. Tim's absence was felt throughout the room and Lilliana was gearing herself up to be as professional as possible while Valerie dusted glitter powder across her eye lids.

"It's perfect, isn't it dear?" Valerie said quietly in her sing-song voice, before brushing Lilliana's lips with clear gloss. "The name of this product after everything you endured."

"Mmm." Lilliana responded.

The fact that the main event had been broadcast into the Underworld, then hacked and shared on mainstream media for all the world to see, had been the first reason the company wanted to shoot on the Given's land.

Having the world's beloved Dark Angel as their campaign face was divinely perfect after all Lilliana had endured and survived, branding it, 'New Beginnings.' And partnering with the talented Rupert and his team had simply been a bonus.

"Valerie, are we all set love?" Cam called out as he walked through the doorway, smiling when he spotted Lilliana looking breathtaking in a sheer emerald dress. "Always a pleasure, Valerie," he greeted her as Valerie collected her equipment and smiled, leaving the wide balcony.

"Gorgeous girl, how are you feeling? Ready?"

Lilliana took a deep breath, nodding.

"I hope so." She took the emerald glass vial he handed her. "Thanks."

"Welcome, darling." He tapped the end of her nose with a fingertip, making her laugh.

"Oh Cam, don't you ever change." She kissed his cheek.

"What's that for?"

"Just remembering my first shoot with you and Tim."

They stared silently at each other for a moment, each deep in thought remembering Tim, missing him. Cam took her hands gently in his.

"You were, and have always been, such a great friend to me, Cam. I'm so grateful to have you in my life."

"Ditto, gorgeous," Cam's smile faded. "Are you going to be alright Lilly, with that Felicia coming into Main House?"

"You don't need to worry about me; I'm more concerned about how Damon and Nadia are going to handle having her in our home."

"Damon is going to be fine, sweetie. I think you are right to be concerned about Nadia, though. It's just as well Eric is her Guardian at the moment."

"I agree, I just wish…" but Lilliana didn't have a chance to finish because the producer, Dean, began calling out.

"You're up, Mrs Night!"

"Just call her Lilliana, thanks Dean," Cam called, as he stepped into the room. "You've got the brief, now do your thing and sparkle." He winked at Lilliana before disappearing out of the camera's range.

She closed her eyes as they cued the music, taking a deep breath for four counts, holding for seven then releasing, then she stepped into the room smiling, holding the vial up, doing what she had to do to make the product shine perfectly, in one take.

It was done and dusted in five minutes, followed by a half hour photo shoot of stills to be used for their marketing campaign. Just as they were finishing up, Damon came in, accompanied by Nadia and Eric.

"Good to see you, Damon," Dean shook Damon's hand enthusiastically. "Did you review the proposal for Beast's set of commercials?"

"Yes, I signed the contract yesterday." Damon smiled and turned towards Nadia. "I wanted to introduce you to a new member of our family, Nadia."

When Dean laid eyes on Nadia they lit up like sparklers as did most men when they saw her for the first time.

"Nice to meet you, Nadia; if I'd known you were here I would have commissioned you to be a part of this shoot too. You're simply beautiful."

Nadia shook Dean's hand, blushing. Not that she wasn't used to such compliments, it was just that she didn't want them from anyone other than Eric.

"Nice to meet you."

Damon crossed to Lilliana and kissed her softly, not wanting to smudge her dark emerald lipstick that had been used for the photo shoot. She smiled up at him, taking his hand and squeezing it in joy at seeing him.

"Once you finish your session with Richard this afternoon, would you be up for the meeting we have scheduled?" Damon was referring to the meeting where Felicia and David Reid were to be introduced to their set house rules and notified of all expectations.

Lilliana nodded, "Yes, I definitely will be there."

Fox smiled at Damon with black lips. "You want me at this meeting too, Sir?"

"I would—thank you Fox."

"Great. Nadia, I'll just get out of this gear then we'll set up for our next round of clients. We have several of our nursing staff booked in for massages and facials."

Nadia smiled enthusiastically, loving the feeling of being part of Fox's team. "Wonderful, I'll set up."

Fox waved a hand in appreciation as she disappeared into a side room to get changed, and Cam thanked the crew who had gathered up their equipment, ready to say goodbye to everyone.

Natalie stood back watching the conversations unfold around her. She wiped the white lipstick off with a cloth as she listened, intrigued about the Reid's coming into Main House. *Things were certainly going to get interesting around here,* she mused to herself

"You want me to walk you down, Natalie?" Lilliana asked her.

"Nope. Later all." She waved her hand as she left, Cam calling out behind her, "Good job Natalie."

"Yep," came her muffled response as she disappeared downstairs.

"Eric, can you bring Orlando and Nadia to my office a half hour before the meeting starts," Damon asked, rubbing Lilliana's arm.

"Yes Sir," Eric nodded, before situating himself near the doorway, watching Nadia set up.

Lilliana looked up at Damon as he said, "I hope your session with Richard goes smoothly, darling." He brushed a kiss over her cheek.

"I'm sure it will. I'll see you afterwards," she smiled before walking past Eric, lightly punching him in the arm as she set off to get changed for her session with Richard, praying it would not be as uncomfortable as she envisioned.

***

Richard closed the hour session with a mindfulness activity on gratitude; it was an exercise where Lilliana had to list five things that gave her life meaning and happiness at the present time. The only hard thing, she told him, was having to list only five.

"And that's what makes it powerful. If you can list even one a day, then you truly have much to be thankful for. As you know, we deal with many individuals that can't find anything to be thankful for."

"Yes, I know. It breaks my heart for them," Lilliana stood. "Thanks for today."

"I hope it begins to assist you in eliminating your nightmares." He stood, looking over his glasses at her. "I think twice a week would be good for you to see me, especially now. Having the Reid's present in our home may trigger more trauma."

Lilliana nodded. "Okay. Are you coming to the meeting downstairs?"

"Yes. As I attended to Felicia from day one, Damon thought it necessary I be included."

"Makes sense."

"Lilliana, I…" he paused, which Lilliana thought was very unlike him, and he cleared his throat.

She felt mildly uncomfortable. With Richard, one could never quite guess what would come next.

"I just wanted to say, despite my… *our* differences over the years, I am very proud of the way you have handled yourself, both while you were away, and since you've returned."

Lilliana was slightly gob smacked at his open compliment. He was right about one thing; they had had many differences of opinion over the years.

"Thank you Richard."

He nodded.

"I better head down. I'll see you there," Lilliana said and quickly left the room. *Like a mixed bag of lollies*, she thought. *You never know what you might get from one day to the next in this place.*

Lilliana headed for Damon's office to see Scott talking to a clearly shaken looking Orlando. When Scott spotted his sister, he patted Orlando on the back and walked across to hug her. "Hey Sis."

She squeezed him back, "How are you?"

Scott nodded. "Good. Although the same can't be said for my friend here. Do you know about the bullshit that's going on in this place?" He exploded. "The Reid's are coming in like they've done nothing wrong—I mean, what the hell, Lilly!"

"Scott, please calm down."

She squeezed her brother's arm, before turning towards Orlando.

"Orlando, are you okay?"

"How can a woman that has done so much wrong, be allowed to live in our home? A woman that Nadia told me made her life hell. It doesn't make any sense whatsoever!" Orlando was visibly frustrated.

"Did Damon and Johnson explain everything to you, the reason why?"

"Yeah, of course they did. I know all about the contract with Gregory Reid. And I have just been informed that we are basically going to have to kiss his ass from now on, as he may have more Bioweapons tucked away that could go off. I mean, seriously Lilly. This isn't the way we run things here."

She felt for him and understood his exasperation.

"I know, I know—it's a lot to take in, but it's out of our hands at the moment, Orlando. We just have to be patient, do what we must for things to transition smoothly, especially for Nadia."

He ran his hand through his hair and concern for his sister filled his eyes.

Lilliana worried, wondering if this were possibly the worst idea ever, and hoped Jessica would be able to calm him down. *Speak of the Angel,* she thought as Jessica walked through the front entrance with a group of Given and crossing over to them, her pretty smile instantly turning into a frown when she saw Orlando's body language.

Her heartbeat uncomfortably. "Orlando?" she ran a hand along his arm, which was now folded tightly across his chest.

He looked down at her, shaking his head. "I'm okay, Jess," he said, even though clearly he was not.

Jessica looked at Lilliana who reached for her to give her a hug. "Everything will be okay, Jessica. I think a nice walk will do him the world of good. Get him away from all the noise for a while."

"I need to be here for Nadia when this meeting is over." Orlando went to sit, but not before Jessica took his hands and tugged him towards her.

"No you don't. We have got two free hours, and I need to show you how the healing centre is coming along. It's almost finished, and Rachael wants our input on the new arts centre. Scott, do you want to come?"

"Sure." He agreed.

"I'm sure Nadia will come and find you when it's all over, Orlando. Don't worry, Eric and I won't leave her side, I promise."

Orlando nodded, before saying quietly, "Thanks, Lilly." He turned his gaze to Jessica's pretty face, running a finger along her check. "You and the healing centre now have my undivided attention."

She brushed her lips across his. "Let's go then. Come on, Scott."

Scott waved to Lilliana as he followed the others out the front entrance.

Lilliana sighed, rubbing the throb that was beginning to beat at her temple. She hadn't even stepped a foot inside the room, yet she felt the negative energy pervading the space. She took a deep breath and walked into Damon's office.

"Sorry I'm late," her eyes met Damon's, and she froze momentarily. Her husband looked like a predator, ready to leap and rip out his prey's throat. He stood by the fireplace, arms folded, his back ramrod straight; he resembled an imposing figure, as he faced the group seated in the room.

Lilliana knew the dangerous glint in Damon's eyes were not

directed at her, but this didn't make her any less nervous. She was unsure where to sit, what to do and was relieved when Richard walked in behind her.

"Excuse me for being a little late," he said walking by Lilliana to sit on the edge of the group beside Nadia. Eric stood behind her with David seated to her right, and an empty seat beside him, near Josephine and Cam. Fox and Marcus were seated beside Felicia, with Rocco behind her. Lilliana presumed Rocco was here to play the role as Felicia's Watcher.

"Lilliana, please take a seat." Damon gestured to the empty chair between David and Josephine. Lilliana sat, and Josephine bumped shoulders with her in greeting.

"Good to see you again, darling…er, Lilliana," David quickly corrected, as Fox glared across the room at him.

"David." She said quietly.

Nadia offered her a nervous smile which she returned, hoping to calm her new friend. Johnson quickly walked in the room, giving his apologies as he stood beside Damon.

"Now that everyone is here, let me make one thing crystal clear." Damon's voice held a note of frost, as he looked from David to Felicia. "You have both been gifted with a position here in our home, as the result of a threat made by your father. You are not, in any way to be considered a Given—nor will you receive any benefits as such. You will address all with respect, and cause harm to none. You will be assigned a role now, in which you can start giving back to our community."

Fox held up her hand. Damon nodded.

"Does Romeo still have a bomb in his head?"

"Yes." Johnson responded.

"I'm feeling slightly offended here," David interjected. "If it weren't for me, I don't think we would all be in this position in the first place."

"Makes you wonder if that wasn't your plan all along." Fox folded her arms, throwing David a nasty look.

"You can't hardly think this was all orchestrated, surely?" David scoffed, looking to Lilliana for back up. "Darl…er, Lilliana, a little help please?"

Lilliana shifted uncomfortably in her seat while looking across at Damon.

She could feel the daggers look that Felicia was sending her way and hoped this meeting would be a quick one.

"It's kinda 'bullshit…'" Fox didn't get a chance to finish as Damon cut in.

"Enough, please," He pinched the bridge of his nose, eyes closing briefly, before placing his hands on his hips.

"David; we are grateful to you for the part you played in helping us to obtain your father. But you are intelligent enough to know that we are not just going to allow you to walk around free as a bird, without taking the necessary precautions."

David nodded, pleased that at least he was considered intelligent in this scenario. "I understand completely."

"Good." Damon reluctantly turned towards Felicia. It pained him to have to address her at all.

All eyes shifted to Felicia as Damon spoke quietly.

"Yes, contracts have been signed to allow you some freedoms among my people. But be warned. If you step out of line, disrespect anyone, cause any disruption to the way I run things here, then despite anything I have signed, punishment will be dealt. Richard."

Richard cleared his throat before addressing Felicia. "I have permission to treat you in accordance with the Official contract which includes shock treatment, and an array of other physical treatments I discussed with you earlier today."

"Treatments?" Felicia spoke in a whiny, nasal tone, her skinny pale arms folded across her chest. "Don't you mean torture?"

Johnson and Damon exchanged looks.

"If you follow the rules then I will not have to treat you in any way, other than a polite conversation twice a week."

Lilliana appreciated, possibly for the first time, the arrogant look Richard cast Felicia over the top of his horn-rimmed glasses.

"Sir," Rocco said assertively. "I will not allow Ms Reid to create any disturbance whilst she is under my watch."

Marcus smiled proudly.

"Yes, thank you Rocco, that is why you were suggested for this role."

Lilliana could see the exhaustion on Damon's face and felt guilty knowing that for the past month she had partly been the cause of it.

"Cam." Damon motioned to his brother.

"Righto, roles. David, you are going to work alongside the horticultural team that grows the stock feed and prepares the soil for rotation crops, along with fencing detail. It's good, outdoor work that I consider the best kind of therapy."

"Sounds fabulous, actually." David nodded enthusiastically towards Cam. "Thank you."

Cam turned towards Felicia. "You will be working in the laundry four days a week, and for the other two you will be in the textile department."

"Washing other people's clothes... and making them? Seriously? With one day off?"

"I'd be grateful if I were you, sister." David raised an eyebrow.

"All good for you to say; I've been stuck in a cell for almost a year!"

"You're lucky it wasn't longer, or permanent darkness." Damon said, dangerously quiet.

"Oh honey, don't be like that." Felicia said coyly, before bending at the waist, clutching her head. "STOP, STOP!" She screamed.

"Rocco, thank you, that's enough." Damon signalled.

Lilliana watched as Rocco released a button on the side of his intricate looking wristwatch that triggered a pain point in Felicia's chip that had already been inserted inside of her head.

"I am so impressed," Josephine whispered, giggling to Lilliana. "I want a go."

Lilliana hid her smile as Cam patted Josephine's knee lovingly, hinting at her to be quiet.

"Does anyone have any questions?" Johnson looked at everyone waiting.

"Why doesn't he have a Watcher?" Fox nodded towards David.

"He doesn't require one." Damon answered, his tone final.

"Okay then." Fox sat back, folding her arms.

"I want to know when I'll have the chance to spend some quality time alone with my brother and sister?" Felicia inclined her head towards Nadia, who paled at Felicia's attentions.

"No thanks." She replied stonily. "I am no sister of yours."

"I beg your pardon?"

"She said, no. End of discussion" Eric replied, wishing he could zap her himself.

"You are to stay away from Nadia. You will not speak to her unless she addresses you first. The same applies to my wife." Damon folded his arms.

Felicia's eyes rested on Lilliana. She bit her tongue halting her hateful response. Her head was still throbbing after the brutal pain Rocco had just inflicted via the implant. "Sure thing."

"Right, that will be all for the moment." Damon nodded. "Thanks Rocco."

"No worries, Sir." Rocco motioned for Felicia to walk ahead of him as Johnson followed.

"I'll escort you down to the laundry, we have a staff member waiting to instruct you to your duties."

Richard stood and left, along with Fox and Marcus. A team member from the HD knocked at the door.

"I'm here for David Reid."

"Thanks Simon." Damon said and indicated to David.

David stood and walked towards Simon. "Thank you, Mr Night."

Damon silently watched David leave, before addressing Nadia.

"Are you alright?" he asked kindly.

"I am, thank you."

"You are in the best hands now." Damon nodded to Eric.

"Thanks, Sir. Lilliana, I'll see you at my session tomorrow."

"You sure will. Nadia, Orlando is pretty concerned about you; he and Jessica went for a walk, but I did promise him you'd find him when you were done here."

"Okay." She looked at Eric.

"Where to?" Eric asked Lilliana.

"The new healing centre."

"Let's go then." He smiled.

Josephine let out a sigh as the room cleared, leaving the four of them alone. "Jesus, Joseph and Mary. Was that insane or what?"

"Slightly insane love." Cam agreed, looping his arm around her shoulder.

Damon crossed to Lilliana, and, reaching for her hands, pulled her to her feet and up into his arms.

She sighed against his chest, wrapping her arms about his waist, as he kissed the top of her silky head.

"You okay, love?"

"Stop worrying if everyone else is okay, Damon." She tilted her head back to look up into his eyes. "We are all going to be fine, because we have you."

"Oh, perfectly spoken, angel." Cam winked at Damon. "Brother bear is our hero."

"Yes, but even heroes need us to take care of them sometimes." Lilliana kissed Damon's chin. "Don't they?" she whispered, concern in her voice.

He smiled down at her, feeling such love. "And you always do, sweetheart."

"I think we all need a night up at the cabin. Wouldn't you agree?" Josephine looked at Damon. "Imagine; the fire roaring, nothing but trees to fill our view, no interruptions, good wine, scrumptious nibbles and great conversation in the most relaxing atmosphere."

Cam nodded. "Sounds fabulous, actually."

"I couldn't agree more." Damon kissed Lilliana; his phone started to ring, and he crossed to his desk, calling over his shoulder. "You organise it, Jose, love, and I will be there."

"Done, Lilly. Let's go do this." Josephine took Lilliana's hand and they left, waving at Damon as they left to go and organise a well-deserved break.

CHAPTER 15

Lilliana sat, laughing with the others, feeling the most relaxed she had in a long time. It was their second night at the cabin, and they had invited Fox, Marcus, Allie, Christopher, Nadia, Eric, Orlando, Jessica, and Scott to join them earlier that afternoon, to spend a night with them. They were a few bottles of wine in, apart from Scott and Josephine, who were enjoying Rupert's non-alcoholic flower wine. The food was delicious, and although it wasn't cold, the fire roared, casting dancing shadows across the room.

The wide, glass doors had been rolled open, allowing the forest to wrap its arms around them. Fox and Cam were relaying a story about a Tantrum Fox had had over a decade ago, before most of the group had arrived in their home. Between the two of them retelling their own version of how the scenario had played out, everyone was laughing at the hilarity of their story.

Lilliana sat on the floor nestled between Damon's long legs as he ran his fingers through her hair; they were both content in that moment, after having spent a peaceful night together.

Damon had heard the story before and was pleasantly lost in his thoughts as he reflected on the night before, making love to Lilliana.

They'd shared a pleasant afternoon together, walking, swimming in the lake, relaxing by the fire with Cam and Josephine, covering many topics before sharing a scrumptious meal they had all made together. Josephine's spaghetti bolognaise. Then each couple had gone to their private section of the cabin, for a romantic spa bath before they turned in for the night.

Lilliana had slept like a baby after they'd made love for hours, talking and laughing in between. Damon left her to sleep in late, slipping out in the early hours to head back to Main House for a conference call and meeting with several of the hospital staff.

A group of new Given were due to arrive, but Richard had assured him he would take care of them, which Damon was grateful for as it enabled him to get back to Lilliana.

Before heading back, he left an invitation for the others to join them that afternoon, if their schedules allowed for it. They had all made sure their shifts were covered to make the afternoon together possible. As the laughter died down, a comfortable silence settled over the room, and glasses were topped up and plates of sandwiches were shared.

"I think we should all share some juicy stories from our earlier days together," Allie said, raising her glass towards Eric, then Lilliana. "I mean, you two wren't the best of friends for a very long time."

"I can't imagine why that was, can you, Eric?" Lilliana smirked.

Damon laughed quietly. "I do recall wanting to wrap my hands around Eric's throat at one time or another."

Eric shrugged, "What can I say, I thought I was charming."

Nadia was intrigued as everyone laughed around her, as they remembered the cocky young man Eric had been when he had first joined them in group therapy.

Christopher shook his head smiling. "Man, you weren't the one I was worried about."

Orlando laughed.

"Oh God, please do not reenact her!" Allie referred to what the others were thinking; the first time they had all met in their first group therapy session, along with Natalie grinding into her chair, pretending she was riding Damon.

Jessica's checks flushed as her eyes met Damon's, causing everyone in the room to burst out laughing once more.

"Please, no Natalie stories tonight," Lilliana begged, rubbing Damon's calf muscle through his jeans.

"Agreed," Orlando wrapped his arms around Jessica, pulling her onto his lap, kissing her head.

"Nadia, I've heard from several of the nursing staff that you have the hands of a goddess. I think I need to book in with you," Josephine said.

"Oh, that's so lovely to hear. Would you like a massage now?"

"No, gorgeous," Fox interjected. You are off the clock. We highly value self-care here, and this is time for you to relax and unwind."

"Thanks, though." Josephine smiled.

"You were always the kindest soul," Orlando affectionately reached across and ruffled his sister's hair.

Nadia beamed at Orlando.

"You know what's interesting," Allie commented. "I think we have the highest number of actual siblings in our establishment."

"I for one, feel like the luckiest brother around to have been sent here." Scott saluted Lilliana with his punch, who returned his smile.

"Rocco coming in makes five." Marcus nodded.

"Six," Damon took a mouthful of wine. "We had the twins arrive, and they joined Main House this morning."

"They are adorable," Jessica smiled. "They're in our group," she announced proudly.

"On that note," Cam said, as he got up to add another log to the fire, "We have recently been approached by United, which, as some of you may know, is the world's leading magazine that reports on all things Given, to run a feature on all of our siblings. They'll be rapt we have a set of twins in the mix."

"All?" Lilliana asked, her fingers reaching for Damon's.

"Yep. All."

"Could be fun." Orlando looked at Nadia.

"*Will* be fun," Scott enthused. "My first photo shoot with my Sis!"

"And an interview which will touch on your journey before coming to us, along with your story since settling into life here." Cam sat back down, putting his arm around Josephine.

Orlando and Lilliana exchanged a look, before Lilliana asked. "How much detail are we expected to go in?"

Damon leaned forward and wrapped his arms around her before quietly whispering into her ear, "They have been notified what they are permitted to discuss with you. You can cover your work here, your passions, your safe houses and of course, meeting Scott for the first time, and having him in your life now."

She turned to look up at him, her heart skipping a beat. His beautiful face was inches from hers, filled with concern and love. She smiled. "Thank you."

He brushed his lips across hers, making butterflies dance in the pit of her stomach, as images of all he did to her the night before, beat behind her closed eyelids.

"Well, I think we need to call it a night." Josephine knew Lilliana would thank her in the morning.

"When are United coming, Cam?" Orlando stood, pulling Jessica up with him.

"Three weeks. They will be doing a group photo shoot, and yes, this will include the Reid's." He looked apologetically at Nadia.

"It would make sense, the magazine wanting the story of two of the most infamous siblings now housed at the Given. It doesn't even sound real when I say it." Fox shook her head, throwing the contents of her wine down her throat.

"And the proceeds from this particular article and shoot will be going towards two extremely important charities."

"Well, that's always a bonus." Allie took Christopher's hand. "I think a spa before bed is in order for us. Goodnight everyone."

The six couples, plus Scott, bid each other farewell, before tucking themselves away for a long night of romance and rest.

✳✳✳

"This has been just what the doctor ordered," Lilliana whispered against Damon's chest as they lay beneath the warm covers. His fingers were gently running up and down her back, sending shivers of delight over every inch of her skin.

"It has," he agreed. "I'll make sure to thank Richard tomorrow."

Lilliana laughed. "Not quite what I meant."

He chuckled, knowingly.

"Damon?"

"Hmm." His voice was sleepy, deep, and sexy. They'd made love over an hour ago and had snuck downstairs for another bottle of wine, then had been discussing the twins and several new arrivals. They briefly touched on the topic of Felicia and Gregory and were pleased they could have a chuckle regarding David's progress and attitude, before happily changing the conversation to discuss themselves.

"Can we do this more often, you, me, and our friends?"

He reached up to stroke the length of her hair. Soft, silky. It tickled his skin seductively as she moved to sit astride him, running her fingertips lightly over his sculpted abs.

He sucked in a breath as her warm, moist centre rubbed against his thighs. He immediately went rock hard.

"Yes," he managed to get out before she leaned down to nibble on his lips.

Her fingers lightly ran up and down his sides as she took her time kissing him, loving the feel of his swollen shaft nestled against her buttocks.

His fingers circled her waist as he adjusted her, placing her throbbing core gently against him, waiting for her to take her time, as he kissed her thoroughly.

She sighed against his lips as he caressed her breasts, gently rubbing her nipples, causing a flood of pulsing juices to flow as she felt a wave of desire throb against her bud. She moved against him, then, loving the moan that escaped Damon's lips as his tongue mated with hers; she sucked on him gently before lowering herself, taking his thick, engorged shaft all the way into her tight centre.

"Absolute paradise," he whispered against her lips as she rocked against him.

"Mmm," she murmured, her eyes clouding over as delightful

sensations stole her thoughts.

His hands gripped her waist as she sat up, flinging her head back. Her hair brushed against the top of his thighs as she arched back, looking like a sexy goddess rocking back and forth against him, sliding up and down, pulling him into a sexy haze as he felt close to exploding with every shift of her lush body, her nipples beckoning to be sucked.

He sat upright and reached one arm around her back as she rocked sensually against him, the other cupping a heavy breast as his lips sucked in the plump nipple, causing her to cry out as her core throbbed. She reached for his head, fingers sweeping into his thick, silky hair, pulling his lips away from her swollen nipple, to her lips. He ravished her mouth, gripping her hips as she thrust against him a final time, as together they released into a powerful orgasm that left them speechless and breathing heavily, as they continued kissing, arms bound lovingly around the other.

"Luckiest man alive," he murmured appreciatively.

She kissed his check, then the other before finding his lips. "Luckiest girl alive."

They fell back into the sheets tucking the blankets around them and fell into a deep sleep, cradled in each other's arms in pure contentment. They weren't the only ones who woke the following morning with spirits high, wearing grins like Cheshire cats.

***

Four days later, Allie and Lilliana were finishing up with their last group session for the afternoon, before a private one on one with Eric and Natalie.

"I've got a question," Sophia sat forward in her chair.

"Fire away." Allie smiled. She had always liked Sophia's spunk. Even when she attempted to disrupt the flow of group therapy when they were on a boring topic. She stirred conversations that got the others in the group thinking about more than just the here and now.

"If I wanted to go to, say, the Australian Given, you know, the new one they are building in Glenormiston South—what do I need to do?"

"Right, like you just get to decide where you want to go overseas, and Mr Night is going to click his fingers and make that happen," Josh, a fairly recent addition to their group, scoffed. "Get real."

"No, it's a fair question, thank you Josh." Allie nodded to Sophia, before continuing. "As more Given establishments are built and set up there is going to be an exchange program where students and workers can experience life at another Given, and where the individual's skills can be matched to, and can benefit that establishment."

"That sounds so cool." Sophia nodded. "But hasn't that program already been around for a while?"

"No," Lilliana answered. "Not so long ago there was a recruitment replacement program that had been operating for decades where Given were forced to leave their home and be repositioned permanently in a foreign Given. It made a lot of people extremely unhappy, and, as you can imagine, an unhappy soul doesn't perform to the best of their ability in any situation. Fortunately, Mr Night and other like-minded directors put an end to that system of rotating Given against their will."

"So can anyone apply for the exchange initiative?" Annabelle asked.

"Yes; once interested applicants meet the required criteria, and after serving at any Given establishment for a minimum of two years, they can send in a request to Mr Night. After several interviews with the directors of your present and future Given, if you are successful, all will be set for your transition."

"I love it here, though; I could never imagine going to another Given," Fee said shyly.

"And we love having you," Lilliana returned her smile.

"Okay you gorgeous animals," Allie stood, clapping her hands. "I believe you all have training for the upcoming Ultimate Given Games."

"When are teams being selected, Ms Allie?"

"Next week, so train hard and give them all a good go."

"Thanks Ms Allie, see you, Ms Lilliana."

"See you. Good work today." Lilliana followed them to the door as Allie went to make a coffee.

As the room emptied Lilliana turned to Allie, who was pouring her a tea, and passed it to her. "Thanks."

"How do you think Josh is doing?"

"I think he is actually doing amazingly well considering what he has been through and the short amount of time he has been with us."

"Mostly I agree—but did you hear him tell James there should be a rodeo section in the games so that he could hogtie Sammy and drag her behind his horse?"

Lilliana shook her head. "That sounds like cruel and unusual punishment. He's just testing the waters, seeing who he can impress."

"Yep… we've known a few of those in our time."

"Speaking of," Lilliana said quietly as Natalie walked into the room for her session with Allie, Eric five steps behind her. He politely knocked on the door as he walked in.

"Eric, what two events are you hoping to participate in?" Allie asked keenly.

"Running and swimming."

"How dull," Natalie sniggered.

Eric raised an eyebrow. One day she was all over him, the next, she was typical nasty Natalie.

"What about you, Natalie?" Lilliana asked over the top of her teacup.

Natalie stared at her, making Lilliana wish she hadn't bothered asking.

Allie hid her smile. It was always entertaining watching these two interact.

"What are you interested in?" Lilliana tried again after a few moments of awkward silence.

"I'm interested in knocking you out... and go fuck yourself." Natalie sneered, before walking into Allie's closed room, screaming out, "It's all Bullshit!"

Eric, Allie, and Lilliana looked at each other.

"Alright then," Allie grinned. "Not to worry, I'll go see what's wrong with Natalie."

"You'd be the first." Lilliana mumbled.

Eric chuckled, "Bloody hell." He shook his head and motioned for Lilliana to walk ahead of him into her private room.

"Coffee?"

"Thanks."

"What's Nadia up to?" She poured him a coffee and put it on the desk as she sat.

"She's got a meeting with Rupert and Josephine. Something about certain blends of herbal hair dyes and conditioners." He shrugged, grateful that his appointment with Lilliana coincided with Nadia's meeting, allowing him to skip all the ins and outs about herbs and all the other stuff that got Rupert excited. "You know, girl stuff, no offence to Rupert."

Lilliana laughed. "I don't think anything could offend Rupert."

Eric nodded in agreement. "Nadia fell in love with him as soon as he started talking about organic lotions for this and that." Eric took a mouthful of coffee.

"Speaking of love?"

Eric sighed, leaning back into the comfortable chair, looking down into his coffee cup and went silent.

Lilliana waited, wondering if Eric would steer the conversation where he needed it to go.

"She asked about my time before I came here," he started quietly, finally looking up at her.

"That's natural. When we care for someone, we want to know all sides of their story. It's sharing our stories that can bring us closer together, help us understand the other person."

"My story is like a thousand other stories, Lilly; it doesn't define me."

"Your story is your own, and what defines you is the strong, caring, supportive man you are today. Sharing your story with Nadia will only strengthen the bond you have."

Eric shook his head, placing his cup on the desk. He sat back, folding his arms. "Why does she need to know what my mother did to me? Why would telling her about the men who had their way with me from the age of five until the day I came here, do anything other than disgust her?"

"Eric, I know you now know that none of what happened to you in the past is anything to be ashamed of. Please tell me you know that?"

"Yeah, alright. I know. But Lilly—all these years I've dealt with what happened and I had just put it behind me; but now, with Nadia? I don't know. She's got into my head, stirring up memories I don't want to think about, bringing it all to the surface. It hurts." He finished, sounding frustrated.

"I know, I understand. And me telling you this is a good thing will probably only annoy you."

He smiled a little, "Yeah, definitely."

She grinned. "Sorry, but it's true."

"This thing. Nadia, it's all so unexpected." He ran his hands over his face. "I have fallen for her. Hard. I can't imagine her not being in my life. It's insane. I met her less than five months ago." He sighed.

"Yes, but five months under those circumstances, and after everything you have been through together can feel like a lifetime."

Eric nodded, agreeing with her.

Lilliana wondered what was going through his mind and she wasn't expecting what would pass from his lips next.

"I'm going to ask her to marry me."

Lilliana was speechless for a moment, as happiness filled her heart for her friend.

His eyes met hers and he was slightly shocked to see them fill with tears.

"Oh shit," he reached across the desk for her hand, and took it. "They are happy tears, right?"

Lilliana shook her head laughing as one slipped down her cheek. "Oh my God, yes—of course they are!" She squeezed his hand and, letting it go, walked around the side of the desk as he stood, throwing her arms around him. "This is such wonderful news!"

He chuckled as he hugged her back before they drew apart. "I wanted to talk to Damon about getting a ring for her, and Christopher and Orlando are the only others that know. I kind of felt I had to ask Orlando's permission. When the time comes Christopher is going to organise a romantic picnic so I can propose."

Lilliana leaned against her desk. "It sounds perfect, I'm so happy for you."

"But I'm guessing you want me to disclose all my deep, dark troubles first?"

"Only you can decide when that time is right for you. But, if it's sooner, rather than later, you can get it all out of the way and focus on the good times ahead, building a gorgeous life with Nadia."

He nodded. "Yeah, I'll suss things out. Just need to think a bit more on the matter. But thanks Doc." He grinned.

Lilliana shook her head. "It's all in a day's work."

He checked his watch. "I better head off; Nadia will be finished soon."

"Keep me posted on all the excitement will you?"

"You'll be one of the first to know when the big proposal takes place. Hey, do you know when the couples' residence is going to be built?"

"I know Damon wanted to get the healing centre and the additional wing finished before they started on the next build. I think it should be within the next three months?"

Eric nodded as he walked to the door, "Great." He spotted Natalie coming out of Allie's room and quickly headed out, calling, "Thanks Lilly, see you."

"Bye." She stepped right out of the way, to hopefully prevent Natalie from saying anything, and was surprised when she stopped in front of her, saying quietly. "Sorry about before."

It took Lilliana a couple of seconds to react before saying, "No worries, thanks."

Natalie looked over her shoulder at Allie. "See you later."

"Sure thing. Stay out of trouble."

Natalie nodded and left the room.

"I don't know about you, but I am done for the day. You?" Allie stretched her arms above her head.

"No, I've got a session with Richard."

"Oh joy," she winked. "Well, I'm off to go and get a blue rinse." She ran her fingers through her long blue locks that needed touching up at the roots.

"I'll see you at dinner."

"Be Zen my friend, see you then."

Lilliana chuckled as they walked separate ways, looking forward to getting this next hour with Richard over with.

***

Lilliana walked into the dining hall two hours later, her mouth, watering as the aromas of freshly baked bread and pumpkin soup wrapped around her.

She spotted Scott waving frantically to an empty seat beside him, and looking down at the head of the table, saw Damon smiling at Scott. She walked towards her brother, eyes on Damon, watching his smile fade as he looked at her. She frowned, puzzled as to why he would be frowning, when suddenly a body slammed against hers, almost toppling her over.

"Sorry Ms Lilliana," a breathless boy panted. He was fairly new and didn't attend any of Lillian's groups.

"That's okay."

"No running in the dining hall, Jacob!" Cam yelled from his seat.

"Sorry Sir." He dropped his head and walked slowly to where his friends were saving him a seat. Lilliana smiled, taking her seat beside Scott as she shook her head at Damon, who was now looking more relaxed.

"This looks delicious," Lilliana reached for a spoon and a bowl of sour cream, adding a healthy dollop before reaching for the chilli salt to sprinkle on top.

"You know, it's Greek night in the third dining hall, and my God, the scent of those souvlaki's!" Scott moaned, closing his eyes and stuffing a piece of buttery garlic bread into his mouth.

Lilliana laughed. "Maybe you can sneak out of here once you've finished your soup and go beg Cook for an extra snack."

"Oh, I wouldn't dare. Christopher took me into the kitchen once. That man terrified me. Nope. I can wait for the next Greek night to roll around and make sure I've put my name down."

Lilliana smiled, tucking into her soup and absorbing the happy noise around her of quiet chatter, the clinking of cutlery and relaxing music playing quietly from the p.a. system.

Her eyes drifted from one face to the next, checking on the newer Given and making sure they seemed comfortable and taken care of. Allie and Jessica waved to her from two dining tables over. She blew them a kiss before finishing off her dinner, while Scott continued talking nonstop throughout the meal about what he hoped to participate in, in the Ultimate Given Games.

"Of course, I am a pretty decent swimmer, and I know I can earn a good score for my team—but I really hope I make it into the archery team and the escape house."

"Escape house?" Why hadn't she heard of that one?

"Yeah, I heard your friend Leon telling Eric about it. It's the psych team's contribution to the games… something about mind muscle?"

"It sounds intriguing." Lilliana couldn't wait to check that one out.

"What's that?" Damon's velvety voice brushed over her as he placed his hands on her shoulders.

Lilliana turned to smile up at him. "Apparently we have mind games as well as physical games happening in the Ultimate Given Games."

"But of course—the escape house. Are you up for a night stroll?"

"Absolutely. Scott," she leaned over and kissed his check before getting up. "Thanks for saving me a seat. Have a good night."

"You too Lilly. Goodnight, Mr Night."

"Goodnight Scott." Damon took Lilliana's hand and they walked out of the dining room, calling out goodnight to those who waved. Once they hit the front door, they walked down the steps towards the stables, Lilliana tucking herself under Damon's arm.

"You alright my love?" He kissed the top of her head as they strolled under the moonlight. "How was your day?"

"Always interesting," Lilliana laughed. "There's never a dull moment around here. Ever."

"I had a visit from Eric while you had your appointment with Richard." He smiled down at her. "He told me he spoke to you about his decision to propose to Nadia."

"Oh Damon, I'm so happy for him... for them both." They drew closer to the stables; a figure was standing in the doorway.

"Good evening Sir, Ms Lilliana," Thomas called out.

"Hello Thomas, are you calling it a night?"

"Yes, I was just heading up now. Goodnight."

"Night," they called after him as he headed to his upstairs apartment above the stables. Damon drew Lilliana further into the stables until they reached the end stalls that housed Beauty and Beast. Lilliana stroked her palomino's soft snout, cooing gently to her before turning to see Damon watching her, his hand rubbing Beast's neck affectionately.

She smiled at him and leaned back against the stall's wall as Beauty nuzzled at her neck.

"I need to discuss something important with you, Lilliana."

"Oh?"

He nodded, remaining silent for several moments.

"What is it, love?" She was only marginally worried about his silence, and knew that, whatever it was, he'd get it off his chest when he was ready.

"It's concerning children."

"Yes."

"Our children."

"Oh." She wasn't sure where he was going with this. She had been sterilised when she'd arrived here. Had he forgotten? There would never be any 'our children'.

Damon could see she was looking confused and knew he was going about this the wrong way. He walked over to her and held her hands.

"Sorry sweetheart, come." He led her up the stairs to the above loft, the opposite end of Thomas's apartments. He remembered the last time he had been up here with her. The day he had left to go undercover. He let go of her hand and she crossed over to the window seat to look out over the property, the moon casting shadows of trees and slumbering cattle and sheep in the distance. She took a deep breath, turning and waiting to hear what Damon had to say. He sat on a bale of hay, watching her.

"Please Damon," she smiled. "You're making me nervous. Just say it."

"I want us to have a child—together. To create our own little family where they can grow up happy, loved and protected. Where we can raise them to be the most caring, nurturing, giving little beings." As he spoke, Lilliana's heart melted. His voice held such passion.

"Oh Damon, I would give anything in this world to have a child with you, but have you forgotten, my darling? I was sterilised when I came here. I'm so sorry." Her heart broke as she crossed over to him, and she put her arms around his shoulders, letting his face drop against her chest. Damon's arms wrapped around her waist, and he held her tightly, pulling her onto his lap.

"There was something Gregory Reid said to you when you were at his compound."

"I'm trying to forget most of what he said at all."

"Maybe, but there is one thing he said that started a conversation between Dr Ryan, Rachael and me."

"And that conversation was?"

"A reverse sterilisation procedure."

A spark of hope ignited inside Lilliana. The thought of having a beautiful little dark-haired boy with Damon's blue eyes, set a flicker of excitement within her.

"Damon," she whispered. "Is it truly possible?" Her eyes grew misty at the thought.

"It is, my darling." He kissed her softly and ran his hand down her back.

She laughed against his lips and sprang up from his lap, whirling about in glee. "Seriously, our own baby? Oh Damon, I didn't think I even wanted—no, needed that—but now, with the possibility being so real, I *do* want it, a baby of our own, oh my!"

Damon loved seeing her so happy and excited; it lifted his own heart. He smiled. "Well, we can have a chat with Rachael tomorrow. Once the procedure is done, your body will need time to recover and it will take twelve months to resume a normal cycle, but it's the first step." He stood and held out his hand, which she gladly took.

"I feel like I'm walking on air," she whispered as they walked down the stairs and headed out of the stables back towards Main House.

He raised her hand to his lips and brushed a kiss over her hand. "I'm glad, Baby; you deserve every kind of happiness."

"Damon, I'm gathering you want this as much as I do?"

"More darling," he smiled down at her. "Or at least equally as much. You have no idea. The thought of seeing you in bloom, carrying our child." He shook his head. "You are going to be magnificent."

"Can I talk to Josephine about this, Allie, Jessica?"

"Sweetheart, of course."

Lilliana dropped her head against his shoulder as they walked down the rose lined path, both blissfully happy with thoughts of a beautiful dark-haired baby.

CHAPTER 16

The United crew were rather a serious lot. Very business-like, straight to the point, wanting to get in and out and get the job done to perfection.

It was unlike any other photo shoot Lilliana had experienced, but she enjoyed it all the same. The separate interviews had been intense, but when they had time together in front of the camera the banter between her and Scott had been light and fun and had created the space for a warm and entertaining interview.

Lilliana, Scott and the twins, Karen and Kiera had been asked to wear white.

Damon, Cam, Rocco, and Marcus had all worn black. Both their interviews were filled with accounts of their roles both in and outside life at the Given. The interviewer engaged in easy conversations with both sets of brothers, creating an interesting dialogue the audience would relish.

Nadia, Orlando, David, and Felicia had worn royal blue, and both their interviews were interwoven, revealing the tragic tale of their past and the web in which they now found themselves tangled in, but together again, after all this time.

David and Felicia's interview was interesting to say the least and would no doubt cause a stir when it was released into the world.

It was the group photo shoot where nerves became most strained, and tensions were high. As much as Nadia and Lilliana didn't want to be near Felicia, they really didn't want the twins anywhere near her. Luckily, Damon had some input into the placements for the shoot, and the line-up was impressive.

Taken out in the east paddock, Rocco, Marcus, Damon, Cam, Nadia, and Orlando sat along the thick wooden railing with Felicia standing in front of Rocco. David stood beside Felicia who was in front of Marcus. Lilliana was beside David in front of Damon, with Scott, Karen, and Kiera in front of Orlando.

All were placed a safe enough distance from Felicia, who had her Watcher right behind her. It would all be mentioned in the article, how ironic some of these couplings were.

Josephine, Eric, and Jessica watched on from a respectful distance as the photographer did close ups, sibling shots and shots of the overall group.

"Beautiful day for it." David said to Lilliana as the photographer was discussing possible wardrobe changes with the producer.

"Yes, it is." She could feel Damon's knees pressed against her shoulder blades and enjoyed having him so close.

"How are you enjoying the physical outdoor work?"

"I could not be happier; seriously, I am so rapt with my position. The team is brilliant." David had a genuine smile plastered across his face which made Lilliana happy for him.

"I'm glad."

Felicia was furious listening in on their easy conversation. She wanted to do something to wipe the look off Lilliana's face.

She turned, looking up at Damon and smiled, cat-like. "They really should do an interview on *us*, our past and now—don't you think that would be entertaining?"

Everyone fell silent around them, waiting.

"No." Damon replied curtly, not even bothering to look at her.

"I think it should definitely be considered though," Felicia said, raising an eyebrow, pushing the subject.

Rocco sat on the fence, ready for Felicia to step out of line.

"Not in this lifetime," Damon ran a hand over his face as Cam gave him a brotherly nudge with his shoulder.

"Mr Producer," Felicia sang out, turning to Rocco. "I dare you to zap me while the world looks on. I wonder what they'd make of your Royal Director then?"

"Are you serious?" Cam scoffed. "The world knows you are only in this position because of your evil, disease-spreading, Bioweapon-plotting, miserable father." He almost looked apologetically at David but continued. "Open your mouth again and I'll tell Rocco to zap you right now."

Lilliana looked across at Nadia and was pleased to see Orlando had his arm protectively around her shoulder as they sat on the fence together.

Damon rubbed her neck and Lilliana reached back to close her fingers around his. Scott seemed oblivious to any of the tension around him as his focus was on the very pretty Karen beside him. They were quietly discussing the possible dilemmas of the escape house for the upcoming games.

Lilliana could see by the way Scott was focused so keenly on the conversation; he was trying to impress the attractive girl. It warmed her heart.

"Okay, we've got plenty of shots. We're wondering if we can do some candid footage Mr Night, maybe shoot Lilliana in her therapist role? Maybe have Scott doing some artwork, as well as shooting Nadia in the HBR? Of course, we would be thrilled to get some footage of you and Mr Night too," he indicated to Cam. "In the main office or attending your Given duties?"

"That shouldn't be a problem," Damon nodded. He couldn't really say no. This was a great opportunity to share their day-to-day lives with the outside world.

"Can we also film Felicia performing her duties in the laundry? I think it would be beneficial for society to see her at a lackluster role."

"Agreed." Cam slid off the fence, almost taking Scott down with him, causing laughter to erupt from the group—everyone minus Felicia who was mortified at the thought of being filmed doing laundry duties.

Eric stepped forward and reached his hands around Nadia's waist, easing her gently to the ground.

"Thanks," she looked up into his brooding eyes, wanting to kiss him then and there.

"Alright girls," Orlando smiled. "Let's get you back to class."

Jessica walked over. "Was that fun?"

"It was," Keira nodded as Karen was still talking to Scott.

"Excuse me, Scott," Jessica said, politely butting in. "I need to get Karen back to class now."

"Sure Ms Jessica, sorry."

"It's alright." She smiled.

"Will I see you this afternoon at training?" Karen asked as she walked backwards following her Team Leaders.

"You sure will." Scott sighed, as Karen turned around and jogged to catch up with her sister.

Lilliana shook her head and chuckled as Damon's arm slid around her waist. "Are you ready for your next shoot?"

"I guess. This was unexpected."

"Yes, but it should be quick enough. You've got time to change; they're going to do Felicia first. After they do you, they're going to follow Cam and I around for the rest of the afternoon."

Lilliana nodded. "Well, that gives me an opportunity to get the girls together. Do you mind if I have a little gathering in our rooms?"

"Of course not sweetheart." She smiled, leaning up for a kiss, which the photographer happily, quietly snapped.

"This may be a great opportunity for you to tell the girls about your meeting with Rachael and Dr Ryan?"

"I believe so, love."

He dropped another kiss against her lips. "I'll see you later. Enjoy."

"Go dazzle the world." She smiled as he walked off to resume his afternoon duties.

Running upstairs to change, Lilliana felt excited to have extra time with her friends, and the thought of sharing her news with them sent a charge of energy through her. She was more than ready to spend an hour in front of the camera and share the important work they did behind the scenes with the rest of the world.

***

"Well my friends, I have something to share with you." Allie stood, tapping her nail against her glass. She walked over and stood under Damon and Lilliana's wedding portrait. Looking up at it, she felt a bubble of excitement well inside her chest as she contemplated her big announcement.

"We can hardly wait." Josephine had something to share herself and couldn't believe the timing of all the girls being able to get together this afternoon.

Allie turned and faced the three women she considered her sisters.

"Christopher and I are signing up for the exchange program in Australia!" She cried enthusiastically.

The room fell silent. None of the three were expecting that, and all their expectant cheers anticipating a possible wedding announcement sat deflated inside them as the moment fizzled into nothingness.

"You're leaving?" Lilliana could barely whisper. The thought of Allie being gone from her everyday life filled her with utter sadness. Not having her in their groups where she always lit up the room with her support, advice, and best of all her humour and sarcastic comments was almost too much to bear.

"Oh Allie." Jessica too, was lost for words.

Josephine stood. "Please, explain?"

Allie looked at their faces and tried to hold her laughter in a moment longer, but she couldn't. She bent over at the waist, laughing her head off, tears spilling down her face. "God, I'm sorry! I am so evil! Totally kidding, Christopher proposed, I said yes, and here we are."

It took the others a few moments for the shock to wear off before laughter filled the room. Lilliana shook her head as Josephine tackled Allie backwards, body slamming her against the couch.

Jessica shook her head, meeting Lilliana's gaze; both were feeling so grateful that Allie wasn't leaving them.

"Bloody Hell!" Allie laughed and Lilliana pulled her up after Josephine got off her. "I simply didn't want to give you a boring wedding announcement."

"And that is why we love you and couldn't imagine life without you! My God, Allie," Lilliana reached for the champagne to top up their glasses. "I thought you were leaving me to partner up with Richard." She let out a nervous laugh.

"As if I ever would." Allie winked.

"You are too cruel." Jessica wiped the tears from her eyes as her laughter settled. Thanking Lilliana for her refill, she sat back, raising her glass. "Congratulations to you and Christopher."

"I don't know if I want to congratulate you or kick you," Josephine smirked. "But congratulations."

"I'll take it all," Allie raised her glass. "To my friends, my sisters, thank you." Allie took a mouthful of bubbly. She looked at each of them, feeling slightly guilty for putting them through a mini emotional roller coaster. She raised her glass again to each of them. "I'd also like to take this opportunity to thank each and every one of you for adding sparkle and shine to my life, close to eleven years now. I'd be lost without you all."

"Oh now you've gone and done it." Josephine grinned, putting her arm around Jessica's shoulders as she began to cry.

"Sorry," Jessica smiled through her tears. "Big day, with a lot going on."

Josephine finished her champagne, thinking she might save her news for another time as emotions were already high. Plus, she didn't want to take the shine away from Allie's announcement. Maybe she'd wait until she was alone with Lilliana.

"Have you picked a season?" Jessica asked.

"No, we only just spoke to Damon last night."

Damon sure had been busy regarding wedding proposals, Lilliana thought.

"Well, enough about me; Jessica, what's happened today?"

Jessica put her glass down and tucked her legs under her as she sat on the rug. "Orlando is not in a good headspace with the fact that Felicia gets to walk around in Nadia's space. The stories Nadia has shared with him from her years with the Reid's, has him seeing red."

"You certainly can't blame him," Lilliana took a sip of champagne.

"Even the short time I was with Gregory…" she glanced at Allie, not wanting to dampen the mood of Allie's sparkly news.

"Go on Lilly, it's fine, really." Allie nodded.

Lilliana sighed, "Being in his world, the way he views it, and then watching him deal his absurd sense of 'justice' on people, and encouraging thousands of others to do the same…" She shook her head. "He thinks it is to make the world 'a better place,'… but he's just so sick."

The girls nodded in agreement.

"His ideas of population control, ridding the world of those he sees as worthless," she shrugged. "I get why Orlando is annoyed. Having Gregory here in custody, and Felicia walking amongst us because of his threats—that we can't ignore due to his past record, is beyond irritating."

"She has made a friend in the laundry and none of you will be surprised who it is."

"If you say Natalie, I will be so disappointed." Josephine cringed, waiting.

"Bingo."

"It's hardly surprising though, is it?" Lilliana held out her glass for Jessica to top it up.

"You know what pisses me off about Natalie?" Allie said, thanking Jessica for the pour.

"Um—is that a trick question, do you only want us to give you one answer?" Lilliana raised an eyebrow.

"Funny. No. She has been with us from day one and none of us have given her a single reason to be a nasty bitch to any of us. Okay, I know she is polite to me, but she kind of has to be, being her therapist and all… but the rest of you?"

"She's nice to Fox." Jessica added.

"Sometimes." Allie shrugged.

"It's in her nature to be unpleasant. Remember what she said to me when she tried to frame Allie for Sapphire's attempted murder?" Lilliana was referring to the hunting accident where Allie had been in some deep water with Damon and Cam's cousin.

"She said, and I quote, 'It's more fun this way.'" Lilliana shrugged.

"Being nasty gives her joy, fulfilment. We are all made differently."

"Amen to that, sister. But kindness is free, and it gives you such a warm, fuzzy feeling, simply by being a good person." Josephine grabbed a handful of pistachios. "It's what makes our world a better place."

"Yet, it is so difficult for some." Allie walked over to the music file and selected some cool, chill-out beats to sway to with her champagne.

"How can we help Orlando, Jess?" Lilliana asked.

"I wish I knew." Jessica sighed. "I haven't seen him this distracted and distant for an awfully long time. He is not himself at the moment."

"Well, we will just have to get him and Nadia engaged in a uplifting activity. Any ideas?" Allie asked.

"Yeah, I have a few," Josephine nodded. "Just need to run something by Cam first..." she trailed off as someone began pounding at the door.

Clearly, someone who didn't have the code.

Lilliana walked over and opened the door as Scott practically fell through the entrance, his face as white as his t-shirt.

"Lilliana, It's bad!" he screamed, before spotting the others.

"Scott?" She reached out to rub his arm. "What is it?"

"It's Nadia! Natalie stabbed her!"

"What!" Allie turned the music off and joined Jessica and Josephine as they crossed over to Scott.

"Where is Nadia, is she alright?" Jessica rubbed her hands over her face. "Let's go." She brushed by Scott and started out the door. They all quickly followed Jessica down the stairs, as Scott continued to fill them in on the details.

"Nadia and Orlando were spending time together when Christopher asked Orlando and Eric to be his best men—so they were all huddled in a group, talking excitedly... I'd been hanging out with

Orlando beforehand, so I saw the whole thing." He took another deep breath as they ran down the stairs.

"Anyway—Nadia was walking towards me just as the blokes were, you know, celebrating, when Natalie ran up behind her and slashed her with a knife; she was screaming out, 'Sorry, but I have to' then, Eric punched her in the face, and she went down hard."

"My God, this is insane!" Allie said as they got to the crowd of fifty plus gathered around the front entrance of the library, the open double doors revealing more people gathered inside.

Damon was calming people down as Dr Richard was bent over Natalie, attending to her as she lay there, her nose swollen and bloody.

Eric and Nadia were nowhere to be seen. Lilliana presumed they had already been taken down to the hospital.

Josephine quickly crossed to Cam, who reached out his hand when he saw her. "Everything's fine love. Nadia's going to be okay, and Natalie will recover."

"Wish I'd seen Eric knock her out," Josephine whispered mischievously.

Cam smiled, shaking his head.

Damon addressed the crowd. "Can everyone please return to their previous activities before calling it a night, thank you."

"What's going to happen to Natalie, Sir?" Keira asked, Karen standing nervously beside her.

"She will be dealt with accordingly. Girls, please," He searched the room for the girls Team Leaders, and, spotting Jessica, waved her over. Jessica crossed over to Damon. Scott, seeing Karen, quickly followed.

"Jessica, can you take the girls for a relaxing activity before bed? Maybe a hot chocolate and a chat?"

"Absolutely Sir." Jessica smiled at the girls. "Come on, Scott's going to join us." She continued after she saw him reach out for Karen's hand, who quickly took it.

As the chatter settled down and people began moving on, Allie and Lilliana joined Damon and Richard. Allie bent down, watching Natalie stare at her. "You alright Natalie?" Natalie was uncharacteristically quiet.

Richard peered at Allie. "Apparently, she hasn't said a word since Eric punched her."

Lilliana looked at Damon, wondering what he was going to do with Natalie.

He met her gaze, and she could see the tension in his eyes. He was acting intense and dark, and all too serious looking for her liking. She put her arm around his waist. "It will be okay. We'll sort this out."

Damon sighed quietly, shaking his head as he looked back down at Natalie. "I hope so, and quickly."

Brett and Johnson arrived as Natalie sat up. Allie moved, giving the men room to take an arm each and get Natalie to her feet.

"We've just taken statements," Johnson said to Damon, who nodded.

"Thanks. Get her downstairs and I'll be along shortly once I've spoken to the others. I've already got Scott's account of what happened."

"No worries, we'll see you soon." Johnson and Brett took Natalie out of the room and headed down to the hospital so she could get checked out. She'd be held there until Damon had received all the eyewitness accounts, before deciding what was to be done.

"I'll go with Natalie, Damon, see if I can't get her talking."

"Sure Allie, good idea." He exchanged a look with Cam, looking over at Lilliana. She was looking up at him with so much love in her eyes; she always made him catch his breath, just by the sheer beauty of her.

"What can I do to help, Damon?"

"Check on Nadia and Eric would you, darling?"

"Of course."

"Cam, let's go and see if we can't find out why the hell this happened."

"Sure thing." Cam dropped a kiss on Josephine's lips.

"Lilly, I'll come with you," Josephine said as Damon kissed Lilliana.

Lilliana nodded and they followed Damon and Cam, out of the library. The girls took off in the direction of the hospital as Damon and Cam headed into Damon's office, grateful United had left just ten minutes before the incident had occurred.

CHAPTER 17

"Okay gentlemen, let's see if we can't figure this out." Damon addressed Orlando, Christopher, and Marcus, who had all been waiting to give their accounts of what happened. Their versions were the same as Scott's, and it seemed Natalie was going to be in a whole lot of trouble.

"It seems simple enough, Natalie is going to get her ass…"

"Thanks Cameron." Damon cut him off.

"It doesn't make sense," Christopher said, leaning back into his chair. "Natalie says and does a lot of stupid things, but she has never physically hurt someone before."

"It is out of character. Rocco was telling me that Felicia and Natalie have been spending most of their working days together, and what with Natalie saying sorry…" Marcus shrugged. "Somethings off."

Damon nodded. "I agree. I'm hoping Allie can get the reason out of her, as to why she did it. She is extremely lucky that Nadia wasn't severely injured, or worse."

"My God, you should have heard the crack when Eric punched her," Orlando shook his head, sounding much too pleased about it.

"Shattering, I'm sure," Cam grinned.

"Yes, well, as much as she deserved punishment, I can't say I'm too thrilled about Eric breaking her nose." Damon shook his head as he began walking to the door.

"Well, he was doing his job protecting Nadia, it was probably just reflex," Christopher jumped in, in defence of his friend.

Damon gave him a wry smile. "Probably. Thanks everyone. Cam, let's go."

Cam nodded. "Keep your ears open, fellas, and if you hear anything, let us know."

Orlando, Marcus, and Christopher exchanged a look before following their directors out of the office, deciding to go up to Marcus's room to get a drink to celebrate Christopher's announcement, which had been interrupted.

***

Allie waited patiently as Rachael attended to Natalie's injury. Richard stood silently by the door, arms folded, wearing a stern expression.

"Right then, Natalie, that's all I can do for you at the moment. The pain should go any moment now. Dr Ryan will come and see you after Mr Night has spoken to you."

Natalie didn't respond; she just sat, staring at the wall.

Rachael looked at Allie. "I'll be at the nurse station if you need me."

Allie nodded, "Thanks Rachael." She watched as Rachael stopped outside the door, quietly talking with Johnson, who was guarding the door with Brett.

"Well Natalie, I think you have some serious explaining to do. Out with it." Allie had no desire to make Natalie feel any better, after the shitty thing she had done to Nadia. Natalie shifted uncomfortably, before glancing in Richard's direction.

"I can handle this, thank you, Dr Richard," Allie addressed him politely.

Richard nodded. "Alright then." He knew Allie hoped that with him gone, Natalie would open up and disclose her reasons. He turned and left the room, closing the door behind him. Allie let out a breath and stood at the end of the bed, blocking Natalie's view of the wall, forcing her to look at her.

"I can't tell you how interested I am to hear the reason why you decided it would be a great idea to attack Nadia. I'd spill the beans if I were you, and I'd do it quickly. Mr Night is no doubt on his way." She folded her arms.

Natalie simply stared at her.

"Look Natalie, I am here to help you. Just tell me why you did what you did? What were you thinking?"

"Clearly, I wasn't." Natalie spat out.

Well, Allie thought, at least Natalie was now sounding like her old self. "Well, that explanation isn't going to fly."

Natalie shook her head as a frustrated breath burst from her. "What does it matter why I did it? I did it, end of discussion!"

Allie shook her head, unfolding her arms, and gripped the bar at the end of the bed. "You do realise that Mr Night is about to walk through that door—and you will be dragged up to Black Ops, where you will await a dire decision about your future?"

"Just piss off." Natalie turned her head away, looking unhappy.

Allie softened. "Natalie, just tell me why?"

Natalie shook her head. "I can't!"

"Yes, you can."

"No, you don't get it. I can't."

The door opened and Damon walked in, looking frustrated. He looked at Allie who shook her head, letting him know she didn't have an answer. Cam walked in with Nurse Billy.

"Look who we've got here, Natalie; he comes bearing a gift."

Allie smiled at Billy as he walked to the bed, holding up a vial.

"Truth serum," Cam smiled. "And it hurts like a son of a bitch as it travels in your blood stream. Burns apparently." He looked at Billy for back up.

"Oh yeah, the pain is intense. Like fire ants running under your skin." He nodded.

He placed the vial on the side table before reaching across and strapping Natalie's left arm, then the right to the bedrail.

Natalie looked at Damon as panic filled her face. "You can't do this."

"You shouldn't have injured your fellow Given, should you?"

"She's no fellow Given of mine; she doesn't even belong here! Shacked up with Gregory Reid since she was young, she's infiltrated our home! Why can't any of you see that?" Natalie screamed at Damon. "You should be thanking me, not punishing me!"

Allie inwardly groaned. Silly girl.

Damon gave the nod as Billy advanced with the vial, slamming it into Natalie's arm.

"You don't need to do this; I've just told you why I did it!" She writhed in pain, her screams echoing throughout the hospital as the burning serum rushed through her blood stream.

Damon didn't like seeing any of his Given in pain, and the tears that fell from Natalie's eyes did make him uncomfortable. But he didn't trust her after her past indiscretions with telling the truth, and this way at least, they'd be sure.

***

"My God, it sounds like someone is being slaughtered." Josephine looked at Lilliana as they sat with Eric in between them. Nadia was in with Dr Ryan, who was applying stitching serum to her knife wound.

"What I want to know is, what did it feel like, slamming your fist into Natalie's face?" Lilliana really wanted to know. There had been so many occasions over the years where she had imagined doing just that. Not very therapist like of her, she knew. But the woman deserved it.

He grinned at her as he folded his arms. "Therapeutic."

"Good answer," Josephine stood, as Damon walked towards them, looking far too serious for Lilliana's liking.

"What's happening, Sir?" Eric stood, curious if there would be any sort of punishment for himself, for breaking Natalie's nose. He knew he could have restrained her in another way, but it was his first instinct to knock her out, eliminating further harm to Nadia.

"The truth serum has revealed that Felicia was behind this attack on Nadia. She has been threatening Natalie. Telling her that David would slit her throat if she didn't do what Felicia wanted her to do.

Cam's bringing David in now so we can find out if there is truth to this. Obviously, it's Natalie's truth. She can't lie with the truth serum, but Felicia could be using Natalie to cause trouble. We'll check with The Guardian's footage."

"Where's Felicia now?" Eric asked.

"Johnson's got Rocco bringing her up to Black Ops. She will be detained until all of this is cleared up."

"There's no way she can remain in Main House now, right Damon?" Lilliana stood, folding her arms. "No matter what agreement you have with Reid, or the contract you signed via the Officials; if she poses a threat to our own, you cannot be expected to uphold that agreement?"

Damon nodded, holding out his hand. Lilliana entwined her fingers in his, her eyes searching his for a clue as to what he was going to do. "Paul is waiting upstairs with Mason on call. We'll head up there now. Eric—once Nadia is ready, can you bring her up to Black Ops?"

"Yes Sir."

"Johnson's office."

Eric nodded.

"I'm coming too," Josephine headed off in front of Damon and Lilliana. Several minutes later they walked into the office, facing a room full of commotion.

"Reid needs to be given the truth serum, then he'll be thoroughly questioned regarding any bioweapon locations and future threats. He and his offspring need to be eradicated!" Johnson jabbed a finger towards Mason's face, that was projected in the middle of the table. "We need to deal with this situation once and for all!"

Lilliana balked at the idea of David being killed, simply because of his father and sister. She looked at Josephine and watched as Damon walked up to the front of the room and stood beside Johnson. Josephine tugged on her hand and they sat in the chairs at the back of the room.

"I see this situation with having Felicia Reid in your Main House being much more difficult than we first anticipated. We did not think she would make any allies in order to be a threat to anyone." Mason addressed Paul. "Paul; you've been overseeing the day to day running's, what do you suggest?"

"Reid has been extremely cooperative, and the intel he's provided has led us to secure three separate underground compounds. But I am in total agreement with Johnson. We need to use all means necessary to get answers from Reid Senior, and end this precarious situation once and for all." The door opened and both Rocco and Cam arrived with the Reid siblings.

"Good evening all," David smiled charmingly as he entered, oblivious to the dire situation.

"David, take a seat please." Damon pointed to Josephine and Lilliana.

David sat beside Lilliana. "This all looks very official."

If only you knew, Lilliana thought.

Cam sat beside Josephine, whilst Rocco walked Felicia up to the front.

"Felicia Reid," Mason addressed Felicia. "What have you got to say for yourself, for influencing an innocent Given to attack another?"

Felicia raised a thin, pale eyebrow. "I'd say I've never heard anything more ridiculous," she scoffed, looking over her shoulder towards Lilliana. "Then again…" she trailed off, looking pleased with her innuendo.

"Careful." Damon said, dangerously quiet.

Lilliana met his steel blue gaze and shook her head a fraction to signal that it wasn't worth it.

"And would you also say it's ridiculous to imply that your brother was going to slice someone's throat open if the Given did not do as you bid?"

"What?" David flew out of his chair, looking as angry as Lilliana had ever seen him. "What lies do you tell, Sister?"

Damon held out a hand. "Easy David, we are trying to get to the bottom of this situation."

"What situation? Being accused of participating in my nutcase of a sister's scheme, leading to my inevitable demise?"

"David Reid, please calm yourself and sit down." Paul addressed David.

As David sat back down, Lilliana couldn't help herself, and rubbed his arm. "It's going to be okay," she whispered, hoping that were true. Surely Damon would not allow David to be eradicated. Her eyes met with Josephine's, who was looking worried herself.

"I think we're done with the antics now. Rocco, if you would please." Johnson pointed to a seat with restraints, and Rocco forced Felicia into the seat and strapped her down in record time, despite her resistance.

A knock sounded and the door opened, and Eric led a pale Nadia into the room.

"Nadia, how are you?" Damon motioned for Eric to take a seat near Cam.

"I'm fine, thank you. The cut wasn't deep." She sat beside Eric.

"You always get away without a scratch; don't you, little Miss Perfect!" Felicia hissed.

Nadia stared at the hateful woman but didn't acknowledge her.

Paul stepped toward Felicia and, without saying a word, stabbed her neck with a needle, releasing the truth serum into her bloodstream. He waited.

In seconds, the room was filled with Felicia's agonising screams. They were angry and pain filled. "How dare you do this to me! Wait till my father hears about this!" She threw her head back, screaming and thrashing about, trying to get out of her restraints.

Lilliana and Nadia shifted uncomfortably in their seats. Eric calmly placed a hand on top of Nadia's knee, squeezing gently until she stilled.

She nodded, letting him know she was okay.

Felicia's screaming quietened to moans as Paul stood in front of her.

"Felicia, what is your surname?"

"Reid."

"Have you been plotting to cause mayhem from the moment you entered this Given's Main House?"

"Yes."

"Did you ask the Given Natalie, to hurt Nadia?"

"No. I asked her to kill her." She laughed, not quite hysterically.

"Did you threaten Natalie?"

"Yes."

"Did you ask your brother to slit her throat?"

"Yes, but he told me to go to hell. Idiot!" She looked across at her brother.

"What's happened to you? You used to rule the world, now look at you! A simple soldier. You shame the Reid name!"

"Enough." Damon snapped.

Paul continued, as Felicia stared eerily at Damon.

"Did you tell Natalie that David would slit her throat if she didn't do as you instructed?"

"Yes, the stupid, fat ugly thing wouldn't know if I was lying, would she?"

Lilliana was offended that she called Natalie fat and ugly. Okay, stupid too. Natalie may be, well, Natalie; but she was considered 'theirs.'

Paul looked at Damon. "There's really nothing more to ask regarding this situation. I think we should move onto Reid Senior."

Damon nodded curtly. "Agreed. Johnson?"

"Yes, let's get this done."

"Rocco, can you please escort Ms Reid to a cell?" Damon folded his arms, tired of having the woman in his line of vision.

"Yes Sir."

As Rocco turned to collect Felicia, Lilliana's blood ran cold, as Felicia crooned.

"Don't you remember our good times, *Will*?" She used the name he had gone by back when he had been undercover. "The times when you worshiped my body?" Her voice dropped, attempting to sound sexy.

Damon froze, but only for a moment before casting a disgusted look in her direction. "There were no good times—you delude yourself, even now. You were a job. An unpleasant means to a successful end."

"You keep telling yourself that, Will; but I will love you forever, and one day, you'll be mine again." she smiled, unattractively.

Damon nodded to Rocco as he jerked Felicia up out of the chair and out of the room.

As she went to walk by the group sitting at the back of the room, she coughed up a lungful of phlegm, but before she could project it towards Lilliana, Rocco zapped her, causing her to clutch her head, screaming as she fell, choking on the contents. Rocco continued dragging her out of the room by her arm.

Cam shook his head as he looked at Lilliana, "The fun never stops around here." He grinned.

Lilliana met Damon's eyes as he addressed David. "At this stage, you are free to go."

"Is that another way of saying don't leave town?" David stood, attempting to make light of the situation, though he looked unsettled.

Damon shook his head. "No. Look, I don't have all the answers as to what will happen."

"So what—I have to just wait around until they decide if I'm to be put down?" A panicked look crossed his face as he ran a hand through his hair. "You may as well lock me up now then!" He shouted in frustration.

"I am sorry, David." Damon felt for the man. "We'll sort it all out as quickly as we can."

His tone broke Lilliana's heart. Damon was filled with regret and tiredness. His eyes met hers. She tried to force a small smile, as David turned to her.

"Can we talk tomorrow, after my first shift?"

She nodded. "I'll meet you by the front door at one."

"Okay." He left the room, looking deflated.

Lilliana felt sorry for him and understood his panic. She knew exactly what it felt like to have the fate of one's future decided by others.

Eric stood and reached for Nadia's hand. "Is that all, Sir? Nurse Rachael suggested that Nadia have plenty of rest after this meeting."

"Yes, thanks Eric. Nadia, take care—we'll talk soon." Damon offered her a strained smile.

Lilliana reached out and hugged her. "I'm so glad you're okay."

"Thanks, Lilly." Nadia smiled as Eric gently led her from the room.

Damon walked over to her as Paul, Johnson, and Mason finished their conversation. Cam stood up with Josephine. "Hey Brother; I don't think we should be including David in all this eradication chit chat. He is a good worker and I believe he has repented for his sins, so to speak."

"I have to agree," Lilliana nodded.

"I'll third it," Josephine added.

Damon smiled softly, looking at the three most important people in his life. "Let's just wait and see what the powers that be have to say about it all, shall we?"

Both Damon and Cam looked at their wife, and said simultaneously, "Did you get a chance…"

Lilliana and Josephine each shook their heads, both replying, "No…"

The four looked at each other, laughing.

"Jinx!" The girls said.

"I'm glad someone is still enjoying the little things around here," Johnson said. "Damon, are you ready?"

Damon sighed, regretful at having to tear himself away from his love's laughing eyes. "Yes, I'll be there in a minute."

Johnson followed Paul out, leaving the four looking at each other.

"Damon—about David," Lilliana began.

Damon reached out and cupped her chin. "Not now, love; let me deal with the situation at hand. Then we'll see what our options are. Okay?"

"Sure," she replied softly. "I just want to give him some kind of assurance…"

"It's not yours to give, love. Please." He hated not being able to offer her some sort of guarantee; but the Officials were included in this decision now, and ultimately David's fate would be their decision.

Cam could see a potential altercation brewing over differences of opinions between his sympathetic sister-in-law and his Official-abiding brother, and decided to intervene. "Come on Lilly, it's getting late. We'll walk you to your room." He nudged her arm.

Lilly nodded and claimed a quick kiss from Damon, who happily obliged. "I'll see you later."

He watched as his brother and sister led his beloved woman out of his sight. Sighing, he ran a hand through his hair and went to find Johnson and Paul, mentally preparing himself to deal with Gregory Reid, hoping upon hope it would be for the last time.

***

Tall ghost gums stood guard along the weathered, wrought-iron fence that wrapped its arms around the graveyard. Sweet scented magnolias and wildflowers brightened the mood for all who visited.

Lilliana found a walk to the cemetery soothing but didn't realise her mistake of bringing David here, where the dead lay, until they had entered under the archway dripping with the yellow glow of Golden Bunny roses, filled with the buzzing of bees.

"Are you trying to tell me something?" David gestured to the tombstones where headstones of angels protectively looked over the dead.

"I'm sorry, I just find it so peaceful here. I wasn't thinking…" she trailed off.

"It alright, it's nice here." They walked amongst the towering headstones and along a path towards one of many bench seats. Lilliana sat, as David paced silently back and forth for several minutes, deep in thought, before saying, "Surely Damon must have some inkling as to what the Officials are going to do with me?"

She remained quiet, allowing David to release the fear he held about his predicament.

"I just don't understand." He threw his hands in the air as he paced. "It doesn't make any sense! I've done everything I've been asked to do, at all times! Hell—if it weren't for me, they wouldn't even *have* my father in custody." He shook his head as he kicked at the gravel path.

Lilliana felt for him, wishing there were some way she could soothe his ruffled feathers.

"I mean; I know I have made grave errors in the past, and maybe I deserve to be simply put down like an injured animal. But, I have finally, after all my years being raised in purgatory and programmed to be an evil wrong doer of society… have discovered another path, a path where I can be useful—and I like it, and I'm not ready for it to end!"

He threw himself against the headstone of an enormous Celtic cross, his arms folded, holding them over his eyes.

Lilliana felt a stab of pity as she heard his voice break.

"It isn't fair. I don't want to die."

"David, come, sit."

He dropped his arms, looking at her, despair etched in his features. "I'm good here, thanks."

She sighed, nodding. "Look, whatever the Officials decide, I'm sure Damon will do everything in his power to help you."

"Yes, well that may be so. But that's not usually how these things work, is it?" He shook his head, sliding his hands into his pockets, a little more relaxed after his rant. "I know deep down that I can never atone for the things I have done in my past. I do acknowledge this. I also realise that I was only kept alive in the first place to bring down my father's empire. But people—some people—can change for the better when other options for a different way of life are presented." He raised his face towards the afternoon sun and closed his eyes.

Lilliana watched him silently, hoping that an outcome would be reached soon to put an end to his internal torment. "Why don't we head back, get something to eat?" she suggested.

He sighed, nodding. "Sure."

"I am sorry I can't help you, David," she added regretfully.

He shook his head, engaging a charming smile. "You can't save the world, can you? Even the great, Dark Angel has her limits. Come on, I am quite hungry, actually."

They walked quietly back along the path and out of the cemetery before David broke the silence. "I can't believe I'm about to say this, but I hope Felicia gets what she deserves. I don't think she has any redeeming qualities to her. Poor Nadia, she was always such a sweetheart, despite the life my father thrust her into."

"Yes. She is amazing to have kept her kind heart after everything she endured."

"She deserves Eric."

"Eric is one of the best," Lilliana agreed.

"You know, these past few months I've spent in getting to know you on an entirely different level, other than the one the world perceived you to be, has been both rewarding and entertaining."

Lilliana looked at him as they continued towards Main House. "How so?"

"Well, you were known to many as the Avenger when you escaped Simon Grey; and of course, since then you've become a beacon of hope to those who found themselves in similar situations. It wasn't just your beauty that caught the world's attention when you fortuitously became the Dark Angel—but your humility in that role. That first moment you sat in that interview room with me…"

"Oh God…"

David laughed. "Who would have thought we'd be here now, sharing a conversation after all that transpired in our first couple of face to face meetings."

"Who indeed. I could have happily ended your life then and there on that second meeting."

"You certainly tried." He said, rubbing the scar under his jaw.

"Oh you deserved it."

"True."

They walked up the steps into the large foyer, just as Scott ran up to them.

"Hey Lilly, Josephine asked me to tell you to meet her in the hot house when you came back." He looked at David. "Mr Night asked if you could meet him in his office."

David nodded. "Thanks for the walk."

"Make sure you get something to eat," Lilliana reminded him.

"Lilliana," Damon's velvety voice caressed her. She turned towards his office to see him standing in the doorway, hands in his jeans pockets, black tee shirt hugging every inch of sculptured perfection. His dark eyes held such a look of intensity that made her heart flutter.

"Can I see you alone for a moment? David, I'll be with you shortly."

"Sure thing." David nodded as he watched Lilliana disappear into the room, the door closing behind her. He turned back to Scott who was watching him closely and raised an eyebrow.

"You know, I appreciate that you tried to take care of my sister when you were at your father's." Scott shoved his hands into his hoodie pockets. "It must have been tricky, what with playing the role of the loyal son and all the while you were manipulating him."

"Not really, one learns a great deal when you've been raised by a despicable mastermind."

Scott nodded. "I guess. I'm glad you're not as evil as you dad and sister."

David simply raised an eyebrow and said, "Thanks."

Jessica and Orlando were walking a group out of the library towards the front door. Orlando called out, "Scott, it's time for work."

Scott waved, "I'm coming." He looked back at David. "I hope it all works out for you."

"Me too," David said quietly as he watched Scott turn and run after the group as they headed off to do a few hours of work, cleaning out the goat and sheep enclosures. David wished he could join them. Instead, he sat on the bench that wrapped around the Koi pond, willing the sound of water trickling from the fountain to soothe his jagged nerves.

***

Damon ran a hand down the river of silky hair that spilled down Lilliana's back. She reached up to stroke his face, wishing his eyes weren't filled with such stress. He lowered his dark head, claiming her lips in a soft kiss, trying to give them both a moment of normality and comfort.

She returned his kiss with a deeper kiss and sighed against his lips before he pulled away. She ran her hands along his biceps, resting them on his shoulders, wishing she could ease his stress.

"I missed you last night."

"I know, Baby; I missed you too. A decision will be made soon enough."

"Please, tell me it's good news."

He closed his eyes briefly, pulling her against his chest and burying his face into her neck. Her soft scent gave him a brief moment of peace.

"Damon?"

"I wish I could." He kissed her forehead, before turning to his desk as his phone rang.

She watched him click on the call as Russell Meek appeared before them. "Damon, Lilliana—it's good to see you again."

"Hello Russell," Lilliana smiled.

"The votes have been sent to the Officials," he addressed Damon. "For now, the decision regarding David Reid's future is out of our hands."

Damon folded his arms as he leaned a hip against his desk. "Thanks for letting me know, Russell. It shouldn't be too long now."

"It's harsh, considering all he did to bring his father down. Hopefully, they will take all our feedback into consideration."

Damon nodded. "I hope so too. I'll see you on the conference call."

"Sooner than later I hope, for the poor bastards sake." Russell said and ended the call.

Damon's eyes met Lilliana's. "There is nothing we can do but wait," he said quietly.

Lilliana shook her head. "Who would have thought we would ever be so perplexed about a decision regarding the life of one who has caused us so much damage and destruction in the past?"

"Crazy world we live in." He forced a small smile as his eyes roamed her beautiful face, wishing he could take her upstairs and give her hours of pleasure and conversation. Simple time with his wife.

"What has happened with Felicia and Gregory?"

He shook his head. "Gregory won't be with us after tomorrow."

"Termination?"

"No, the Officials have decided to hold him at their facility of the damned. They've deemed him too valuable to kill, because he holds information that we need in bringing other organisations down."

"Seriously? Yet they are considering killing David?"

He shrugged, folding his arms across his chest, watching her watch his movements.

Her eyes met his. "Felicia?"

"She will be terminated tonight," he said quietly.

She let out a breath, nodding. "Good."

He smiled, "I knew that was one decision you wouldn't have a problem with."

"I'm sorry." Lilliana felt a small moment of guilt for wishing anyone dead.

"Don't be. None of us will lose any sleep over this decision."

He crossed over to her and picked up her hands, raising them to kiss her palms. "This will all be over soon, and we can get back to concentrating on the good again."

She nodded, squeezing his fingers. "I so look forward to that."

He cupped her chin, watching her lips part in anticipation as his head bent to hers. He whispered, "I want only to see you happy, my darling, just to see your beautiful smile." His lips slid over hers, gently back and forth, before he deepened their kiss, taking a moment to appreciate her gasp of delight as his tongue mated with hers.

Her heartbeat quickened, as a delicious warmth spread to her loins, and a throb of pleasure pulsed deep in her core. She was always surprised that a simple kiss from Damon could have her insides melting in a molten wave of pleasure. She had a constant insatiable hunger for him.

A sudden knock at the door before Johnson briskly walked in, had them parting from their embrace. But not before Damon swept another kiss over her swollen lips. He smiled, watching her dazed eyes cloud over as she took a deep breath, finally looking away from his lips.

"Sorry Damon, Lilliana. We have a situation in common room four that requires your attention. Cam thought it best you sort this one out."

"What is it?"

"It's a small protest rally concerning Nadia's placement here. There are those that are joining in Natalie's opinion that she doesn't belong here."

Damon shook his head, before saying under his breath, "Bloody dills."

Johnson nodded in agreement.

"Can you bring David here, make him a coffee? I'll sort this out quickly and hopefully be back before David's verdict is announced."

"Of course."

Damon dropped a kiss against Lilliana's check. "Sweetheart, I'll see you after."

She nodded as she watched him walk briskly out of the room. Her eyes met Johnson's. He could see how anxious she was.

"I hope it's a good verdict for David."

He nodded, understanding her stress, given the relationship that had developed between her and Reid.

"I'll see you later Johnson."

"Yep."

They both headed out the door; Johnson, to bring David in, and Lilliana to find Josephine, hoping that this moment would be a good one, to share her news of a reverse sterilization procedure.

CHAPTER 18

"Finally I've got you all to myself." Josephine hugged Lilliana hard. "Let's head upstairs."

"Perfect."

They walked up the narrow stairway that encircled the hot house, four levels high. Reaching the top floor, Lilliana glanced down, appreciating the spectacular sight of striking, hanging baskets dripping in colour. Their scents gifted her with a sense of calm.

Josephine hit a lever that had the glass roof opening, allowing the breeze to ruffle their hair with gentle fingers.

"I see you came prepared," Lilliana sat on a bench seat beside a basket with two glasses and a champagne bottle nestled inside. Josephine laughed as she sat down opposite Lilliana.

"Well my friend, I think we've both been waiting to share some news, and I know mine is worth popping a bottle of bubbly over. Also, with everything that's been going on lately, I thought we needed it."

"Totally agree." Lilliana picked up the glasses as Josephine opened the champagne with a loud pop.

"Ah, it's like music to my ears," she laughed. Filling their glasses, Josephine clinked hers neatly against Lilliana's, and they both took an appreciative mouthful.

"Mmm, delicious," Lilliana smiled.

"Right, who's going first?"

"Please, go ahead."

Josephine's eyes twinkled as she took another swallow of the delicious bubbles. "Mr Cameron Night and I are going to become parents in eight months!"

"Josephine! Oh my God!" Lilliana squealed in delight as she placed her glass on the table. Standing, she reached for her friend who had done the same. They wrapped their arms around each other, laughing in sheer excitement and joy. Lilliana leaned back, looking into Josephine's warm brown eyes. "You are going to make the most beautiful mother, and Cam, well, he is extremely suited for fatherhood."

Josephine laughed, "Words can't even begin to describe how happy I am Lilly; I've been busting to tell you and the girls."

Lilliana nodded. "Well, on top of you becoming a gorgeous, nurturing mother, I'm sure you will also make the most fabulous aunt... to your baby's cousin." She grinned.

"You and Damon?" Josephine's voice was filled with absolute happiness.

"Well, not yet, but we will be—and not that much longer after your delightful little bundle arrives." They looked at each other quietly for a minute, smiling, thinking about the future.

"Can you imagine, our children growing up as cousins and best friends?"

"It is going to be so fabulous, Lilly. Damon will make such a wonderful father."

"I know he will. How did we get to be so lucky?" Lilliana shook her head in disbelief as Josephine handed her the champagne glass as they sat back down.

"Well, it's not like we are complete assholes," she laughed.

Lilliana smiled. "True." She indicated to the champagne. "I'm guessing that this is Christopher and Rupert's non-alcoholic brew?"

"But of course." Josephine drained her glass. "What's happening with David?"

Lilliana shrugged, "We're waiting for the verdict now."

"Bloody harsh if you ask…" Josephine was interrupted by a voice from below.

"Hey, Josephine, you up there?"

"No." Josephine grinned at Lilliana.

"Well get your ass down here please," Sammy called up sweetly.

"We've just had an order from Uganda that needs filling immediately. The cargo plane is on the way. Rupert's waiting for you, it's all hands-on deck. We need to pack absorption soil, compost, mulch as well as all the plants."

"Oh joy," Josephine whispered to Lilliana. "Lucky I love my job." She stood and looked down at Sammy. "Be right down," she called. Sammy marched out of the hot house as Lilliana and Josephine made their way down the stairs.

"What are you up to now?" Josephine asked as they hit the ground level.

"Allie and I have two groups, then I'll see how Nadia's doing."

"Hey, do you know what's happening with Natalie?"

"No, but I'm sure it won't be long till we find out what's happening with everyone."

They walked outside to see a crowd of people bustling outside HD, along with the crew from the agricultural department. The bobcats were filling containers with the animal manure and hay that had developed into perfect organic matter that would benefit the drought afflicted soil for this delivery to Uganda, along with Rupert's absorption soil. Pallets of plants were lined up, waiting to be loaded on the flat trailer before being taken to the cargo plane strip. Josephine smiled as she headed off towards Rupert who was enthusiastically motioning for people to complete the tasks quickly.

"Have fun," Lilliana waved.

"Always. See you later," Josephine joined Rupert and took the tablet off him to go over the impressive order they had to fill, happy to dive in and get the job done.

***

"For anyone who is feeling any stress towards any event they have been placed in, please have a chat with your Team Leader. I know they are more than happy to work with everyone to make the games as enjoyable as possible." Allie stood. "We'll see you next week." She spied Natalie lingering outside the door as their second group for the afternoon began to leave.

Lilliana began gathering up the water jugs and cups to take to the hospital cafeteria's kitchen to clean up. "I'll leave you to it."

"Please don't." Allie whispered, before saying brightly, "Natalie, what the hell can we do for you?"

Natalie walked in. "Nice. Do you greet everyone so warmly?" She raised an eyebrow as she tucked a lock of brown hair behind her ear.

"Only those that I am super pissed off with and passing their care onto Dr Richard."

"Seriously?"

"You have no idea how serious I am. After your last stunt with Nadia, I am done with you." Allie folded her arms.

Natalie scoffed, mirroring her stance. "Just like that? You know I was being threatened."

"Get completely real, and over yourself Natalie! What came out of your mouth had nothing to do with Felicia's threat. You are an awful person who has the decency of a cockroach."

Lilliana was enjoying Allie's lecture a little too much. She enjoyed watching her petite friend turn into a spitfire occasionally. Especially when people deserved it. And Natalie certainly did.

"And, I also have the pleasure of informing you that your privileges have been revoked."

"What's that supposed to mean?"

Allie looked across at Lilliana. "Would you do me the honour of informing Natalie as to what this means?"

Natalie looked across at Lilliana, who was still holding a tray full of jugs and cups.

"You will no longer have the privilege of working on modelling projects or commercial shoots. You will still have your role with the design team, but your days have been cut from three to two, increasing your duties in the laundry to a four-day week." Lilliana took no pleasure in telling Natalie this, and watching the unfriendly girl's face fall tugged at her soft heart.

"This is utter bullshit." Natalie said quietly.

"Are you seriously for real?" Allie scoffed. "What is utter bullshit is the fact that you think you can put a knife in someone's flesh and have nothing in your world change. You are nearing thirty; it's time that you figured some stuff out Natalie, and fingers crossed, Dr Richard can help you do that."

"I'm going to speak to Mr Night about this!" Natalie slammed the door open and stormed out.

"Knock yourself out," Allie called behind her. She smiled at Lilliana, "And I mean that, literally."

Natalie screamed behind her. "You are a pair of…"

"Hey," Eric's voice snapped, stopping her next word. "Get going."

"You touch me again and it will be the last thing you do." Natalie screamed at Eric, pointing to her swollen nose.

"And if you give me any reason to touch you again, it will be the last thing *you do*." Eric clipped out. "Piss off, Natalie."

Allie and Lilliana exchanged a look as they listened to Eric and Natalie's exchange in the corridor.

"Fun times," Lilliana smiled.

"Oh yeah," Allie agreed.

Eric strode into the room and they listened to Natalie's cursing drift away as she made her way down the corridor.

Eric shook his head. "She is lucky I didn't tear her throat out."

"How's Nadia?" Lilliana asked.

"Wanting to see you. Orlando had a quick visit with her before he had to take a group out to work, and Christopher just gave her some food."

"I'll just clean these, and I'll be up then."

He nodded, looking at Allie. "I'm rapt for you and Christopher, congrats."

"Thanks, I'm rapt myself," she smirked. "Although, a congratulation gift would be to see you punch Natalie in the face—that would have been delightful."

He grinned, "Trust me, it was reflex 101."

"I think I can speak for us all when I say, job well done."

He saluted before reaching for the tray Lilliana held, as her phone rang.

Walking over, she pressed the speaker on. "Hello."

"Lilliana, it's Damon. I need you come to my office immediately." His voice held a certain edge to it she couldn't discern.

"Of course, I'll come right now." The call clicked off on Damon's end.

Allie raised an eyebrow. "David's verdict?"

Lilliana nodded as she headed towards the door. "I believe so."

"I'm coming with you."

"I'll take this to the kitchen and tell Nadia you'll pop in later."

"Thanks Eric, see you."

Lilliana and Allie hurried down the corridor and out of the hospital section and headed up the stairs to Damon's office in record time.

Lilliana was surprised at the number of people in the room. Damon and Cam were standing up the front beside Johnson and Paul. David was seated beside Dr Richard, Marcus, and Rocco. On a large glass monitor, thirteen faces were looking back at them, including Russell, and Mason.

"Lilliana, Allie." Damon held out a hand for Lilliana to come forward, as Allie went to stand behind Marcus's chair. Lilliana stood close beside Damon, taking comfort in his presence as Mason addressed Lilliana.

"Mrs Night, we have been debating the future of David Reid, and due to your influence on him, he seems to have developed a conscience since being in your presence. We wanted to hear from you personally, regarding your thoughts as to whether he deserves to be spared due to his past crimes, and the influence his father may have had on his actions and his part in helping us bring the Reid Empire down."

"Of course," Lilliana nodded before looking across at David. He was paler than usual; his knees were bobbing up and down in a nervous movement. His eyes seemed to be imploring her to save him. Feeling an immense amount of pressure, she looked back at Mason, as all eyes were fixed on her. Damon shifted his stance, so the side of his body brushed against hers.

"When I first met David Reid, I thought he was one of the most despicable humans I had ever met. I did not think he had a redeeming bone in his body, or that he could perform any task that would benefit anyone other than himself. My initial thoughts, after interviewing him on two occasions, were that his life should be terminated, and that we should stop wasting our resources on the likes of him."

Everyone looked across at David as he winced out loud, arms folded tightly across his chest, dripping in a light sheen of sweat. Lilliana took a breath, feeling terrible for him, before continuing.

"His past crimes are deplorable and unforgivable, indeed. However, when we look at his upbringing, his being conditioned by his depraved, controlling father from the most impressionable young age, what hope did he ever have? I know where the Officials Law stands for those that have committed crimes as David has done in the past, and, for the most part, I agree with it. But I think it is time the Laws were reviewed and amended in situations like this. David Reid's actions have shown him to be capable of great remorse and regret. Yes, The Guardian may have influenced him in bringing his father down, and so we should ask ourselves if his actions and good intentions were due only to The Guardian? I for one, have seen a side to David that is decent and redeemable, and I believe he can be a valuable member to our home here." She looked up at Damon, who had a look of pride in his eyes as he looked down at her.

Damon looked across at Mason, as he ran a hand lovingly down her back, resting it around her waist.

"Thank you, Mrs Night. I just need a few moments." Mason's screen went blank, along with several of the Officials screens as they went to discuss the verdict privately.

"Good job Lilliana." Russell smiled. "You're lucky to have her in your corner, Reid."

"It took me a moment to wonder which corner you were in." David said to Lilliana, shaking his head, still looking shaken.

Lilliana met his gaze. "Won't be long now," she said quietly.

A knock sounded at the door before Christopher entered pushing a trolley loaded with sandwiches, pots of tea, and coffee.

"Thanks Christopher, perfect timing." Cam went to grab a sandwich as Christopher began pouring him a coffee.

"How's it going?" Christopher asked Allie, as she leaned in to plant a kiss on his cheek, grabbing a tomato and cheese sandwich as she did.

"Just waiting for the verdict now."

"Nerve wracking for the bloke," Christopher nodded towards David.

"Yep," Allie agreed, before turning to Richard. "Are you in agreement to take over Natalie's care?"

Dr Richard filled a plate, and silently passed it to David as he sipped his tea. "I am."

"Thanks." Allie and David said together. David was starving but didn't know if he could keep it down. Allie poured a tea and took it across to her friend.

Damon pulled Lilliana close against him, as she put her arm around his waist. He dropped his head and whispered against her ear. "If this decision sways in David's favour, it will go down in history."

She nodded. "We're doing the right thing; I hope they do, too." She looked up at him. "What are your thoughts?"

He shrugged, looking over her head towards David, before replying. "It could go either way, but your input should sway the decision in David's favour." His eyes dropped down to hers as he offered her a smile. "My beautiful girl." He leaned down and swept a kiss across her lips. "You did well."

"Thank you." She smiled up at him, wishing this were all over so they could be alone.

"Here you go Lilly," Allie said, passing her the tea.

"Thank you."

"Anything from the trolley, Sir?" Christopher asked from across the room.

Damon smiled, shaking his head.

Christopher wasn't the only one in the room who had noticed how tired their director had been looking lately. Always kindly commanding, strong and in control, but Damon was tired, nonetheless. He hoped all this drama would die down soon, so life could get back into a normal pace.

"Are we still on schedule for the healing center's opening tomorrow, Damon?" Allie asked.

He nodded. "We are. Katy, Emile and Adam are extremely excited to be attending."

"I cannot thank you enough, Damon, for everything you have done for my siblings. They have healed so beautifully."

"I'm only sorry they couldn't be a part of the United photo shoot."

"No, I understand completely, it was for blood relatives only."

"Still," Damon said, looking at the screen as the Officials came back on. "It would have been nice for you."

"I think it would have been too much for Adam; although he has made so many steps forward, he is still too fragile for certain situations."

"Agreed." Damon nodded.

Everyone's focus turned to Mason as he commanded their attention.

"Thank you for your patience. We have reached a verdict and I thank you all for your testaments. David Reid, you have been fully pardoned and are now under the sole care of the Louisiana's Given and under the protection of Damon and Cameron Night. If you break any rules or laws pertaining to their lands, they have free will to terminate you at their discretion."

David leaped out of his chair, knocking the plate of sandwiches from his grip.

"Thank you! Thank you so much!"

Mason nodded. "Does anyone have anything further to add?"

The room was silent for a few moments before Damon spoke. "I'd like to thank you and the Officials for your decision and time, Mason. We are certain David will make a fine contribution to our home here." Damon nodded to David.

"I won't let you down, Sir." David nodded back to Damon.

"Until next time. Damon, the Official jet will come for Gregory Reid in the morning. Paul and my team will escort him, and several of the other prisoners off your property. Any questions?"

"None."

"That will be all." Mason's screen, along with the other Officials, went blank leaving Russell and the other Given's Directors a few minutes to say goodbye, before ending the conference call.

Damon turned to David, who was ravenously eating his sandwiches, still looking a little stunned. Marcus and Rocco were enthusiastically congratulating David. Having spent plenty of time with him on their latest mission, they had seen his good qualities and were happy he was sticking around.

Cam walked over and held out his hand. "Congratulations, I'm glad you get to stay in the land of the living."

David put his sandwich down as he stood to shake Cam's hand, and then Damon's, as he came up behind his brother.

"You won't regret this." David nodded, still shaken.

"I think you may need to call it a day. A session with Richard would be beneficial. Richard?" Damon turned to the older man.

"Yes, I agree." Richard looked down at David over his horn-rimmed glasses, pushing them up with his middle finger.

Allie and Lilliana exchanged looks, trying not to roll their eyes.

David turned to Lilliana. "I can't thank you enough. What you said really swayed them."

"Happy to help. Just make us… proud." She wasn't sure of the word that she needed for what she hoped David would do here on in, but it seemed fitting in the moment.

David nodded, smiling.

"Let's go then, shall we." Richard led the way and the room applauded David as he walked out, a free man at last.

"Thank God that's done and dusted," Cam sighed.

Johnson approached Damon quietly, saying, "It's time."

Damon sighed, "Of course."

"Time for what?" Allie asked.

Lilliana knew they were referring to Felicia's termination and took Allie's arm. "Let's go visit Nadia."

"Righto," Allie took the hint and turned to Christopher who was packing up cups and plates.

"I'm going to see Nadia; will you be in the kitchen for a while?"

"Yeah, I've got a heap of prep work to do for the brunch at tomorrow's opening ceremony. I've got a few new staff coming to help, but I'll be at it till at least eleven."

"Okay love, well, if I don't pop down, you'll know I've passed out from this exhausting day."

Christopher laughed, knowing full well that Allie could last another twenty-four hours without passing out. "I'll see you later, babe."

Damon took Lilliana's hand. "Won't be long darling, and things will finally be back to normal," he said quietly. She pulled his hand up to her lips and kissed them.

"Come on Brother," Cam sauntered out. "Let's get this thing done."

Damon followed Cam up to Black Ops, to finally rid the world of one more polluted piece, the evil Felicia Reid.

CHAPTER 19

Opening day for the healing centre saw a fresh breeze billowing through dancing clouds as the wind blew and the sun leaked through. Lilliana was dressed like most of those who had turned up for the special tour and brunch in jeans, jumper, and boots.

The building was impressive, and the word 'healing' radiated from every corner, beam, and surface of the natural looking four level glass and timber structure.

Damon and Rachael stood at the wide front doors as the crowd gathered, waiting for it all to quieten down. Damon smiled as he began.

"Our healing programs, along with our highly trained staff who work tirelessly and with such dedication and passion to help the injured, is what makes our Given nonpareil to any other Given establishment." He smiled. "I hope that makes you all as proud as I am. I'd especially like to say thank you to Rachael and the wellbeing Team Leaders who have helped make this centre possible. Thank you, Rachael." He turned and dropped a kiss on Rachael's cheek as the crowd clapped.

"Thank you, Mr Night," Rachael turned to everyone. "I am so

grateful to be sharing this moment with you all and I'll be quick so you can all get out of this wind and come in and look at our fabulous new centre in just a moment. Healing takes time; and what may work for one individual, may not necessarily work for another. Inside these walls is an opportunity for healing for all those who have suffered trauma, anxiety, depression, and addiction, amongst other forms of mental illness, as a result of negative life experiences before they came to us." She turned, raising her hand behind her.

"The healing centre leads us onto a path for healing, starting with the physical, and then the mental, which encompasses the emotional, energetic, and the subconscious minds."

"Trippy, troppo stuff," Josh snickered to his mate Zac, before receiving a gentle scuff over the back of his head from Cam.

Rachael continued. "The benefits of our new healing centre impacts one's mindset, offering emotional wellbeing and development of self-confidence through working on all levels of consciousness. Through these efforts towards building mindfulness, we aim to achieve profound and long-lasting results as we lead sufferers towards realising their potential. Encouraging them to let go of their limitations and move towards places of healing by letting go of old patterns trusting in the arms of our phenomenal and highly experienced wellbeing leaders, to embrace and guide them."

"This is going to be such fun," Allie whispered to Lilliana, who nodded vigorously.

Rachael concluded. "Of course, the beautiful thing about our new healing centre is that it will work in symmetry along with our already existing programs, with HBR, our expert in-house counselling, and so many other areas. A list explaining our mergers is posted inside for you to view. I'm thrilled so many of you came to support and celebrate this auspicious opening with us; thank you. Please, come in and explore our new facility as tours will be starting shortly." Rachael turned to Damon and laughed nervously as the crowd applauded. "I hate public speaking," she whispered off the mic.

Damon smiled, putting his arm around her shoulder, and leading her inside as people started walking in. "You were wonderful." He rubbed her back once before walking towards a long oak desk in the middle of the room where Jessica, Orlando and Fox were waiting along with a handful of volunteers for the morning's tour.

"All set?"

"It's going to be a knockout, Sir." Leon smiled, joining him with a warm cheesy muffin in his hand.

"Oh, that looks good," Scott, Karen and Keira walked up behind Damon, eyeing Leon's muffin.

"Help yourself," Orlando pointed to the far wall where a delicious spread of gourmet sweet and savoury muffins sent mouth-watering aromas into the air as the large room began to fill with the hungry and excited crowd.

Rachael allowed fifteen minutes for everyone to grab a muffin and a drink before getting the ninety odd people to return their attention to her.

"Jessica, Orlando and Fox are taking the tour today. If you miss anything, don't worry—the centre will be open around the clock, and we have a fabulous booking system that will allow you to experience all the benefits," she added, gesturing to Jessica.

Jessica smiled. "Please follow me."

Damon looked across the crowd to see Allie and Lilliana at the back, looking over the list of merging practices. He hoped they would be happy to see their names on the list, allowing them to work in the mental health wing.

Lilliana and Allie looked at each other simultaneously and smiled, seeing their names on the list, high fiving each other.

Looking across at Damon, Lilliana smiled, and Allie saluted. He returned Lilliana's smile and pointed to the crowd as people began following Jessica up the stairs. The girls nodded, and quickly followed.

The first two floors formed the Physical healing area, organised as a perfect open plan design layout that flowed from the gym and yoga area to acupuncture, then to a kinesiology space, naturopathy and nutritional healing, and ending up at a meditation and massage space.

Cam rubbed his hands together in excitement as he turned to Josephine. "My gym has always been pretty decent—but this is spectacular!"

"It is fabulous," Josephine agreed, rubbing his arm before turning to catch up to Jessica.

"Wait till you see the next floor, Jose," Jessica turned to her friend. "Allie and Lilliana will be in their prime."

They walked up the stairs that were tucked away behind the wall of each floor. As they continued, the view beyond the thick glass windows offered stunning views as fields of wildflowers ran all the way towards the edge of the forest.

"It makes one feel instantly relaxed," Billy said to Rupert, who had jogged up to join the group.

"The entire purpose of this centre is to achieve a complete sense of calm. Every single element to this building was carefully thought out to increase the peace and wellbeing of its dwellers." Jessica then led them up into the mental health wing that wrapped one in serenity from the moment of entering.

An entire glass wall lit up and gently changed colour as water flowed along its length, and the most angelic music played softly, floating throughout the level.

"This floor taps into some pretty powerful healing," Rupert said, having read the list downstairs. "Mindfulness meditation, Psychology, Life coaching, Hypnotherapy, Timeline therapy,"

"Don't forget the Inner Child Healing," Cam piped up.

"Oh yeah," Josephine said, walking around the huge space that offered stunning views from the three massive floor-to-ceiling windows. "Allie and Lilliana are going to go nuts in here."

Rupert slung his arm around Josephine's shoulder. "Probably not the best term to use in here my friend," he chuckled.

Josephine laughed quietly as one of the younger Given asked Orlando a question.

"Why would you need a life coach in here?"

"Well, when people first enter Main House after their initial months evaluation, sometimes they can feel disconnected, missing their old life, family or friends. A life couch is just another term for Team Leader, really; their role here is to help you build confidence, find activities that engage you and help you make clear goals, help you be accountable for the goals you set. They also encourage you to form better relationships and create a more meaningful life as you become a happy Given."

Jessica looked proudly at Orlando. He was certainly a Team Leader who did all those things for his Given, and more. Just then Karen slowly raised her hand. Damon spotted the shy blonde girl and was pleased to see she was interested enough to ask a question.

"Yes Karen?"

"If this is supposed to make you feel good about yourself, why is this level just called 'mental?'"

"Great question, Karen. Unfortunately, the word 'mental' has always had a negative stigma attached to it. Which it should not. Mental within these walls stands for: Mindfulness, Energy, Nurture, Transform, Adapt and Love." Damon smiled at her.

"Very nice," Allie approved.

Karen blushed with the attention coming from Damon and looked up at Scott, who was looking at her adoringly, which then made her pretty pink blush turn to red.

"How about mad, ego nut twat asshole losers," Zac laughed to Josh.

Lilliana stepped up behind them and said quietly, "How about you can get more creative with that in detention tonight?"

They spun around as their laughter fell from their faces, realising both of their counsellors stood right behind them.

"Come on, boys, surely you can be smarter than that and check behind you next time." Allie raised an eyebrow. "Kids today, no respect."

Lilliana hid a chuckle, thinking they were only eight years younger than her.

"Sorry Ms Allie, Ms Lilliana," Josh at least had the sense to look ashamed.

Allie pointed a finger forward and the two boys turned to face the front again as Jessica explained the many forms of healing in the mental centre. "There is also reiki, crystal healing, art expression and Nurse Rachael's energy medicine—oh, and acupuncture." Jessica smiled at Rachael.

Cam clapped his hands in applause, and everyone joined in.

"It's phenomenal," Lilliana clapped, looking around her. "I can't wait to have the chance to dive in."

"Ditto," Allie agreed.

"Please, everyone, feel free to look around at your own pace, grab another muffin before returning to your obligations for the day," Damon called to the audience, and people began drifting away down the stairs.

"That was received well," Rachael said to Leon after several minutes answering further questions. Leon nodded as Johnson joined them.

"It's wonderful, Rachael. It all looks great now that everything's in place."

Rachael nodded. "It was such a team effort."

"We'll need a meeting this afternoon with all the staff that will be involved," Damon waved Allie over, who joined him with Lilliana.

"Allie, Lilliana; Dr Richard is waiting to escort Katy, Emile and Adam up through the psych entrance. Do you have time to show them around once the area clears out?"

Allie nodded, "Yes Sir."

"Good. Rachael and Leon will show you the entrance. It is only for psych and hospital staff clearance." Lilliana and Allie both nodded.

Damon looked at Johnson. "Time we prepared Reid and the others for transport."

"Yes Sir, the Officials plane arrived twenty minutes ago. I've already organised for the bodies to be taken to the airstrip." He referred to Felicia and several of the other prisoners they had terminated per the Officials instructions.

Johnson turned and followed Rachael and Allie as Damon took a moment to plant a kiss on Lilliana's cheek. "Do you like the centre, Baby?" he asked, taking her by the hand and leading her downstairs behind Johnson.

"It's gorgeous," she smiled up at him feeling lighter with every step, knowing that soon Gregory Reid would be out of their lives forever, and the sanctity of peace would return.

As they hit the bottom level almost everyone had cleared out and gone to classes or work for the day.

"I'll see you later, darling; the meeting will be after three pm."

She tilted her head to claim his kiss before he quickly followed Johnson out.

"Lilliana," Rachael called.

She quickly walked over and joined Rachael, Allie, and Leon near a solid blue glass divider, that from the front entrance and reception desk looked like a simple solid wall.

Rachael waited for Christopher's last kitchen hand to leave, carrying a basket of the remaining muffins.

Once they were alone, Rachael stepped behind the glass panel and stood in front of a large oval mirror that reflected the beautiful scenery outdoors. A door in the glass panel opened automatically, revealing a set of stairs leading underground. "Follow me ladies, if you please."

"In the dark?" Allie questioned, pointing to the dark descent.

Rachael took the first step, and the next five steps lit up. "I know it seems a bit dark and creepy, but once you start walking along, it really is quite beautiful. Come, you'll see." She walked ahead and Allie followed.

Lilliana turned to Leon who waved his hand. "After you," he bowed.

She smiled, shaking her head, and followed Allie down the steps. Twenty steps down was a path that gently curved in the direction where the psych ward would be located if one were walking above ground. The tunnel was warm and well lit, with a ceiling of fairy lights powered by solar panels that resembled dancing silver leaves in the trees above. The ground had been levelled out and was covered in a thick layer of moss, which felt more like walking on plush carpet.

"Glad I'm not wearing heels today," Allie commented.

"It is actually pleasant, you don't sink down, due to the foundation being firm," Rachael explained as they approached another door, which this time used a retina scan. Once Rachael's eye was scanned, the door opened revealing Richard, Katy, Emile, and Adam.

Allie's eyes lit up on seeing her adopted siblings, who, like her had been abducted from a very young age and held as prisoners by a couple who stole young children. As they grew older, the couple had them lay with each other in order to bear children, only to sell their babies on the black market. Karma eventually knocked on the couple's door as a fire burned them alive, which led to the discovery of the underground door to the children's prison, where the Officials finally found and rescued them.

"Allie," Emile cried, throwing herself into her sister's arms.

"Hey guys, are you ready for an experience?"

"Oh yeah," Adam said, rubbing his hands together as Katy hugged Allie.

Lilliana smiled at Leon. They were all so pleased with the progress Adam especially had made. He was no longer harming himself, and both the girls had been taken off suicide watch.

"Lilliana," Dr Richard peered down over his nose at her.

"Yes?" She looked away from Leon and met Richard's eyes. He had a peculiar glint to them.

"Jaycee needs to see you in room 47."

"Richard? Have you checked with Damon about this?" Leon had a concerned look on his face.

"Damon has had his hands excessively busy, I'm sure his wife can handle this situation," he retorted, before addressing Lilliana again, more insistently. "Room 47."

"Okay," she turned to Allie and the group. "Enjoy upstairs, Allie, I'll see you in the group soon?"

"I'll be there." Allie smiled. "Come on you lot, let's go explore."

They followed Racheal and Leon, with Richard taking up the rear.

Lilliana shook her head at Richard being so... well, Richard-like, and made sure the door was shut firmly behind them before making her way to the psych desk where Brad was holding up the fingerprint sign-in for her.

"Hello Brad, almost done for the day?"

"Yep, just about ready to call it a night." He smiled; the permanent night shift suited him more than the endless rotations.

"Hey Lilly—be careful, we've got our hands full of some real cases at the moment," he said, raising an eyebrow suggestively as if she would know what he meant.

Lilliana chuckled as she began walking down the corridor. "Okay Brad, thanks." Taking a deep breath as she walked, she put herself in a calm and caring mindset as screaming and crying echoed throughout the ward. Reaching room 47, she knocked gently on the door so as not to startle before entering.

"Hey Lilly," Jaycee smiled softly and sympathetically as Lilliana returned her smile, puzzled at everyone's behaviour, before noticing the figure standing in the corner of the room, arms folded, a glare across his handsome face as he stared back at her.

"Damon?"

He pinned her in place with his brooding dark eyes, his stance that of an angry Damon. Dressed in psych ward attire, he looked a misfit in the white pants and tee shirt.

Lilliana looked at Jaycee and back towards Damon. "I don't understand what's happening here?"

"Don't you?" He asked. His voice sounded so similar, but not quite the same.

Lilliana stared at the man, trying to wrap her head around what she was seeing. What was she seeing?

Jaycee watched Lilliana and the man stare at each other intently in uncomfortable familiarity.

He stepped toward her, hand reaching out. "Come here, come to me."

She shook her head and hastily took a step back. He frowned, dropping his hand, staring back at her in puzzlement.

"Jaycee, outside now," she ordered. She was feeling a rush of unpleasant heat the longer this Damon stared at her and had to get out of the room.

Turning, she fled, with Jaycee three steps behind.

The door closed quickly behind them, and Lilliana turned on Jaycee. "What is going on? What is this?"

"I'm sorry Lilly, I thought Dr Richard would have warned you." Jaycee looked flustered. "He's not the only one. Come."

Jaycee walked along to the next room and knocked on the door before opening it. Shelley turned around and there, sitting on the bed, was another Damon lookalike.

"Lilliana," Shelley said softly.

"Hi Shelley," Lilliana said and stared in shock once more, as this Damon quickly stood to attention when he saw her. A handsome yet all too familiar frown flashed across his face.

Lilliana felt a wave of dizziness hit her as her breath seemed to leave her body. "I need Damon," she whispered.

"I'm here Lilliana," he said and stepped toward her, a puzzled anguish crossing his face at her distress.

"Lilliana," a voice called from behind them.

Lilliana turned to see Dr. Hillary, who stood in the doorway. "A word please."

Lilliana stood frozen, staring at this Damon. A firm, but gentle hand took her elbow and turned her around, leading her from the room.

Out in the corridor, Hillary asked Jaycee, "Who sent Lilliana down here?" She sounded as displeased as Jaycee had ever heard her.

"Dr Richard."

Hillary remained quiet as she led Lilliana towards Brad and into a room near the sign-in desk. "Brad, can you make Lilliana a cup of chamomile tea; Jaycee, hunt down Leon for me please." Jaycee nodded and took off to the healing centre.

Hillary sat a noticeably quiet Lilliana into a comfortable chair and drew a blanket across her lap. "Just sit here dear, and I'll fetch Mr Night for you. Okay?"

Lilliana nodded, staring at the beautiful seascape painting on the opposite wall.

She heard Hillary say in a quiet voice to Shelley, "Has she seen the others?"

"No, just the two."

"Let's leave it that way until Mr Night arrives, shall we?"

"Yes, Dr. Hillary."

"Brad, once you give Lilliana her tea, get Richard up here, please."

"He is with Leon, leading the healing centre tour with Nurse Rachael and Allie."

Hillary nodded, "I'm sure he'll be back soon enough."

It may have been his knock off time, but Brad was not going to miss out on the fireworks that were sure to go off once Mr Night and Dr Richard arrived. He almost laughed as he poured Lilliana's tea, but remembering the shocked look on her poor, sweet face sobered him. She had never been anything but a sweetheart to everyone.

"I'll be back shortly; make sure she does not leave that room," Hillary instructed as she left the psych ward.

Brad walked into the waiting room. "Hey Lilly," he sat in the chair beside her, watching her beautiful sea-green eyes as she stared at the seascape.

"I've got you a nice cup of herbal tea." He reached out and took her hand, gently pressing it in his.

Lilliana turned her eyes on him, blinking. "Thank you," she said and quietly took the cup.

"I know it must be a shock. Bloody Richard, not warning you." He shook his head.

Lilliana sipped her tea; she was thankful Brad had dumped enough cold water in it so she could take a couple of decent mouthfuls to quench her dry throat.

Two Damon's, possibly more by the sound of it—but how?

"Excuse me a minute, Lilly." Brad got up when the psych door opened as Joe, one of the attendees, walked in.

"G'day Brad, what are you still doing here?"

"Just… finishing up a couple of things," Brad shrugged.

"How's it all been?"

"Yeah, busy as always."

"Great, I'll get to it then."

Brad nodded, turning as Lilliana walked out of the room.

"Hey Lilliana," Joe said as he headed off towards his shift.

"Hi," Lilliana said quietly as Joe disappeared down the corridor and around a corner.

"Do you want another tea?" Brad asked.

"No thanks, I'm just going to go to the… bathroom." She hoped he wouldn't pick up on her little white lie.

He looked at her for a moment, before replying. "Sure Lilly."

She headed along the corridor and turned in the opposite direction to Joe and headed towards the female staff toilets. She waited around the corner for a moment, before peeking back towards Brad. He had his back towards her, leaning on the sign in desk, scribbling on a pad. Lilliana felt a flash of guilt as she darted into the opposite corridor and headed past the two doors she had already entered. Stopping in front of the next door, she let the high security fingerprint scanning, installed throughout the psych ward, record her fingertips, before unlocking the door.

The tall man had his back towards the door when she entered. He smiled joyfully when he saw her.

"Lilliana."

"What is this?" she whispered, "who are you?" Seeing the third Damon wasn't helping the situation.

He took a step forward.

She took one step backwards and spun around, opening the door she had just stepped through, and quickly shut it behind her, her heart pounding as she could hear his desperate cries.

"Lilliana, don't leave me!"

Oh my God! What the hell is happening? She opened the next door, and the next, and the next, all leaving behind grieving Damon's.

She paused outside the first door again, that she had entered with Jaycee, her heart accelerating and sweat dripping down between her breasts. She felt faint and pulled off her jumper that had fought off the chill of the windy day. Dropping it on the ground, she pushed open the door and stepped into the room. She needed answers, and for that, she had to ask the right questions.

"Back again, Lilliana?" The first Damon raised an eyebrow.

How could he look like her Damon? Slowly she approached him, comforted only by the fact that he felt so familiar. Stopping a foot away from him, she asked, "What are you doing here?"

"I'm here for you of course, my Lilliana."

"No," she shook her head. "I don't think so."

He angled his head, arms folded as he looked down at her. "I've missed you, love." He stepped forward.

Hastily she stepped back.

"We've never met."

"Are you not my Lilliana?"

"Your Lilliana? No, I'm not." Lilliana frowned. This felt so wrong. How the hell was this happening?

"If you're not my Lilliana, how can this be? Where is she, what have you done with her?" He sounded desperate, angry. "If you've hurt her!" His hand shot out and he grabbed her arm, jerking her up against him.

She felt it then. The complete difference. He may have been as tall as her Damon, as dark and hell yes, almost as incredibly handsome, but he felt all wrong. Dangerous.

"Let me go," she forced herself to stay calm as she stared up into his eyes, imploring him to do the right thing. "I can help you, but you need to let me go."

He stared into her eyes. "How can you be more beautiful than my Lilliana?" he frowned, confused, his other arm bound around her waist, bringing her body hard up against his, his breathing heavy. "How is that possible?"

Lilliana froze, feeling her judgment cloud over as fear enveloped her; he lowered his head to kiss her and she squeezed her eyes shut and whispered, "Don't, please don't."

He had to taste her; make sure she was real. His lips slid across hers, tasting her utter sweetness, a sigh of pure pleasure escaping his lips.

"Stop," She pushed against his chest, moving her head to the side as she heard a stampede of footsteps charge down the corridor. The door flung open with a crash.

"Get your hands off her," Damon shouted as Jaycee rushed in ahead of him.

"Hey," she soothed her patient. "This isn't your Lilliana, Damon— you have to release her, okay?"

The Damon lookalike frowned, confused. "I don't know what's going on here. What is happening, where's my Lilliana?"

Lilliana stepped back quickly as he released her and Damon reached out, grabbing her protectively and pulling her under his shoulder. He was cross that she had snuck off on Brad to explore this, well... whatever the hell this was. Looking at the other Damon, he felt a flash of pity for him as he led Lilliana out of the room past Richard, Rachael, Leon, Allie, and Hillary and down the corridor.

Calling over his shoulder, he shot out, "I want to see everyone who knew about this, in Johnson's office in one hour. Do *not* be late."

Brad had never heard Damon so furious.

Leon at least had the decency to look guilty.

Lilliana peeked at Damon through her lashes as he marched her along and out past Brad's desk. She hadn't seen him so angry and was grateful he hadn't walked in when the other Damon's lips had touched hers. Looking away from his darkness, she felt flushed with guilt, thinking that right now he looked as dangerous as the other Damon had felt.

He opened the door to the secluded passageway and led her up towards their room. After several minutes, he opened the door and took her inside, releasing her.

He walked into the kitchenette and poured a coffee for himself and a tea for Lilliana.

She walked over to the balcony door and slid it open, stepping out into the wind, that pushed the sheer curtain inside, performing a furious dance with its maelstrom partner.

Damon rested her tea on the railing in front of her and stood beside her, watching her hair fly around her like a silken cape. He took a gulp of coffee, waiting for his own emotions to get under control before he spoke. Seeing her in the arms of another man just about sent him over the edge. And witnessing her struggle to free herself from his embrace had him seeing violent, rageful reds. He was on fire.

Brad had told Damon that she had said she was going to the toilet and had felt guilty he hadn't watched her properly. Poor Brad had thought he was gearing up for some entertainment, instead he got his head chewed off by Hillary and Damon. He'd have to apologise next time her saw him. Of course, it made complete sense that she would be curious.

Meanwhile Damon was still trying to get his head around what Hillary had told him on the walk down from his office, as the Officials and Paul had just escorted Reid and the other prisoners off towards the plane.

Just as one situation seems to get sorted out, another begins, he thought. He sighed, rubbing a hand over his face.

Lilliana turned to face him, her heartstrings aching. "Damon, are you alright?"

He turned to face her; he was silent as he carefully contemplated his answer. She flushed under his stare, praying he wasn't cross with her.

"I'm so sorry… I didn't know what was going on… I still don't. I was so confused, it was like… it was you, but I knew it wasn't… I was trying to get an answer, but he almost seemed as confused as I was, and then... well, he just…"

"Stop Lilliana, stop," he said quietly, cupping her check. "It's okay."

She closed her eyes and leaned against his hand and a tear escaped, running over his palm, breaking his heart.

"Darling," he whispered, placing his cup on the rail beside hers, pulling her against his chest, as he wrapped his arms protectively around her. Her arms slid around his waist. He dropped his cheek on top of her silky hair that flew around them both. They held each other silently, both deep in thought about their visitor's downstairs, wondering how long they had been there and why they hadn't known about them.

"Let's get you in out of this cold wind," Damon said, rubbing her bare arms that felt naked without her jacket to protect her from the chill.

Walking back inside, Damon closed the door and followed Lilliana over to the couch, where she sat, tucking her legs underneath her.

He flicked a switch on in the fireplace, grateful as the hot flames leaped about in the large grill, licking the fake logs, spilling instant heat towards them both. Damon looked up at their wedding portrait for a minute before turning to face his beautiful wife.

"Someone has a lot of explaining to do, and I cannot wait to hear it."

"Richard?"

"For a start. I don't know what the hell he was thinking, sending you down there." He shook his head as anger spread across his features.

"On top of that, what are these lookalikes doing here?"

Lilliana watched as he began to pace the length of the fireplace, hands on hips.

"I can't imagine what has been done to them all. They each believed I was their Lilliana; I did feel sorry for them in their confusion, Damon."

He turned to her as he stopped his pacing. Crossing over to her, he knelt, taking her hands.

"Of course you did, my darling, because you have a kind heart." He raised her fingers to his lips and kissed them.

"Can you imagine what it must be like for them to have their own identity stolen, their faces, transformed? Let alone what's been done to their psyche, to believe that they are you, and I am theirs?" She shook her head.

"We'll get to the bottom of this. Are you okay? Do you want to join me for Q and A?"

"Definitely. I am not ready to leave the real Damon Night's side just yet."

He smiled, standing as he pulled her up with him. "Do you want to get changed?"

"Yes." She paused, before saying, "Damon, I know this is wrong of me, but I seriously cannot do my group this morning with this situation cluttering my head."

He nodded. "Totally understandable. I'll run down and chat to Allie now. Are you okay to be alone for a few minutes and join me in Black Op's when you're done here?"

She nodded and smiled as he headed to the door. "Thank you love."

He stopped, turned around and marched back towards her. Placing his hand under her chin, he gently tilted her head back. "Just know, that whatever this situation is, we've got it covered, you and me, okay?"

She placed her hands upon his chest and nodded. He bent and gently dropped the sweetest and most tender kiss against her lips.

"I'll see you shortly." He smiled, dropping another kiss on her lips before turning and walking out the door.

Lilliana sighed, alone with her thoughts and hurried down to their room and into their walk-in robe. Stripping off her boots, jeans, and shirt, she pulled out a long sleeved, black jumpsuit and slipped into ankle socks and boots, before quickly running a brush through her windblown hair.

Heading towards their side door, Lilliana hoped the meeting hadn't started yet. She did not want to miss a single detail or see Damon rip Richard's conniving throat out.

CHAPTER 20

Lilliana walked into Johnson's office within twenty minutes of Damon leaving her side, feeling a rush of peace fill her at the sight of him.

Johnson looked irritated but offered her a smile as she crossed over to Damon.

"How are you?" he asked kindly.

"I'm fine Johnson, thanks." He nodded, hoping she'd continue being fine once she had been filled in with the other half of the story.

Damon ran his hand down her back appreciatively, marvelling always at her beauty.

She smiled up at him as Rachael approached her. "Lilly, I am so sorry Richard sent you in to that confusing situation."

"It's okay, Rachael. Did you know?"

Rachael shook her head.

"How did they get past you in the hospital section without you knowing?"

"All will be answered shortly; why don't you both grab a tea and sit?" Johnson gestured to the trolley in the corner of the room.

Rachael and Lilliana exchanged a glance, knowing both their men had been under a lot of duress with the Reid's case, amongst other things, and complied, pouring a beverage, and joining him around the oval table. Shortly after, Cam walked in followed by Richard and Hillary. He crossed over to Lilliana and dropped a kiss on her head.

"Hey Angel, you okay?"

She patted the hand that rested on top of her shoulder. "I'm fine, thanks."

Cam sat down on the other side of her and nodded to the coffee pot, winking at Damon, as Jaycee, Brad, Shelley, and Leon walked into the room, anxiously waiting to be seated.

"Please, sit everyone." Johnson stood at the top end of the table, and Damon joined him after passing Cam his coffee.

"You are all aware why this meeting was called," Johnson began. "And we don't have any time to waste. Richard, when the replicas arrived, why did you not notify Damon immediately, and why were they not processed in the normal way, as our protocol stipulates, before taking them to psych?"

All eyes shifted curiously to Richard.

Rachael's fingernails tapped against her teacup in pent up anger. Cam crossed an ankle over one knee as he leaned back in his chair, looping one arm over the back of Lilliana's chair, the other hand around his coffee mug. He sure as hell was interested in hearing this answer.

Richard reached for the water jug on the table and took his time filling a glass, before taking a mouthful. "It's quite simple, really. The replicas, as you call them, arrived a few weeks ago when Mr and Mrs Night were having time away up at the cabin. Mr Night did check in the second morning, and, as the new arrivals were running late, I offered to take care of the matter."

Lilliana watched Richard; her eyes glued to him as she held the teacup between her hands.

His eyes met hers briefly before continuing.

"When I saw the new arrivals I assumed that they had been made to create some disturbance, so I had them transported immediately to the psych ward with the help of Leon and the psych staff." He gestured to the others around the table. "I didn't get a chance to tell Rachael at the time, and as you all had your hands full with the Reid situation, I decided it was best for you to focus on one dilemma at a time."

Damon stepped forward angrily jabbing a finger at Richard's face. "That was *not* your decision to make, Richard! And as for the rest of you—did you not think it a little strange that I hadn't even been to see our new arrivals? No one thought to report that we had seven rooms filled with Damon lookalikes?" His voice raised in frustration and disbelief, incredulous that none of his staff had approached him with such a serious matter.

"Sir," Jaycee said, quietly but firmly. "I'm sorry Sir, but Dr Richard informed us that you knew about our latest arrivals, and that you were too busy at the time to come down."

"Jaycee, I'm sorry you were all misinformed. I'm sure you thought it was very remiss of me, not bothering to check out such a precarious situation."

Jaycee nodded. Brad and Shelley remained apologetically quiet.

Hillary looked at Damon. "I honestly thought you were aware of the situation, Damon." She looked across at Richard, a frown pinching her features.

Leon looked at Lilliana then towards Damon. "Sir, I also cannot apologise enough. I was also told that you had been notified, and that, due to what Lilliana had already endured at the Reid compound, I was not to notify her regarding the arrivals under any circumstances." He looked back at Lilliana. "I'm so sorry, you know I would never do anything to hurt or upset you, Lilly."

"It's alright Leon," she said, feeling sorry for her friend who had done nothing but work to the best of his ability. She hoped Damon wouldn't come down on him too hard.

"You were only doing as you were instructed Leon; I'm beginning to see that, as a team, you are not to blame."

He turned back towards Richard. "May I ask, Richard, why you thought it was a grand idea to place my wife in such a stressful situation, if you were so concerned about her welfare in the first place?" His voice was colder than ice, as he folded his arms across his chest, fists tightly clenched.

Cam could easily spot his brother's temper, a temper that Damon usually held in check, as he saw it now, creeping dangerously close to the surface.

Richard was obviously thick or too arrogant to see it, as he cast a bored look in Lilliana's direction, pushing his glasses up with his middle finger.

"I simply thought that, as Reid Senior was evacuated into the hands of the Officials, that is was time to sort out this ordeal, and as her physician, thought she was ready to handle it."

Lilliana looked away from Richard, feeling her own dismay and fury at his complete inconsideration for her. He'd helped her so much with her nightmares the month after she'd returned, and she was disappointed in his lack of regard for her mental health.

"You will no longer be her physician." Damon spat out.

"Well, I disagree with that decision," Richard countered in a dry, arrogant tone.

Cam rubbed Lilliana's shoulders as he took a mouthful of coffee, considering his next move. He knew it was the wrong place but couldn't help himself.

"You're a real prick Dick, do you know that?"

Brad burst out laughing before he had a chance to stop himself. "Sorry Mr Night," he held up his hands, "I get a bit delirious at this time of the day."

Damon looked away from Cam, to address Brad. "You're free to leave, sorry we kept you from your sleep. I will check in with you during the night."

Brad got up from his chair and pushed it under the table. "Sure thing, Sir." He looked across at Lilliana. "I'm really sorry."

Lilliana offered him a small smile before he left.

"Well," Johnson sighed. "That's only the first half of the problem, I'm afraid."

He turned to his glass monitors and tapped seven screens on.

A collective gasp could be heard from Lilliana's, Cam's, and Damon's lungs in response to what was being shown to them. There were seven rooms, all holding seven identical Lilliana's.

"What the hell?" Cam exclaimed, standing up.

A question I've been asking myself all morning, Lilliana agreed quietly, wondering if anything else could shock her further.

"Johnson?" Damon ran his hands through his hair before looking at his wife, shaking his head before dropping his hands on his hips.

"Seriously, Richard; you actually thought I was too busy to not want to deal with this?" He looked at Johnson, "I am almost speechless with the arrogant stupidity of some people around here!" His voice rose to a shout.

Johnson held up a hand, trying to calm Damon as he addressed the room. "I think we'll have another meeting this afternoon once we have seen the replicas for ourselves. I'll let you know the time. Thanks." He dismissed them all.

Damon looked at Hillary, "Can you help Allie out with Lilliana's sessions today?"

"Of course, Sir, I'll get onto that immediately." Hillary turned and left the room.

"Are you okay Lilly?" Rachael asked quietly as she got up from the table.

Lilliana turned away from the seven screens where seven Lilliana's moved about their rooms.

"I am fine Rachael; I just worry for them." She nodded, looking back at the women.

"It's right of you to worry, Lilly," Leon stood. "Sir, if I may?" He looked at Johnson and Damon.

Damon had his back to everyone, focused entirely on the women on the screens. He was listening, but he couldn't respond just now. Johnson nodded.

"In the time we have spent with these Lilliana's and Damon's, we note that they have shown no aggressiveness, no intent to harm. They are all simply desperate to be with their, well... partners. We don't know who goes with who just yet, as we were just following protocol in that regard. And waiting for you to come on board."

"What did they do to be sent here?" Lilliana finally asked.

"I sent the report through to Johnson just minutes before I came to this meeting," Richard said, turning from the door.

"How good of you." Damon snapped, crossing over to Johnson's glass screen, logging in and flicking across until he saw the file.

"Get out Dick—I think we are done with you for the moment," Cam waved him away.

Richard frowned. "In time you will thank me for my consideration."

Damon turned around, furious with the man. "Well that time is certainly not now, Richard. Now. Get. Out."

The room cleared as Cam headed towards the door. "I'm going to find Josephine. Be back soon."

Lilliana rose and walked over to view the files with Damon and Johnson. Damon put his arm around her shoulder as he read, absently stroking her arm.

"They were dumped anonymously at the Officials head office, bound and unconscious. No fingertips for a clear fingerprint, looks like they've been sliced off. Eye scans were invalid, and their DNA could not confirm who they were," Johnson stated, running his finger down the screen, before flicking a file across, pulling it up on another screen beside it. Reaching across, he tapped on the fourteen individuals' photos.

"It's uncanny; they are identical in every way."

Damon continued reading the psych team's reports for several minutes.

"They have no recollection of who they were, or what they did before they were taken, except that they remember their other half. All of them claiming to be Damon and Lilliana Night."

Damon sighed, "This is absolutely mind blowing."

Lilliana turned to him. "This doesn't make any sense."

Both men turned to face her.

"We never announced our wedding. Nobody outside these walls knew us as Damon and Lilliana Night." They stood silently for a minute.

"The United crew knew, although that article hasn't been released yet." Damon looked at Johnson.

"They're professionals, and under contract. They wouldn't say anything." Johnson ran his hands through his hair.

"Russell Meek knows." Damon folded his arms.

"Let's get him on the line now," Johnson said, wiping the photographs from the screen and pulling up another file, finding Russell's number, and pressing it.

Within minutes Russell's face filled the screen.

"Hello," he smiled, his usual friendly self.

"Russell, we have a situation here. I need to know if you told anyone about Lilliana and myself?"

"About you being together? Absolutely not. Why?" Russell looked concerned.

Damon swiped a finger sending the file to Russell, who spent the next few minutes reading over it, opening the fourteen photographs and staring in disbelief. He looked up, horrified. "What the hell?"

"Something we've all been saying a lot this morning," came Cam's reply as he and Josephine walked into the room.

Josephine quickly pulled Lilliana into a hug. "I can't believe this is happening."

Lilliana nodded, "That makes all of us."

"What's the purpose behind this, Damon?" Russell said, glancing back at the file. "I mean, why would someone go to all this effort, let alone the expense of cloning yourself and Lilliana?"

"That's what we need to find out; the trouble is, none of them are aware of who they were before they woke up in our psych ward."

Russell shook his head, reading through another file. "The Officials state that they were kept separated the entire time they were at their facility, and sleep serum was used on them before transporting them to you. I'm gathering from this report that they have no knowledge of each other, as in the Damon's aren't aware of the other Damon's?"

"It seems that way," Johnson said. "The men have seen Lilliana however; and all presumed she was *their* Lilliana."

"Although," Lilliana said, looking at Johnson. "I noticed one of them looked confused when he realised I was not '*his*' Lilliana; he was genuinely distressed, so he knows there are at least two of us." She shook her head. "If you know what I mean."

"How will they react upon seeing you two, or the others, do you think?" Josephine asked.

"That's my concern also," Lilliana added. "At the end of the day, we have to care for these people as though they are any of our other Given. I think we need to be as gentle as possible." She looked at Damon. "I think you should speak to the females and I should speak to the males to begin with, explain who we are, and our roles here."

Damon nodded, watching her face for any tell-tale signs of stress as she spoke. But in typical Lilliana fashion, whenever she stepped into her role as a carer all thoughts regarding her own comfort or anxiety disappeared.

"Perhaps after we have explained everything to them and reassured them that they are safe, you and I could speak to them together, and then bring them together as a group?"

"It's a start. I want to begin this process immediately. Are you up for it Lilliana?" His concern filled her with warmth.

"I am."

"I'll go with you Damon," Johnson said.

"Can I go with Lilly?" Josephine asked.

Damon smiled at her, shaking her head, "Sorry darling, but I think it will be better if the person going with Lilliana have the right training. Leon?" He asked Johnson.

"Perfect." Johnson nodded.

"Let's do this."

"Good luck," Cam clapped his brother on the back. "I'll buzz Leon and send him down and we'll take care of the meeting in the healing centre this afternoon." He picked up Josephine's hand.

"Thank's Cam, I have a feeling we are going to be at this well into the night." Damon took Lilliana's hand and led her out of the room and downstairs to the psych ward with Johnson. Jaycee was there to greet them.

"Jaycee, Johnson and I are going to speak with the women. We'll need who was attending them to introduce us, to put a familiar face in the room to begin with."

"Yes Sir, that's a very good idea." She nodded. "Joe is already attending one of them at the moment, you could start there?"

"What room?" Johnson asked.

"Room 72."

Damon turned to Lilliana, "Darling, Leon shouldn't be long. Are you going to be okay?"

She reached up and stroked his face lovingly. "I am totally fine, please, don't worry about me."

He nodded and dropped a kiss on her cheek before turning to follow Johnson to the first room.

Lilliana sighed, looking at Jaycee as they waited for Leon.

Jaycee smiled. "I hope they are all going to be okay Lilly; they really seem like such nice people as individuals. My heart kinda breaks for them."

Lilliana nodded. "Mine too."

"I really am sorry about what Richard did." She shook her head.

"Don't be; we shouldn't really be that surprised."

"True."

The door opened and Leon walked in. "Cam told me what you and Damon are about to do; I think it's a good idea."

Lilliana smiled, "I hope it is."

"Lilliana, you won't need an attendee; Leon has met with all the Damon's and they are comfortable around him."

"That's great. Shall we?"

"Yep, follow me." Leon led the way to their first Damon of the hour.

Lilliana took a steadying breath as she followed him, grateful that at least this time she was prepared, and felt she could do her job with a clear head.

***

Joe opened the door to Damon and Johnson's last interview with the seventh Lilliana. It was well past eleven o'clock at night, each conversation having lasted roughly two hours each. Damon couldn't help feeling unnerved every time he entered the next room to see a lovely replica of his Lilliana. Yes, maybe not quite as perfect, or beautiful, but gorgeous all the same. Their pain and anguish pulled at his heartstrings. As they entered the room the figure on the bed rolled over and sat up, blinking tears out of her eyes. She'd been crying.

"Lilliana, this is…"

"Damon," she whispered, just like all the others before her had, and she launched herself happily toward him.

Johnson gently blocked her path, taking her arms and holding her at bay as Damon waited, for Joe to introduce Johnson. As he did, he quickly pricked her arm with a calming sedative. She stopped struggling immediately and stepped away from Johnson.

"Damon?" she asked again.

"Lilliana, please sit down." He said gently, gesturing for her to sit on the bed before he dragged a chair over from the corner of the room, putting it a couple of feet away from her.

She tucked a strand of hair behind her ear; it was so like Lilliana.

Damon took a deep breath and smiled. "Sorry for disturbing you so late at night. How are you?"

"Better now that you are here." She smiled, breathtakingly.

Johnson stood against the wall, totally baffled by how someone could clone these women almost perfectly as mirror images of Lilliana.

"I know this has been an extremely difficult time for you, so please bear with me while I explain a few things."

She nodded, simply happy to be seeing her lover's face again. Although the more he spoke, the more she too got a prickling feeling that something wasn't quite right.

"Firstly, I must tell you, that I am not your Damon."

"My Damon? Yes, I think you are right. But how?"

She was the first one who hadn't become hysterical.

She was more like the real Lilliana than the others.

"Someone has created a number of lookalikes to resemble me, one of them being your Damon. There are seven Damon's in this facility. I've been told you know where you are?"

"Yes, the Louisiana Given. Although, I don't know why," she replied sadly.

Damon looked at Johnson, who could see that all these

heartbroken Lilliana's were taking a toll on his kind director.

"I've only been told that I needed caring for, and that horrid Doctor told me that my situation was on a 'need to know' basis. As though my being here was none of my concern." Her voice raised in irritation.

"I'm presuming that was Dr Richard?"

She nodded, tucking her feet underneath her and wrapping the blanket about her shoulders.

"Would you like something to drink?"

"Yes, tea would be lovely, thank you." She smiled.

"Joe?"

"Right on it, Sir." He left the room, knowing how this Lilliana liked it.

"Lilliana, I am Damon Night, head of this facility, and it is my role here to look after anyone who has been delivered to my door. Along with my staff, we want nothing more than to care for you in every capacity. This includes physical and mental."

She nodded, hanging on his every word.

Joe returned with a tray, handing Lilliana her tea, and passing Damon and Johnson a coffee.

"Thanks Joe; you're good to go now," Damon smiled before taking an appreciative mouthful as he watched the lady sip her tea.

Joe nodded and left the room.

She looked back at him. "How can there be seven of the same person?"

"Well, technically they are not all the same person, but they have been created to look the same."

"Why?"

"This is something we are trying to find out."

"Is my Damon, the real Damon?"

He slowly shook his head.

"Then who is he?"

"Once again, this is something we're working on. There's something else I must tell you, and it may be difficult to hear." He paused as her eyes became wary.

"Something more difficult than learning about several Damon's?"

"I'm afraid so. There are several Lilliana's, too, that look identical to you."

This piece of news startled her equally as much as it had the others.

"What?" She cried, shaking her head. "That doesn't make any sense, I am Lilliana, there's only one of me." She got off the bed, placing her tea on the side table and walked over to the door, knocking on it, "I want my Damon, now! Please, I can't do this anymore, none of this makes sense!"

Her small fists pounded on the door as she began to cry.

Johnson went to comfort her, but Damon got up quickly, placing his cup beside hers, walking over and gently placing a hand on her shoulder. She spun around, fright filling her face as she looked up at him, tears running down her cheeks.

"It's alright, I promise you; tomorrow you will see your Damon, and we will get the answers to all your questions," he nodded, hoping that were true.

"Okay." She collapsed against his chest, crying softly as her small hands clung to his shirt. Damon felt he had no choice but to put his arms around her and comfort her.

"I think that's about all for tonight, Damon," Johnson said.

Damon nodded and he led the small figure back to the bed, gently holding her at arm's length away from him. She looked up at him, wiping her tears away with the back of her hand.

"I'm sorry," she shook her head and stepped back, sitting on the bed.

"Don't apologise, your reaction is completely understandable after everything you've just heard. Tell me, do you think you'd like to meet the other Damon's and Lilliana's tomorrow?"

She looked thoughtful, before nodding slowly. "Yes, after being here for so many weeks, I'd like that."

"Do you have any recollection at all of who you were and what you did before you were delivered to the Officials?"

She frowned, shaking her head. "I've already been asked these questions, I'm sorry; all I know is that my name is Lilliana, and I belong with Damon."

He nodded. "Thank you so much for helping us tonight. Joe will be here in a moment to give you something to help you sleep. We will come and chat to you after lunch tomorrow, before we take you to meet the group. Okay?"

"Sure," she scooted into the bed, pulling the covers up to her chest and waited for Joe.

"Goodnight," Johnson nodded to her as he followed Damon out of the room.

"Goodnight," she called back as they closed the door behind them.

Damon let out a long breath as Johnson nodded. "I'm beat," he said.

"Oh yes, I'm absolutely drained, " Damon agreed as they headed to the sign-in desk.

Brad was back on for the night shift. "Mr Night, how did you go?"

"A bit overwhelming, but manageable. Has Mrs Night left yet?"

"Yes, she and Leon went to her office."

"Thanks Brad. Have a good shift."

"Sure thing."

As Johnson and Damon walked out and into the hospital section heading towards Lilliana's office, they saw Rachael talking to Josephine, who spotted Damon and interrupted the conversation.

"How did it all go?" Josephine asked; she herself was desperate to meet all the Damon's and Lilliana's.

"Fine, sweetheart. What are you still doing up?" It was well past midnight.

"Waiting with Lilliana for you."

Johnson put his arm around an exhausted looking Rachael. "We'll call it a night. I'll see you in the morning."

"Night," Josephine and Damon called together.

Entering Lilliana's office, they saw Allie, Leon, Cam, and Cristopher sitting around the cosy round table with a spread of late-night sandwiches, all discussing the replicas. Damon's stomach rumbled; the only thing he'd eaten all day had been a muffin at the brunch opening. When Lilliana spotted him, she got up and practically threw herself into his arms. He held her tightly, understanding exactly how she felt. After spending hours with the other Lilliana's, to hold his very own in his arms was precisely what he needed.

Allie patted the seat beside her. "Come on Damon, sit and eat before you crash and burn."

"Probably a good idea." He led Lilliana over to join their friends.

"What was it like?" Christopher asked, pushing a plate of food in front of him.

"Exhausting and shattering. I don't know where to start." He sighed, biting into a sandwich as Josephine jumped up behind him and began to massage his tense shoulder muscles.

"If you really want to relax, get Nadia to do this to you tomorrow," she suggested.

Damon tipped his head back as he chewed and smiled up at her.

He looked at Allie, "How did the meeting go at the healing centre?"

"Just fine Damon—don't you worry about a thing."

He nodded, grateful to those who held high positions, that he knew valued, and cared for the running of his establishment as much as he and Cam did.

"I know this is probably not the right time," Allie continued. "But, no time like the present, huh?"

Lilliana smiled at her, hiding a yawn behind her hand.

Damon reached under the table with his free hand and rubbed her knee before placing his hand in her lap for her to take.

"Absolutely agree there," Cam saluted.

"Christopher and I want a simple wedding as soon as possible." Damon looked across at Christopher, who was smiling at Allie.

"You don't want to wait a bit longer so we can organise something special for you, Allie?" Damon reached for the water that Leon had poured and washed down his sandwich.

"Having a day with a handful of my most favourite people and marrying the man I love is all I need; this is what will make it the most special occasion ever."

"We're trying to get in before Eric asks Nadia, too." Christopher added.

"He still hasn't asked her yet?" Leon shook his head.

Josephine laughed. "I'm surprised Nadia doesn't know about it yet; everyone else does."

"Poor Eric, he's fighting demons in his head and wanting everything to be perfect for Nadia at the same time." Lilliana sighed.

"And it will be," Damon said pushing his chair out and standing. He pulled Lilliana to her feet.

"Everyone, I'm calling it a night. We've got another big day tomorrow, and only a week until the Ultimate Games. We've got a lot to organise, and unfortunately time is going to be tight with this added dilemma we now have to sort out."

"Don't worry, we will all work as a team to get things done," Cam assured him.

"Allie, Christopher; it will be my pleasure to make your day a special one. You both deserve nothing but the best. Are you happy to wait for the week after the games?"

"Absolutely, Sir." Christopher smiled as Allie wrapped her arms around his waist.

"Great; well, goodnight all." He tucked his darling under his arm and led her from the room, the others following as they took themselves off to their beds for the night.

***

As the stars twinkled high in the sky, the moonlight cast soothing shadows around their room from the glass ceiling. Damon had one arm tucked around Lilliana, the other behind his head as he stared up at the night sky.

Lilliana's soft breathing comforted him in a moment when his nerves felt stretched beyond all comprehension, his mind racing.

What were they going to do, with these poor, lost, conflicted souls that had no identity other than their names and a love for their partner?

He finally fell asleep, only to have to wake three hours later for a conference call followed by another early morning meeting. Before heading downstairs to start the day, he left a note on his pillow for Lilliana to find when she woke.

CHAPTER 21

Waking to an empty bed had been hard that morning for Lilliana but finding Damon's note had filled her with love and had eased her sadness, giving her the boost of energy she needed to join the early morning running group.

After breakfast, Lilliana had a group session with Allie, followed by two private sessions before taking Nadia and Eric on a tour to the healing centre, filling them in on the replicas.

"My God, it sounds insane," Eric shook his head. "I'd love to see them."

Lilliana shook her head. "It's actually quite sad. Damon and I are doing all we can to lift their spirits and get them all together as a group after lunch. I'm hoping that when they connect with their other half things may start to make a bit more sense for us all."

"I've heard of this being done before," Nadia said, worried. "And it never ended well."

"What do you mean?" Eric turned to her.

"It's just that replicas, especially in large numbers, are used simply as a diversion or to cause harm."

"There's no need to be concerned," Lilliana assured her. "They are harmless. According to the psych staff, in all the weeks they have been held, not one of has exhibited any signs of violence or aggression. The only thing they have been wanting is to have their own Damon or Lilliana, and, seriously—there is no way they can cause any damage where they are, being twenty feet underground; the psych ward is one of the most secure places for them to be."

"Sounds good to me," Eric said, bending so he could look Nadia in the eyes. "Nothing for you to worry your gorgeous self about. Come on, let's get lunch."

"This really is such a wonderful centre," Nadia said, referring to the healing centre as they were leaving. "I can see how it will benefit many."

"It sure will," Lilliana agreed as they walked back to Main House and up the front entrance stairs. Upon entering they spotted Natalie walking into one of the dining rooms and automatically chose another room to dine in.

As Nadia walked ahead, Lilliana grabbed Eric's arm. "Have you asked her yet?"

Eric quickly made sure Nadia was out of earshot, but not too far from his protection. "Not yet, I'm waiting until after the games, and Christopher and Allie's day."

Lilliana nodded, smiling. "Just so you know, everyone's talking about it."

"Everyone?"

"Well," she laughed, "Just us, everyone, if you know what I mean."

He smirked. "Yeah, I know what you mean. Tell everyone to chill and quieten down, I don't want anyone giving it away."

"Sure thing, I'll see you later."

"Hey," he grabbed her hand and pulled it up to inspect her gorgeous cut emerald in its ornate antique setting. "This is pretty nice; I'd love something with a blue diamond."

Lilliana smiled, "To match her eyes, you thoughtful boy."

"Yeah, that's me. I better go." He took off after Nadia.

Lilliana walked by the entrance to the koi pond and crossed over to knock on Damon's office door.

"Come in," he called.

Walking in, she was relieved to find him alone and closed the door behind her.

"Hello love," he smiled, moving away from several screens and walking towards her.

"Hi," she reached up and wrapped her arms around his neck as he pulled her close. She pushed her face into the softness of his neck and breathed him in, before murmuring, "Can we not move from this position for an hour?"

He laughed into her hair, rubbing her back. "Wouldn't that be something."

She tilted her head back so she could look up at him. "Did you sleep well?"

"Well enough—when I did sleep."

She ran a hand along his strong jaw, the light shadow of stubble gracing his usually silky soft skin. "Darling, I'm worried about you."

"There's no need my angel, I am perfectly fine because I have you by my side."

She smiled up into his eyes as she reached to give him a solid kiss which gently deepened. They stood, arms around the other, taking their time with a kiss that felt as though it would last forever; sadly, it didn't because Damon's phone rang.

Lilliana rolled her eyes, which caused him to roar with laughter. He ran a hand over her hair before turning to answer his phone, calling over his shoulder, "That's very unlike you, but I like it."

She snorted quietly, shaking her head as she walked over to glance at the books lining his shelves. Picking one of her favorite's, the Haunted Castles of Ireland, she sat on the arm of a chair and flicked through its scenic pages as she listened to him speak.

"I get it," Damon said, "We were making our way to you in an hour." He paused, listening to Leon explain that one of the Lilliana's had been inconsolable and wanted the meeting with the others right now. Dr Richard had apparently wanted to sedate her, but Jaycee had intervened.

"Jaycee's right, we don't want to sedate any of them; they need to be alert in order to take this meeting in, and hopefully recognise their partner. We're on our way now."

He ended the call and watched as Lilliana slipped the book back into its slot. "Do you want to change, love?"

She looked down at her white dress and sandals. "No; maybe it will make the other Lilliana's more comfortable seeing me in the same colour as what they are in?"

"Okay, lets head down," he held out his hand for her to take and they headed out the door and down towards the hospital, through to the psych ward.

They spent an hour visiting all the replicas; Damon introduced Lilliana to all the Lilliana's and Lilliana introduced Damon to all the Damon's. It was surreal, to say the least. They found it emotionally difficult dealing with all the replicas in their distress, especially since they had visited with them the night before. But to be standing opposite another human that looked practically identical to themselves was completely unnerving. Even their voices, their mannerisms were almost spot on. The last visit before the group meeting was to the last Lilliana that Damon had spoken to the night before. Knocking once he gently opened the door, leading Lilliana in.

"Hello Lilliana, how are you this afternoon?"

The other woman's eyes widened in shock as she sat on the bed. "Oh my, you look just like me," she whispered, fascinated.

Lilliana smiled. "Yes."

"Do all the other Lilliana's look just like us?"

"They do."

"How can this be? Who did this to us?"

"We wish we knew," Lilliana clasped her hands in front of her. "Are you almost ready to meet everyone?"

She nodded.

Damon gestured to his wife. "Lilliana and I are going to be waiting for you in a very peaceful room called the garden room. Shortly, someone will come and collect you and bring you in to join us. For the sake of confusion and for everyone's safety, you will be taken to a seat where you will sit quietly and wait for further instructions. I know you will be overwhelmed and excited to see your partner, but do you think you can do that?"

She nodded enthusiastically. "I will do whatever it is you need me to do to make this work." She smiled sweetly at them both.

Damon beamed as he took his Lilliana's hand. "Wonderful. We will see you shortly."

"Thank you." She smiled as they left the room.

As they made their way to the garden room, Lilliana released a deep breath. Damon raised her hand to his lips and kissed her fingers.

"It's a perplexing situation, isn't it?"

She nodded as they walked into a beautiful, large room lined with the brightest plants and greenery that made one feel as though they were in a rainforest. The ceiling that had once been painted as a sky in the style of trompe l'oeil had been removed, along with twenty feet of soil, allowing for a thick, clear glass roof to let sunlight stream in, gifting the plants below with natural photosynthetic light.

Long wooden benches were positioned around the room, each lined comfortably with colourful cushions in which to sit and absorb the energy of the tranquil space.

Johnson and Leon entered shortly after them.

"All set?" Johnson asked.

"Just waiting for Richard," Damon said with a touch of annoyance. It would be a while before he could forgive the insolent man, not only for his deception but for placing Lilliana in such an uncomfortable position the day before.

He had often wondered about Richard's motives over the years as it seemed like as time wore on, he gained some perverse pleasure in seeing Lilliana in dangerous or uncomfortable situations. He simply could not work the man out.

Richard breezed in, unaware of Damon's negative thoughts towards him in his usual blasé manner.

"They're on their way," Richard said nonchalantly in way of greeting, before joining them.

They stood in a row, a united front. Richard was the only constant, familiar face that all the replicas had known since first arriving.

The attendees for the day entered, along with Jaycee, Shelley Joe, Hillary, and Billy; they were led one at a time, to their seats in a very orderly manner.

The Damon's sat on one long bench seat, while the Lilliana's sat opposite on the other long bench.

Lilliana and Damon were both feeling a little discombobulated the longer they stood there, staring as their identical selves entered the room.

All of the replicas were now staring at each other in awe, trying to figure out which one was theirs. It would have been difficult enough, even if they had all been wearing something different; but being all dressed in the white pant and tee shirt attire of the psych ward only added to their confusion.

"Everyone, thank you for your co-operation," Damon began, as all eyes moved to him. "We know this is a difficult situation, and we are here to help make this process as easy for you as possible. Just take your time sitting; see if you can recognise your partner—and no stress whatsoever if you can't. There's no rush. If anyone would like to speak, please just raise your hand."

The room fell silent, as the replicas eyed not only the opposite sex, but their own.

Leon had to admit that if he threw the real Lilliana in with the other Lilliana's it would be beyond difficult to tell them apart. All their eyes were the most piercing of greens. The Damon's, too; their intense dark blue irises were identical. It made him dizzy just looking at them all. He looked at the real Lilliana. She felt his stare and gave him a small smile, before looking away. One of the Damon's raised his hand.

"Yes," Damon nodded to him.

"What is going to happen to us after today? I mean, after meeting and seeing which Lilliana is ours, where are we to go?"

Johnson answered for Damon. "This, as I'm sure you will all appreciate, is a very unusual situation that needs to be treated with delicacy. We will keep you here for a while longer, just to make sure you are all cared for and receive the best possible treatment as we endeavour to ascertain your history before you came to us here at the

Given."

One of the Lilliana's raised her hand.

Johnson nodded to her. "I think that Damon is mine," she said softly, pointing to one of the Damon's at the opposite end of the bench

Richard walked over and put his hand on the man's shoulder.

"This one?"

She nodded.

"Are you sure?" Richard had an odd glint in his eye as he waited for the Lilliana to confirm.

"Why don't you stand and come over here," Richard nodded, leading the tall, handsome man to a space at the opposite end of the room.

"Come now," he gestured to the Lilliana who immediately stood and made her way towards Richard. She stopped a few feet in front of Damon and smiled.

"Damon?"

Hesitantly he reached for her hands. As they connected, their smiles lit up and they laughed with excitement, both calling out, "It's really you!" before embracing.

Lilliana looked at Damon, unable to conceal her smile. Her heart lit up for the couple.

Johnson and Leon circled the other couples, encouraging them to explore and see if they could find their partner. Soon, happy chatter filled the room, with occasional tears of joy as more couples made connections with their other half, before removing themselves from the group, preferring to sit alone and talk quietly with their loved one.

Damon ran his hand through his hair.

"What to do now?" he whispered to Lilliana.

"I think they deserve some time together, the poor dears. Why can't they have afternoon tea in here?" Lilliana suggested. "I've got time, I can stay with Leon and look out for them."

Damon looked around the room. They were all sitting respectfully, not bothering the other couples, focused as they were on their own partner.

"If only all that came to us behaved this beautifully," Johnson said quietly as he joined them.

"Indeed," Damon agreed. "Lilliana suggests they have afternoon tea here, instead of in their rooms."

"Which Lilliana?" Johnson joked, adding a dark chuckle.

"Shouldn't be a problem by the looks of things. We'll leave Richard and Leon here." He nodded. "I'll head upstairs, see if I can dig up some more information."

"I'll pop out and chat to Hillary about afternoon tea then." Damon turned to Lilliana, sweeping his hand along her neck, running his fingers gently over her skin. "You okay for a few minutes?"

"Of course," she smiled.

He crossed over to Leon. "I'm just ducking out for ten minutes. Things seem to be going smoothly."

"They certainly do," he nodded across to their Lilliana. "She'll be fine, Sir."

Damon smiled as he clapped Leon on the back in thanks before following Johnson out of the room.

Lilliana sat down on a seat positioned between two large Birds of Paradise, enjoying their bright, colourful flowers.

The room was abuzz and Lilliana felt an energy of peace and harmony fill the room as she watched all the couples as they connected as much as they could, given that they hadn't been able to recall even as much as their names or the one they loved.

Her eyes fell on Richard who had his back to her across the room, fiddling with the front of his pant pockets as he was watched one of the Lilliana's. He had always been such a strange man, she thought.

Leon was busy answering one of the couple's questions as he leaned casually against a tall tree with his arms loosely folded, laughing at something they said.

She sighed, feeling the tension of the day drift away. Just then Richard headed in her direction. Great, just what I *don't* need, she thought to herself as he stopped directly in front of her, blocking her view of the room, a peculiar look in his eyes.

"Can I help you, Richard?"

"Indeed I believe you can," he said, almost gleefully. "Goodbye,

Miss Lilliana."

She frowned as he reached into the front of his pants, and with lightning speed, pulled out a syringe.

She gasped and jumped up from her seat, shouting "Leon!" as she attempted to run past Richard.

Leon saw what Richard held in his hand, but before he could reach the man to stop him, Richard had slammed the needle into the back of Lilliana's neck.

She staggered backwards as pain began to spread throughout her body overwhelming her, and as she fell onto her hands and knees, crying out in pain, all the Lilliana's ran to comfort her.

The Damon's stood around the room, somehow immobilised, stressed that they could not take a step towards their loved one.

Leon tackled Richard to the ground and Richard slammed his knuckles into Leon's throat.

"What the hell is wrong with you?" Lilliana gasped from the floor as Leon struggled to breathe, clutching at his throat. She screamed as the pain increased to an intolerable level, and she panicked, thinking her bones might break from convulsing. Suddenly, her body went completely still, and she found that she was unable to move. She could barely think, a fog was slowly consuming her thoughts. She became aware as one of the Lilliana's stood and began removing her clothes; now two more were removing her dress, shoes, and underwear. She felt helpless as she could do nothing to stop them.

Oh God, please, no! Do not let Richard see me naked! Her foggy mind began to drift, and everything around her looked to be moving in slow motion.

Staggering to his feet, Richard pulled a small device from his pocket while smiling eerily at Lilliana, wishing he had more time to enjoy her naked vulnerability. He raised his hand and made a show of pressing the device's switch.

Three of the Damon's walked towards one wall and stood along it; their eyes had lost all colour and were now completely white. Within seconds, their heads blew off, sending out a blast that knocked everyone off their feet. Lilliana was swept along the ground, the powerful force of the explosion propelling her into the trunk of a tree, knocking her out in an instant.

***

The explosion could be felt throughout the establishment. For some, it felt like a soft rumble of the earth, while for others it had been more like thunder in their eardrums. For Damon, it had sounded like the world had come to a standstill, before ripping his heart in pieces.

He'd been talking to Hillary, making the afternoon tea arrangements, and taking a quick call before heading back to the garden room. The first blast sounded when he was just forty feet away. That didn't stop him from charging in the direction that Lilliana was in, and just as he did, the second blast hit, which sent him reeling into a wall, along with Jaycee, knocking them both out.

Upon hearing the explosion, Cam had the Team Leaders take their groups quickly out of Main House and into the recreational centres until they could determine that Main House and its structure was safe.

Although the explosion was to the rear end of the psych ward at the back of Main House Cam didn't want to take any chances until they could be completely certain there were no more explosions set to go off.

Damon came to as chaos erupted all around him, the eerie sound of their lockdown siren echoing off in the distance. He watched as Richard carried a Lilliana down the corridor, her long black hair a matted mess, her limp arm swinging behind him.

"Richard," Damon called out.

He turned around. "It's alright, I've got her," Richard said quickly, leaving.

The psych ward and hospital staff were taking the psych patients up to Black Ops and placing them in any available cells, while back in the garden room staff members picked their way through the debris and destruction.

Johnson pulled Damon to his feet as he looked about the corridor that had been impacted by the explosion; for the most part, the building seemed to be intact, apart from one gaping cave-like hole visible from the garden room.

"You alright?" Johnson squeezed Damon's shoulder as Rachael arrived to help Jaycee to her feet.

He shook his head, trying to clear the buzzing in his ears. "Head hurts," was all he could say as he stumbled towards the opening.

"Damon, you should really go to the hospital to get checked out, it's likely you'll have a concussion. You too Jaycee." Rachael raised her hand to a staff member.

"Yes, Nurse Rachael?"

"Get Jaycee in for a scan immediately, would you Toby."

"Of course," he immediately took Jaycee's arm and led her away.

"Damon," Rachael called as he entered the danger zone.

Several staff members were already carrying the unconscious bodies out on stretchers. Damon stood in shock seeing the once beautiful room now look like a war zone. Body parts hung in the tall branches, and the earth above had collapsed inside the room, along with glass shards from the ceiling. It looked like the result of a dangerous mudslide. The blue sky shone cheerfully above, oblivious to the destruction.

Damon looked about desperately trying to find Lilliana, his hands shaking.

"All the bodies have been cleared, Nurse Rachael; Dr Richard took the last one," one of her staff said.

She nodded her thanks as she turned to Damon. He cursed softly. She quickly put her arm around him. "Johnson," she called in a calm, yet authoritative voice. "I need you to get him out of here—right now."

"Where is she?" Damon's voice filled with despair.

"She would have been taken out already, Damon; you were out for almost ten minutes, which is why I want you scanned ASAP."

Their eyes took in the gruesome scene of broken, bloody limbs scattered in the foliage.

Rachael met Johnson's eyes, and gestured towards Damon. Johnson caught her meaning and placed his arm around Damon's waist, pulling his arm around his shoulder and leading him out of the psych ward.

The hospital operated like a well-oiled machine, where not one movement was wasted by the staff. Dr Ryan spotted Damon looking devastated and quickly helped Johnson get him into a room and onto a bed.

He held a clear glass screen in front of Damon's face, and within seconds it beeped, confirming there were no lesions to his brain. "All clear for any brain injury. Just a slight concussion, but we can monitor that."

He lay Damon back and rolled the bed into a clear glass cylinder to scan for further injuries. All results came back clear.

"You're good to go, Sir; but make sure someone is with you at all times for the next twenty-four hours, okay?"

"Thank you Ryan." Damon got off the bed and walked out of the room, just as Josephine ran down the corridor, crying. When she saw Damon, relief swept over her face and she threw herself into his arms.

"Damon—thank God you're alright."

He wrapped his arms around her as he saw Allie and Cam race down towards them.

"What happened?" Cam asked, bewildered.

Damon shook his head and rubbed Josephine's back as Leon was rolled by on a stretcher, looking worse for wear.

"I think it would be a good idea for us to get out of here, out of everybody's way," Johnson suggested.

"Where's Lilliana?" Allie searched the corridor.

Josephine pulled her teary face away from Damon's chest and looked about them.

"Damon?" Josephine whispered, "Where's Lilly?"

"Brett has taken the surviving replicas to Black Op's for treatment, I wasn't in the room when the explosion went off, I…" but before he had a chance to finish, Rachael called out.

"Damon, Johnson, it's Lilliana, she's alright!" Damon closed his eyes briefly in a silent prayer and Allie cried in relief.

"Come on," Cam motioned for them all to head off and they jogged down to meet Rachael, stopping outside the room.

Richard stepped out, a disheveled mess himself. "She's unconscious, but she looks like she's all intact. Billy just finished the scan—there's no internal bleeding, no head injury. She's extremely lucky."

"Thank you." Rachael nodded.

"What the hell happened, Richard?" Damon asked

Richard shook his head, "By the looks of things, three of the Damon's had been implanted with a tampering detonator. One of them took Leon down, and then they set off the explosions.

Damon met Johnson's gaze. "How could our scans have missed any explosive implants?"

"I don't know—we'll get to the bottom of it, but first, why don't you check in on Lilliana."

Damon nodded before entering the room.

Lilliana lay on the bed, hair a bloodied mess, her white dress torn and her sandals missing. She looked like a beautiful, pale broken porcelain doll.

"My poor baby," Damon whispered, aggrieved, leaning down to stroke her face before picking up her hand, her fingers bloody and bruised. He wiped the blood off her emerald ring.

He felt a small hand on his back, turning to see Allie, tears pouring down her face. He took a deep breath and put an arm around her shoulders.

"It's all right sweetheart, see? She is going to be fine. Isn't that right, Rachael?"

"Absolutely; you go clean yourself up, Sir," she said with compassion. "I will get her cleaned up and as comfortable as possible, and when she wakes I will notify you."

Cam put his arm about Josephine's waist and a heavy sigh escaped his lips; he was relieved both his brother and Lilliana were safe.

"Come on Damon, the Buildings Team has declared the building safe. Let's head upstairs for you to shower."

Damon took a final look at Lilliana and placed a kiss against her brow. "Get her cleaned up please, Rachael."

"Of course." She patted his arm as Allie led him out of the room, and up towards his. Cam and Josephine followed, ready to take care of their brother.

Rachael sighed in relief once Damon was out of sight. His hovering would have made it take twice as long to get Lilliana cleaned up, and he had to take care of himself.

"Rachael, I'm heading up to Black Ops; see what Brett has found out about our replicas and if any of them know anything about this explosion. Will you be okay, love?" Johnson looked worried.

She smiled reassuringly. "I am fine, Johnny—go do what you have to do to make our home safe again."

Johnson forced a smile and disappeared down the hall, determined to get to the bottom of this. One of the replicas had to know something; there was no other explanation for it, and he would get to the bottom of it, even if he had to kill one of them.

***

Damon spent the next couple of hours getting cleaned up and having a meal with his brother, Josephine, and Allie, before calling Rachael to see if Lilliana had woken.

"Not yet, but she is all cleaned up and has had the best treatment. Now she's wrapped up warmly, sleeping like a baby. Sleep is the best thing for her now Damon, it's her body's way of healing."

"Thanks Rachael, what about everyone else down there?"

"Everything has started to slow down. Four have died in the explosion, being the three Damon's with explosives. The others are being held in quarantine with Johnson's team and are separated from each other. Unfortunately, we have lost one of our own," she paused, her throat catching in tears. "I'm so sorry to have to break this news to you, but Leon died an hour ago, Sir. There was nothing we could do."

Damon closed his eyes as he pinched the bridge of his nose, trying to focus. "I'm very sorry to hear that, Rachael," he said quietly. He could feel an uncharacteristic rage flicker to life. "I'll let you go," he said, ending the call.

Damon stood, his back ramrod straight as a million questions began racing through his mind. How could this happen? Who made it happen? How could these replicas be responsible for this when they seemed so genuinely innocent, so harmless?

"Damon?" Josephine called.

He turned slowly, and she forced herself not to cry as a look of utter rage shadowed his handsome features.

Cam stood, immediately alerted to the look of fury on his brother's face. "What is it?"

Damon met his brother's stare as he answered stonily. "Leon's dead."

Allie gasped from across the room, covering her mouth.

She needed Christopher, and she needed him now. Standing, she quickly excused herself and fled from the room to search for her love who would no doubt be in the kitchen at this hour.

Cam and Damon stared at each other as Josephine stood to the side.

"You know," she began. "I need to keep busy; Rupert and I can make some flower arrangements to brighten the hospital rooms."

Damon looked at her and smiled gently, saying quietly, "That's a lovely idea, sweetheart."

Josephine returned his smile then turned to her husband and hugged him tightly, before leaving.

"Right," Cam began, but didn't know what else to say. His brother was making him nervous.

Damon was dangerously quiet as the unforgiving rage flowed through him; it was so unlike the professional, always together, forever calm Damon Night.

"We have eleven out of the fourteen replicas; I don't care what we have to do to get answers out of them, but answers we will get."

Cam nodded. "I agree. Let's do whatever it takes."

Damon followed Cam, hoping to get justice for Leon. Ten minutes later they walked into Johnson's office to meet with a very frustrated looking Johnson, Brett, and Clair.

"What's going on?" Cam asked.

"They are all saying the same thing. The blokes are saying that they are Damon Night, and the women all claim to be the real Lilliana."

"They've been saying that all along." Damon didn't know what the fuss was about.

"No Damon," Clair turned to face him. "All the Lilliana's have just given us an explicit account of events that occurred at Gregory Reid's main event. All of them are saying the exact same thing."

Damon exchanged a look with Johnson and thought for a moment. "It was broadcast to the underworld. Plenty would know the details of that night." He shrugged.

"Yes, but before this incident they'd claimed to have no recollection of who they were before they were delivered to the Officials, and then to us. They only knew their first name."

"Maybe the explosion triggered their memories?"

"Well, that makes entirely no sense," Cam shook his head. "They can't all have the same memories; only the real Lilliana has those."

"I think they need a little help from the water chamber." Brett suggested. "The cold usually clears up a foggy memory."

"I tend to agree." Cam was keen; it would get them the answers for sure.

"That room is used only for the most highly rated criminals." Clair stated and turned to Johnson.

He folded his arms, giving it some thought. "We have just had an explosion go off in our home, killing one of our family members and destroying part of this building!" He shook his head angrily. "Right at this moment, I don't care if any of them freeze to death in the process!"

"Once again, I tend to agree." Cam echoed his earlier statement.

"Brett, grab a team member, and start the questioning. Cam and I will speak to Richard; see what we can learn. We'll meet you in the water chamber as soon as we're done." Damon said.

"Yes Sir." Brett strode out of the room.

"Is this really such a good idea?" Clair folded her arms.

Johnson, Cam, and Damon exchanged a look between them.

"Fine," she nodded. "I guess we don't have a choice."

"Oh, there's always a choice, Clair." Damon said quietly, nodding to Cam and leaving the room.

***

"Alright Richard, can you explain what happened?" Damon leaned his hip against the desk as Cam poured everyone a coffee.

Richard sat with his legs crossed, nodding his thanks to Cam as he passed him the steaming mug.

"It was all a muddle, really. Lilliana and I were having a conversation when Leon became quite frantic, insisting he heard one of the Damon's say it was time to detonate their bombs."

He shook his head, feigning a puzzled look. "I knew that was impossible, because there hadn't been any implants or destructive materials found anywhere on them when we performed the initial body scans." He took a mouthful of the black brew, pausing, before continuing. "I was extremely thorough with those scans, too. One of the Damon's knocked Leon out, and then three of the Damon's stood by the wall and set off the blast, causing their heads to explode before a second blast from their bodies sent a shock wave throughout the room. I shielded Lilliana with my own body, of course, wanting to protect her." He tried to look regretful as he finished off, saying, "If only I could have protected them all…"

Damon watched as Richard answered several more of Cam's questions before saying, "The security feed to the garden room had been tampered with. Only staff can access that room. How do you explain that?"

Richard sighed, looking like he was carrying a burden. "To be honest Sir," he said with more respect than usual, "I do believe Leon had been acting particularly uneasy this morning, quite jittery in fact. Not his usual self. I hate to speak ill of the dead, but could he possibly have had something to do with this mess?"

"Highly unlikely," Damon said quietly, absorbing Richard's story.

"Highly unlikely?" Cam scoffed. "How about totally bloody inconceivable. Leon is the best, he's one of the good guys!"

"Was," Richard said quietly, wiping under his eyes, feigning fake tears. "Was one of the good guys."

"Thanks for your time, Richard." Damon pushed away from his desk and walked towards the door.

Richard stood and followed Damon. "I'm only glad I saved your Lilliana, Sir."

"We're extremely grateful to you, Richard," Cam clapped him on the back as they headed out to join Johnson.

***

"Any results?" Damon asked as they walked into Johnson's office.

"The surviving Damon's are saying that Leon had something to do with the explosions."

"Corroborating the story we have just heard from Richard, then," Damon ran a hand through his hair.

"And the women?"

"The Lilliana's are devastated about the three dead Damon's and are denying any knowledge about the explosion."

"How convenient." Cam scoffed.

"One of them is deferring from the story, however, saying Leon had nothing to do with it—when questioned further, she screams in pain before going blank, then barely remembers her own name." Johnson shook his head before continuing. "Lilliana's fingerprints were taken five minutes ago, confirming she is the real Lilliana. The others, as we knew, had no fingerprints, although all of them have suffered further injuries because of the explosion. So, all fingertips, bar Lilliana's, have been burnt off. Strange though, their palms aren't burnt—just their fingertips." He shrugged, perplexed.

Damon let out a sigh of frustration. "This entire situation is getting us nowhere."

"We're yet to put that Lilliana, into the tub, though."

Damon ran his hands over his face. "Let's get her in the water. The cold might motivate her to tell a different story."

Johnson buzzed Brett. "Brett, take the forgetful one into the water chamber. We're on our way."

"Yes Sir."

Johnson hung up the call. "Let's hope we get some clear answers."

Several minutes later they entered the viewing room and, looking through the one-way mirror, saw one of the Lilliana's standing alone in her tattered, bloody, psych ward clothes, shivering with her arms bound around her waist; her hair was a mess, face still dirty and bloodied from the explosion. Her piercing, green eyes darted around the room in fright, as she looked at the large, raised tub filled with icy cold water.

Brett walked in to speak to Damon. "This one has a concussion, but a cold dip certainly won't do her any harm."

"Do what you have to do." Damon folded his arms, watching the beautiful, frightened rabbit inside the chamber.

"No, " Cam said. All eyes shifted onto him.

"I'd like to do this one, if you don't mind." Cam often missed the days when his interrogation skills had been put to good use.

Damon raised an eyebrow. "Do you really think that's such a good idea, Cameron? Interrogating the woman who is the spitting image of your sister-in-law?"

"But she's not, is she brother? So there's no problem."

Johnson looked at Brett, who leaned against the wall, shrugging a shoulder. "There's no harm giving him a crack at it."

Cam waited for Damon to give the go ahead, before folding his arms and turning his attention to the Lilliana in the room. He rubbed his hands together and walked into the room next door. When the Lilliana saw him, she paled further if that were at all possible, given that her skin had already paled considerably from waiting in the freezing room.

"Okay, little one; what's your name?"

"Um, I think," she frowned looking confused. "It's Lilliana?"

"You think?"

"Yes, Lilliana Night," she answered hesitantly.

"Okay, Lilliana Night. You've said Dr Leon had nothing to do with the explosion?"

She nodded, rubbing her arms briskly, trying to get warm. "I think so," she whispered, trying to recall the events before the explosion as a sharp pain pierced her skull. She cried out, rubbing her temple as though the pain was blocking her ability to retrieve any knowledge, as if remembering information seemed to cause the most horrific agony. Coupled with the temperature of the room, the pain was growing close to unbearable.

"Please, please can we leave this room."

Cam felt a rush of protectiveness envelop him as her beautiful face filled with torment and terror.

It's not our Lilly, he sternly told himself; he needed to get a grip.

"If it was not Dr Leon, then who was involved in planting and detonating the explosions?"

She pushed her hair away from her face, shaking her head. "I don't know," she whispered.

"Sorry, I need you to give me more information than 'I don't know.'" he said, using air quotes with his fingers for added emphasis. "How about a little dip, to freshen your memory?" He walked towards her as she looked at the tub full of icy water and continued to back away.

She shook her head. "No, no, no, please."

"Who are you?"

"Lilliana Night!"

"And I'm Father Christmas," Cam grabbed her arm and dragged her towards the tub. "This will all be over as soon as we get some truth out of you, okay?"

"No, you *really* don't understand..." she screamed as he grabbed her by the back of the neck and slammed her face first into the sub-zero water.

Cam stood close behind her, leaning on her back as she struggled under the water, petrified as the frosty needles stabbed at every inch of skin that came in contact with the water. He held her down for the approved time before pulling her back out, coughing, spluttering, and gasping for air. She wanted to cry but knew breathing was the more important priority.

"What do you know about the explosion? Was it your Damon that detonated the device?"

She struggled in his arms, still gasping for air as the cold stole her breath.

My Damon? My Damon? She struggled to recall who her Damon was as pain slammed into her skull. She cried out, clutching at her head.

"Please, please, I can't, I can't...I don't know anything," she sobbed.

"Who are you? Who do you work for?"

I'm Lilliana, I think I am? Haven't I always been Lilliana? She felt so confused, and when she tried to recall anything before the explosion, shards of pain pierced her skull.

"Let's try this," Cam picked her up effortlessly, as she struggled against him, and placed her legs into the tub, pushing her away from the side and into the middle. She almost fell but regained her balance.

"Be a good girl now, answer the question, and I'll let you out."

She was shivering uncontrollably and pushed at her hair that was dripping over her face.

"I don't know anything, except, I think I am the real Lilliana?" She exhaled painfully.

"Yeah, about that. We have the real Lilliana downstairs and her fingerprints have confirmed that she is in fact the actual, real Lilliana." He reached out, snatching at her wrist, and held up her burnt fingers.

"And yours are like the other Lilliana's we currently have locked up. Explain that!"

She shook her head, shivering uncontrollably, teeth chattering.

"I can't, I'm sorry, I can't!" Her voice broke and she began slurring her words, convulsing as her eyes rolled into the back of her head and she fell backwards into the icy tub.

"Christ!" Damon ran out of the viewing room and into the water chamber, pushing Cam out of the way, before plunging into the freezing tub. Pulling her stiff, cold body out, he dropped her onto the heat blanket Johnson had laid out and wrapped it about her tightly before picking her up and heading out the door. He made it to the hospital in record time and passed her to Billy, who raised an eyebrow in confusion.

"Water chamber."

"Right. Ah, you should get warmed up yourself." Billy turned on his heel and took off to warm the replica up.

"Cuff her to the bed, Billy," he called as Rachael spotted him.

"Right. Go get warmed up yourself." Billy turned on his heel and took off.

"Damon," Rachael smiled. "Lilliana's just woken."

His heart lifted instantaneously. Even his icy wet clothes did nothing to dampen his spirits. He walked towards Rachael, who, noticing his wet clothes, immediately set off to get him a blanket.

Passing it to him she said, "Do not hug your wife and make her cold, please."

He grinned, feeling as though a weight had been lifted, simply knowing that his Lilliana was alright. "Yes Ma'am."

After instructing a staff member to mop up the trail of water, Rachael led Damon into the room and smiled.

"Lilliana, look who's here to see you," she announced.

Lilliana pushed her hand through her hair, her emerald ring mimicking the glorious colour of her eyes. Damon crossed to her side and picked up her hand before leaning in to drop a kiss on her forehead.

"How are you, Baby?"

Lilliana nodded. "I'm fine Damon, I promise."

"You gave me such a fright."

"It was all so terrible." She shook her head. "I thought I'd lost you."

"Never going to happen," he said, trying to stop his uncontrollable shivering. The cold must have been affecting his hearing, as her voice was wavering and didn't sound at all like his Lilliana.

But she was. She'd been in her own dress and was wearing her ring. He was simply exhausted, he thought; and his mind was playing tricks on him, the concussion playing havoc with his thoughts.

Rachael was pottering in the background, listening, when a niggling feeling dug its fingers into her. She crossed over to the bed and looked down at Lilliana.

"Damon, I think you need to get out of those wet clothes immediately."

He looked down at Lilliana and smiled. "I'll come back and see you shortly and take you up to our room, okay?"

She smiled her beautiful smile, albeit with less glow; but of course, Damon thought; she's been through hell.

"Lovely." She nodded.

Rachael led Damon out of the room as more screaming could be heard further down the corridor. He moved to head in that direction when Rachael grabbed his arm. "If I have to strip you naked myself, God help me, I will. Now, go get some warm clothes on or you'll be no help to any of us."

She pointed for him to leave; as Damon turned to go, Allie, Jessica, Josephine, and Fox all walked towards him.

"She's awake," he said. Allie beamed.

Damon nodded. "Keep her company till I get back?"

"Sure thing—get out of those wet clothes," Josephine scolded him.

Damon went upstairs for a steaming hot shower, pain killers and a shot of awake serum before heading back down forty minutes later, feeling more like his usual self.

CHAPTER 22

It was the day of the Ultimate Given Games. Despite the gut-wrenching events of the week before, the atmosphere surrounding the event was of one filled with competitive excitement, all the teams abuzz with enthusiasm.

There were sixteen competitors per team, comprised of all levels of Main House. Teams ranged from new Given to older Team Leader's, senior staff, and the Watchers, when necessary. There was a relay that included several events from running to swimming, archery, and the steeple chase course. Then there were the mind games, which began in the escape house and led to a rescue mission, where teams had to decipher codes and follow a set of instructions in order to rescue a team member in a set amount of time from another team that had them hidden at a secret location around the property. Once the teams had rescued their stolen member, it was another race to the finish line.

Allie, Jessica, and Fox were partnered with Marcus, Scott, Thomas, Edward, Karen, and Keira, amongst others. Josephine was thrilled to have Rupert on her team, along with Jaycee, Shelley, Billy, and other members from HD.

The games ran for eight hours in total, and by the end everyone was feeling exhausted and exhilarated. The winning team got to spend a weekend at the cabin with the person of their choosing, and all those who participated in the games, celebrated a massive night with awards and dancing.

***

Damon and the Black Ops team had not had a moment's rest in the following week that passed, and Damon was concerned that Lilliana wasn't healing as quickly as she should have been. She had insisted on staying in the hospital wing, claiming her head was constantly throbbing, and she didn't seem too disappointed for missing out on the games, although in the weeks leading up Damon thought she had been excited about them.

When her friends had the chance to visit her, she remained quiet and slept often. Even when Damon sat with her, she said little and closed her eyes often.

"I'm worried about her, Rachael," he said quietly while Lilliana was sleeping.

"Yes, she certainly has taken Leon's death awfully hard. Rest is the best thing for her, Damon. Surprisingly, Richard has had a good effect on her." Rachael shrugged her shoulders at Damon looking mystified as she had no explanation for it.

"We need to sort out why the replicas are here." She shook her head.

"Johnson isn't sleeping—he is just that perplexed by the entire thing."

Damon nodded, running his hand through his hair. "That makes two of us."

Lilliana moaned in her sleep, tossing the hospital blanket from her.

Damon crossed over, running a hand gently over her forehead, before tucking the blanket around her again. "Shh," he soothed.

Her eyes flickered open and were vacant for a moment before she closed them again. Damon sighed and walked out of the room, heading up to Johnson's office. It was time to see if the truth serum could help them out.

***

The other Lilliana's sat in their cells, exhausted, devastated and confused. They had been kept awake for the better part of three days, all away from their Damon's. When the door opened to one of the cells, one Lilliana got off the bed and quickly moved to the corner of the room as far as possible from the man who came to take her. She knew him, she was certain; but when she tried to think of his name, it felt like knives were shredding her skull.

She closed her eyes, missing the glint in his as she grabbed at her throbbing temples; his strong arms steered her forcefully from the room.

Damon and Johnson watched as Richard led the Lilliana into Johnson's office, strapping her unceremoniously to a chair.

She winced at his manner of rough handling.

The replicas had all been given clean white clothes after the water chamber interrogation, and this Lilliana, who had been hospitalised after convulsing, had had to wear special gloves to heal her fingertips, which seemed to have been more severely burned than the others, which Damon thought could indicate that she'd had something to do with triggering the bomb.

"Good afternoon," Damon said as Richard stepped away from the beautiful woman.

She looked up at the handsome man they all called Sir or Mr Night, or Damon. Was he familiar? She tried to recall if she knew him.

She closed her eyes, sucking in her breath as pain slapped at her temple.

He grasped her chin gently, and her eyes flashed tiredly open as she gazed up into his gloriously handsome face.

"Lilliana?"

"Yes."

"We are going to try another method to extract information from you. Unfortunately, it is rather painful; but honestly, we are at our wits' end with this situation."

She tried to pull her chin out of his grasp, but his fingers were too firm. He did not hold her unkindly, only in a determined way. Looking into the depths of his intense gaze, she felt a flicker of familiarity; then came another sharp and sudden slap of pain.

Damon frowned before stepping back, nodding to Johnson. So far, the truth serum had only revealed that all the Damon's thought they were the real Damon Night, and all the Lilliana's thought they were married to him. There was nothing more about who they were, who they worked for or any other helpful information about the explosion.

Richard picked up the truth serum vial and stepped towards her.

She flinched as he jabbed it into the flesh of her arm, sucking in her breath as a slow burning, pain spread instantaneously throughout her system, building in such intensity that made it hard to breathe.

"Why do you think you are the real Lilliana Night?"

"Because that's all I know, all I'm really sure of," though she didn't sound convinced herself.

She felt so confused, so exhausted. It was a double assault, the pain she felt when she tried to recall information, along with the pain of the truth serum when she tried to answer their questions, overwhelming her already fatigued system. Tears of frustration fell from her eyes.

"How did you burn your fingertips?" Richard asked.

"I… I can't remember."

"Did you set off the explosion?"

"No," she said before crying in pain again as the truth serum did its work, coursing through her body.

"I think so?" She cried. *Did I?* she despaired. *Could I have?*

Damon and Johnson exchanged a glance. This was the first time they were getting more of an answer than the standard 'I don't recall' responses they had been getting.

"Why did you do that?" Richard asked, hiding the delight in his voice.

"I… I don't know?"

It disturbed Damon though, that with almost every answer she gave, it sounded more like a question.

"Who hired you? Who do you work for?"

"Gregory Reid, I work for Gregory Reid…" tears were flowing down her face, along with more confusion. *Why am I saying this?*

As the session was being recorded, Johnson rang the Officials office and spoke to the team that had handled the replicas before they were sent to the Given; quietly he filled them in on the confession and said he'd patch the video through to them shortly. After hanging up, he turned his attention back to Richard.

Damon was standing silently to the side, feeling a sense of fury for Leon. Someone knew something, and the way her answers seemed more like questioning answers was really starting to bother him. He felt sure she knew something.

"What was your plan? Why have you infiltrated our home?"

She shook her head again, not wanting to answer as the answer that was automatically being conjured by her mind was too frightening, even to her.

The look on Damon Night's face was terrifying as he said, "Answer the question." Each word he spoke was clipped, cold.

She shook her head again, squeezing her eyes shut; her body trembled with the torture that was taking place inside her body.

Damon stepped towards her and bent down so his eyes were level with hers. Her eyes opened in fright at his close proximity, startling her as his cool breath caressed her face.

"We don't want to hurt you any more than we already have," Damon said steadily, dangerously quiet. "But you need to answer the question."

He had her pinned in place with his look, like a butterfly caught on a silver web; he simultaneously mesmerised and terrified her.

She swallowed nervously. Why was she so torn? She knew another answer, but it seemed to be locked away in the hazy cloud of her mind, as another answer pushed her first one out of the way.

"I can't," she cried quietly, shaking her head. "Please, don't make me," she whispered. "Please, just stop," she begged.

"I think we need to inject her again," Richard declared.

"No." Damon shook his head, moving away. "She's been through enough."

He turned around, folding his arms, looking down at her. "You will answer though, if you have to sit here all night."

"How did you get the explosives into our building?" Johnson asked.

"It was implanted in three of the Damon's before we arrived, through someone at the Officials head office, a friend of Gregory's." *How do I know this?*

"What was the plan? Why did you set the explosive off?" Cam asked.

"To kill Lilliana or Damon Night and take their place, to infiltrate the Given." She choked out. *I am stuck in a nightmare!*

"You could not have pulled this off alone. Who were you working with in here?"

"Leon," she cried, sobbing. "Leon!" *Why! Why am I saying this!* she was screaming on the inside, totally distraught and trapped in her own body.

"Liar!" Damon yelled.

"I'm sorry, *it's true!*" she screamed back at him, sobbing.

Richard looked over at Damon as he pushed up his glasses. "Well, I think you finally have your answer," he cocked his head, seeming extremely pleased with himself.

Johnson nodded. "It seems so."

Lilliana dropped her head, shaking it side to side as she cried. "No, no," she repeated. "It's all wrong. It's twisted."

"Tell Brett that his team can stop the rotation shifts and let them all sleep."

Johnson nodded as Richard began unstrapping Lilliana. He grabbed her by the arm to take her back to her cell.

"No Richard, I'll take her."

"It's alright Sir, I've got her," Richard said determinedly.

"Richard." Damon snapped. He hated it whenever Richard tried to undermine his authority.

"I *said*, I'll take her back."

Richard paused, looking slightly worried, before releasing her arm as he walked out the door.

As Damon stepped towards her, she stumbled back, and would have fallen with fatigue if he had not acted and quickly caught her up in his arms, scooping her soft body against his.

Fresh tears mysteriously fell from her eyes as she covered her face, sobbing quietly and he carried her out of the room and to her cell. He gently placed her on the bed, and she rolled over, curling into a ball with her back towards him.

"Is there anything I can get you?"

"Please, can you please just keep that wicked man away from me" she begged, her voice a mixture of pleading, fear and pain, as the truth serum still coursed through her viens.

"Richard?"

She rolled over, looking up into his face. "Yes—Richard. Please, I answered all your questions. Just please keep him away from me. He's dangerous. I don't know why, but he scares me."

Damon felt a flicker of warmth wash over him as he watched her. Her eyes were, in fact, full of terror. It broke a part of him inside. He nodded.

"You have my word."

She closed her eyes and whispered. "Thank you."

He stood there for a few moments, feeling sorry for the poor shell of a woman who had been used as a pawn in a game, someone wanting to make an attempt on his, or his beloved Lilliana's, life. He shook his head sighing as he closed her door, locking it, before heading down to the hospital to check on his wife.

It had been almost three weeks since the explosion and Damon was hoping she would start to feel more like herself soon.

Allie and Christopher had delayed their wedding as they wanted Lilliana to be one hundred percent well again for the occasion. Damon continued to pray that Lilliana would return to her beautiful, strong self again soon.

Reaching the hospital Damon walked down the corridor and ran into Grant, who was the head of the Building Team.

"Grant, how's the construction going?"

"Just about done, Mr Night. The shelter above will continue to stop the weather from getting in, and as soon as the new plants are in, the new glass dome will be mounted without a hitch."

Damon nodded. "Good work; I'll pop in tomorrow to thank the team."

Grant smiled. "Cheers, Sir. See you then."

Damon continued along the corridor before walking into Lilliana's room. It made him smile seeing her sitting up in bed, talking to Scott. Scott looked at Damon and forced a smile.

Whatever the explosion had done to Lilliana's head, she wasn't the same sister he had had a conversation with a few weeks prior, and he worried about her.

"I was just telling Lilliana how my team came second in the Games, Sir."

Damon smiled. "You certainly did very well, Scott, that's for sure. I think the team was lucky to have you and Karen on board."

Scott's smile reached his eyes. "True story."

"It's getting late. Why don't you head up to bed? Big day tomorrow, I recall you have exams?"

"Yes Sir," he groaned, looking over at Lilliana. "Official Law first thing—kill me now," he said jokingly, pretending to choke himself.

Lilliana blinked, not thinking it funny at all as she lay back down under the covers.

"Okay, okay," Damon could see the distress on his wife's face. "Assembly is early in the morning, so off you go."

Scott nodded before saluting. "Night," he said as he headed out.

Damon turned to Lilliana and picked up her hand. "How are you, sweet heart?"

"Tired."

"I know, that's why you're here, so you can rest." He planted a kiss on her brow. His beautiful girl, even laying here, miserable, and unwell, she was still stunning.

The spark that was usually between them had been doused, both by her fatigue and his fright of losing her, along with all the stress dealing with the replicas. He sighed as he tucked the blankets around her.

"I need to see Richard," she said quietly.

He looked down at her. "Now?"

She nodded. "Alone, please Damon."

He stood for a moment, realising his exhaustion was messing with his mind. Shaking it off, he nodded. Kissing her brow once more he said, "I'll send him in at once. Goodnight."

"Goodnight."

Damon walked out, looking to see if Rachael was still working, and found her behind the nurse station talking to Billy about the next shift.

"Damon, how's it going?" Billy smiled over the top of his teacup.

"Ah, you know. A bit all over the show at the moment. Rachael, I want only yourself or Billy handling the replicas health or medication needs from now on. No one else is to enter their cells for any other reason."

"Of course." She nodded. "Any reason?"

He nodded, meeting her eyes, but not answering beyond that.

"Also, Lilliana wants to see Richard."

"Okay," Rachael kept her thoughts to herself. "He's actually just down the hall, room 122."

Damon nodded. "Thanks."

Finding Richard in the room, Damon leaned against the door, watching him attend to the patient, unaware that he was being watched.

Richard turned and was startled but for a moment as he caught Damon watching him. "Can I help you?"

"Not me personally, but Lilliana wants to see you now."

"Of course, Sir," Richard said, looking pleased with himself.

"Richard, from now on, you are not to go anywhere near the replicas—I have Rachael and Billy looking after their needs."

A flash of panic crossed Richard's face, but it happened so quickly Damon wasn't sure if he'd actually seen it or not.

"Oh, that doesn't seem like a good idea; I have been handling their needs from day one. I think it's in their best interest that they see only me, as their mental health may decline if they are put into the hands of a stranger…"

"Richard—I don't care. I don't want you anywhere near them."

"Well, I think that's the wrong decision…"

"*Richard!*" Damon barked impatiently. "That is my final decision.

Are we clear?"

Richard stared frostily at Damon for a moment. "Crystal clear, Sir."

"Good." Damon turned on his heel and left, wanting to put this day behind him and hoped that whatever comfort Lilliana found in having Richard tend to her would benefit her, so that she could return to him, sooner rather than later.

***

The replicas were having withdrawals from the truth serum that had ran its course through their systems. Some had been vomiting due to the stress it caused their bodies, while yet others had turned to self-harming. Rachael was distressed seeing them suffer. Poor pawns in some depraved mastermind's game, she thought.

"Billy, hot showers now please, for those that are awake. It may ease the tension in their muscles that the serum has caused."

Billy nodded. "No worries, Rachael. You want me to take the Lilliana's or the Damon's?"

"Probably best you take the men first; I'll start on the ladies." He nodded and set off as Rachael opened a cell.

The Lilliana whose questioning had revealed the most answers was in the most amount of pain. She was curled up tight in a ball, crying and moaning, her arms wrapped as tightly as she could around her waist, gently rocking herself back and forth.

Rachael approached her quietly, gently saying her name. "Lilliana?"

Her eyes met with Rachael's, as tears continued to fall down her face. It broke Rachael's kind heart to see the girl suffer.

"There now, it's going to be alright. Let's get you into a hot shower, it will help with the aches, okay?"

She helped the pitifully frail girl up and into the showers, getting the water bearably hot and undressing her as she set her under the spray. The girl's body spasmed constantly under duress, stress and withdrawal overtaking her nervous system.

Rachael had seen what the truth serum did to bodies, and its aftereffects were never a pretty sight. But this girl's reaction to it had been something else. Taking out a syringe, she gently pricked the needle into Lilliana's buttocks and drew a vial of blood.

This Lilliana barely noticed the needle pierce her skin, so focused as she was in trying to relieve her aches under the hot shower spray. She turned and smiled a tiny smile at Rachael and whispered, "Thank you."

Rachael fought back her own tears and forced a bright nurse's smile. "You're welcome sweetie, just enjoy."

Rachael squashed her suspicions. She would wait until she had the results before she spoke to anyone.

***

The questioning of the replicas continued over the next fortnight, with some of their stories altering during that time. All of the Lilliana's became distressed, wondering which one of their Damon's had been killed.

The Lilliana who had confessed her crimes, sat in her cell, her mind becoming clearer as the fortnight passed without Richard's constant medical administration. At first, every thought she'd had, had been a painful cyclone of disturbed thoughts, none of them making any sense, which confused her even more. Rachael had been kind to her, and the healing vitamins she'd been giving the girl were making her spirit strong again.

When Brett or Johnson came to speak with her, Lilliana begged them to listen. "I am the *real* Lilliana, and I need to speak to Damon— please, please listen to me. I didn't do what I confessed to doing."

"The truth serum never lies, lady," was Brett had said.

"Look at me! Really—look at me! I *am* Lilliana Night! Get Damon this instance! Brett, please!"

Brett sighed, shaking his head. If he'd heard this statement once, he'd heard it six times already this night. "You're all the same. You all say you're Lilliana. Enough! Now, goodnight." He slammed her door, leaving her to sit and dwell in frustration.

They are going to regret this, she thought, falling back onto the stiff bed, and throwing her hands over her eyes, swallowing tears of frustration and helplessness.

CHAPTER 23

Five weeks after the explosion the fate of the replicas were being discussed with the Officials and the Given's Black Ops team. Gregory Reid had, of course, denied all allegations that the Lilliana had made about her working for him, and after being administered a double dose of truth serum, along with further questioning, Gregory Reid had not altered his story.

Lilliana had still not returned to her duties or to her and Damon's apartment, and her peculiar bond with Richard was frustrating Damon to no end.

After a team meeting with all senior staff to discuss the overall running of the establishment, as well as a conference call and a quick chat with Allie, Damon spent the late afternoon checking in with the progress of all the replicas. He found himself growing more frustrated with them, and for them.

"Damon," Johnson called out from the next room. "Rachael just called; she has some information to share."

Damon nodded, pointing to the cell that housed the last of the Lilliana's. "Ok—I've just got this one left to talk to, then I'll be done."

"Sure," Johnson left as Damon entered the cell, closing the bar grill gate behind him.

He leaned against the bars and pushed his hands into his jeans pockets, his tee shirt hugging every inch of his chiseled form.

Lilliana sat on the bed looking exhausted, but finally, seeing him clearly for the first time in weeks.

"Have you had enough?" Damon asked, sounding weary, frustrated.

"Oh I have definitely had enough." She sounded awake, alert and pissed off. Much like his Lilliana would have been.

She pushed at the heavy waterfall of hair slipping over her shoulder. So very Lilliana-like, too.

"Good," Damon replied shortly. "I have to ask: why are you now changing your story, stating that your confession was a lie? You can't lie when the truth serum permeates your blood."

"I cannot explain why; all I know is that, I felt that if I told you the truth, it would kill me. Whenever I thought to speak the truth or even tried to remember what the truth was, there would be this unbearable pain in my system, as though my head would explode."

"Like your Damon's head exploded?"

"No!" Lilliana shook her head, clearly frustrated. "None of them were my Damon."

"Come on, you must be getting tired of all this. I know I am."

She stood up and walked across to him. Standing a foot away, she folded her arms, trying not to glare at him. "*You* are my Damon."

"Ugh, Please," he sighed. "Don't make this any more difficult than it already is."

Lilliana's eyes flashed emerald fire. "Are you ready to listen? To hear me?"

Her tone of voice caught his attention; he raised an eyebrow, watching her now. She seemed so much braver than she had previously been. Stronger, too. Not so frightened and vulnerable. He felt something stir in his groin that he had not felt in the weeks since the explosion and immediately felt a rush of guilt. How dare he lust for this beautiful Lilliana when his own angel was still struggling to find herself!

"Are you ready to *see* me?" Lilliana said, softly, pleadingly.

His eyes roamed her beautiful face. There was no denying how very much like his Lilliana she was. His Lilliana before the explosion.

"Can you share anything with me that would help clear this all up?"

"I was injected with a substance before the explosion. I couldn't move to save myself. My clothes were removed, my ring was removed." She held up her small hand as proof.

"You are the second Lilliana with this story." Damon shook his head; they were constantly going around in circles with these replicas.

"I believe I was injected with an amnesiac serum, followed by the power of suggestion serum—trust me, it's the only thing that makes sense, Damon!"

He looked down at her in silence as her frustration became more palpable.

"You all truly believe you are the true Lilliana."

"Yes—they believe they are the real Lilliana because that's what they've been programmed to believe! They are not lying, it's the only truth they can tell!"

"Makes it all so neat, doesn't it?" Damon folded his arms, ready to end the conversation.

Lilliana could see the look in his eyes, the doubt; she knew Damon too well, his stubbornness, and it flared up her banked temper. She stepped forward and jabbed a finger hard into his chest, surprising him with her anger and force.

"How the *hell* can you not know it is me, Damon!" she cried out in despair.

"Careful," Damon said, becoming dangerously quiet, taking a step forward.

She pushed him back hard against the wall with the flat of her palms.

"No—you be careful!" Her eyes blazed a furious shade of verdant green, her lips parted, breathing heavily, partly in anger, partly from lust. Her eyes dropped to study his lips, and he could see she was intending to kiss him.

He grabbed her shoulders in part to hold her away from him, also to keep himself from crushing her mouth with his.

She shook her head. "Have you kissed your Lilliana? I mean *really* kissed her since the explosion?" She raised a perfectly sultry eyebrow, before stepping out of his hands and moving across to lean against the other wall, mirroring his stance.

"Go on, go and kiss your Lilliana then, Damon. See what she pours into that kiss. I'll be here waiting for an apology." She looked away, but not before he detected a hint of hurt creep into her eyes.

He frowned then, thinking of the blur the last month had been. His Lilliana was downstairs, and her prints were her own; all the other Lilliana's, including this one, had come to them with no fingerprints. But his Lilliana downstairs was not the durable, resilient, and loving Lilliana he knew. Meanwhile, he knew that this Lilliana, this one right here, right now, was exhibiting *all* the signs of his true Lilliana; even throughout all of the gruelling interrogations, he'd thought she'd acted more like his Lilliana, had reminded him more of her than all the others—even the one waiting for him downstairs.

It was all impossibly confusing, but... could she be right?

Had amnesia and suggestion drugs been used on all the replicas before the explosion? Had those drugs fought against the truth serum, conflicting the results? It would at least explain why this Lilliana had been in so much anguish.

Oh Christ, and if it were true—what they'd done to her in the water chamber!

Damon felt his heart thud uncomfortably as he watched her in silence, suddenly feeling overcome by a flood of emotions as he realised she was telling the truth.

Her eyes lifted, slamming into his, making him catch his breath. He pushed off the wall and walked towards her, stopping just inches away from her beautiful porcelain face.

She looked up at him, hopeful as the breath left her body in anticipation and relief. "Finally," she whispered.

Damon reached out and cupped her chin, raising it up, to capture her lips in a sweeping kiss. Her kiss tasted like sweet nectar and wrapped itself around him in a silken whisper of familiarity. She kissed him like no other could, full of love and hope, and with promise of tomorrow.

Feeling overwhelmed and close to tears, he broke off their kiss, plunging his face into her neck, taking a deep breath. *Oh my*, he thought, unable to speak and in shock. *What have I done?*

Her lips sought out the smooth soft hollow of his neck; it was one of her favourite places to kiss him, and as she did so, memories flooded them both, back to when she was seventeen and had been whipped by Richard in detention.

Damon had taken her into the kitchen that night so many years ago to care for her bleeding palm, and after attending her cuts they had put their hands on each other in wild lust, each with such wanting of the other's flesh, and she had kissed the hollow of his throat that had almost sent him over the edge.

She was one hundred and fifty percent, his Lilliana.

"Lilliana," he breathed her name, begging for her forgiveness as her fingers curled in his silken hair at the nape of his collar.

"Damon," she sighed, wanting to cry. Finally, finally, he saw her.

He kissed her again, relishing the taste of her.

"Damon?" Brett stood at the door of the cell wondering why their director was behaving so unprofessionally.

Damon pulled away from Lilliana to address Brett, his eyes never leaving her face. "We have a problem."

"Yeah, I can see that, Sir."

Lilliana raised an eyebrow and folded her arms as Johnson approached the cell.

"What's going on?"

"Mr Night has a problem. He can't keep his hands off the Lilliana's."

"And this is what *I've* been dealing with," Lilliana whispered under her breath.

Damon smiled, running his hand under her delicate jaw and shook his head. "It's really you. I'm so sorry darling," he whispered back to her. "Will you ever be able to forgive me?"

Her eyes kept him glued in place. "Time will tell," she said, returning a cheeky smile. Lilliana could forgive all under the circumstances. It had been one hell of a debacle for everyone involved.

"Damon?" It was Johnson's turn to look puzzled.

"Seriously, you are all such intelligent men, when are you going to get it?"

She turned to Johnson. "Instead of asking me a 'Lilliana-replica' question, why don't you try asking me a 'Lilliana-Given' question."

"We've been asking you all the same sorts of questions, and for the most part, you all have had the same answers."

"Do you think it's possible then, that we could have a mole on the inside who has been feeding information to the replicas? I've been watching the way each Lilliana pushes her hair, the way each Damon stands or moves. Even the way they articulate an answer, has been pretty identical."

"It would have to be someone who knows us both very well, no one else could share such information," Damon added.

"Who organised for the replicas to be delivered to this Given? Who had the means to place explosive implants in the Damon's heads?" Lilliana took a breath before continuing.

"Who injected me before the explosion went off—and who the hell burnt my fingertips to a crisp? And more importantly, who killed Leon?" Lilliana's last word ended on a sob.

"Richard." Damon whispered, wrapping his arms around her, pulling her into his chest.

Lilliana took a deep breath, wiping her eyes as she looked up at Damon. "Who had the means to replicate my fingerprints and have them grafted onto the other Lilliana's fingers?"

"Bloody Richard." Johnson's fury almost choked him.

Lilliana nodded. "Indeed. The one and only."

Damon stared at his wife, feeling an overwhelming rush of guilt. All that she had endured during and after the explosion. Tortured and nearly dying in the ice bath; being roughly handled by Brett and the other Black Ops staff, thinking she was a replica! Days of not being allowed to sleep; being interrogated around the clock. And yet here she was, frustrated and somewhat mystified by their lack of insight, but in typical Lilliana fashion—in real Lillian fashion, she was ever the calm and graceful centerpiece of the Given.

"Bloody hell," Brett gushed. "Lilliana, I'm so sorry…"

She shook her head, smiling a little. "I feel sorry for the replicas; they were once someone, and they have been erased—to be used as empty shells, pawns in a game." Lilliana felt safe for the first time in weeks. While she stood, warm in Damon's arms, she was filled with sadness for the replicas who might never find their loves again.

Damon ran his hands along her back. "Get Cam up here right now Brett." He grabbed Lilliana's hand and led her out of the cell past Johnson.

Brett went to make the call as Damon and Johnson took Lilliana into Johnson's office. Damon sat her in a chair and made her a cup of tea, standing behind her he rubbed her shoulders.

"I don't know what to say, Lilliana…" Johnson began as he shook his head, knowing he would never be able to apologise to her enough.

"It's alright Johnson; you were simply doing your job, and you were dealing with a very difficult situation."

He sighed. "Rachael has some information for us; I'll let her know we're ready." He left to go make the call to ask her to join them.

Damon knelt in front of Lilliana, placing his hands on either side of her knees, before looking up into her eyes adoringly, full of love. They remained silent, embracing the moment, each drinking in the other.

Lilliana cupped his cheek and stroked his smooth skin. "God I've missed you. I've missed not knowing who I really was at the time."

"Oh my darling," he whispered, his voice filled with remorse. "How can you ever forgive me? I don't think I'll ever be able to forgive myself."

"Damon, don't you dare," she shook her head. "Please, I couldn't bare it if you carried this burden of misjudgment. Let it go, I'm alright."

He shook his head. "Now."

"Yes, now, but she was under my watch the past week and a half, and I was caring for her," Rachael breezed in.

Damon stepped up and moved out of the way as Lilliana stood.

Rachael put her arms around her. "Have all your memories returned?"

Lilliana nodded. "Yes… all."

"What have you been keeping from us, Rachael?" Damon asked.

"What's going on in here," Cam said, walking in with Josephine.

They both looked at the replica, wondering why Rachael's had her arms around her.

Lilliana looked at them both, and the image of Cam dragging her to the ice bath filled her with momentary dread.

"This is our Lilliana," Damon sighed. "We've been fooled. Lilliana's mind was tampered with."

Josephine's grin was as wide as a Cheshire cat's. "Let me get this straight, please dear God! You mean to say that the Lilliana downstairs in the hospital is not our Lilliana?"

"Correct."

Josephine let out a scream of delight as she charged at Lilliana, grabbing her in the tightest bear hug as she laughed and laughed. It was contagious, and Lilliana joined in, her arms bound around her friend's frame.

Lilliana was shocked to hear a deep, pitiful sobbing and was even more shocked when she realised it was coming from her. The past five weeks had been, to put it bluntly, hell on earth.

Cam stepped forward and pulled Lilliana out of his beloved wife's arm's and into his own, rocking her gently.

Damon swallowed the lump in his throat as he realised his younger brother must be feeling like absolute hell too, reflecting on the water chamber incident.

"Lilliana, why didn't you tell us who you were at the start?"

She shook her head at Cam, looking up at him. "I couldn't. The drugs altered my every thought, and when a memory finally surfaced, the pain took it away before I could think clearly," she shrugged as she let her tears subside.

"I'm so desperately sorry, my angel," Cam whispered, kissing her cheek. "So, so sorry," he said and his voice broke and her arms bound tightly around his waist, tying to offer him some comfort.

Johnson sensed Lilliana's exhaustion. "Alright everyone. I think Lilliana is due a shower in her own room, a feed and a good night's sleep in her own bed."

"I can't do that just yet, Johnson."

All eyes looked at her, waiting.

"There is only one reason these replicas were programmed and sent here," she said, stepping back into Damon's arms, relishing his warmth. "And this was to have Damon—or myself—eliminated; and for a replica to take our place, and infiltrate our facility."

The room fell silent as they absorbed her words.

"Not just a pretty face, are you," Brett smiled.

Rachael turned to a screen and pulled up some information. "These are Lilliana's blood results that I took a fortnight ago when I began her care. Her blood contained confusion parasites, on top of the amnesiac serum and power of suggestion drugs she was dosed up with. She also endured severe psychological abuse at Richard's hand; given what her body has been through, this young lady is lucky to be standing here in front of you in such good health."

Johnson flushed. Brett fidgeted. And Cam and Damon's guilt couldn't have been any higher.

"Rachael," Lilliana said gently. "They weren't aware of the other drugs in my system—so they didn't know they were putting me in danger."

Rachael softened as she turned to her young friend who had always shown such warmth and courage, no matter what situation she had been in.

She smiled. "You're right, of course. Still."

Damon smiled, though Johnson was looking increasingly uncomfortable the more Rachael spoke.

"What are you suggesting, Lilliana?" Damon asked her point blank.

She turned to face him. "Well, Rachael told me that the other Lilliana—the one who you thought was your Lilliana—asks for Richard to attend to her. I want to know why. I propose that we do a switch; I take her place and we slip a video feed into the room and catch Richard out, once and for all."

"Lilliana, this is the man who just tried to have you killed. He has been pushing for the replicas to be destroyed via counsel with the Officials." Cam shook his head. "It's a dangerous game, I don't like it."

"Well, I didn't like having an ice bath, Cameron—but we all do what we must."

Cam flushed, his eyes filling with sadness as he looked at her.

She smiled, reaching out to take his hand. "I'm sorry, it may take me a little longer to get over that, but I still love you dearly." He squeezed her hand back.

"Well, I for one am excited at the thought of finally wiping that arrogant, smug look off Dr. Spock's face!" Josephine put her arm about Cam's waist. "Can we make it a movie night? Live stream it to your room, Damon?"

"One thing at a time, Jose. Rachael, where's Richard now?" Damon asked.

"He's not on till the morning shift."

Damon nodded. "Okay, that gives us roughly six hours. Let's get the other Lilliana up here, see if the truth serum can get us any information that will help our Lilliana settle into her role without raising any suspicion in Richard." He addressed the room before looking down at his love. "Then we'll settle you in before Richard's shift, okay?" Lilliana nodded.

"I'll bring her up," Cam said, quickly exiting the room.

"I'll get the serum." Rachael nodded, following Cam out.

Damon turned to Johnson, "Let's get Brett and the team to set up a video feed." Johnson nodded.

"Can I stay for this?" Josephine asked.

"I think it's best if the other Lilliana doesn't see you," Johnson said to Lilliana. "Grab a hot drink and step behind my privacy screen."

Damon poured two teas and walked them into Johnson's corner office while Johnson had Brett go down and set up the video feed. A thick, reflective glass screen slid out, blocking them from the rest of the room.

"Neat." Josephine sat, cupping her tea in her hands.

Damon ran a hand over Lilliana's hair, dropping a sweet kiss on her lips. She nuzzled into him, wishing they could stay like that. "I love you," she whispered in his ear.

"I love you." He kissed her again, helping her get situated and passing her the tea.

He smiled at his favourite girls. "Try to remember, this is detention. No whispering."

"Yes, Mr Night," they whispered together, almost wanting to laugh.

He smiled, stepping around the screen from where they could no longer be seen from the rest of the room. Whatever feeling of laughter they had felt soon disappeared however, when the other Lilliana was led into the room.

"Damon, what's going on?" she asked as she was strapped gently into the chair.

Rachael passed Johnson the serum.

"Well," Damon began, not wanting to call her darling, Lilliana, or any other name. "We are wondering how much you really know— if you are simply a pawn being used, or if you are more of a power player, a partner to someone higher, perhaps?"

"I truly don't understand what you mean?"

"You're about to," Cam said, watching as Johnson slid the needle into her arm, injecting the serum.

Her screams were horrendous, and Lilliana braced herself but couldn't help the tears of sympathy that fell from her eyes.

Josephine took her hand, squeezing it; their eyes met, and they nodded silently to one another, hands held tightly as the interrogation began.

"Who do you work for?"

"Richard Grey?"

Lilliana felt the hair raise on the back of her neck. *Grey… it can't be.*

Her thoughts were interrupted by the next question.

"What has been your mission?"

"I… I can't remember." Confusion flooded her face before she started to scream, shaking her head from side to side.

Rachael exchanged a look with Johnson, and Damon pressed on, asking the next question.

"Why do you ask for Richard so often? What does he do for you?"

"Richard…" she whispered, her voice fading away. "He… he helps me?"

"This isn't useful," Johnson shook his head. "Gauging by her reaction, she has been administered the same drugs as Lilliana to prevent the truth serum from having its desired effect."

Damon nodded, folding his arms. "Place her in a cell until we can rid her system of it; we can try again in the morning." He reached for her hand and pulled Lilliana's ring off her finger. "And I want her prints removed."

"Damon?" Rachael raised an eyebrow.

"Just do it, please." Damon closed his eyes, pinching the bridge of his nose and trying to release the tension in his head as the Lilliana was taken out of the room and to a cell.

Small fingers wrapped around his wrist, pulling his hand away from his nose, holding it to her cheek.

He smiled down at Lilliana and pulled her into a tight embrace. Josephine's heart melted just seeing them together. She hadn't realised Damon had been so miserable all these weeks. Seeing him now, with his arms around the 'real' Lilliana, made him glow.

"Listen, I'm going to round up the gang and quietly let them know what's going on. Allie will be so thrilled. She thought someone must have performed a lobotomy on you," Josephine said jokingly.

Lilliana couldn't contain the laugh that burst from her. It felt like she hadn't laughed in years. It felt so good, that she almost cried.

Damon nodded to Josephine. "Thanks sweetie. Keep it nice and quiet."

Josephine gave Damon a light peck on the cheek, then another one on Lilliana's.

"See you soon gorgeous."

"Bye Jose."

As Josephine left, Cam turned to Damon. "What information do you hope Lilliana can extract from Richard?"

Damon picked up Lilliana's small hand and slipped her ring back on her finger where it belonged

"As much as we can to end him."

Lilliana stared up into his eyes, lost in the unmistakable look of desire and affection.

"Damon," she leaned in, waiting for his kiss.

He obliged, wrapping his arms around her, and holding her close.

Cam cleared his throat. "I can help you guys get a room if you like," he chuckled.

"The room's been set up. Let's go," Johnson announced, returning to the room.

Damon tucked Lilliana under his arm. "You ready?"

"Oh yes—like you wouldn't believe."

CHAPTER 24

Soothing music drifted through the hospital room and Lilliana woke to the relaxed blend of sounds coming from the speakers; it was the pleasant sound of waves as the backdrop to an ancient, Celtic harp. She tried to focus on the sweet music, though try as she might, it did little to settle her nerves. She was grateful Damon had insisted she be given a low dose of sleep serum to help her sleep before having to face Richard.

Looking across the room, Lilliana's heart melted at the sight of her handsome husband asleep, arms folded, long legs stretched out in the small, uncomfortable looking hospital chair.

Never, ever am I letting this man out of my sight again. With that thought, she gently pushed off the covers and slipped from the bed, tiptoeing over to him, and tucking herself up onto his lap, nuzzling under his chin.

His strong arms held her tight as he breathed her in.

"My Lilliana," he whispered, kissing her head.

She leaned back, lighting up the room with her smile, her breath catching as she saw the glint of hunger in his eyes.

"Oh, if only," he mumbled, sweeping his lips across hers, turning her into a purring kitten in his arms. She kissed him back with everything she had, feeling tears of desire ready to overtake her.

Their igniting passion had to be quickly banked as the door closed with a bang. Rachael stood, looking nervous. "He's coming."

Damon didn't hesitate; in one quick movement he swept Lilliana up in his arms and placed her back in the bed.

"Play demure Lilliana now; not my beautiful angry, vengeful angel, okay?"

She looked up into his eyes, that only moments before were filled with love and lust. Now, only concern and a deep fury burned in his intense gaze.

"I'll be fine Damon, please don't worry, Baby."

He leant down and swept a kiss across her lips as the door opened.

"Morning all," Richard sang out smugly.

He really thinks he's in charge. Lilliana concentrated on the task set before her. Be demure.

"Richard." Damon checked himself before he turned around to face the traitor.

Richard nodded, practically ignoring Damon as he crossed the floor to greet his favourite patient. "How are you this morning, dear?"

Lilliana nodded quietly as Rachael had instructed her to do the night before. She had been given as much information as possible as to how the other Lilliana had acted when others were in the room with her and Richard. Unfortunately, when the two had been alone they had little insight to give, which frayed her nerves again. She watched in awe as Damon remained stonily silent, while Richard pranced around her bed, as though he was her knight in shining armor.

"Richard, I want Lilliana returned to our room by end of day; I feel she is ready to return to her duties," Damon said, expecting an argument.

"That sounds like a very good idea, Sir," Richard said, shocking them all.

"I'll do a blood scan," Rachael suggested, waiting for Richard to react.

Of course, he did.

"No, no—I've got that all sorted, thank you Rachael. Why don't you go attend elsewhere so Lilliana and I can do some hypnotherapy, get her prepared for her return?"

"Of course," Rachael said. She knew just as Damon did, that they weren't going to get any proof of Richard's culpability unless they left Lilliana alone with the man.

Damon leaned in and planted a kiss on Lilliana's lips.

Lilliana desperately wanted to meet his gaze, but she did as she'd been instructed and remained demure, aloof.

"See you later, sweetheart."

Lilliana watched as Damon and Rachael left the room, leaving her alone with Richard. She felt afraid, then. Her fingers gripped the blanket, building up enough courage to meet his eye.

He smiled at her as he sat on the side of the bed. She said nothing and waited for him to speak.

"Everything is going according to plan, my dear. Soon, you will in charge as Mrs Lilliana Night, and the demise of the great Night name, along with this prestigious establishment, will be set in motion."

He sounded so gleeful; Lilliana's stomach rolled, she thought she might be sick. Instead, she nodded demurely. "What would you like me to do first?" she said, playing along with the charade.

"I want you to slip back into Damon's bed like a good wife and go about your day-to-day duties. Within a month, you will have gained much more insight on how things run, and soon you and I will have the means to kill him and replace him with one of our Damon's." He chuckled gleefully.

"I can't believe it has all worked out so well. And the joy I will have when I can get my hands on the real Lilliana!" Lilliana retorted, trying to sound equally as joyous. Richard's eyes glazed over as he ran a cold fingertip along her cheek bone, relishing in her soft skin. "The things I will do to her," he whispered, sending chills of disgust down Lilliana's spine as he did.

"Any questions?"

"I've forgotten something you said," she asked, looking at him shyly.

"Yes?"

Her heart fluttered uncomfortably as he raised an eyebrow, looking arrogant.

"You told me your name, Richard Grey."

"That's right, and—?"

"I was visited by an Orlando and Nadia Grey."

"Yes, my nephew and niece; although they've never met me before coming here. Their father, my younger brother, was slaughtered because of Lilliana." He shook his head.

"I have been working towards her downfall, for quite some time. Certainly, in many ways it has been since the moment I first saw footage of the blood bath that led her to our doors here."

Lilliana's mind secretly flew back to the night that had ultimately led her here, and eventually into Damon's arms. She could never regret the events that led her to have the life she had now, no matter how much they may have scarred her on the inside. Healing hearts, she now knew, could open their arms wide to embrace all who had been so wronged in this world.

So, Richard was the elder brother of Simon Grey. Richard, who had worked for this establishment for over two decades before she had even heard of Damon Night. The same Richard, who, had had an unusual and instant dislike for her, from day one. Well, at least now she knew why.

He blamed her for his brother's death. Probably did not care one iota that his brother was a foul human long before he had abducted her and Jessica.

Being near him disgusted her and she wondered how long she could go along with this charade. He moved closer to her and ran his fingers through her tresses, down and over her collar bone and along the top button of her nightgown. Her sudden rapid breathing made him curious. Was she finally showing her attraction to him after weeks of tirelessly programming her in the hopes that she would eventually be his, to have in secret? She knew her next question would not sound so demure, and she ran her tongue over her lips, hoping to distract him as she asked, "I forget who made me?"

He leaned forward, mesmerised by her pink tongue, her plump, moist lips; he was wanting to taste her now after lusting for weeks over all the Lilliana's.

Lilliana knew she would knock his head off if he came an inch closer, so she leaned back further into the pillows. She had him right where she wanted him. Bait.

"You were a crack whore, stolen from the streets and sculpted by the Replica Organisation. They can create a double of anyone for the right price," He leaned into her chest now, his arms pinning her down on either side of the pillows. "And you, my dear, were worth every penny."

"Stop," she cried as his lips almost made contact with hers. She covered her face with her hands. "I'm… I'm not ready." She had to force herself to sound apologetic.

"Oh, my dear, that's quite alright." He took her hands away from her face, holding them in his cold clutches.

"All in good time," he said gleefully, looking forward to the time when he would help her run this facility. His eyes dropped to her delicate hands, and he turned them over to run his fingers over her soft flesh, freezing when he spotted her fingertips. Although the burns had healed with the burn cream Rachael had been applying, her fingertips were still badly scarred.

Her breath caught as her eyes met his. Her cover was blown.

He stared at her silently before saying in the deathly quiet, "Well now, we have a problem."

"I think you've always had a problem, Richard." She tried to push him away so she could get up, but he wrapped his hands around her neck, lightning fast.

She gasped in fright, always surprised by his strength, and she dug her fingernails into his wrists; she hated having to touch the man, but she was desperate to get away from his vice-like grip.

The door flew open and Damon stormed in like a demon on a rampage. "Get your hands off my wife!" He marched over to Richard, who leapt from the bed, and was by now standing against the wall. Cam, Johnson, and Rachael were just steps behind, and they watched with great satisfaction as Damon punched Richard square in the face.

Richard's head gave a satisfying crack as it connected with the wall, his nose producing a steady stream of blood.

He cursed as he stumbled forward before falling to his knees. "I can explain…" he attempted.

Damon let out a pained laugh as Johnson dragged Richard to his feet.

"Don't even bother. You're done. Get him out of my sight."

Johnson twisted Richard's arm painfully behind his back and marched him from the room. Lilliana got out of the bed and jumped into Damon's waiting arms, wrapping her arms around his waist, pushing her face into his chest. "We've got him."

Damon met Rachael's gaze as he ran his hands down Lilliana's back, soothing her, loving her for her bravery. "We sure as hell do."

"What now?"

"Right now, what I need is five minutes alone with my wife before we clean this mess up."

"Take all the time you need. Welcome back, Lilly."

Lilliana turned to Rachael, smiling. "Just about."

As Rachael left, Lilliana looked up at Damon. "I can only imagine what has to be done now and I want to be there every step of the way with you. But please, can I shower in our shower, and get my own clothes back on first?"

He kissed her soft, plump lips. "Of course, darling. Come, I'll walk you up. I'm not ready to let you out of my sight just yet."

With arms tightly around the other, they went up to their room so Lilliana could freshen up and feel more like herself before tackling the duties of the director's wife.

***

"What was your main mission with the use of the replicas?" Johnson had to ask.

"To kill Lilliana Night." Richard's replica puppet answered.

"To what purpose?"

"I am here to be Mr Damon Night's wife in every capacity. I am here to infiltrate this Given facility, and in time, through my modelling and other roles, bring disgrace and chaos to the Night name and undo all the good of the Louisiana's Given."

"What other objective's did Richard Grey have?"

"In time, we are to kill Damon Night and replace him with our replica as well as reach into other Given establishments in an effort to destroy the Official's Law and decimate the facilities into the ground."

Damon pressed pause on the screen after playing it for the seventy Officials around the globe and the fifty Given Directors who had all been requested to attend the broadcast. Over one hundred and twenty faces all looked on in bewilderment.

The conference call had been going for nearly forty minutes already, and this final footage confirming Richard's mastermind betrayal had them all talking.

Lilliana sat in a chair by Damon's legs while he stood running the meeting with Cam, Johnson, Clair, Brett, and Rachael.

Josephine sat near Lilliana, relieved that this nightmare had finally come to a close.

"The only question now, Mr Night," Mason sighed, "Is what do we do with these poor shells that were once victims on the street?"

"Whatever you decide; but they cannot stay at our facility." Damon took a sip of the coffee that Christopher had poured for him.

"Agreed," Russell shook his head. "Although innocent puppets, the fact that they hold the faces of two of the most well-known individuals on this planet makes things very complicated because we need to ensure they are never used again for harm."

"We could place them at the Ruins?" Paul suggested.

Mason nodded; they could work their days out there.

"They shouldn't be punished," Lilliana said quietly, causing all eyes to shift to her.

She looked up at Damon. "They can't stay here, but they shouldn't be placed somewhere as harsh as the Ruins. They were innocent people who were stolen and turned into doubles. They've already suffered enough, even if they can't remember half of it."

"Why can't you people just turn them into another version of themselves?" Josephine waved her hand in the air as though it were that simple. The room fell quiet for a moment then suddenly it seemed as though all the Officials were talking at once. Cam smiled at Josephine and Lilliana leaned into Damon's legs while all the commotion continued on screen. After what seemed like a minute, fifty of the seventy Officials screens suddenly went blank as Mason addressed the online room.

"We acknowledge that your establishment has indeed undergone an enormous amount of stress this past year, and we wish to eliminate any further stressors that would contribute to your current situation. Therefore, we will collect all of the replicas and, additionally, we will have your replicas identities refashioned and moulded to fit new identities as something other than you and your wife, as a measure for your protection." Mason nodded specifically to Damon, before nodding to Lilliana as well.

Lilliana smiled, grateful for all the assistance from the Officials in bringing closure to the case.

"It's obvious we have a leak in our building, and I'm sure once you hit Richard with enough truth serum, he will reveal who it is. We'd be grateful if you could do this immediately, so we can resolve that situation."

"Of course." Johnson said.

"What you do with your traitor, is up to you and your establishment, of course."

Damon nodded, trying to ignore the excited look on Cam's face.

"—but we would prefer you use lethal injection."

Damon watched as Cam's face fell in disappointment. "Thank you Mason. Anything else?"

"No, we will have the plane there before dark. Until then."

The Officials screens went blank leaving only the directors from the other Given facilities.

Damon chatted to them briefly before they all ended the call, leaving Russell to have a final word with Damon.

"Take it easy, hey—it sounds like it's been hell."

"That's one way to put it." Damon smiled as Lilliana stood. He looked down at her and Russell noticed the hunger in his eyes.

"Well, I've got to go. Keep in touch, good luck with it all. I'm so glad you are safe, Lilliana."

She turned her eyes from Damon to smile at Russell. "Thanks."

"Bye Russell."

"See you." The screen went blank.

"Okay, what next?" Josephine enthused as she jumped up. "How about you two have some time out?"

"I can organise a nice meal for you?" Christopher added.

"Oh yes; then we can all come for brunch and have a catch up in the morning to discuss your wedding?" Josephine nodded to Christopher.

Damon looked at Johnson.

"We have to extract information from Richard. Immediately."

"Brett and I can do that; why don't you take an hour or two, be with Lilly?"

Damon looked down at his wife, who looked at him, begging with emerald eyes. Like she'd ever have to beg. He smiled. "Sounds perfect."

"I'll organise the replicas for transport. Make sure they're fed and comfortable."

"Thanks Rachael, I appreciate that." He nodded, knowing that the replicas comfort meant a great deal to Lilliana and gave her peace of mind.

"Okay, well off you go." Cam hugged Lilliana as Damon reached for her hand.

"Christopher, can you organise a tray in an hour's time? I think we'll have something to eat first and then go for a ride."

"Absolutely, Sir," Christopher nodded as he tidied up the cups to take back to the kitchen.

The entire group were relieved and happy once their director took Lilliana out of the room, retiring upstairs.

***

They stood holding hands, looking into each other's eyes, neither wanting this moment to end. He slowly drew her to him until her soft body brushed against his hard-firm skin.

"Never letting you out of my sight again." Dropping his forehead down to hers he closed his eyes, breathing her in.

Her fingers floated up his biceps to caress his chest, then she let them drift lazily up and around his neck, feeling his silky black locks. "And I'm never letting *you* out of mine," she whispered back.

They swayed together to the music of their beating hearts.

She watched his lips part in a sexy smile. She moved her body into his, his eyes opening wide in anticipation, swallowing her whole as his gaze caressed her face. They smiled in joy as their lips softly met, hands entwined, each clinging to the other. Lilliana moaned in delight just being with him again, and he swept her up into his arms and carried his treasure into their bedroom. The sun kissed the bed through the dome ceiling where he gently placed her down like the goddess that she was to him.

"Damon, come lay with me." She ran her hands over the soft cover. He happily obliged, slowly sinking into the bed, leaning down on his elbow as he kicked off his shoes.

"This is going to be slow," he whispered, thrilling her as her eyes glazed over with the thought of their love making. Taking his time, he ran his fingers along the edges of her soft, stunning face, kissing her chin, and mumbling sweet nothings. She reached out and undid the top button on his shirt, running her fingers teasingly along the inside of his chest, feeling his firm, warm skin. Her eyes met his as she undid the second button, her foot caressing his calf as her fingers explored his chest.

"I love you more than life itself, Lilliana Night." He gently cupped her chin and stared into her eyes, reaching down until he was a breath away.

"And I love you more than words can say, Damon Night," she whispered back as his lips swept over hers.

He relished the feel of her, and God knew he wanted to take it slow. She wriggled beneath him, trying to get as close to him as she could, driving his gentle passion closer to an insatiable hunger.

He almost laughed with delight, but soon enough she had swept his thoughts away from laughter and over to the ledge of lust.

She pushed him onto his back and straddled him still fully clothed, as her lips glided over his. Her hair shrouded her face, a dark curtain around them. He was rock hard now, but he was grateful they both still had their clothes on to slow down the process of things as she started to rock against him.

"Lilliana, you are driving me wild," he gasped as she sucked his tongue deep into her mouth.

"Good," she whispered against his lips, her fingers working below as she tried to unzip his jeans.

He sat up, dropping her onto her back and ripped his shirt over his head before reaching for her dress. Pushing it off her shoulders, he tugged it down over her waist to reveal a snug fitting black bra, hugging her luscious breasts. He became ravenous at the sight of the pretty lace edge holding her smooth, soft flesh and ran a finger ever so gently along the top of her bra, loving the way her skin turned to goosebumps under his touch.

She sighed, watching his eyes darken as he drank in the sight of her. She removed her dress to reveal matching black underwear and she melted with the look he gave her.

"My gorgeous girl." Sitting above her, he ran his hands in a tantalising massage across her flesh that caused her insides to melt like molten lava. Damon took his time, as hard as he was, enjoying her sighs as his fingers floated down her neck and along her rib cage, then up again to cup her swollen breasts.

She looked up at his devastatingly handsome face through eyes heavy with desire, her body soft, pulsing, and ready.

He lifted his hips, discarding his jeans and underwear before laying back against her sexy, underwear-clad body. He smiled into her eyes again as he ran a hand down her back, bringing her flush up against him. Sweeping a hand over her curvy bottom and then lower, behind her leg, he hooked his long fingers behind her knee and slowly drew it up to rest across his hip.

She moaned softly in anticipation as his fingers went back down to massage her throbbing bud through her slick underwear. Wantonly she rocked against him, pushing herself closer to his swollen shaft before reaching down to wrap her fingers tightly about him, stroking back and forth. He sucked in his breath again as she moved the tip of his engorged head towards her moist entrance, rubbing against him. She was making him see stars. In one move, he rolled her onto her back, and with two hands ripped her knickers in half. Her breath whooshed out in delight as he lay against her, cupping her face, and he kissed her breathless. She opened her legs and wrapped them about him, feeling his shaft as it throbbed against her bud before it finally eased into her molten cave.

"Damon," she sighed as he thrust gently, in and out, rhythmically, building up to a pleasant wave as he rocked against her. Each deep, slow thrust went on forever, leading her to free fall into a colourful vortex of pleasure until she didn't think she could take it anymore.

He kissed her tenderly as he worshiped her body. Every thrust he made was with her pleasure in mind. Every touch, every caress. He unclipped her bra and tossed it aside, one hand holding her head in place for a deep kiss while his other hand gently cupped her heavy breast, flicking her swollen nipple as he thrust up again and again, deeply hitting her core, over and over until a dizzying wave washed over her, pushing her over the edge of bliss. She cried with intense pleasure; her hands swept through his hair as she held him to her and sucked his tongue, kissing him endlessly.

"Lilliana," he whispered huskily. He rocked against her, feeling her explode around him and with one final deep thrust, he allowed himself the blissful release into her soft, warm body. Both lay there breathless, thankful, and completely satisfied, silently relishing the peace.

"I have a million things to say," she began. They both lay on their backs, looking up into the sky.

"I can't wait to hear them." He kissed her head.

She rolled over onto her stomach, dropping her chin into her hands as she crossed her ankles, swinging them behind her.

"Damon Night, I hereby declare, I am never letting you out of my line of vision again. Ever."

He ran his hand over the creamy flesh of her back and slowly smiled up at her. "Done. Next?"

"More of that, really."

He laughed. "Darling, I feel the same way." He shook his head. "I wonder what a normal day in the outside world must feel like for the average couple?"

"Well, there's absolutely nothing average about you, Damon Night." She raised an eyebrow. He smiled, leaning up to claim her lips for a soft kiss that had her insides melting in a heartbeat.

"That may be so, but my partner matches that statement too, in every sense."

She ran her fingertips lightly over his chest. "These past few weeks," she shook her head. "Leon," she ended, barely above a whisper.

His smile slowly vanished, and he wrapped his fingers around hers, meeting her eyes. "We will have Leon's service tomorrow afternoon."

She nodded, taking a slow, deep breath.

His face couldn't fall any further. Yet it did. "I can't forgive myself for the way we treated you and the other replicas."

Her heart lurched at the look of regret that shadowed his face. "Damon, don't—please. It was truly an impossible, dangerous situation. Can you imagine if I had continued in Richard's care with his mind-altering medications? What would have happened?" She shook her head.

"Thank God for Rachael's all-seeing eye," Damon sighed.

"Yes, Rachael always has her ear to the ground and her eye on the ball. Her medical knowledge was a godsend in this case. But you and the team did what you had to do, and if you hadn't, you might be rolling around here right now with a completely different Lilliana."

"That would never happen. Even Richard can't replicate your charming, vivacious personality." He grinned, trying to lighten the mood for her sake. He could beat himself up privately later, but for now, he wanted to see her smiling.

"True." She dropped a kiss against his jaw.

"He will pay for his crimes."

She looked silently into his eyes before saying, "That is one man I do not wish to discuss right now."

"I understand that completely, sweetheart." He ran his hand over her back and pushed his own feelings of frustration and anger towards the traitorous man, aside. "Are you hungry?"

She smiled, nodding, "I am starving."

"Good, Christopher will have a tray here shortly; let's shower and get our riding gear on, and by the time it arrives we'll be ready."

She nodded, "That sounds perfect, thank you Damon, I really needed this."

He kissed her again. "So did I, sweetheart." He got off the bed, pulling her up with him and into a rejuvenating shower, before feasting on food followed by a therapeutic horse ride for their souls.

***

The air seemed fresher than any air Lilliana had ever breathed. Riding over the luscious pastures were wildflowers raised their bright faces towards the sun, filling the air with a delicate scent, had Lilliana's soul filled with complete happiness. She knew the tears would come. It was inevitable after everything she had gone through not only these past weeks, but the months before on Reid's compound. But right in this moment, watching Damon gallop ahead on Beast as she rode her beloved Beauty under the afternoon sky, she allowed the breeze to blow every worrying thought away.

***

After their two-hour ride, Lilliana sat quietly in Damon's office while he attended to some urgent matters.

Rupert had got wind through Christopher, that Lilliana was waiting for a pot of tea and took it in to her, himself. As Damon was on a call, Rupert and Lilliana had to keep their squeals of excitement low upon seeing each other, and they hugged each other hard.

"I tell you, Lilly; you need to think about writing a book, given all the adventures you've had this year." He shook his head as he poured her a black floral tea.

"Food for thought," she smiled, thinking she could pack all their adventures over the years into a trilogy at the very least. They sat down on the couch and huddled together so they could talk quietly without interrupting Damon.

"How's Luke, how's everybody? I feel like I've been away forever."

"I can tell you this; you've been missed. Everyone is great and tickled pink that zombie Lilliana didn't take your place for any longer than she did." He chuckled, leaning closer. "Eric and Allie knew it wasn't you after only ten minutes, but Dr. Dick insisted your strange behaviour was because of the explosion, concussion and all." He shook his head, bumping his shoulder against hers. "Did you know there was almost a biffo' between Eric and Dick... but your superhero saved the day."

Interesting that Damon hadn't mentioned any of that, she thought. They looked across the room to where Damon was listening intently to a problem another Given Director was having, his eyes immediately locking on hers, pinning her in place. She couldn't help the flush that crept over her face; the intense look he was giving her made her feel naked in front of Rupert.

Rupert's chuckle had her quickly looking away from Damon. She smiled at Rupert. "It's nice to see love lasting." He winked. "Drink all of that, it is full of healing blossoms."

Lilliana nodded. "I can smell Lavender and Hawthorne."

"And a wee touch of Passionflower." Rupert took an appreciative sniff from her teacup before meeting her eyes. "We need you well and ready for the wedding day, Lilliana. Will you be up for it in about a week?"

"Absolutely, I'd be ready for it even if it were today."

Rupert wrapped his arms around her, holding her silently for a few moments. "You've always been such a good friend to me."

"And you've been such a good friend to me," she said, hugging him back, careful not to spill the hot tea on him.

"If you need me for anything, anything at all... please, just come find me, Okay?"

"Of course."

The door burst open and Allie marched in. "Why the *hell* wasn't I informed sooner that you were here?" she practically shouted.

"Shh," Rupert pointed at the other end of the room where Damon stood, arms folded, repeating himself over the background interruption. He raised an eyebrow and tapped his lips just then, which Lilliana thought she would have loved to march on down and kiss.

Allie waved a hand apologetically before reaching down and scooping Lilliana up for a bear hug. They giggled quietly as Allie bounced up and down in excitement. "I told them you know! I told them that other Lilly-thing wasn't you, but would they listen to me? No." She grabbed Lilliana's face, staring into her eyes.

"Where did we first meet?"

"At the lake on a morning run and swim."

"What did I say?"

Lilliana thought for a moment, thinking back over a decade. "Something like, if you knew you were going to be splashing around with snakes and toads, you wouldn't have bothered showering?"

Allie squealed again in delight, unable to contain her excitement as she yelled, "It's really you!" and she danced Lilliana around in a circle. Lilliana couldn't suppress the laughter that burst joyously from her, and hugged Allie.

"Dwayne, I'm sorry, I'm going to have to call you back." Damon ended the call and made his way back down to the other end of the room where the two girls stood clinging to each other.

"Sorry Sir, I couldn't help myself," Allie smiled through her tears at Damon as she released Lilliana, keeping her arm about her friend's waist.

He ran a finger along Lilliana's cheek, saying, "I think perhaps a quiet dinner can include our friends tonight, what do you think, Baby?"

"She thinks hell yes!" Allie answered for her.

Lilliana laughed, "She does think that, actually."

Rupert grinned. "Am I included in this gathering?"

"Of course Rupert. I'll speak to Cook, see if we can organise a nice informal meal after hours in the library. I still have a few hours' worth of meetings." He looked apologetically at Lilliana. She didn't want to leave Damon's side, and he could see it written all over her face.

"Baby," he drew her out of Allie's arms and into his. "You are completely safe. The Replicas will be collected in an hour's time. Richard is locked up tight. There is nothing to fear."

She looked up at him, nodding. "I know, it's so silly; I just don't want to be away from you at the moment."

His eyes bore into hers. "I know," he said quietly.

"Lilly, why don't you stay here and finish your pot of tea that I clearly interrupted," Allie grinned. "And I'll come back in an hour, see if you're up to having some drinks with the girls before the men join us for dinner?"

"Good idea," Damon agreed as he tucked a strand of hair behind Lilliana's ear.

"I have to go; I have a quick session with Hillary taking our final group for the day."

"How is everyone?"

"Everyone's fine, if you don't count Max taking a dump in the middle of group!" Allie rolled her eyes. "What is it about people using our sessions as toilet breaks?"

Rupert chuckled. "I'm off, Lilly; it's been great seeing you again."

"We'll see you later." Lilliana smiled at him before he left.

"Thanks Damon, and sorry again about the interruption," Allie said, smiling genuinely, and turned and kissed Lilliana on the cheek before spinning out of the room with as much energy as she'd arrived.

Lilliana smiled up into Damon's face. She shook her head in wonder at her life.

He ran his hand over her silky hair. "What, love?"

She sighed, "Moments like these, I just want to pause everything, have our world quieten around us, so we can simply be."

He cupped her face in his hands. "Beautiful girl, you take as much time as you need before you leap back into your role. I really don't care if you remain my shadow for the rest of my days. It will certainly prevent me from having heart failure."

She laughed and leaned up into his kiss. They held each other for a few moments before he said, "I have to go return that call now."

She nodded as Damon took a step backwards towards his desk. "Don't mind me, I'm going to sit here and enjoy Rupert's tea," Lilliana said and sat, tucking her legs under her as she reached for the teapot to top up her cup, enjoying the hour that followed.

True to her word, Allie returned on the hour and she was not alone. Fox, Jessica, Josephine, and Nadia burst through the door enthusiastically. Lilliana smiled at Damon as she got up to meet her friends for a group hug. Damon was grateful for the timing as he'd only just hung up from his call before they all entered, laughing, and talking all at once.

"My God—it's so good to see you!" Jessica cried.

"You too, Jess." Lilliana squeezed her friend's hand.

"You certainly find yourself in the most unusual situations," Nadia grinned.

Lilliana laughed, shaking her head at her new friend. "Tell me about it."

"I hope you are planning on drinking a month's worth of wine with me tonight," Fox crossed her arms.

"Not if you want to see the sunrise tomorrow, she won't." All eyes went to Damon who was standing a few feet away, hands loosely tucked in his jeans pockets.

Josephine laughed, "Oh you gorgeous guardian you," she crossed over and put her arms about his waist, smiling up into his face.

Damon returned her hug, smiling down at her fondly. "I was only half kidding."

Allie laughed. "Sounds like me half the time. Right?" She clapped her hands. "Are we doing this, or what?"

Everyone looked at Lilliana, waiting to see if she would leave Damon's side. She felt so surrounded by the love of her friends, and although she didn't want to leave Damon, she had really missed her girls. A knock sounded at the door, interrupting them.

"And that's how it is usually done," Damon said, before calling out. "Come in."

Johnson and Brett entered, hesitating for a moment upon seeing the crowd of women.

Damon waved his hand. "Please, come in."

Johnson nodded at the others as he said to Damon. "It's time to escort the Replicas to the airstrip. The Official jet is touching down as we speak."

Damon nodded, his eyes meeting Lilliana's.

"I'm fine, love," she reassured him.

"We will not let her out of our sight, Sir," Jessica smiled, a hint of a blush filling her pretty cheeks.

Damon smiled at her; she was always such a darling, he thought.

"I've made sure the library is free so you will have it all to yourselves. We won't be with you all till after seven, so you'll have plenty of time to catch up."

"Excellent. Let's go." Fox spun on her heel and led the way.

Lilliana threw a smile over her shoulder at Damon as Allie and Josephine flanked her, following Fox with Nadia and Jessica in tow.

Damon sighed, running his hand through his hair as he watched her disappear from his sight.

Johnson waited, appreciating the effort it was costing Damon to let go of her after only just getting her back last night.

"She will be completely fine."

Damon met his calm gaze. "Yes, she will. Thanks, Johnson. Let's get these poor souls onto the jet and out of here."

Damon led the way up to Black Ops as Brett filled him in on Richard's interrogation. "Once Richard gave us the name we immediately called Mason. The name meant nothing to us, of course. But Mason recognised it instantly."

"Good, that's another step towards cleaning up this entire mess."

They crossed the walkway and opened the gate.

"This incident has certainly got the other establishments talking about cleaning up any issues they may have hidden inside their walls." Johnson pushed the door open.

"And we'll be taking measures to do the same here." Damon shook his head, angry that they would ever need to doubt their staff to begin with. Johnson could sense his frustration. They had all been taken for fools as far as Richard was concerned. Clair stood with Rachael outside the waiting room, watching the men approach.

"They've all been given a calming sedative, Sir," Rachael nodded as Damon looked into the room. His heart ached for them. He saw all three Lilliana's sitting alone, mourning their Damon's who had died in the explosion; it left a hollow feeling in his chest. The others quietly sat together, holding hands.

"It's too sad." Clair said quietly.

"It's a disgrace what Richard has done." Rachael sounded furious.

Johnson placed a calming hand on her shoulder, gently squeezing it.

"Brett, let's grab a few more Team Members to escort them down to the plane."

"Yes Sir." Brett left to round up spare hands and Damon turned to Rachael.

"The girls took Lilliana to the library; why don't you get Jaycee to help Billy cover tonight's shift so you can join them. I know Lilliana would love that."

"You know, I think I will do that. God knows the past month has sucked a bit of my energy. A fun night could be the recharge I need."

Damon smiled. "Great. We'll see you all later."

Rachael nodded and looked to Johnson. "Treat them kindly," she implored him.

"Of course Ray, you know we will."

She kissed his cheek before leaving, hoping the replica's future would be brighter than what the past month had been.

CHAPTER 25

The library had always been one of Lilliana's favourite rooms; she drank in its grand feel and opulent furnishings around the large, central ornate fireplace. Bookcases twenty feet high were crammed with books in every genre to delight a range of readers, accessible by long wooden ladders that rolled along long, oak stained shelves. Thick candles had been lit and the chandeliers lowered and set to dim, creating an atmosphere of romance and mystery.

"This looks gorgeous!" Jessica exclaimed as they walked by the Koi pond that trickled soothingly. They crossed to the fireplace where a table sat filled with silver ice buckets topped with mixed drinks and champagne. Splashes of flora filled vases that were placed on tabletops, the fireplace mantel, and the bookshelves, adding to the stately vibe. Fox reached for the champagne and began to pour.

"Even I feel a little underdressed for such an occasion," she said and passed Josephine a glass.

"Should we get changed?" Josephine wondered out loud.

"That could be fun, getting a little dolled up?" Allie added, her eyes lighting up. "It would be fun to surprise our men."

"What do you think, Lilly?" Nadia asked.

Lilliana could see the enthusiasm on all their faces, and after having spent a month in a psych ward outfit, the decision was a no brainer for her. "I think it's a great idea. Let's have a drink first."

"Or two," Fox smiled, passing Lilliana a glass. "Have to get as much into you before Mr Night arrives."

Lilliana laughed, enjoying the cool bubbles that fizzled in her throat, feeling tingly inside at the mention of Damon. The door opened and an elderly man appeared, pushing a trolley that carried an assortment of delicacies and their mouths watered instantly.

"Here are your starters, ladies," Cook took a bow, looking over at Lilliana.

Cook's father had served Damon's grandfather; and he had served Damon's father and had a great respect for the way Damon did things at the Given, taking over after his father had died. Although he preferred to keep to himself and his kitchen duties much of the time, Cook had quietly been watching from the sidelines for many years and admired the woman Damon had taken to be his life partner.

And secretly, he had always quietly adored young Josephine.

Lilliana smiled at him. "Thank you so much. Would you like to join us for dinner tonight?"

"Thank you, but no. Ms Bonnie and I are sharing a meal tonight."

Jessica was listening in, and hid her smile. She hadn't seen Ms Bonnie much over the years; their roles keeping them busily apart. But she would always remember her as, the 'cutlery count lady,' after she had first arrived.

"I hope you all have a lovely evening." He bowed again before turning on his heel and briskly leaving the room.

Josephine popped a baked goat's cheese ball into her mouth as Nadia reached for a tiny sweetcorn pancake topped with avocado.

"I swear—between Cook and Christopher's cooking, I am going to be as fat as a pig before I say, 'I do.'" Allie placed a mouthful of asparagus wrapped in crispy pancetta and dipped in melted parmesan into her mouth, moaning with pleasure as it hit her taste buds.

"If Mother Nature didn't like curves so much she would have made the earth flat," Lilliana said, washing down a piece of olive bread.

"Nice, I'll remember that." Allie smiled.

"Right, a toast—" Fox wiped her fingers clean, reaching for her glass. "Here's to life rolling smoothly, good friends and cold champagne."

Josephine laughed as they clinked their glasses together. "Always the sentimentalist of the group, hey Foxy-Loxy?"

Fox shrugged her shoulders. "You know I love you all."

"Indeed," Allie nodded. "Right. Drink up, then let's go change. Lilliana, you are not leaving my side, so we'll grab my get up and then we'll go up to your rooms to get changed."

Lilliana smiled. "Sounds good to me."

"Alright then," Fox said, walking to the door. "Let's see what we can drag out from our wardrobes for an elegant night."

***

When Damon and the others joined the ladies in the library after seven their eyes just about fell out of their heads when taking in the spectacular sight of their women all dressed up in tantalising outfits that revealed creamy skin and curvaceous shapes in the most delightful of ways.

The party of eighteen finished a delightful dinner around colourful conversations before Allie requested to have private time with the ladies upstairs to discuss her big 'I do' day, leaving the men to enjoy their drinks by the roaring fire. Eric passed Damon one of their distilled beers that he, Christopher and Orlando had been working on in their spare time. Cam had had the Brewery built a few years ago opposite the cheese and milk building, all of which were surrounded by spectacular gardens and seating for those wanting to taste test their beers on special occasions.

After taking his first mouthful, Damon looked at the three men. "This is unlike anything I've ever had before."

"I'll be the judge of that, Brother," Cam held out his hand as Orlando passed him a beer. "You not really being a consumer of beer, and all."

He smiled before taking a decent swallow, then echoed Damon's verdict. "Totally unique."

Orlando smiled. "We've been working on it for several months now."

Jessica watched Orlando become animated as he discussed the flavours and techniques that they had used to create the mouth-watering ale. She was so proud of him, and looking across at Nadia's face, knew that she felt the same.

"Rupert contributed also to this fine batch." Eric saluted in Rupert's direction.

Luke put his arm around his shoulder, smiling with pride.

"There's an interesting flavour, I can't quite put my finger on though," Johnson held the glass up to the flickering firelight, as if it would tell him what it was.

Rupert shrugged. "Just a few special little ingredients to make it pop. I believe in organic all the way."

"Do you want to distribute it?" Damon took another swallow, appreciating the flavours.

"Absolutely." Christopher nodded. "I know we have to contribute to the profits here in order to continue improving our facility; but we also wanted to contribute to the funding of Lilliana's safe houses and see what other projects we might help out in the future."

"It's something we can certainly work towards," Damon nodded. "I'll always support a Given's passion project that can grow in order to help others. Well done, all of you."

"Cheers to that." Marcus raised his glass.

"I'm thinking of a photo shoot, or mini ad campaign to launch it into the market already." Cam looked thoughtful. "This will be fun." He grinned at the men.

Scott and Karen sat on the spiral staircase, nursing hot chocolates, whispering quietly between themselves. Karen had been thrilled when Scott invited her to be his special 'plus one' for this get together, and now, watching the group below, made her participation in the night seem even more surreal.

"Look out, you two cuties," Josephine smiled at Scott and Karen, who were blocking the staircase.

"Do you want to join us for another hot chocolate before we call it a night?" Lilliana asked her brother.

"Sure thing." Scott picked up Karen's hand and led her downstairs to the men below as Lilliana linked arms with her brother.

Damon's eyes lit up as Lilliana walked towards him.

Wearing an off-the-shoulder bright red dress with matching pumps, her hair, black as night swept over her creamy skin; she looked like a hot, sultry vixen. Damon's heart pounded.

He quietly wondered if every other man on earth adored and wanted his woman as much as he wanted Lilliana. The thought of sharing his life with her from this day forward made his gut clench in excitement. To love and protect her, to laugh with her; they had all they needed in the family they had here now; and then to create a little family of their own... the emotions of gratitude riding up inside him were almost too much.

Running the establishment was often challenging and difficult at times and certain events weighed heavily on him. But he knew that, with the right people by his side, it was all completely worth it. They truly did make a difference in the world. Lilliana smiled as she sat beside Damon, running her hand lightly over his back, wondering what he was deep in thought about.

He kissed her softly, which she happily returned.

Nadia smiled at Eric as he handed her a glass. "We've got an announcement that we're sure will come as no surprise to any of you here," Eric said and smiled down at Nadia, turning to face all their friends.

"And we've been waiting for the real Lilliana to return to us so that we could share this with you all." He nodded, acknowledging Lilliana.

"I finally got around to asking Nadia the question, and she said yes," Eric announced, grinning proudly as everyone applauded and cheered. They were all grateful that the news was finally out so they wouldn't have to hide it from Nadia anymore.

By the look on her face though, Nadia had always known.

Orlando swept his sister up in a hug. "You deserve all the happiness in the world."

She smiled up at him. "Thanks, Orlando."

Damon got up and shook Eric's hand before turning to embrace Nadia. "Congratulations."

"Thank you, Sir… sorry, er Damon," she laughed.

"Okay, who's next in line?" Allie winked at Jessica.

Orlando picked up Jessica's hand, smiling into her eyes. "We don't feel the need to commit via a ceremony," he shrugged a shoulder as he glanced around the room at their friends. "We're just happy to celebrate every day as we are now."

"And that's what matters," Rachael smiled.

"Not to bring the celebration down," Cam began after everyone had hugged the happy couple and poured another round of drinks. "But how do you two feel about Richard being your Uncle?"

"Nice one, Cameron," Fox raised an eyebrow.

"No, we're all friends here. If we can't talk about it with you, then who can we talk to about it." Orlando sat beside Jessica, who placed her hand on his knee for support. She herself, still couldn't believe it.

Luke nestled beside Rupert as they both sat back with their cold beers.

Rachael, Allie and Lilliana's eyes met. They each shared many conflicting emotions where Richard was concerned.

Allie bit her tongue, not wanting to add acid to the flame, of unsavoury relatives.

As the room turned silent, Nadia began. "My mother had only met her brother-in-law a handful of times when he had been on leave. We didn't have any other family, so she would speak of him occasionally. I never met him."

Orlando nodded. "I was five years old the last time he visited our family home, which is why I had no idea who he was when I came here. One thing our mother always said was that our father wasn't half the man his brother was."

"And how disturbing is that statement?" Marcus shook his head.

Orlando nodded.

"So, he wasn't always a freak then." Fox finished her champagne.

"Not possible," Allie shook her head.

Damon and Cam exchanged looks with Johnson, knowing Richard

needed to be dealt with immediately but neither was wanting to think about it tonight.

Damon changed the subject. "We have Dr Ryan speaking at Leon's service tomorrow. Would anyone else like to say a few words?"

The room grew instantly quiet.

After a moment of silence Rupert put up his hand, awkwardly returning it to Luke's. He looked around the room. "He saved me twice from getting sliced open by Franklin, remember that time?" He looked at Lilliana and Jessica.

"Yes," Jessica smiled fondly. "Franklin cut you one morning before breakfast, and Leon stepped in to rescue you."

Josephine laughed, "I remember that day like it was yesterday. Big, strong Leon, saving the day."

"Franklin knocked his Watcher out to get to you," Lilliana shook her head.

"Every morning before breakfast he was so determined to cut you." Jessica laughed.

"Persistent little weasel." Cam chuckled.

"Well, I'd be honoured to have the chance to speak tomorrow," Rupert said to Damon.

"Wonderful." Damon said quietly.

"I know we've given Natalie a hard time over the years," Allie began.

"Can't imagine why?" Josephine interrupted, grinning, before Allie could continue.

"But, on this one occasion she did everyone a huge favour. Remember the time she smashed her face into Leon's package, when he was laying out by the pool?"

Rupert laughed. "Most of you missed it; but Allie and I had the pleasure of seeing Leon pick her up and drop her into the water."

Nadia wondered why that was so funny.

"Yes," Allie continued, "When she went down she took Leon's trunks with her… and boy oh boy, did everyone get an eyeful!"

Josephine laughed with Jessica as they remembered Allie sharing a different version of the story way back when, when they were younger.

Lilliana was happy that Allie had edited this version for their current company.

"What ever happened to Franklin?" Eric asked as the laughter quietened down.

"He volunteered to go to the Washington Given when the last recruitment came through," Cam answered.

"We had five hundred leave at that time, too," Johnson added.

"Your charming cousin and uncle, hey. Fun times." Allie winced, recalling when Sapphire had come into their home and caused chaos well over a year ago.

"Your Uncle, Seth Night?" Nadia asked.

"Yes." Cam answered. "Unfortunately, we can't always choose our relatives." He held his glass up to Orlando.

"Even in the circles that Gregory operated in, you and your Given were always highly spoken of—and I know you were the envy of a few other directors." Nadia nestled against Eric's side as he put his arm around her, rubbing her arm gently back and forth.

"Every director and Given facility has the potential to excel as we do here. We commit one hundred percent of our time and effort into benefiting our establishment and caring for every single soul that comes into our home. Whether it be the psych ward or Main House."

"Amen to that." Allie interjected.

"How does it all work, if you don't mind me asking?" Nadia asked.

"How does a facility not become overpopulated?"

"Sterilisation program," Fox muttered under her breath.

Damon ignored her comment as Cam moved on to answer the next question.

"The Officials delegate how many Given are sent to each facility throughout the year, and this depends on each Given's capacity and ability to handle the flow of new arrivals."

"I heard that once you entered a Given facility you could never leave?" Nadia was so intrigued about the world of the Given, and Damon seemed more than happy to answer her questions.

"Yes, even as recently as a decade ago, once you entered a Given establishment, most would never step foot outside the walls again unless they were recruited by another Given facility. But, the Officials have changed the way we run things now, and over the past two years we have been working on a volunteer program whereby, once you've received your education or training, depending on how old you were when you arrived, you are then free to work for any organisation of your choosing to help those in need; or, you could enter one of the Given's exchange programs where you can assist at another Given facility expected to be operable by the end of the year."

"So one can choose to leave, but only to work elsewhere at another Given?"

"Correct. Those that enter our doors—as you have seen for yourself—are given an exceptional life in order to continue supporting those in society who have fallen. The world is a cruel place at the best of times, and those of us in the position to continue lending a helping, supportive hand, must continue to do so."

"You all seem to go above and beyond here."

Damon nodded. "We certainly do everything in our power to do what we can."

"Like Lilliana's safe houses?"

Damon smiled proudly down at Lilliana as he put his arm around her. "Exactly."

Nadia nodded, not wanting to monopolise the conversation, but with everyone finally together after a month of mayhem, it seemed like the perfect time to get more information.

"How many Given facilities are there?"

"There are many; there is one in every major state in the remaining functioning countries that exist around the globe, with supporting facilities in regional areas."

"Everyone here seems so loyal to you, dedicated to working hard and making the most of their situation. How do you achieve such fierce loyalty?"

"Forced loyalty is just another form of slavery. We may have rules here—and a fierce work ethic. But like anything in this world, anything worth having is worth working hard for. People either follow our rules to benefit themselves and their future, or they don't. Those that don't, do not enjoy their time as much as those that do."

Nadia nodded. "Makes complete sense. Josephine was telling me that at one time, this establishment only took in children?"

Karen was glad Nadia was asking questions, as she was genuinely enjoying listening to the answers.

"That's correct. In the time of our great, great, Grandfather's reign, babies to eighteen year old's were taken in. Then, halfway through my father's reign the Officials decided we were to take in only teenagers to mid thirty-year old's."

"Just made it in before the cut off day," Josephine grinned, joking at Damon. "My lucky day."

Damon smiled fondly at his sister of choice. "It was we who were lucky."

"I'll cheers to that." Cam kissed his wife's cheek.

Nadia glanced at Eric before asking her next question. "And what about now, for those here who want to start a family of their own?"

Cam and Josephine shared a smile.

"I'm sure you're aware of the Official Law which had decided decades ago that only a select number of women per state could bear a child?"

Nadia nodded. "The world's been overpopulated for too long."

"Yes, but not everybody obeyed that rule, did they?" Fox said as she walked around, topping up everyone's glasses.

"No, they did not. And it was decided at the very beginning of the Given's foundation that only the director and his wife could bear a child within the walls of their home, to carry on the family legacy."

"No one else?" Nadia raised an eyebrow.

"The world was overpopulated and dying then. We couldn't overpopulate the Given, given that it was a sanctuary that had been set up to save and support the many injured souls we took in." Cam got up and poured another coffee.

"Hence, the sterilisation program," Fox repeated.

"Yes; sadly there are some things I don't agree with, but they must be carried out for the greater good." Damon took the mug of coffee from Cam.

"But luckily the sterilisation procedure can be reversed," Rachael explained.

Damon nodded. "I have spoken with several other directors about this issue, and we did petition the Officials for the laws to change within our establishments."

"There are plenty, however, who do not want to have kids." Marcus said.

"Christopher and I have spoken about adopting a child if the day comes where we feel the need to be parents, but, quite frankly, I'd rather put my ongoing energy into doing what I do, every day." Allie agreed.

Rachael nodded. "Johnson and I made the same decision fifteen years ago not to have children, and many who live within our walls feel the same way."

"We become like parents and supportive siblings to so many of the Given we treat and care for in our roles here," Lilliana joined in, covering her yawn as she nestled against Damon and laying her cheek against his shoulder.

"That's so true," Allie nodded. "We have been called sister, or aunty. It feels good."

"Was the petition granted?" Nadia asked, steering the conversation back to her original question.

Damon smiled. "We, along with four other facilities, have been granted to select no more than ten couples every second year to bear a child, starting next year."

"Can you imagine? Where will the little darlings go?" Fox asked, not quite horror struck.

Marcus hid a smile.

"We were so confident with our petition's being granted that we had our Buildings Team design a small family village well before the Officials gave their verdict."

"Very cool." Rupert nodded.

"Just one child?" Nadia asked.

"Correct—unless it's a multiple birth. That is the way it's been for twenty years."

"There's so much to be thankful for in living here." Nadia smiled at Damon, then looking over at Eric, stars in her eyes. She still could not believe her good fortune.

"Absolutely." Damon took the last mouthful of his coffee, wondering what else the pretty young blonde was curious about. He could feel Lilliana leaning heavily against his side, and, looking down, saw that her eyes were closed. "Q and A will have to resume tomorrow," he smiled at Nadia.

Nadia returned his smile, grateful for his taking the time to explain things.

"Sorry Damon, what time again for Leon's service tomorrow?" Orlando asked.

"It's going to be an afternoon service, three pm."

"Assembly at eight am, Sir?" Scott asked as he and Karen stood to leave.

"Yes, it's an early assembly, but one that won't go for too long, so you can get breakfast in after your morning run."

"Yippee," Scott smiled, masking his sarcasm.

"Well, it's been lovely to spend time with you all. Thanks everyone." Rachael smiled as Johnson took her hand and led her from the room.

Damon kissed Lilliana's cheek and whispered. "Wake up Baby, so I can put you to bed."

Her eyes flickered open, apologetically. "I fell asleep in a flash; did I miss anything important?"

"Nothing that you don't already know. Come on." He pulled her up into his arms as they bid their friends goodnight, going upstairs where Lilliana could finally tuck herself back into her own bed, and back into the safety of Damon's arms.

CHAPTER 26

The breeze blew kindly on the hundreds of mourners who stood under the sinking afternoon sun as they bid Leon a peaceful farewell.

Damon spoke proudly and fondly of the young, injured man who had come to them and had worked his way up to become an invaluable member of the surgical team.

Rupert, along with Dr Ryan, Rachael, and Billy, spoke with hearts full of love, mateship and respect, as they shared stories about a man who would be dearly missed and grieved for deeply.

Tears were expected after such a great loss, due to such tragedy; and Leon's spirit was sent off with heavy hearts and fond memories.

Lilliana stood by Damon's side, devastated by her good friend's death. There was a time when Leon would have liked more than a friendship with her; but even before she knew she was in love with Damon Night, her heart knew there could be no other.

Memories of their time together washed over her now as the service came to an end.

Damon looked down at her tear stained face as the cemetery emptied out. "Sweetheart," he whispered tenderly, worried about all that she had been through lately. He knew Lilliana was strong, but everyone had a breaking point.

Lilliana looked up into his devastatingly handsome face, lost for a moment in his unblinking gaze. She reached up and cupped his cheek. "I love you so much Damon," she whispered, as a tear cascaded down her face.

He sighed, overwhelmed at times by his love for her, and he bent down, kissing her tears away and wrapping her up in his arms. "I love you too, my sweet girl," he murmured against her soft hair. He rocked her silently for several minutes and let her cry softly into his shoulder. The songs of a wood thrush swept over them from above, wrapping them in a private orchestra of peace.

***

Five days later Hillary, Damon, Cam, and Natalie were waiting in a questioning room, sitting opposite a snarly Richard.

It amazed Damon that the man could still be looking so arrogant, so conceited and smug, despite the charges he was up against, let alone his impending doom.

"Where is she?" Cam whispered to Damon, nodding to the empty chair that sat between Damon and Hillary.

Damon shook his head. Maybe she'd changed her mind about being part of Richard's last request panel?

It was not unusual for a high-ranking staff member to request a final meeting with the people of his choosing before his judicial execution.

Natalie sat, unusually nervous, as she fidgeted with the hem of her skirt. She had no idea why she had been excused from her duties in the laundry to attend this meeting. She felt Dr Richard's stare bore through her, so she deliberately averted her eyes towards Damon. Natalie had always found comfort in Damon's presence, despite the trouble she had enjoyed causing him in the past.

The door opened and Lilliana entered hurriedly; cheeks flushed, a curtain of silky hair billowing behind her.

She met Damon's gaze, returning a guilty yet apologetic look for being late and crossed over to sit beside him.

Damon knew instantly that she'd had something to drink as her sparkling eyes smiled and gave her away.

"Sorry—I'm a bit late." She smiled at Cameron, who was looking at her, clearly impressed. It was unheard of for Lilliana to ever break the rules. Although it was the day before Allie and Christopher's wedding, and although the girls had been celebrating out in the garden, Lilliana knew it was still unacceptable for a staff member to turn up to any official meeting with alcohol in their system, even a small amount.

Damon held in a sigh as he forced a smile. "Not a problem, darling."

"Yeah, why would it be a problem for the director's wife to turn up late to a meeting?" Natalie leaned back in her chair, folding her arms.

"Seriously, this place has gone to the dogs."

"Why don't you transfer then?" Lilliana shot back at her sweetly.

"Enough," Damon snapped, before adding, "please," in a softer tone towards his wife.

"Sorry," Lilliana muttered, already feeling guilty enough for being late; she didn't want to add any more stress to the situation.

"Let's get this meeting started, shall we?" Hillary sighed, clicking on her tablet to record the session. "Richard Grey, you've called this meeting in order to have your final word before our justice department rightfully terminates your life, based on your attempts to murder both our director and his wife; your execution is further warranted by the fact that you laid out plans to hijack and overthrow this facility with the intention of running it, as its new director, along with kidnapping charges as well as the creation of illegal replicas, having performed illegal procedures on unwitting victims. You have exactly one hour to speak." Hillary nodded towards Damon.

"Right, Richard; where would you like to start?"

"An apology would be mighty decent of you, Dick." Cam leaned back in his chair, his arm around the back of Damon's as Damon sat forward, his arms resting on the table.

Richard and Damon stared each other out silently, unblinking. The tension in the room was building to an uncomfortable level as Lilliana and Cam exchanged looks behind Damon's back.

"I guess am I somewhat sorry for the events that took place."

"Somewhat?" Lilliana interrupted. She couldn't help herself. The hell she and those poor replicas had been put through made her see red. Richard ignored her as he looked at Damon and continued.

"Somewhat sorry—but that's neither here nor there."

Richard's nasally tone irritated Lilliana more than usual. It reminded her of someone else.

"I've asked for this meeting to discuss your parents," he said, nodding towards Damon and Cam.

"You heard that your father blackmailed me to poison your mother?"

"From your own lips, Richard, do you remember telling us that our father was having affairs and participating in illegal operations involving other Given directors, and that our mother became suspicious?" Damon said.

"Yes—" Cam continued, picking up where Damon left off. "Mother was going to report him but she told you first; once Father knew his secret was in your hands he was going to send you to another establishment. But you were in love with a doctor here at the time and didn't want to leave, so you did as Father bid you to do, and killed our mother."

"Wouldn't that be nice and neat? Yes, I did kill your mother in the end—but it was not in the way you think." Richard pushed his glasses further up onto his nose.

"For the most part, that story is true. Your father was a disgrace to the Night name just as his brother, Seth was. It was your mother, and her father before her, and his before him, and so on, who gave this establishment its good name. Along with your work, also, which has made the institution a great one."

"I bet it hurt to say that," Lilliana scoffed, very out of character.

Richard giving Damon any sort of compliment must have felt like swallowing nails.

Damon sat back in his chair placing his hands in his lap, before slowly reaching under the table, covering Lilliana's knee with his hand, squeezing gently. She covered his hand with her own, stroking his flesh, wishing this to be over soon so she could go back to the pre-wedding celebrations with her friends.

"Your father wasn't the only one to have had an affair, and it wasn't a doctor I was in love with at the time. Your mother and I were in love, and she fell pregnant through our lovemaking."

Lilliana tried not to make a gagging sound. He used the word love making in the same way he used the word latrine. It was disturbing.

Cam flew out of his chair then, yelling. "That's a *lie*! Our mother would *never* have lain with you, let alone have a child!" Cam's face had gone stark white, terrified that Richard was about to tell him that he was his son.

Cam looked down angrily at Damon. "This is bullshit."

"Cameron, it's okay, please, sit down." His brother soothed.

Lilliana looked at Cam's worried face as he slowly sat back down, wishing she could somehow comfort him.

Cam looked over at Richard angrily, pointing a finger at him. "If you tell me that I'm your son I'm going to punch you in the face then choke you out right here, right now!"

Lilliana could not help the squeak of a giggle that escaped her lips. She would later let Fox know that giving her that double vodka shot before the meeting had not been the best idea.

Damon let go a long sigh. He put his arm around the back of Lilliana's chair, brushing his fingers over her shoulders.

"Continue Richard," he said, wishing too, that this nightmare was over.

"Your mother and I had an affair for three years. No—you are not my sons; neither of you. Your father found out what had transpired between your mother and I when she was eight months' pregnant. Your mother gave birth to the child, who was then sent off. Your father said he would have the child murdered if I did not poison your mother. Once I told her of your father's plan to have me poison her, she begged me to go through with it, in order to protect our child, which I would not. She then drank the poison herself, which caused her fatal heart attack."

Damon silently stared at Richard, feeling an intense fury at both of the men in his mother's life. He would gladly strangle his own father if he had had the chance.

Lilliana glanced up to see Damon swallow hard as his jaw clenched. He must be in such turmoil right now listening to this, she thought.

Richard continued. "Your father wasn't the only one who had connections, so I had my friend from the Officials keep their eye on the child's progress over the years. She was in and out of foster homes, enduring terrible abuses before we had the luck—and chance—to coordinate her being sent here."

All eyes suddenly shifted over to Natalie. It must have been the reason she had been asked to attend Richard's final meeting, Lilliana thought.

Natalie was Richard's daughter.

That's it, Lilliana thought; *she had the same nasal whine to her speech as Richard when she complained.*

Natalie's arms folded tightly over her chest as she stared back at her father. "So am I to understand that I get a father—who is about to be terminated—as well as two brothers who can't stand the sight of me, all in the space of thirty minutes? Great. That's just great."

Cam looked at Hillary. "Hillary, you've been here as long as Richard; can you confirm this?"

"It's all true," Hillary nodded quietly. "I'm the only other soul who knew about your mother and Richard's affair. Natalie is your half-sister. I delivered her myself, before she was taken away. I'm sorry I never told either of you," she said with great remorse, looking at Damon and Cam.

"What could have you said?" Damon ran his hand up and down Lilliana's arm, trying to comfort himself as much as her.

"Natalie," Richard spoke to her, addressing her as his daughter for the first time. "With this knowledge, that you are a Night, it is now your chance to do something positive with your life. Make a difference, make smart choices. I'm only sorry we didn't get to have more time together."

"We had the past decade together, but you never thought to tell me that I was your daughter. More importantly, that I was their sister?"

"Half-sister," Cam muttered under his breath.

"Whatever. I'm of your blood, and therefore should have the distinction of being addressed as a Night."

"Natalie," Damon spoke to her curtly. "You having the Night name doesn't change the fact that you tried to harm another Given. Even being our half-sister doesn't entitle you to any privileges after committing that deed."

"Actually," Richard interrupted, peering over his glasses at Damon. "It does."

"Bullshit." Cam was unapologetically Cam.

"It's true," Hillary added. "Being related by blood or marriage to a director allows certain privileges. You yourself have taken a life, Damon." Hillary was referring to their cousin, Sapphire, whom he had killed once he had learned of her evil crimes and deceptions.

"Yes— but that was after the fact that I had knowledge of her crimes, and once again to protect our people here. This was the act of some young girl's fanciful revenge, just because she thought another Given didn't belong."

Lilliana expected Damon's voice to rise in anger. It didn't, though; he became cold and quiet, which to her was always a dangerous sign of things to come.

Her eyes met briefly with Natalie's; they both had the same thought.

My God, she's actually my sister-in-law. They both looked away at the same time.

Cam wanted to divert the current conversation away from Natalie's future and back to the man on trial. "What else do you have to say, Richard?"

Richard looked at Natalie a while longer before answering. "I've nothing further to say," he said looking down.

Lilliana was relieved. It looked like this meeting was finally over, and she felt relieved to be able to go back to her friends.

Damon nodded as he stood, picking up Lilliana's hand as he did.

"I just want to know," Lilliana asked as she stood with him. "Why betray us in such a deplorable way? How could you so casually cause such grave physical and mental harm to those innocent replicas in the process? What is wrong with you?"

Richard sat back, crossing his arms as he stared stonily back at her. "Do you really want to hear my answer?"

Cam looked at Damon, thinking he should stop this conversation. He knew it wasn't going to lead to anywhere good.

Damon stilled himself, waiting. Lilliana deserved an answer after all Richard had put her through, he thought.

"It's simple really, Miss Lilliana. I've always wanted you."

"Richard," Damon cut in, his tone icy.

"No, I am allowed to have an hour, and I don't believe it's up yet. Miss Lilliana asked a question. And so, I'll answer it." He looked away from Damon, back to Lilliana.

"From day one, I wanted you. Of course, I knew that was never possible, but I did what most intelligent people do. I bided my time, until the timing was perfect. Once I knew of your mission on the outside, I put my plan into action, behind the scenes. You see, I knew that with you venturing around for the greater good, our esteemed director here would be totally preoccupied, allowing me time to source out the homeless and get them to a replica lab with the help from my Official friend, and your DNA." He sat forward, placing his long, pale fingers upon the tabletop.

"It was all so easy." He sighed quietly, eyes glazing over as he fantasised about what his plan would have looked like, had it succeeded.

"Once I had you replaced with the replica, I planned to undergo the procedure myself… then I would have ended you," he nodded towards Damon. "And I would have lived happily ever after with a similar version of the woman I have lusted after for years, while causing chaos and debauchery within our walls and beyond."

"As if I wouldn't have noticed that my brother had turned into a dick, you Dick." Cam snarled.

"Oh, you foolish boy; I had plans for you, too. Mind altering drugs would have taken care of your suspicious nature." Richard shook his head. "I should have made a move on my plans years ago, but like everything in life, the timing wasn't right."

"Richard!" Hillary sounded so disappointed. "You have held an esteemed position alongside the best all these years. Was your life so bad that you felt the need to betray us all?" She shook her head sadly. "I am utterly disgusted and disappointed."

Cam patted Hillary's back, his eyes never leaving Richard's smug face.

"You are one person I am sorry to have upset, Hillary. But it was my revenge against your father." He looked at Damon.

"What was the point of revenge? The man's been dead for years."

"Yes, but I had planned on killing him and taking his place beside your mother to run this Given, as you are now. I would be the one in charge, not you—making decisions, taking liberties with those I desired, just as you did years ago with Miss Lilliana here."

"That's not true!" Lilliana spat out. "Damon was always the perfect Guardian over us all!"

Richard raised an eyebrow as he curled his lip. "I saw things, Missy. Can you deny what occurred between you?"

"I don't owe you anything. Even now, you're consuming too much of my oxygen," Lilliana spat angrily, wishing she could knock him out.

Damon looked at her; beautiful with her angry, flushed cheeks, he felt a niggle of guilt as he remembered the times he had wanted to do more with her younger self than what he had wrongly done, when he had been her protector.

"Give it a rest, Dick," Cam shook his head. "This meeting's over."

Damon looked across at Natalie. "Do you want to spend your father's last ten minutes with him?"

Natalie looked unsure as she stared at the man who seemed even more disturbed than she could have imagined. She felt angry, and slightly ripped off, that this was her father. This pathetic human stain. Sure, she had done some crazy things herself over the years; but come on, she had reason to, her childhood hadn't been that great. She glanced at Damon and Cam and couldn't believe that she shared their mother's blood, although by all accounts, their mother had been a truly kind, decent human. Maybe she could make a change? She actually felt like she wanted to, with all this new information coming to her now. It felt like a gift. Could she make these two men—her brothers—see her in a different light?

Natalie knew she had to start somewhere.

"No thank you," she said respectfully, "I don't think I will."

"Natalie, please—" Richard implored.

"An hour ago I didn't even know I was your daughter. And hearing about the things you've done, the things you'd planned on doing, certainly doesn't endear you to me. I am not your daughter, but I am the daughter of Lynette Night. And that is what I will take with me from this meeting." She stood up as gracefully as she could and exited the room.

Cam and Damon exchanged a quick look as Hillary followed Natalie. Lilliana then turned to follow them.

"Lilliana," Richard called.

She stilled, her back to him, waiting.

"Your face will be the last thing I think about before they take my life." His cool voice washed over her, giving her unwanted chills.

"And I won't think of you at all," she replied and quickly departed.

Damon and Cam followed, and Johnson and Brett met them outside the door. "The Officials are waiting online in the injection room."

"Good, we'll meet you in there." Damon said, before he called out to Lilliana.

Lilliana stopped walking and turned around, waiting.

"I'll see you in a minute, Cam," he nodded to his brother.

"Sure." Cam took off to the injection room where Richard was to be put to death. He was, however, disappointed with the Official's verdict for Richard's being sentenced to death by injection. He personally had had visions of hanging the man up in the forest and using him as a piñata.

Lilliana watched Damon walk towards her. Tall dark, and sexy as hell. He stopped just inches from her and looked down at her.

"Sweetheart." His voice was full of love and reprimand.

"I'm sorry Damon," she said softly. "I almost didn't come after Fox gave me the shot. I shouldn't have." She looked up into his eyes and took hold of his large hands.

He raised her hands to his lips, his eyes staring into hers as he kissed the back of her hands. "No, you shouldn't have." He said quietly. "And if it had have been any meeting other than Richard's, I'd be upset."

"Still, I am sorry, love." She reached up and kissed him apologetically.

He cupped her face in his hands, angling her head gently to deepen his kiss. Her fingers stroked the back of his neck in response, and she sighed, heady with pleasure.

He smiled as he drew away from her.

"Go and be with your girls and tell Fox I'll have a chat with her later."

"You wouldn't!"

He laughed softly. "Only to give her something to think about," he grinned.

Lilliana smiled, placing a kiss on his jaw. "Come find me soon?"

"You know I will."

Lilliana spun on her heel and, leaving Damon behind, she called out playfully to him again over her shoulder. "Can't wait."

CHAPTER 27

"I'm sorry, but can you please repeat that?" Josephine's eyes weren't the only ones practically boggling out of her head as Lilliana shared the news that Natalie was not only the daughter of Dr Richard, but was also Damon and Cam's half-sister.

The girls had been enjoying massages in the Balinese garden, drinking cocktails and sharing funny stories about Allie and Christopher's decade-long escapades, when Lilliana returned to them.

Josephine was however, on second thought, wishing she had had more than a mock-tail for this mind-blowing news.

Fox paused halfway through downing her drink as she stopped and stared at her friend.

Lilliana wanted to laugh at their expressions, but in all truth she was still processing the news herself, allowing for it all to slowly sink in for her too, so it was hard for her to consider it funny. They were all shocked, and all returned her gaze, gob smacked.

"My God, Lilly! Sit down. Someone please get her a drink and rub her poor shoulders so we can get this story in full." Allie pointed to an empty chair.

Lilliana nodded as she sat down, thanking their server for her cocktail, as small, warm hands rubbed at her tense shoulder muscles.

She sighed and was silent for a moment, enjoying being pampered, before she started at the beginning, telling them all about Richard's final meeting.

There was total silence when she finished.

"I always knew Dick had a thing for you," Allie shook her head, looking at Nadia. "So I guess that makes you and Natalie killing cousins?"

"Don't you mean kissing cousins?" Jessica asked.

"No, I mean she did try to kill you," Allie nodded to Nadia, "And that makes you killing cousins." She shrugged. "Ok. Whatever. It sounded funnier in my head."

Fox laughed. "I'll pay it." She looked at Lilliana and Josephine. "Then does this make her your sister-in-law?"

Lilliana and Josephine exchanged looks and Josephine just shook her head and said, "I need time to process all this. It's just too much."

Lilliana nodded, "I think Cam and Damon feel the same way."

"Imagine if Damon and Cam's father had been killed, and Richard had taken his place? He would now be your father-in-law," Jessica uttered, feeling even more disgusted.

Josephine and Lilliana looked at each other in mock shudder.

"It feels strange to have gained an uncle and a sister, all in the space of a fortnight." Nadia walked across to the food table and picked up the platter of fruit, taking it around to the group.

"If Richard's your uncle, that would make Damon and Cam your cousins, too." Lilliana finished her cocktail and selected a piece of pineapple.

Fox got up and took Lilliana's empty glass, handing her another full one, laughing, "By this rate we'll all be related somehow."

Allie chuckled. "How novel worthy."

"Speaking of which, I know we encourage journaling with all of our patients, but I've been thinking; how about we incorporate journaling, writing and poetry as part of the program in the healing centre? What do you think?" Lilliana asked Allie.

"Sounds perfect."

"Speaking of 'perfect,' Allie," Josephine said. "Are you *perfectly* happy with your afternoon?"

Allie smiled as she settled back into the cushions, sighing contently.

"It has been divine."

"How do you want to start your morning tomorrow?" Jessica asked.

"With a run and a swim. And I want you all to join me."

"No thanks, Sugar, not even for you on your big day." Fox inspected her nails, avoiding Josephine's glare.

"Um, I'm sorry princess—but if our friend wants us to join her for an invigorating morning run on her special day then that's what we are going to do. Comprende?"

Jessica and Nadia smiled, and Allie laughed. "Thank you, Jose; I always wanted my own cheering squad."

"You've always had one with these three," Fox sighed. "I'd be delighted to sweat my backside off for you, on your special day." She grinned at Allie, who mock bowed in response.

"Why, thank you. Okay, now that we are all loose and limber, who's ready for the couple's tennis match?"

Fox stood up with unexpected enthusiasm. "Now you are talking. Marcus and I will have this in the bag."

Allie's eyes lit up at Fox's competitive streak. "Ok, the teams are Marcus and Fox, against Orlando and Jessica. The winner takes on Lilly and Damon, against Eric and Nadia."

Nadia smiled at Lilliana. "This will be fun."

"Oh yeah, especially after two cocktails."

"Two for you, maybe; the rest of us have had five!" Nadia laughed, hiccupping. "Who's next?"

"Christopher and I against Josephine and Cam, and then the winner plays the winner, of the winner."

"That doesn't really make sense." Lilliana laughed.

"And *that's* why you need another cocktail," Fox said, passing her another full glass.

"I'm only halfway through this one! You're going to beat us

anyway, I'm out of practice." She shrugged, noncommittally.

The small, warm hands on her back were suddenly replaced by large cool ones. "You're not giving up on our game, are you darling?" Damon's velvety voice brushed over her.

She felt a rush of warmth spread through her as she arched back, looking up into his glorious face. "I wouldn't want to lie to you, my love." Lilliana smiled as he dropped a soft kiss against her rose petal lips.

"I hope so," Marcus grinned, as he walked across to Fox, pulling her against him for a juicy kiss.

Orlando grinned at Jessica as he reached for her hand and Eric joined Nadia on the pile of cushions. Cam chose a cocktail and took one large swallow, downing the drink until the glass was empty.

Josephine wrapped her arms around his waist, resting her cheek against his back. Cam patted the top of her hands as he winked at Allie. "Game on!"

"Oh this is going to be fun!" Allie clapped her hands before she was grabbed from behind and spun around in a circle. Her squeals of delight lit all their hearts as Christopher's laughter floated amongst them.

Damon stroked Lilliana's cheek as he watched Allie throw her head back laughing, her pretty blue wisps of hair fluttering in the breeze. His heart swelled with love and respect for the young girl that Allie had once been. Kidnapped and imprisoned for too many years. Abused beyond belief. And yet, despite her horrid past, Allie had radiated nothing but decency from the first day she had come to them at the Given, excelling in her studies and in every aspect of her career.

Lilliana was thinking similar thoughts, as they all were, watching the happy couple kiss, reflecting on their first memories of Allie and Christopher both.

"Righto," Christopher yelled enthusiastically. "Prepare to be whipped, people!"

Cam pointed back at him. "Oh you are on!" He bent over, patting his back and gesturing to Josephine, who immediately leapt on. "Let's do this." He hooked his elbows through her knees and piggy backed her towards the tennis courts. The couples held hands all the way, with Christopher doing one better than Cam, bending down and shoving his head through Allie's legs and making her laugh again as he gave her a shoulder ride in hot pursuit after Cam and Josephine.

Eric looked down at Nadia and raised a suggestive eyebrow in her direction.

Nadia just laughed. "No, sorry, don't even think about it."

Eric put his arm about her waist. "I wouldn't dream of it," he whispered into her ear, making her shiver.

She smiled up at him as they followed behind Orlando and Jessica.

Lilliana finished her cocktail and placed the full one back on the table.

"That's cheating." Fox called out behind her.

Damon smiled down at her as he put his arm about her waist as they headed after the others. "Worry about your own game, Fox," he responded good-naturedly.

Fox smiled back over her shoulder as Marcus led her in the direction of the tennis courts.

"How did it go?" Lilliana looked up at Damon as they walked.

He kept his eyes looking forward, silent in himself, before looking down at her again. "It's a moment that I'm glad has passed, and now I have this exact moment right here, to focus on."

Her eyes remained on his as he stopped walking and turned to face her fully, cupping her chin. "My mother used to say, 'The present moment is the only moment that actually matters. That's why it's a present.' So, I'm taking this moment, my beautiful, sweet girl, to tell you that I love you more than anything in this world. You are the moonbeam that lights my way when I'm lost in darkness, and I could never navigate this life without you by my side."

"Damon," Lilliana whispered, holding her hands over his. She stared into his eyes, as tears of love spilled from hers. She swallowed hard on the other tears of joy that wanted to follow. He was, and always had been, her absolute hero. She nodded, letting him know that she felt the exact same way. He lowered his head and kissed her gently, his kiss deepening with intensity.

"Righto, love birds!" Eric yelled. "Game time, prepare to be slaughtered!"

Damon waved a hand in Eric's direction as his lips left Lilliana's.

She smiled up at him. "And I will make sure that this moment repeats itself later."

"I'll hold you to that." He dropped a swift kiss against her lips, and hand in hand, they walked down to catch up with their friends.

***

Lilliana woke to the sounds of waves crashing against the shore, accompanied by sweet Celtic notes. She sighed contently, rolling over to push her face into Damon's pillow, only to connect with a note that read:

'My darling, I hope you slept deeply. Had an early meeting. I'll see you on the morning run. Xx'

She smiled and threw the covers back, dressing in her running gear, excited for the day ahead, for Allie and Christopher's special day.

A half hour later it seemed everyone was filled with equal enthusiasm this day, as the breakfast room she'd entered was abuzz with happy chatter. She spotted her girls and waved as she headed to the buffet, helping herself to a green smoothie.

"Hey, Sis!" Scott bumped into her as he balanced two plates of pancakes and eggs in his hands.

"Hi," Lilliana said, noticing he was in running gear also.

"Whose group are you running with this morning?"

"Neo and Kim."

"Cool. Try to keep up," she grinned, before joining her friends at the table.

"Morning all," she said, smiling at their happy faces.

"And what a morning it is my friend!" Allie's smile was as wide as the sky.

"Yes, just fabulous," Fox muttered into a coffee cup.

Jessica laughed. "You'd feel better with a smoothie in your belly, instead of caffeine."

"Nonsense, Sugar," Fox said, staring at Jessica, before forcing a small smile, making Josephine crack up.

"You cannot be miserable on such a splendid day, Foxy. Come on, drink up, it's almost time to go."

Eric strolled over and sat beside Lilliana as he watched Nadia selecting a piece of fruit. "It's going to be a good day."

Lilliana smiled as her eyes followed his. "It is."

Her heart felt content, watching the Given dressed in running and horse-riding gear as they bustled around the breakfast room. Her eyes lit up as Damon walked in, riding pants hugging his long legs, defining his strong thighs. He threw his head back laughing at something Marcus said while reaching to pour a coffee.

Marcus chuckled, shaking his head and clapping Damon on the back, helping himself to wheat toast.

Damon took a mouthful of coffee as his eyes scanned the room, looking over the faces of his Given.

His eyes connected with Lilliana's and he lowered his cup, offering her a smile, which she returned.

"We're lucky." Eric said quietly as he watched Orlando and Nadia talking excitedly over their breakfast.

"We are so lucky, my friend. Sometimes I can't believe how lucky," Lilliana said, her eyes fixed on Damon's as Neo blew a whistle.

"Running formation outside now, thanks," Neo called out.

"Ah, music to my ears," Allie sang. "Let's go, girls."

"Kill me now," Fox muttered.

"Excuse me," a voice said behind them as they got up, heading towards the door. "Do you mind if I run with you this morning?"

The group turned to Natalie, dressed in the white running uniform of tee shirt and shorts.

"Of course you can, Natalie," Jessica answered for the group as Neo called again.

"Come on, dawdlers," he grinned as Marcus joked about cracking the whip.

They headed out into the damp morning where frost kissed the tops of every plant and blade of grass.

"Jesus," Fox grumbled, rubbing her arms. "You really don't expect me to swim in this, do you?"

"Trust us, by the time we reach the lake you'll want to dive in," Lilliana said as they joined the straight running line.

A whistle blew again, and slowly the line began to move out.

"Just like the old days," Josephine said.

"Speak for yourself," Allie said, taking a deep lungful of air. "Lilly and I run almost every morning."

"Yeah, well I don't want to jostle Baby around too much." Josephine rubbed her belly as the pace increased.

"Can't. Talk. Now." Fox gasped, sucking in a lungful of air.

Nadia laughed as Eric jogged backwards to keep pace beside her.

"Come on, sleepy," he winked.

"Sleepy now, is it? We'll see." And with that, Nadia's stride quickened, and she left them all in her wake.

"Nope," Allie panted happily, "I'm not racing anyone this morning, I'm just enjoying the moment."

"That's the way," Lilliana said approvingly, watching the horse riders in the distance, admiring Damon's form.

Jessica kindly kept pace with Natalie.

"Our earth angel," Lilliana said to Allie, who nodded.

"Has always been the kindest of souls."

They arrived at the lake forty minutes later, panting, sweaty and hot, despite the frigid temperature. Without even thinking about how cold the lake was, Allie and Lilliana plunged in and swam to the middle.

The water stole Lilliana's breath, but she pushed on, stroking hard and fast to keep her body sailing smoothly through the water.

Fifteen minutes later they dragged themselves out of the lake, gasping and laughing at the fuss their friends were making, as the eighty odd runners chatted alongside the twenty riders, whose horses were now taking a drink.

Damon sat on Beast, who pranced about anxiously, waiting for the final gallop back to the stables. He stroked his horse's damp neck affectionately as his eyes watched his wife laughing with her friends while she jogged lightly on the spot to keep warm.

"Excuse me, Sir?"

He looked down at young Keira who was shivering and turning a light shade of blue. "Are you alright Keira?"

She shook her head as her teeth began to chatter.

Damon waved to Orlando, who rode over. "I think we need to give Keira a ride back immediately."

Orlando nodded. "Yes, Sir."

"Get into a warm shower as soon as you get back, Keira; maybe skip the morning run and swim if it's too chilly out, and join the afternoon group in future?" He smiled kindly.

"Yes, Sir," she stuttered.

Orlando reached down for Keira's hand, pulling her up behind him on his mount and waved to Jessica, before cantering off in the direction of the stables.

"Now I want a bit of that action," Fox said to the girls, calling out, "Mr Night, Sir," as politely as one had ever heard.

Lilliana chuckled, shaking her head as Damon carefully moved Beast over to them. He leant down in his saddle as Lilliana stretched up to meet him, and they kissed gently. "Sleep well, my angel?"

"I did."

He ran his hand over her wet hair before looking at a very pale, frozen Fox.

He smiled internally, knowing exactly what she wanted.

"What's up?"

Fox almost choked on her too-quick sarcastic response and instead looked as pitiful as she could. "Sir, I can't feel my fingers or toes. And I have the hospital night shift staff coming in for massages in just over an hour. I feel I won't be much good to them in this condition. Do you think you could get me back sooner to defrost and prepare?"

Clever girl, Lilliana thought. Damon would do anything for the hospital staff who worked so tirelessly. His eyes met hers before reaching a hand down towards Fox. "Of course."

Fox suppressed her whoop of delight and took his large, warm hand, allowing him to pull her up behind him, with an added boost from Allie.

"See ya, slacker," Allie laughed at the look of glee on Fox's face as

Fox strapped her arms around Damon's waist.

He nodded to them all before turning Beast away and into a canter, before breaking the stallion into a full gallop.

Neo blew the whistle as the last swimmers climbed out of the lake. "Return run now," he called out. "Then showers, work or class."

"Yippee," Allie turned and started on the run home. "Three sessions left and then it's, I do!"

Lilliana smiled as she kept pace, looking forward to returning to their sessions after being away for so long. She sighed, feeling grateful as she warmed up on their run back thinking about the special day that lay ahead of them as they prepared to celebrate their dear friend's 'I do' day.

***

After she had had a relaxation massage with Nadia, Lilliana met with Allie and they had their last session of the day in the healing centre. After they had all finished their work for the afternoon, the girls pampered Allie as the men had drinks with Christopher.

The white party of one hundred people gathered in the rustic gazebo between the brewery and the hot house. Wisteria and Spanish moss dripped from every rafter and flowers filled every surface, gracing the area in complete serenity. Most of the flowers were white, with bunches of blue hydrangeas and splashes of blue star flowers scattered about, a perfect blend for the happy couple.

Orlando and Eric stood at the front of the gazebo with Christopher as they waited for the bride. Johnson stood beside them, ready to perform the wedding ceremony.

Damon and Lilliana stood holding hands beside Cam and Josephine, next to Jessica, Fox, and Nadia. Like everyone else that filled the gazebo that day, they were all dressed in arctic white, as requested by the bride.

Allie had requested a low-key affair, and Christopher had told her where to meet him. He was hoping she'd be happy with what he and his best men and organised.

Ten minutes later, as the music announced her arrival, it was clear by her beautiful bright smile as she clung to Rupert's arm, that she was deliriously happy.

Dressed in a sea-blue gown, hair arranged romantically on top of her head with long pretty blue curls spilling in wisps about her temple, Allie looked like a sea goddess amongst the flowers.

Lilliana smiled from ear to ear along with her friends and happy tears fell down her cheeks. Damon put his arm about her, holding her tight as they watched Allie with pride walking towards the love of her life. The ceremony was sweet and simple; once over, applause erupted from the gazebo as the wedding party spilled out into the afternoon sun and the kitchen staff circulated amongst the guests, serving champagne and canapés.

Cam had hired Pier to photograph the event, which included a marketing shot of Christopher dipping a glowing Allie, along with Eric and Orlando in the background posing with their ale, promoting this as the ale to celebrate every occasion with.

Hours later, Josephine smiled up at Cam as they danced together. "Can life get any better than this?"

Cam grinned down at his glowing, pregnant wife. "Yep, in just under seven months, it's going to get a whole lot better than this, Baby."

Josephine's honey brown eyes smiled into his. "You know, if it's a girl I want to call her Leah."

He nodded, understanding. "After your twin," he said gently.

She nodded as her hand stroked his face.

"And if it's a boy?"

She grinned, "You're going to hate me."

He kissed her softly. "Never."

"Damon."

He threw his head back, laughing. "Why did I have a feeling you were going to say that!"

Josephine looked up at him, smiling impishly. "Well, he always *was* my superhero, long before you ever were." She laughed.

He smiled into her eyes. "And for that, I am extremely grateful." He kissed her, before saying, "Whatever makes you happy, Baby."

She laughed again as he spun her in a circle, colliding into Eric and

Nadia. Nadia clung onto Eric's strong arms as they nearly toppled over. But he centered them both effortlessly as Cam apologised profusely.

"All good." Eric said as Allie approached them.

"Hey, my friend Pier's taking a final shot of me and my girls."

"Awesome." Josephine kissed Cam's cheek and she and Nadia followed Allie over to find Jessica and Fox.

"A drink?" Eric asked Cam.

"Oh, definitely." They headed to the bar set amongst an ocean of flowers, joining in a group that was discussing brewery matters with Damon, Christopher, and Orlando.

Scott and Lilliana were in a discussion about art therapy with Karen and a group of younger Given, when Allie yelled out to her.

"I'll see you later." She hugged her brother before turning to join her friends.

"Sure thing," Scott said, watching his sister leave, before turning to Karen and asking her for a dance. She shyly agreed.

Damon was laughing with Cam as he saw Lilliana run to catch up with her friends for Allie's requested last photo.

Her long black hair was waving to him as it swayed and caressed her beautiful bottom as she caught up to her girls.

Damon felt a light thump on his arm. Turning, he caught sight of the impish grin on Cam's face.

"Try to focus on the groom's conversation, Brother."

Damon smiled at Christopher. "Sorry."

Christopher chuckled, understanding Damon's train of thought as his eyes too, flickered across to his blue-haired love.

"Don't apologise for that, Sir."

All the men turned, their eyes following the direction of their loved ones, taking the moment to enjoy the view, and feeling blessed before their conversation resumed and their laughter carried across to their ladies in the evening breeze.

***

The sun kissed the earth goodnight as Pier took the last photographs of Allie's wedding at her request. She herself had gotten changed into a white dress and let her long, blue hair down. They stood, backs to the camera as they faced the paddock where horses grazed under the starlit sky.

Pier captured the treasured moment of love, sisterhood, and friendship in an instant. He caught the glow of their dresses highlighting their hair like wood nymphs standing under an old Louisiana moon as it greeted the world.

Blonde, red, black, blue, and brown hair danced in the breeze as Jessica, Fox, Lilliana, Allie, Josephine, and Nadia stood together quietly, holding hands, unaware that Pier had finished and left minutes before. He had seen their bonding and hadn't wanted to interrupt their moment.

The laughter from their loved ones drifted across the way, accompanied by the music and chatter from the celebration as they stood for several minutes, each silently grateful for the bond they shared and the life they'd been gifted with.

Lilliana squeezed Fox and Allie's hands as tears of joy glistened like jewels on her long, black lashes. The girls squeezed in the joining of hands in turn, as an unspoken love whispered in the air around them.

"Lilliana," Damon's velvety voice caressed every inch of her exposed skin, deep into her heart.

The girls turned to find each of their men standing three feet behind them as a slow beat wrapped its way towards them. In a timed dance move, each man offered a palm out to their lady, who gracefully accepted it, allowing themselves to be pulled into the arms of their love as they danced under the moonlight; and in turn, as each couple broke away from the group they called out goodnight as they drifted apart.

Damon and Lilliana walked arm in arm by the stables and down the blue stone path, surrounded by gardens filled with flowers all twinkling under the night sky as beetles joined in the chorus of the night birds singing.

Walking up the stairs that led into Main House, they turned back to view the property and the party goers in the distance, lit up by a thousand fairy lights.

They stood there in silence until Lilliana whispered. "Another moment, that is actually the only moment that matters."

He ran his hand along her back before turning her to face him. He smiled as he tucked a wayward strand behind her ear, running his hand along the length of her cheekbone.

"I got so lucky Damon, coming here, and every moment since that I've had with you, with our friends, being able to help so many." She shook her head, feeling overwhelmed. "I will treasure all of these moments, because of the life you have gifted me with." She looked up into his dark eyes, reflecting the love she felt for him. She placed her arms around his neck, stroking his soft flesh, feeling his silky hair, brush over her fingertips.

"You are the real gift, Lilliana. My life changed the instant I laid my eyes on you." He smiled handsomely as his lips neared hers. "I have been irrevocably in love with you from the moment you called me, Sir."

Her laughter was cut off as his lips covered hers, sweeping her along in a wave of elation, that carried her over the abyss of pure heaven.

"Mr Night," she whispered against his lips as his hands moulded her body against his, all thoughts of laughter had faded with the intensisty of his kiss.

"Yes, Mrs Night?"

"Take me upstairs."

"Gladly." He dropped another kiss against her lips, taking her by the hand and leading her into their sanctuary.

THE END

EPILOGUE

Damon leaned against the tree, watching as the vision of his wife walked towards him holding the small hand of a bright curly haired toddler.

Lilliana smiled, her eyes glowing as she placed a hand against the small of her back. The toddler screamed in delight as she spotted Damon, and slipping from her aunt's hand, started running towards her uncle.

Damon laughed as he swooped her little body up into his strong arms, spinning her around in a circle.

"Keep that up, Brother, and you'll be cleaning up the mess." Cam said, chuckling behind Damon as he walked over to put his arm around Lilliana.

"How are you holding up, Angel?" He gently placed a hand across her nine-month pregnant round belly.

Lilliana smiled. "Your darling daughter has just taken me for a lovely stroll, and I believe she has helped move along her cousin's arrival."

Cam kissed Lilliana's soft cheek. "It's an exciting day for us all. Twins: a boy and girl," he turned to his daughter, who was now in

Damon's arms. "Are you almost ready to meet your cousins, Leah?"

"Dada, Dada!" she squealed, reaching her arms towards him.

Cam plucked Leah from his brother's arms and rained adoring kisses over her face, making her laugh.

Lilliana's eyes met Damon's and they shared a smile as he put his arms about her. "How are you, sweetheart? Ready?"

She nodded, rubbing her back. "It's almost time."

He cupped her chin, raising it gently and covering her lips with his, as Leah joined in, screaming, "Me kiss, me kiss!"

Cam stepped closer so Leah could wrap her pudgy little arms around her aunt and uncle, and they shared playful kisses.

Josephine's laughter was joyous as she joined them. "My baby girl, it's time for your nap."

"Good luck with that," Damon chuckled.

"Thanks." Josephine smiled. "I'll need it. Fox sent me to get you, Lilly. She said it's massage time."

Lillian smiled as Cam slid his arm around Josephine, turning her and Leah towards the house as they walked back.

"That actually sounds like heaven."

"We'll be there waiting for you, Lilly," Josephine said, blowing her friend a kiss and saying, "Kisses for Aunty and Uncle, darling before nigh nigh."

"No Mama, not nigh nigh!"

"Yes darling, then you get to play with baby Natasha," Josephine referred to Nadia and Eric's new baby.

"Sha, Sha," Leah repeated excitedly, blowing her aunt and uncle kisses.

Damon chuckled as Lilliana returned the kisses, before Leah's curly brown head disappeared. Lilliana sighed, watching Cam and Josephine disappear with their cherub.

"She is so adorable." Lilliana smiled up at Damon.

"She's a whirlwind on legs," he replied affectionately.

Damon swept a hand over her hair, looking into her liquid green eyes made all the brighter and more beautiful from carrying their babies.

"I finished your trilogy," he smiled.

She bit her lip nervously. "What did you think?"

"I loved everything about it. *The Given and Beyond*," he smiled. "I love that there could be more."

She smiled brightly. "Always. I was nervous to hear your thoughts. You really love it?"

He laughed, "What's not to love, when you make me sound like a Knight in shining armour?"

She ran a hand along his cheek. "You are that and so much more," she whispered.

Damon rested his forehead against hers.

"Come on, sweet girl, let's get you in to see Fox for some pampering before our angels arrive."

Lilliana nodded, agreeing as he bent to drop a soft kiss against her lips, the breeze ruffling her hair about them. Arms about the other, they walked across the lawns where Given here and there called a greeting, as the sun kissed them gently. A horse whinnied in the distance as Lilliana looked up into the face of the man she adored. As they walked up the stairs, he felt her watching him and looked down at her, smiling. "What, love?"

She sucked in a deep breath as a flash of pain spread across her stunning features. "I think our angels want to greet the world now." She smiled through a sharp contraction.

"Now?" His usually steady resolve froze seeing the look of pain etched on her face.

"Now," she laughed.

He smiled, relieved that, for the moment she wasn't in pain, and swooped her up into his arms. Lilliana laughed again as he strode up the stairs into Main House, spotting Allie.

"Allie," he called. "Can you run and get Rachael? It's time!"

"Oh my God! It's time?" Allie's enthusiasm was contagious as Damon continued for the stairs, taking Lilliana up to their room.

"I'll get Jess too; we'll see you up there!" she screamed in excitement as she disappeared down the hospital stairs to get Rachael.

In the Given's record history, Damon made it up to their room and had Lilliana sitting comfortably on the bed, the blue sky smiling down on her through the glass dome roof.

He knelt down taking her hands in his, his heart full of mixed emotions as he swung from excitement and joy, to terror.

Lilliana smiled down into his eyes as she cupped his beloved face.

"It's okay, my love. Everything is going to be fine."

He kissed her hands as another contraction stole her breath.

"Lilliana?" His voice stole her heart, as it did every time he said her name.

"Damon," she smiled as she leaned forward. "Just kiss me."

"Gladly, Mrs Night."

He stood over her so that she wasn't stooped and kissed her gently while rubbing her aching back.

She sighed against his lips, feeling her world shift. She stood, wrapping her arms around him as he supported her weight, and they rocked together.

"I love you," they both whispered at the same time, smiling.

Thirteen years of memories flashed before them as they welcomed their dark haired, blue-eyed boy and green-eyed girl into the world of the Given.

About the author

MICKEY MARTIN lives and breathes romance into her novels; despite the dark, turbulent situations and plot twists her heroes and heroines must face. Martin is a true romantic writer at heart who feels it important to leave the reader with messages of hope and healing. Her books are filled with casts of colourful, resilient characters who thrive and survive hardships and trauma, allowing the reader to draw endless inspiration from memorable faces who have backbones of steel and hearts of gold as they go in search of their 'happy ever after.'

Martin is also a non-fiction writer under her married name, Michelle Weitering; here she seeks to write and make a difference, inviting the reader to question what more can be done to make our world a better place, with acts of kindness.

As a mental health advocate, she uses her writing to become a voice for those living and dealing with issues such as anxiety, depression, and other important social issues surrounding mental illness in order to raise awareness for mental health.

Many new and exciting projects are developing in the pipeline for Michelle Weitering and her pseudonym Mickey Martin as she embarks on her next project; a collaborative effort with her twin Leah Martin on their first writing journey together, a non-fiction body of work, that will speak to the all-important subjects of childhood abuse, domestic violence, sexual abuse, and child rape, and to celebrate the strength of the human spirit and its ability to not only survive but triumph over trauma against all the odds. This will be Leah's, debut novel. Title yet unknown.

Mickey is an author-shareholder with MMH PRESS, and is a member of the Romance Writers of Australia, Writers Victoria and the Peninsula Writers' Club. She lives in the stunning seaside town of Frankston, in Victoria, Australia, with her very scrumptious, supportive husband Jade, and their two gorgeous son's, Jesse and Zane.